"...riveting...I have enjoyed few series in my lifetime(s) as much as I do Karen Hooper's Kindrily series. The story is perfectly plotted, the characters are fully developed (and fun to follow) and the emotional connection that one feels for them while reading is immense."

~Jenna DeTrapani at *Jenna Does Books*

"Hooper really knows how to bring a character to life. This book is just as magical, if not more, than *Grasping at Eternity* and will leave the reader breathless and wanting more! This series has quickly become one of my favorites."

~Jessica Chiles at *Such a Novel Idea*

"...beautifully romantic, it will have you absolutely melting. I adore this story and all of the characters in the kindrily. I still hold to my first review that this series is the new standard for star-crossed love stories. Karen's writing continues to be impeccable and I remain a devoted follower."

~Jennifer Greeff at *Once Upon a Twilight*

"Hooper is a master storyteller who combines subtlety with intricate descriptions to captivate her audience with a story that takes the supernatural to a whole new level. *Taking Back Forever* is the perfect escape from reality. It is a love story (and awesomely unique story) that will stand the test of time right alongside many of the classics."

~Jonel Boyko at *Pure Jonel*

"...so much romance that makes your toes curl and things get revealed that will make your jaw drop. The book did not leave my hands until I read the very last page. While *Grasping at Eternity* was an amazing, fantastic, scream your head off good novel, in my opinion it doesn't hold a candle to *Taking Back Forever*."

~Inna Mankevych at *Inna's Little Bookshelves*

"I thought that this book couldn't be any better than the first. Boy was I wrong. The soul mates and souls topic is so big and beautiful, it's hard not to believe in it. Honestly, one of the best books I've read in this year. If I had the book in paperback, it would be worn out from the many times I'd read it, mark it, cry in it, and so on. And I'm not a person who can cry so easily."

~Jennifer Madero at *Boricuan Bookworms*

TAKING BACK FOREVER

Edited by Marie Jaskulka
http://mariejaskulka.wordpress.com

Front cover design by Alexandra Shostak
www.coversbyalexandra.com

Cover layout design by Steven Fitzpatrick
http://avurt.com

Visit author Karen Amanda Hooper on the web at
www.karenamandahooper.com

TAKING BACK FOREVER

Bernie

I'm beyond grateful for everything you do. Thank you for being you.

May you shine forever.

Love,

Karen A. Hooper

"The unread story is not a story...
The reader, reading it, makes it live:
a live thing, a story."
~Ursula K. Le Guin

Dedicated to you.
Thank you for being a reader.
May you shine *forever*.

TAKING
BACK
FOREVER

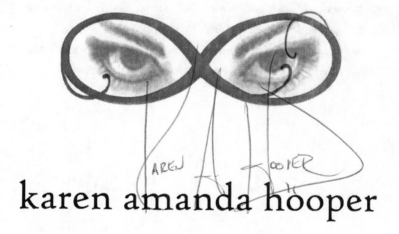

karen amanda hooper

Starry Sky Publishing

Dear Reader,

Welcome back.

I say welcome back because if you are reading *Taking Back Forever*, you have hopefully read book 1 of the Kindrily series, *Grasping at Eternity*.

If you haven't, let me respectfully explain that this isn't one of those sequels where the details of book 1 are recapped. The story picks up right where we left off. A lot of characters and details tie in from one book to the next. For your own reading pleasure, I recommend reading *Grasping at Eternity* first.

With that being said, I love my readers. When they talk, I listen. Keeping track of all the kindrily members in *Grasping at Eternity* was difficult at times for some, so I included a character key with this book for easy reference.

Thanks so much for coming back to read more of the kindrily's story. I hope you enjoy *Taking Back Forever*.

My eternal thanks,

Karen

Kindrily Key

1 **Edgar** Reads the Akashic Records	**2** **Helen** Wields Herbs
3 **Anthony** Freezes Time	**4** **Louise** Views Auras
5 **Dylan** Power of Persuasion	**6** **Amber** Communicates with Animals
7 **Nathaniel** Traverses	**8** **Maryah** Astral Travels
9 **Gregory** Hears Human Thoughts	**10** **Harmony** Communicates with Spirits
11 **Faith** Feels Human Emotions	**12** **Shiloh** Sees in the Dark

13
Krista
Healer

14
Carson
Ultra Fast, Strong, & Smart

15
Michael
Not Yet Known

Eightball
(the Bulldog)
Sleeping & Snoring

SHAKING THE STARS

Maryah

S tars glittered down around the girl as the peacock feather in her hand fanned out into more than a dozen blue and green quills. The figurine's eyes were made from tiny green jewels. The iridescent liquid she stood in shimmered like Louise's paintings or the dream I had where the hallway flooded with a river of green and gold.

I shook the snow globe again, mesmerized by the beauty of the twinkling stars.

"It's you," Carson told me.

"Me?" I suspected the strawberry blonde girl inside the glass was me, but I felt arrogant saying it out loud. Carson said he made the snow globe for a school project, so why in the world would he have chosen me as the centerpiece for his assignment? "I don't understand."

Carson plopped down in a stool across from Krista and me. "All week in science class we've been learning about classical conditioning and our teacher wanted each of us to bring in stimuli we thought would elicit a similar reaction from everyone." He tugged the strings of his hoodie. "So I made that."

A close-lipped grin spread across Krista's face and she lowered her chin. Carson glanced at her and smiled.

I rubbed my thumbs over the smooth glass. "I don't get it."

Carson tucked his dark hair behind his ears. "My experiment went exactly as planned. Every single one of my classmates, without fail, couldn't resist shaking the crap out of you."

Krista held back a laugh, covering her mouth with her hand.

I set the globe on the counter in front of me. "I'm sensing there is a joke at my expense somewhere, but I don't want to know what it is."

Carson blasted a loud and obnoxious air horn. Krista and I almost jumped out of our seats. Eightball had been asleep near my feet. He jumped up and howled.

"What in the world?" I leaned down and rubbed Eightball's head, assuring him everything was okay. He snorted. Then his chubby short legs slid apart until he lazily sprawled flat on the floor again. My pulse returned to normal, but my ears were ringing. "Why did you blow that thing?"

"Yes! Ding, ding, ding!" Carson pulled out a wrapped chocolate truffle from the pocket of his sweatshirt and tossed it across the counter to me. "Way to ask a question."

Krista leaned forward, watching us with an expectant smirk on her face.

I eyed Carson, and the chocolate, skeptically. "What's wrong with the candy?"

He tossed me another truffle.

"Seriously," I said, "what are you doing?"

Another truffle skidded across the counter and hit my hand.

Krista nodded at him. "It's working."

I crossed my arms over my chest, studying the devious duo and replaying our whole awkward encounter. "Are you rewarding me with chocolate every time I ask a question?"

Krista, the traitor, handed me a truffle while Carson grinned smugly.

I smacked the candy away. "I'm not Pavlov's dog!"

"Hey," Carson said. "You're finally asking questions. Pavlov would be proud."

"I still don't see the connection between that and the snow globe."

He leaned forward. "Maryah, for months so much magic has been happening all around you, but you were oblivious. I speak for many when I say we really wanted to shake some sense into you. Now, you know the big secret, but you're still not asking enough questions about us, your kindrily, your power, or your past. You need to try a lot harder if you really want to enhance your ability and recover your memories."

"Or what?" I asked. "You'll blast me with your air horn?"

"For questions, you get chocolate. For obliviousness, you get the horn." Carson smirked. "It's a win-win."

"Okay." Krista jumped to my defense much too late. "Point made. The air horn isn't necessary but I like the chocolate reward."

She unwrapped a truffle and popped it into her mouth.

I stared at the miniature me in the snow globe. All the stars were piled at her feet. The liquid around her was completely still. I folded my hands in my lap, resisting the urge to shake her again. "I still don't get how the snow globe fits into your ridiculous experiment."

He picked it up, turned it upside down, and shook it so hard his bangs fell like curtains over his eyes. "It's a stress reliever. Figured it would come in handy if Pavlov's method doesn't work."

Krista cooed. "I'm impressed that you made it. It's so pretty."

"You like it? You can have it." Carson ate a candy and spoke with his mouth full. "Just leave it in an easily accessible place so I can shake it when Maryah frustrates me."

"Very funny," I deadpanned.

Krista giggled and Carson winked at her in a way that looked sort of flirty. Carson was not Krista's type whatsoever. She was way out of his league, and he knew it.

"Nathan's not here?" Carson asked.

I glanced at the clock above the pantry. "No, but he said he'd be back by dinner."

"It really sucks that you don't have to go to school and I do."

"At least it's Friday. You've got an entire weekend to irritate us." I chucked a candy at his face but he caught it.

"You call it irritate, I call it entertain."

I hadn't been back to school since before spring break. The kindrily—mainly Louise and Nathan—decided my time would be best spent learning about my past, practicing seeing into the eyes of their souls, and hopefully getting a handle on my ability to astral travel. At first, Nathan worried about me being deprived of all the end of the year activities of my senior year, but class trips and proms weren't really my thing. I didn't mind missing them, and I was much happier hanging out with Nathan, Krista, Sheila, or any other member of the kindrily all day. Not to mention the drama with River and his arrest was the big topic of discussion at school. I didn't need to imagine the rumors flying around because Faith kept me updated even when I didn't want to hear them. I was relieved to stay out of that spotlight.

Carson ate the chocolate I threw at him. "So where'd Nathan go?"

"I don't know." I shrugged. "I didn't ask."

He blew the ear-piercing horn again and spun out of his stool. He headed for the hallway and shouted, "Snow globe!"

"He's so funny," Krista said.

I rolled my eyes and patted Eightball's head to stop him from growling. "Yeah, he's a riot."

When I heard Carson's bedroom door shut, I picked up the globe and cradled it in my hands, slowly rolling it from side to side, examining all the stars and the detailed peacock feathers.

Krista leaned over the counter, her forehead only inches from mine. I raised my eyes, and sighed when I saw her eager expression.

"Here." I handed it her. "You know you want to."

She smiled and took it from me. "I do, but not for the reason Carson said."

I crossed my arms over my chest. "Mmm hmm."

After waiting ever so patiently, and with what seemed like great satisfaction, Krista shook me.

∞

Faith had been coming over every day after school to do her part in my diligent training. By the time she sashayed through the door it was almost five o'clock.

"You're over an hour late," I pointed out.

She shouldered her messenger bag onto a chair and spun on me with her hands on her hips. "Clearly, I had a good reason."

I waited for her to continue, but unlike usual, she didn't ramble on. She stood there silently, her blue eyes narrowing under her diamond eyebrow piercing. After a few moments of uncomfortable staring, I shrugged. "Should we get to work?"

"Maryah!" She threw her hands up above her head. "You seriously didn't notice my hair?"

Now that she mentioned it, her mostly white and pink hair did look a little different.

"You trimmed it?" I couldn't say cut because her hair was so short there wasn't enough to cut.

"I razor trimmed it so the sharper angles frame my face and accentuate my petite features. Plus, I touched up the pink sections so they're brighter."

"Ahh." She looked pretty much the same to me. "It looks great."

She shook her head. "You're just appeasing me. You're supposed to be working on noticing details. You aren't off to a good start."

"Yes, between you and Carson I'm well aware of my inadequate observation skills."

"Even more reason for us to work harder." She opened her bag and pulled out an overstuffed folder. "Today's lesson is history."

"Every day's lesson is history."

She grabbed my hand and led me to the couch. She opened her folder and spread out photos on the coffee table. The same photos I'd been staring at since Tuesday when we started "training."

"That's because the key to mastering your ability is remembering your past." Faith pointed to the photos. "Start studying,"

"You have too much faith in me, Faith."

"You don't have enough faith in yourself."

She was right about that, but I was determined to become stronger all around. Being part of a supernatural family sort of forced me to raise the bar for myself. Average was no longer an option, but I was a *seeing is believing* type of person. The kindrily had blind faith in me based on the soul I used to be, but all I knew was the current me. And I still had a lot to prove to myself.

For the next hour I stared at pictures of almost every member of our kindrily. Most of the photos were from this lifetime or the last, but a few members had several rounds of lifetimes documented. I spent the most time on Nathan. He looked so different in his last two forms, but he still had the same intense green eyes.

Krista and Sheila had gone out shopping together. I wished they had stayed at the house so they could answer my questions about the pictures of them. My favorite was an old black and white photo of Mary and Nathaniel with Sheila and Krista as young girls. The back of the picture said it was taken in 1915. I held up another photo of Mary as a young girl with black curly hair. Her arm was around Sheila, who at the time was older than Mary. Me. I was Mary. I was still trying to get used to that fact.

"Weird," I whispered under my breath. If I didn't have the pictures, each lifetime would have been even harder to keep straight. The fact that our kindrily members retained their memories from multiple lifetimes, and could keep them straight, still astonished me. But I kept reminding myself that once upon another lifetime, I was just like them. And I wanted to be again.

I couldn't deny any part of my unique existence. At Montezuma Well, I had seen flashes from my past life with Nathan, maybe more than just the last one, but my recollection of what I had seen became blurrier as time passed. Love for him flooded through me so strongly that I could never question if he was my soul mate. Same with my feelings for everyone in the kindrily. I couldn't remember past lives with them, but I knew I had loved them long before this life. Even Sheila.

I held up the photo of Sheila and Krista as kids so Faith could see it. "We lived in England here, right?"

"Yes, that year you—"

"Stop, please. All I needed was yes or no." My brain hurt from asking questions and having Faith give me lengthy explanations.

I rubbed my temples, and Faith leaned across the coffee table raising my chin with her hand.

"Photo break." Her aquamarine eyes sparkled like always, along with her glittery face powder. "Let's try soul searching again. Look deep—past my irises. Try to find any remnants of our history together."

"How many more times will I have to do this tonight?"

"Until you remember."

I stared at her until my eyes crossed. "I'm sorry, Faith. I feel lots of love for you, but I only remember you." I pointed at her, waving my finger up and down. "This you."

She tapped her glossy pink lips. "There must be a way. Maybe we should drug you like River did. That's when your memories of Nathan came back."

"Faith!" Remembering my drug-induced paralysis sent a shiver up my spine. I never wanted to go through that again.

"I'm kidding. Don't get your panties in a bunch."

I whipped a photo at her like a Frisbee. "You're a twisted little pixie."

She did a pathetic imitation of an evil laugh. Amber was supposedly napping on the couch, but I heard her giggle.

I rubbed the peacock ring on my thumb. The night Mikey was born the ring had lit up and pulled me into what felt like another dimension. Not only was the experience powerful and magical, it's how I knew—before even looking into his familiar blue eyes—that Mikey was reincarnated, and that he was an Element.

I had rubbed and stared at my ring countless times since then, hoping to trigger another vision. I yearned to be pulled into that tunnel of light again so I could come out more knowledgeable, or with solid memories of my other lives—anything that would help make up for my erasure.

"Harmony should be here any minute with photos of Gregory," Faith said. "You need to start focusing on him so you can find him."

Trying to locate Harmony's soul mate by astral traveling put a lot of pressure on me. I didn't even know my soul could leave my body until a few days ago. Now my kindrily was counting on me to learn how to make my soul travel anywhere I wanted so I could watch over a guy I never met. We weren't even sure that he was alive. To me, the task seemed impossible.

"But for me to astral travel to someone I need to be able to picture their eyes—"

"Their soul," Faith corrected.

"Right, their soul. I've never met Gregory or seen his eyes."

"That you remember," she clarified.

"That I remember."

"Yet."

I sighed. Every time I had astral traveled had been by accident, and I thought I'd been dreaming, except for the one time when River was about to kill me. Somehow, that night I had desperately traveled to Nathan on purpose, but I hadn't been able to do it again. "It's like the chicken and the egg dilemma. Which should come first—remembering my past and the people in it, or figuring out how to intentionally astral travel?"

"Both are equally important," Faith said.

Just then Nathan materialized in the kitchen.

"Hello, ladies." He winked at Faith before leaning down and kissing the top of my head. He glanced at Amber asleep with Eightball on the sofa and lowered his voice. "Still working diligently?"

I jumped up. "Yes, but we were about to take a dinner break."

Faith frowned. "But—"

"You've had her long enough," he told Faith. "I'm claiming rights to her for the rest of the evening." He wrapped his arms around my waist, still smelling like godly nectar, but with a musty hint of dust and wind, which meant he'd been BASE jumping again.

My "dreams" about him flying off mountains had actually been me astral traveling and watching him partake in one of his real life hobbies—a hobby that made me nervous he'd hurt or kill himself. He and I agreed that to spare me from worrying, he wouldn't tell me when he was leaping off cliffs. Thankfully, he had survived another round and was home safe. I leaned back against him, and he kissed my neck.

"Get a room!" Harmony grunted, strutting into the living room. "Here Faith, the photos you wanted." She pulled out a stack of pictures from an envelope and tossed them on the table with the others.

"Yesss!" Faith scooped them up. "Maryah, look at a couple shots of Gregory so you'll—"

"No!" Nathan snatched the pictures away before Faith could hand them to me. "I said that's enough for today."

His attitude had taken a 180. He seemed irritated, or maybe nervous. Faith looked as shocked as I felt.

Amber and Eightball stirred awake.

"I'm okay," I assured him. "I can look at a few more while you shower."

"No," he insisted.

"Don't be so rough with my photos." Harmony tugged her pictures out of Nathan's hands. "They're irreplaceable. What's your malfunction anyway?"

His eyes darted from Harmony to me and back again. "Now isn't the time. Maryah can look at pictures of Gregory after she has learned more about him."

"What more does she need to know?" Harmony flipped through her stack. "Dedrick and his mongrels kidnapped him. We have no idea where he is. This is him."

"No!" Nathan swiped at the photo Harmony held up, but it was too late.

I saw him.

I saw Gregory and I yelped. I actually yelped and started trembling like a scared three-year-old who'd just seen the boogey man. Eightball jumped off the sofa and ran to my side.

"Damn it," Nathan hissed, hugging me to him.

"What?" Harmony's eyes were wide. "What's wrong with you two?"

Faith jumped up and placed her hand on my back. "Jeez, she's terrified. What is going on?"

Keeping me wrapped in his arms, Nathan whispered in my ear. "It was him, wasn't it?" I nodded and he took a deep breath. "Harmony, wait for me on the deck so we can discuss this matter in private after I tend to Maryah."

"Screw that," Harmony said. "Tell me what's going on right now."

Nathan's chest rose and fell beneath my cheek. "I didn't want you to find out like this, but Gregory is alive. He's with the

Nefariouns. He is the one who attacked Maryah and nearly killed her."

"No!" Faith gasped.

I pulled away from Nathan to get a better view of Harmony. Her face was icy and unreadable.

My eyes blurred with tears, but I could clearly picture the blood seeping through Mikey's shirt, his arms and legs flailing as he tried to tear himself out of the huge man's chokehold. Nathan and Faith stood on either side of me, holding my hands. My voice shook as I struggled to breathe. "He's the monster who murdered my brother."

Faith wrapped her arm around my shoulder. Except for my heart pounding, the room was silent.

Harmony stepped in front of me. Her face looked paler than usual. The black stone piercing her eyebrow arched into her black and purple bangs. "Your *brother*," Harmony started, "is down the hall asleep in his crib. So quit the melodramatics about *him*."

My breath caught in my throat. At first I couldn't believe she'd be so heartless while I was upset, but then I realized she was right. As horrible as Mikey's death had been in his last life, we had been reunited. Sure, he was a baby, not my brother, and it would be years before I could talk to him about any of this kindrily stuff, or talk to him about anything for that matter, but Harmony was right; Mikey was alive and part of my life.

"Gregory," she continued, "has been in the grimy grasp of Dedrick and his minions for almost two decades and *you*..." She turned to Nathan and stood on her toes, trying to raise her face to his. "You knew about it and kept it from me?"

Nathan backed up. Harmony moved with him. "Harmony, I apologize, but—"

"Don't *but* me!" Harmony yelled. "You knew where he was. You knew how worried, and heartbroken, and miserable I've been not knowing if he was alive, yet you still didn't tell me. You filthy deceiving piece of—"

"Harmony!" Faith interrupted. "Nathan must have had a good reason to keep this secret from you. Why don't you two go outside and discuss it? You're upsetting Maryah."

I was fine. Actually, watching Harmony and Nathan was so shocking it distracted me from thinking about the night my family was murdered. Harmony was attacking Nathan—with good reason—and I was more concerned she might murder him.

Nathan bent his knees, so he was closer to her height. "I'm deeply sorry."

Harmony glared at him then turned away. She paused and clenched her fist then spun on him again, throwing a punch that probably could have knocked him out cold. I yipped a warning, but Nathan anticipated Harmony's reaction and vanished as Harmony's fist sailed through the empty space where his head had been.

He reappeared by the glass door to the deck. "Shall we take this outside?"

Harmony whipped around. "Do I get to beat you senseless outside?"

Nathan opened the door. "We'll see how it goes."

She stomped past him and out onto the deck.

He vanished then reappeared in front of me before I could blink. "I'll return shortly."

He kissed my forehead then traversed outside with Harmony. Her arms flailed as she screamed at him, but eventually he caught her hands and led her away and out of our view.

"Should I be worried?" I asked Faith.

"Nah." Faith waved me off. "They'll work it out."

"What if she really does beat him up?"

Faith sat on the sofa, flipping through photos, not worried at all. "Krista can heal any damage she does."

SWEARING ON LIVES

Harmony

I remained motionless and speechless in a patio chair for nearly twenty minutes while Nate paced the deck confessing everything he knew—supposedly.

He sat across from me on the end of a lounger, offering his final blow about Gregory and his whereabouts. "He goes by Argos. He's obviously being mind-controlled, which means there is hope we can convert him back to his old self. Somehow."

Time ticked away on my watch. Several feet away the pond pump kicked on and hummed. I stared at Nate, wishing more than ever I had Gregory's ability to read minds. Summaries always left out important details.

I took off my sunglasses. "He really stabbed you?"

"Of all things to focus on, *that* is the least of our concerns. Consider it a paper cut."

I racked my brain trying to think of ways to find him, or to find Dedrick so I could rip Gregory out of Dedrick's vile clutches. I had *just* helped Maryah's parents cross over two days ago. If their spirits were still here I could have asked them to help me search in ways much faster and far-reaching than technology or human capabilities. "Why didn't you tell me all of this sooner?"

"Because I didn't want to cause you further heartache. Because I knew you would want to find him, and you can't do that until we know more about what we're dealing with, and hopefully after you graduate."

"Screw graduation."

"Your parents wouldn't understand if you dropped out now. They'd feel like they failed to raise you properly."

"I'll have Dylan ease their minds." I gripped the seat cushion. "I have to find him. What the hell is he doing attacking and murdering members of his own kindrily?"

"I don't know. Louise has been working diligently to find out."

"Louise knew too?" I wanted to punch something. "Did everyone know except Faith and me?"

"Only Louise, Anthony, and me." He bobbed his head to the side. "And Edgar and Helen."

I gritted my teeth. "Dandy, only five of my kindrily members have been keeping the biggest secret of my life from me."

"To protect you."

"That's a cop-out and you know it."

"We have sources all over the world helping us. As soon as we have a strong lead, we'll begin our reconnaissance."

"I can't wait that long. Who knows what Dedrick is doing to him?"

"You have to wait. It's a big planet and you have no idea where to look."

"You saw him in London." I stood, resisting the urge to run inside and demand Anthony get the plane ready. "I'll start there."

"I'm certain they fled London immediately after our encounter. Dedrick is smart. He wouldn't hang around and wait for us to retaliate."

Maryah erasing screwed up everything. We depended on her for search missions like this. How could she have done this to Gregory and me? I positioned myself behind my chair, bracing my arms against its back. "What will you be doing until then? Hanging around here making out with Maryah?"

He ignored the snide remark. "I will continue investigating as much as possible. Our contacts all across the globe are on alert and updating Louise or Edgar whenever they see or hear anything that might be Nefarioun related. I promise to keep you abreast of everything from this point forward."

I nodded, but if he thought I was going to sit around and leave the search up to everyone else, he was an idiot. My mind raced with plans of my own.

Nate stood, bending down and beckoning me to look at him. "We will get him back, Harmony. I swear it on my life."

"Swear on all of them."

He raised his hand. "On all of them."

In the short week since Maryah's momentary remembrance of him, Nate had come alive again. He smiled all the time. His eyes were brighter. I was happy for him, but it left me feeling more alone than ever. He had been my partner in suffering over our lost soul mates. But not anymore.

I gazed at the landscape of Sedona behind him. To myself, I could admit my jealousy of his and Maryah's reunion, but I'd never say it out loud. "How's it feel? To have her back after all this time?"

"I don't have her back. She hardly remembers anything. But I don't have to hide who and what I am anymore, or that I love her.

She knows who she was and where she belongs. I'm patiently waiting for her to figure out who she is now, and what she's capable of."

"She loves you. I can see it."

"I am ecstatically grateful for that. But I still feel the loss of her, of all the time we shared together. It's like we're getting to know each other for the first time all over again. We haven't had to do that for hundreds of years." His head drooped. "What if she doesn't like what she discovers?"

"Oh, please. You two light up around each other. That girl is smitten, and so are you."

His cheeks flushed. "It's amazing how much more you appreciate someone after you've lost them. Her happiness means everything to me. I want to give her the world, the magical and beautiful one she can no longer see, but I worry that's no longer possible."

"Give it time. If there's one thing Mary proved over and over, it's that anything is possible."

His lips pressed together and he slightly nodded.

"Okay, enough of the sappy Hallmark moment." I put on my sunglasses, and turned to go back in the house, but I paused at the patio door. "Gregory really hasn't aged at all?"

"Not one day."

Despite my anger, a grin slipped through. "He still has his long hair?"

"Wears it in a ponytail."

"Good. That'll come in handy when I drag his ass back here and beat him within an inch of his life for what he did to Maryah and her family."

With that final vow I opened the door and went inside.

I knocked on Carson's door. Two taps and a fist thump, like always, so he would know it was me.

"Enter," he called out.

He had an electronic device disassembled on his desk and he was hunched over it with a screwdriver in his hand.

"How's it going?" I asked him.

"I showed Maryah the snow globe."

I grinned. I'm sure she wasn't nearly as amused as the rest of us. "We need to talk."

He set down the screwdriver and swiveled in his chair to face me. "Uh oh. You only say that when it's something bad."

I sat on the edge of his bed and rested my elbows on my knees. Saying it out loud made it hit me that much harder. "Gregory is with Dedrick. He's using some awful alias name. He stabbed Nate. He's working with the Nefariouns."

Carson slumped back in his chair looking shocked.

We stared at each other until Carson lowered his eyes.

"Aren't you going to say anything?" I asked.

"Give me a minute to recover. Your delivery wasn't exactly gentle."

Gentleness had never been a quality of mine. Standing, I reached into my back pocket and pulled out a photo I had put aside for Carson. "Here."

He reached forward and took it, squinting at the image of himself at age three with Gregory and me in our previous life. His grin deepened the dimple in his chin.

"You had that same dimple last go-round," I said.

He held the photo closer to his face. "I did. Gregory had one too. Or has?" He dropped the photo into his lap. "This sucks. Not the update I was hoping for."

"Me either." I rolled my eyebrow ring between my fingers, trying to find something comforting or assuring to say. "He was an amazing father, much better at the parenting thing than I was. Don't forget that."

Carson's eyes met mine. "I remember some stuff from our last life. You were a great mom."

I smirked. "You were four years old when we died, what could you possibly remember?"

He reached for his Howlite necklace and fingered the stone. "I remember a party in a cemetery."

"Dia de los Muertos. Day of the Dead. My favorite holiday."

"Morbid much?"

"Actually, it's a celebration of life, but that's not the point. What do you remember?"

"I remember you in a dress with flowers in your hair, which is so far from who you are now. Sometimes I think I must have imagined that part."

"Nah, I did wear dresses. And flowers." I used to be so happy. I hoped Carson remembered that too. "Continue."

"Your face was painted like a skeleton, but a pretty skeleton, with colorful sparkles and maybe more flowers or something."

"I'm impressed. That's all accurate."

"And I remember Gregory dressed up too. He was wearing a fancy velvet sombrero and he picked me up and lifted me into the air. I knocked his sombrero off and you put it on my head. Music was playing. I think we were all dancing."

I pictured the moment like it was yesterday. Two lives ago, Gregory and I had lived a long life in Mexico. That's when Dia de los Muertos became a cherished holiday for us. But last life, in Peru, we also celebrated the transition between lives. In Peru, parties were held in cemeteries so the dead could celebrate with the living. Most of the time my interactions with spirits were annoying because they badgered me for favors, but during Dia de los Muertos I was just another face in the crowd believing in their existence."

"We really whooped it up in a cemetery with a bunch of family and strangers?" Carson asked.

"Yup."

"Wasn't that overwhelming for you considering your gift?"

"Nah, I actually looked forward to it every year. The dead would sing and dance all around us. So many times I wanted to tell a member of the living that their loved one's spirit was at their side, having the time of their lives—well, deaths. But admitting I could communicate with spirits would kill the buzz. Not to mention I'd be mobbed by spirits all wanting me to communicate everything they'd wished they'd said before they passed. Still, it was fun to be part of the celebration."

"So cool," Carson muttered. "Anyway, I remember being happy. I remember Gregory spinning me around, singing to me, and you doing the same. You were awesome parents."

He remembered all of us being happy. Success. "You were an awesome kid. Still are."

Carson's olive cheeks blushed with pink. "I'm not exactly a kid anymore."

"Oh, excuse me. I didn't mean to imply you were, Mr. Maturity."

He tugged at the strings of his sweatshirt. "I'm going with you."

"Going with me where?"

"To find Gregory."

"I'm not going anywhere yet." I wasn't sure if that was a lie or not. I hadn't created a solid game plan yet.

"I know you too well. You'll go searching for him now that you know who he's with. Just promise you won't go without me."

I rubbed my lips together. "I'll let you know when I figure out my next step."

"That wasn't a promise."

"You know I don't make promises I can't keep."

Carson stood and walked over to me. "But you promise you'll find him, right? You'll bring him back to us?"

"That I can promise."

His dark brown eyes softened. "And promise me we won't lose you too."

I pulled his hood up over his head and flicked his chin dimple. "I swear it on all my lives."

SPARKING OLD FLAMES

Maryah

Faith sat on the counter, kicking her legs against the cabinet doors. Her over-excited energy made me want to slip her some of Helen's calming herbs.

"This isn't all bad news." Faith, forever the optimist. "Now we know Maryah has seen Gregory's eyes in this lifetime. True, he was murdering her brother and beating her to a pulp, but maybe that will make his eyes stand out even more vividly in her memory. If she can master her ability then she can locate Gregory much more easily than if she had never had any contact with him."

Gregory's dark eyes stared back at me from a photograph. Physically, he looked almost identical to the man who murdered my family and tried to kill me, but when I studied his eyes, it was clear the picture showed a completely different person. No question, the smiling guy in the photo looked like a kind, good soul. The hellion who I had the nightmare encounter with was evil. How could they be the same person?

I felt horrible for calling Gregory a monster when I first found out who he was, but Harmony stormed out of the house before I could apologize.

"She's been trying," Krista said, "but Maryah hasn't astral traveled in days, and whenever she did in the past, it was by accident."

I was glad Krista and Sheila had returned. Having them around always made me feel better.

"Except at Montezuma Well," I added. "I intentionally traveled to Nathan that time." I ran my finger over my ring, wishing it would work again. I wished I could rub it and the tiny peacock feather inside would light up and whisk me off to wherever I wanted.

"Again," Faith chirped, "she was on drugs. I still think drugging her is worth a shot."

"We aren't drugging her," Nathan said.

I flashed him an appreciative nod while Faith whined, "Fiiine."

Krista grabbed a juice from the fridge and sat beside me. "I'm sorry to keep bringing up the worst night of your life, but Faith has a point. You saw Gregory. I'm sure you looked into his eyes at some point. Can you picture them in any kind of detail?"

I nodded. "They were gold with black slits. They looked like snake eyes."

Nathan straightened. "On the boat in London, everyone with Dedrick had that same look to their eyes. Dedrick has done something to change them, perhaps with the intention of preventing them from being recognized or tracked down by someone with abilities such as Maryah's."

Faith moaned. "This sucks. Tracking them down the old-fashioned way could take forever."

Nathan was telling us about the progress Louise had made with her search—or, rather telling us hardly any progress had been made—when Carson strolled into the room.

He spooned heaps of macaroni and cheese from the stove onto a plate. "What's going on out here?"

Faith reached for his food, scooping up a heaping bite with her fork. "Wishing Maryah could astral travel at will."

"Why waste your time?" Carson swatted Faith's hand away on her second attempt to steal his dinner. "Nathan said she doesn't sensperience the world anymore, which means she can't truly see into anyone's soul. She only saw Nathan's eyes in detail because adrenaline stimulated her senses and emotions, which allowed her to sensperience long enough to have flashbacks of their past. The first step in this process is for Maryah to start sensperiencing the world again."

We all stared at Carson in silence. I was flabbergasted by how quickly his mind worked.

Faith smacked the counter. "Of course! That makes total sense."

Krista laid her head on her forearm. "Heaven help us."

Confused by Krista's apparent hopelessness I eyeballed Nathan for an explanation.

"Your story," he started, "any kindrily member's story for that matter, is all recorded in their soul. You erased your ability to read those stories. Our eyes should be a way for you to recognize other kindrily, but you don't experience the world in great detail anymore. In a way, you're illiterate."

Why? Why would I give up such an extraordinary way of life? That question plagued me all day every day. "So teach me to read again."

Krista lifted her head. "It's not that simple. This is my third life and I still haven't evolved enough to sensperience the world."

"Really?" Carson set his plate on the counter. "I thought Maryah was our only defect."

"*You* can?" Krista asked with shock. "But you're younger than I am!"

Faith giggled. "It's probably because he's a Scion."

"What's a Scion?" I asked.

Carson opened a drawer then tossed me a chocolate. "Good question, Sparky. A Scion is a genuine descendant of our kindrily. I've never had normal human parents. The only blood to supply my soul with life is Element blood. It's probably why I'm multi-gifted."

Even though I really wanted to eat the candy, I swatted it back to him on principle. "How do you know that? What about your other lives?"

His mouth was full of mac and cheese so he waved his fork at Faith and she answered for him. "Sheila read his history. His last life was his first. He's a fairly new soul."

I sat up straight. "Carson, one of your abilities is that you figure out how to fix things and make stuff work. So fix Krista and me."

Carson looked startled. "I fix *stuff*—bikes, cars, electronics. Not people's souls."

I wasn't giving up that easy. "Think Carson. You sensperience. If you had to make someone understand how to do it, what would you do?"

His focus shifted to the ceiling while he chewed his food slowly. "Ooh!" He moved so fast I only saw a blur leave the kitchen. A minute later he blurred back, not even out of breath. "Cool. I've got a plan. It's detailed and requires a lot of design and assembly. One of the parts, I'll have to order from Anthony's connection on the East Coast, so give me a few days."

"Aren't you going to tell us what it is?" Krista asked.

"No."

"Come on, Carson," Nathan said. "Why does it have to be all hugger-mugger?"

"What the heck does hugger-mugger even mean?" I asked.

"Secretive," Nathan answered.

"Nathan." I sighed. "What'd I say about speaking more mainstream? I swear, sometimes having a conversation with you is like training for the SATs all over again."

He leaned on the counter. The sight of his arm muscles rippling still rendered me speechless at times. He had the sexiest forearms, and his hands couldn't have been more perfectly sculpted. He dipped down, trying to catch my attention with his soul-seducing green eyes. He grinned, probably knowing what I'd been staring at because he moved to stand behind me then slid his hand down my arm until our fingers linked. His chin rested against my ear. "It's not my fault you're a product of limited education with minimal enrichment from worldly experiences."

"Let him use his big exotic words," Carson said. "It makes him feel important."

"You know what they say about men who use big words." Krista shimmied her eyebrows. I was glad Nathan was behind me so he couldn't see me blushing.

"Yeah," Carson slugged Nathan's shoulder. "They have big dictionaries."

Nathan laughed. "We can't all be naturally brilliant like you, Carson."

"Ah, flattery will get you everywhere," Carson said. "But I'm still keeping my plan confidential. It'll be more effective that way."

∞

After dinner Nathan and I laid in bed while he read to me. I loved the sound of his velvety voice. We had started a romantic time travel series that Helen recommended, and some of the scenes got pretty steamy. Nathan was always a gentleman, never losing his composure. He cruised through the racy parts without batting an eye, but during one risqué chapter he sensed my bashfulness and paused.

"Is Jamie and Claire's rendezvous making you uncomfortable?"

My face warmed. "It's not that. It's just..." I sat up, shifting nervously.

"This is me you are talking to. You can discuss anything with me."

"I guess I'm wondering if..." As much as I missed my parents, I was relieved to know they had crossed over and couldn't be invisibly lurking around to hear this. "Well, don't you want to *do stuff* with me?"

His eyes widened and my cheeks burned hotter. How did people talk about sex so casually? I could barely look him in the eye.

Embarrassed as I was, I powered through. "I mean, if you have memories of us..." Oh god, I had to say it. Was it possible to die of humiliation? I took a deep breath. "*Making love* in past lives, isn't it difficult to wait?"

Dear Judy Blume, why didn't you write a book about how to survive talking to your centuries-old, super-duper experienced, smoking-hot soul mate about sex for the first time ever? That book would have been extremely helpful in preparing me for this incredibly awkward situation.

Nathan never looked away. The topic hadn't made him uncomfortable whatsoever. He hadn't even blushed. It was impressive. He tucked a strand of hair behind my ear. "I have learned to control my desires. The reincarnation process is about learning from each lifetime. I've mastered quite a bit throughout the centuries. Delaying gratification is one of the most rewarding human pleasures. In almost all cases, the anticipation of an enjoyable experience is as pleasurable as the experience itself. Not to mention, you have no memory of us being together, and you are encased in a different body since I last made love to you, so those factors make it easier to wait."

Hearing him say the words "made love to you" sent delicious chills throughout my entire body. He sounded so sexy and sophisticated when he talked about it, but I felt like the nervous virgin I was. Nathan noticed my goose bumps and smiled with satisfaction. He caressed my arm while he continued his explanation. "I don't know how your new body will respond to me. It will take time to learn what feels good to you, how you like to be touched and kissed, what makes you…tingle, so to speak."

No "so to speak" about it, I was tingling.

He kissed my wrist and my eyes fluttered closed.

"Every lifetime," he continued, "each body has been different. It's always a challenge to relearn you, but I enjoy each and every drawn out moment of it, and in the past, you did too." He kissed the crook of my arm and my breath caught. I didn't even know people kissed each other there, but it should be on way more top ten lists.

As enchanting as Nathan's words were, it was still hard for me to comprehend that I had lived in other bodies. He set my arm down and I forced my eyes to open. "What was your favorite version of me?"

"What do you mean?"

I spun my ring around my thumb, avoiding eye contact with him. For some reason it was easier to talk about it if I wasn't looking at him. "I'm sure I was prettier and sexier in my other lives. Is there a past version of me that was your favorite?"

Nathan put the book on the nightstand and adjusted so he was sitting directly facing me. "Let me explain this again. It's your soul I'm in love with. The package it comes in makes no difference to me. Your inner beauty and the energy of your being are what attract me to you." He touched my cheek then his fingertips drifted down my neck and shoulders. "But to answer your question, *this* is my favorite version of you."

His eyes followed every inch of my body that he touched. His warm hands ran down my arms then meandered up the bare skin of my legs. I held my breath when he reached the bottom of my shorts, but he stopped.

"This is by far, my favorite version," he said in a huskier voice. My entire body was going to melt into a pool of flesh if he kept touching me, but I didn't want him to stop. I didn't want to live without his touch ever again. My fingers linked with his and his thumbs lightly traced shapes onto my palms.

"Should we, you know," I said breathlessly, "start letting you explore?"

Unexpectedly, he laughed, killing the moment. "No, we should not. We have plenty of time for that."

"Well then when?" I asked, frustrated.

"We'll know when the time is right. It's nothing you need to worry about or plan."

"Will it be soon? Weeks? Months? A year?"

He licked his lips and focused on me with a seriousness that demonstrated his maturity. "I'm amazed and disheartened at how quickly adolescents lose their innocence nowadays. Everyone is in such a rush to give themselves over to someone physically without truly knowing the person to whom they are entrusting with their body and emotions. Unfortunately, it's the only way you understand right now because it's all you have experienced."

"Whoa. Let me remind you I have had practically no experience in *that* area."

"I mean experiencing how the world used to be." He solemnly shook his head. "People used to be much more romantic and patient. The world moved at a slower pace and so did relationships. Sex is a sacred act which sadly, over the past few decades, has been demeaned and demoralized until it means almost nothing to most people. Very few still appreciate the emotional and spiritual connection that can and should take place when two bodies and souls are joined together."

"I would appreciate it." Never in my life had I been even minutely attracted to any guy the way I was to Nathan. My fingers flinched, needing to touch him. "We were made for each other, so of course it will be special."

He leaned in so close that his breath warmed my lips. "When your heart and soul are in it, making love is not just special, Maryah—it's magical. I would never deprive you of experiencing how incredible it can be. You need to know me first, and I need to know you—this you, not the memory of whom you used to be."

How could I possibly argue with that? As much as he made my body tingle and ache, my head and heart knew he was right.

"If I hadn't erased," I said, "would we be...doing it by now?"

He licked his lips again. "Most definitely. You had usually ripped my clothes off by age fifteen."

My eyes bugged. "*Fifteen?*"

"Physically fifteen. In a couple of our lives we didn't live much beyond that age, so time was always of the essence."

"Wow." I glanced around at our luxurious bed. The white canopy draped down and around the tall tree branch posts. I swallowed. "Did we do it in this bed?"

His smile made me smile. "We did it many many times in a bed just like this, but you set that bed on fire."

"Oh, yeah," I frowned. "I'm really sorry about that."

"It wasn't the first time."

"What! I set our bed on fire before?"

"Once, but we were mutually to blame. Neither of us noticed we had knocked over a candle." His brow rose seductively. "We were preoccupied."

He made it sounds like we were nymphos. I tried to picture myself being so confident and unafraid that I'd rip his clothes off, or so engrossed in sex that I wouldn't notice a fire starting. Both scenarios seemed impossible but exciting. I laughed. "We're combustible."

"Yes. Always have been. Especially when we're together." He kissed my hand. "But we burn bright and beautiful."

"I can imagine."

"You don't need to imagine. We're still us. You're just starting with a clean slate."

"I feel awful about that."

"Don't. It's in the past. You're back, and that's all that matters."

"Are you angry at her? At the old me? Mary." It felt so strange to talk about myself as two different people. "Back then, I, *she* knew what she was doing, but she still erased."

He was quiet for a few moments while he thought about his answer. "No, I'm not angry at her or you." He tilted his head toward me. "Especially because you and she are the same. If anything, I'm angry with myself."

"Why?"

"Because I let you down." For the first time he looked away as if he was uncomfortable. "I was so angry and hurt by your erasure that it blinded me to what I should have been doing, which was helping you remember who you are, no matter what. I temporarily forgot how powerful you are, that you of all souls, would be strong enough to recover." His eyes met mine again. "For anyone else an erasure would mean forever. But not you. I should've had faith that you'd find a way back. The rest of the kindrily did, yet I, your soul mate, wasn't there when you needed me most."

"That's not true. You saved my life, twice." I cupped his face in my hands. "Like you said, it's in the past. I'm back, and we're together. That's all that matters."

"I need you to know that I do believe in you." His dark chocolate lashes blinked closed once then he gazed at me so intensely I felt it in my core. "Please know that I have unwavering faith that you will master astral traveling again. I believe with all my soul that you will remember every single memory again, even if it takes you multiple lifetimes to get to that point, I will help and support you any way I can."

I nodded, wanting so badly to click a magic switch right then and there, to be the soul he spent so many lifetimes with, to remember every last detail so we could reminisce together. I wanted to be the strong and powerful person he and the kindrily talked about. I stared deep into his green eyes, studying every line and fleck of color. I mentally begged to connect with those memories I recalled the night at Montezuma Well. I yearned to tell Nathan that I remembered again, remembered more, and remembered with ease. But the person I had been for eighteen years, the person I now was, couldn't find the magic cord that connected me to my past.

"I'll remember more," I promised him. "I know I will."

"I have no doubt." He kissed me so soft and sweetly. "But no rush, we have all the time in the world."

He lay down and I curled up against him. I wanted to kiss him again. Actually, I wanted *him* to kiss and touch me again, but I didn't want to keep throwing myself at him. My mom had told me a lady should always play a little hard to get.

"Listen," he said, "if you wake up and I'm not here, it's because I'm nipping up to Colorado to pack the last of my things. The moving truck will be there first thing tomorrow morning."

Much to everyone's happiness, Dylan and Amber decided to move back to Sedona. A house went up for sale that Amber had admired for years. As she put it, "Fate was giving them the perfect opportunity to buy it." I looked forward to having them live nearby and getting to know them better.

I almost asked Nathan if I could go with him to Colorado, but I would've made the trip unnecessarily long. "You're traversing there and back?"

"Yes." He kissed my hand. "I won't leave until you fall asleep. I'll be back by the time you wake. You won't even know I'm gone."

"How will your car get here?"

"I'm having it shipped."

"Good. I like your Mustang."

"You do?" He sounded surprised. "Why is that?"

"I have fond memories of that car. You brought me hot chocolate, and you had my favorite music playing. It was sort of our first date."

Nathan's body tensed.

"Nathan?" I said into his chest. He didn't answer, so I sat up to make sure he was okay. His expression flickered, like his emotions were battling each other, but disappointment appeared to be the winner.

"Our first date," he murmured. He propped himself up on his elbows. "We haven't even had a proper first date. I've been an inconsiderate git for not thinking of it sooner."

"What?" I gawked at him. "Um, you took me on a hot air balloon ride."

"And almost killed you."

"By accident."

"Still."

"What about the night you gave me the Desoto and surrounded it with candles?"

"If I remember correctly, it was River who ended up on a date with you that evening."

"Only because you didn't man up and tell me how you felt about me, so I had no idea you wanted to spend time with me."

"Touché." He hopped out of bed and subtly bowed. "Maryah, would you do me the honor of accompanying me on a proper date when I return?"

I threw a pillow at him. "Stop being so stuffy."

"You call it stuffy. I consider it good manners."

"We sleep in the same bed together. I'm pretty sure we blew right past first date formalities."

He winced then glanced around the room. His eyes settled on me and all flirting or playfulness was gone. I could practically see the gears churning in his head.

"Uh oh. What's on your mind?"

He swallowed then leaned across the bed and kissed my cheek. "Nothing. Get some sleep. The stars are waiting for you."

"Hey." I grabbed his hand before he could go. "What just happened? Did I say something wrong?"

"Not at all. I'll see you when I return."

Something had shifted in him. I didn't know why or what it meant, but it must have been because of something I said. Had I already screwed up our relationship before it had begun?

I wanted to rewind back to where we were before I somehow ruined everything by opening my big mouth. "Promise me you'll take me out in the Mustang when you get back. And you'll bring me hot chocolate."

A genuine smile returned to his lips. It made me want to pull him back into bed and never let him leave. "You have my word."

"Good, now get back in bed. You said you wouldn't leave until I fell asleep."

He squinted and opened his mouth to say something, but stopped. He laid beside me, on top of the covers—much to my frustration—so I rested my head on the pillow beside his.

"Tell me more of our story."

He reached for the nightstand to grab the book we'd been reading.

I pinched his side. "No, *our* story."

He looked at me and flashed his eternal loving grin. "I have plenty of those. Very well then, once upon another lifetime..."

I drifted to sleep listening to tales of our heavenly history together.

DRAWING A LINE

Harmony

Saturdays at our house were quiet because our parents spent all day at church planning the upcoming week's events. Faith and Shiloh were always out doing something together. Carson and Dakota usually didn't hang out until mid-afternoon. Saturday mornings were bonding time with my little brother.

Dakota was at the kitchen table working on his comics. I sat beside him and grabbed a few pages of storyboard frames. Superheroes, as always. Poor kid, he wanted to be an Element so bad he spent countless hours drawing out his imagined adventures in great detail. He could draw so well that art could have been his superpower.

I read the word bubbles filled with brave and triumphant dialogue. "It's not nearly as exciting as your stories make it out to be."

He finished drawing vapor trails behind one of his flying characters. "What's not?"

"Having supernatural abilities."

"Has to be more exciting than my boring life."

"Hey." I leaned forward and pushed his blond floppy bangs out of his eyes. "You're talented and all-around amazing. I wouldn't want anyone else as a brother."

"Until your next life when I'm replaced by your next brother. Or the dozen you'll have in future lives."

"There is no replacing you."

"Right," he grumbled. He twirled his pencil between his fingers. "How's Maryah doing? Any new memories yet?"

"Not that I know of."

"She still hasn't managed to astral travel and find Gregory?"

"Yes," I said snidely. "She found him and I forgot to tell you."

He smirked and continued sketching. "Will you wait until after graduation?"

Dakota was an intelligent kid. We never played dumb with each other. I respected him more than to dodge his questions or pretend not to know what he was talking about. Knowing how close he and Carson were, I figured Carson had already updated him on the revelations about Gregory and his whereabouts. "I'm not sure yet. It would crush Mom and Dad if I skipped town before graduation."

"Dylan could make them believe it was no big deal. Persuade them to send you abroad to study or some crap that would make them proud but allow you to search for him."

"I'm way ahead of you. Dylan said he'd talk to them if and when we had a firm lead on where they might be."

"When you do go, can I come?"

"No. It's too dangerous."

A frown formed so fast that an onlooker might assume I'd just killed his dog, but he recovered quickly. "If I got hurt Krista could heal me."

~ 38 ~

"No, Dakota."

"Why not?"

"Hurt is one thing. What if they killed you?"

He tapped his pencil eraser on his sketch book. "Her power couldn't save someone from dying?"

"She can heal. She can't resurrect." I picked at my black fingernail polish at the memory of Krista's early and unexpected funeral from two lifetimes ago. Mary and Nathaniel were devastated. Sheila didn't speak for almost a year while she mourned her sister.

"That sucks," Dakota said.

"Told you it wasn't as great as you imagine."

Dakota glanced sideways at me, biting his top lip. "I made something for you, but I don't know if I should give it to you."

"If you made it for me, I'm entitled to it."

He blew his bangs off his forehead then stood up. "Wait here. I'll get it."

He headed down the hall to his bedroom and I ran my fingers over his latest drawings. A flying superhero who very much resembled Dakota—except for the bulging muscles—carried a pretty girl from a burning building. It was the first time I'd seen his character have a potential love interest. I hadn't been paying attention to what he was doing in school lately, or who he hung out with. I'd have to keep an eye out for the cute doe-eyed girl who inspired him to make her a character in his stories.

"Here," Dakota said, handing me a comic book that looked professional. It was in color and bound with a cover.

"This looks like it came from a store."

"Nope, I made it. Carson helped me produce it into a real book."

I whistled and opened to the first page. A lump formed in my throat. There I was drawn in cartoon form, right down to every last detail: my eyebrow piercing, my short black hair with purple streaks, my all black clothing, even my combat boots. I glanced up at Dakota. "I'm honored."

His milky white cheeks flushed a deep pink.

I flipped to the next page and there *he* was. Gregory. Dialogue bubbles hovered over our heads, and I'm sure the story would be enthralling, but my mind couldn't compute words at that moment. All I focused on was Gregory's strong jawline, his long black hair, his bronze skin. Even the gleam in his eyes was perfect. I closed the book and held it to my chest.

"Thank you," I told Dakota. "I will cherish this forever."

"You'll read it?"

"Of course I will." I studied the front cover again. The title was *The Reunion*. "It does have a happy ending, right?"

He nodded then sipped his soda. "Just like you will have a happy ending."

∞

Carson and Dakota were playing basketball in the driveway when Faith and Shiloh pulled in to pick me up. I grabbed my sunglasses and rushed out, hoping Carson and Dakota wouldn't ask too many questions. Faith spewed out information much too easily.

Shiloh was already out of the car. Dakota passed him the basketball.

"No," I said. "We're in a hurry."

"Aw, come on, Harm," Shiloh shuffled his feet while dribbling the ball between his legs. "One quick game."

"In a hurry to go where?" Carson asked.

"Nowhere," I replied.

"Jail!" Faith called from the driver's seat. I turned and glared at her. She shrugged. "You said we couldn't tell Maryah. You said nothing about Carson and Dakota."

"Jail?" Carson walked over to me. Dakota ignored Shiloh as he pivoted around him and dunked the ball. "To see River?"

It's not that I was trying to keep our trip a secret from Carson or Dakota. I just didn't want them to be guilty accomplices if I ended up beating information out of River. "I have some questions for him."

"I don't think that's a good idea," Dakota offered.

"We'll be fine." Faith leaned out her open window and draped her arms over the door. "We'll make sure she doesn't kill him."

Carson leaned on the hood of his Mustang. "You can't visit him."

I rolled my eyes. "I appreciate your concern but I need to speak to him. He's the only accessible connection to the Nefariouns we have right now."

"That's fine and dandy," Carson smirked. "But you literally *can't* visit him. The jail doesn't allow visitors on Saturdays or Sundays. And you need an appointment, which clearly you didn't make or you'd know you can't visit on weekends."

Dakota chuckled. "As advanced as you guys are you still haven't learned to look up basic planning information on the Internet. It's baffling."

I glanced at Faith. Her mouth had formed a surprised "O."

"Great!" Shiloh dribbled the ball again. "Now we have plenty of time for me to wipe the floor with Dakota."

"Bring it," Dakota said, turning to continue their game.

"Why would you know or even research the jail's visitation policy?" I asked Carson.

"Because I wanted to visit him last weekend and couldn't."

"You? Why did you want to see him?"

Carson stuck his hands in his pockets. "I had questions of my own."

That was Carson—always working behind the scenes. Figuring out how to solve a problem before the rest of us could. I didn't know what questions Carson had for River, but they would most likely be better than mine. I should have asked for Carson's help from the get-go.

"We'll take Dylan," I said. "He can persuade them to let us talk to River."

Carson shook his head. "Dylan is in Colorado with the movers, remember?"

"Then we'll take Anthony. He can freeze time and we'll break in."

"And then what?" Carson asked. "You'd need to find River in his cell. Don't you think he'd question how you got in and why everyone and everything was frozen? The last thing we need is him telling Dedrick that our time stopper has the ability to control who and what is frozen." He was right. And I was irritated at myself for not thinking of it first. "Your desperation is making you sloppy. You're making mistakes. That could've been a costly one."

My jaw tightened. I could feel Dakota, Shiloh, and Faith staring at me but I refused to look at any of them.

"It's okay," Carson continued. "I almost made the mistake of visiting him too, but I gave it more thought, and River isn't the key to figuring out where Dedrick is. None of us should visit him in jail. We'd be bringing unnecessary attention to ourselves."

"But he's the only possible lead we have right now," I argued.

"Then we find a new lead," Faith chimed in. "Carson's right. Besides, I promised to keep *you* from hurting him and going to jail, but if I see him again I might break his neck with my bare hands and move into his cell."

Shiloh laughed. I glared at him. "What?" He asked me, wrapping his arm around Faith's waist. "It's funny because she's serious."

I hated not being in control of a situation. "So I'm supposed to sit around here and hope a new lead magically surfaces?"

"It's all we can do," Carson said.

They acted like it was no big deal. That Gregory being in the evil hands of Dedrick was not a red alert emergency. They had no idea what it was like to be without their twin flame for almost two decades, or worry day and night about their safety and wellbeing.

I stormed back into the house and threw my keys at the wall. Our kindrily believed that with time the universe would always provide a solution. I'd given the universe enough damn time. I wanted my soul mate back.

FATE CALLING

Maryah

Nathan wasn't beside me when I woke up. I rubbed my hand over the cool sheets of his side of the bed. I slept in much longer than I had planned. Maybe he had been here but got tired of waiting for me to wake up. Unlike me, he didn't like to sleep in.

I stumbled into the kitchen rubbing my eyes. "Good morning, Louise."

"Good morning to you, Maryah. You missed breakfast." She was drying dishes but motioned toward the foyer with a spatula. "But a messenger left something for you on the table by the front door.

"A messenger? Left me what?"

She flipped a dishtowel over her shoulder. "Go see for yourself."

I was somewhat worried about what I'd find as I walked into the foyer, but sitting on the table in an antique silver tray was a peacock feather and a small envelope with my name written in calligraphy on the front.

At first I didn't touch it. Something about the card on the tray felt familiar, and the scene looked too elegant to disrupt. A wave of pain throbbed from one side of my head to the other. I rubbed my temple and leaned against the wall, taking mental pictures while hoping a memory from my past would break through.

"Aren't you going to open it?" Louise asked leaning against the wall beside me.

I still couldn't peel my eyes away from the card and feather on the tray. "What is it?"

"It's a calling card."

I spun my ring. The pain in my head dissolved as quickly as it had surfaced. My first thought was a long-distance phone card, but then I thought of the book *Pride and Prejudice*. My mom and I read it together and she gushed about how nice it must have been to live in the genteel days of taking the time and effort to hand deliver cards to friends and family. Nobody used calling cards anymore. Or did they? "Who is it from?"

Louise nudged me with her shoulder. "Open it and find out."

"What if it's from Dedrick and laced with anthrax or something?"

"Oh, Maryah." Louise laughed and walked over to the table. She picked up the card and handed it to me. "It's from Nathaniel."

I craned my neck to glance at the hallway to our room. "But he lives here. Why would he leave me a card?"

She shook the envelope and her bangle bracelets jingled. "Just open it."

I pulled the card out of the envelope and ran my fingers along the gold scalloped edges. A message written in calligraphy said:

May I be permitted the honored pleasure of accompanying you on a date this evening?

Eternally Yours,
Nathaniel Luna

My stomach flipped. He had meant it. He was setting up a proper date. Invitation and all.

I looked up at Louise who watched me with a pleased grin. "How do I respond?"

"That depends. What is he calling on you for?"

"A date."

"He does have an upstanding reputation in the community. I daresay you'd not find a more perfectly matched suitor." Clearly Louise already knew about this invitation and was doing her part to keep it genuinely old-fashioned. "Do you wish to allow him to court you?"

It all seemed so dignified and refined. I stood up straight and pulled my shoulders back, wishing I were wearing a dress with a petticoat skirt instead of shorts and a ratty old t-shirt. I pressed the card to my chest and batted my eyelashes. "Well, he is quite handsome. Yes, I do believe I would fancy a date with him."

Louise turned her chin as her smile spread wider. "Fancy a date? My, aren't we well versed in British colloquialisms."

I was giddy. "This is fun." I read the card again. "I want to reply properly. How did they reply in the old days?"

She linked arms with me and we strolled back to the kitchen. "You send a card of your own with your reply."

"But I don't have any cards, and where would I send it? To our bedroom?"

"Helen and I have several styles to choose from. We'll set your reply on the tray when it's ready. But don't use an envelope."

"Why not?"

"Sending a reply in an envelope implies you no longer wish to be called upon."

"Oh. Then definitely no envelope."

She winked at me. "I figured as much."

∞

After some guidance from Helen and Louise, and several attempts at writing in legible calligraphy, I placed my own elegant card on the tray then showered. I tried calling Nathan, but he didn't answer his phone, so I headed back to the foyer to see if he had picked up my card yet. As I rounded the corner I heard Krista and Louise quietly talking in the living room.

"It would be senseless," Louise said. "Her time would come soon regardless."

Krista sounded upset. "I can't accept that."

I turned back because their conversation seemed private and I didn't want to intrude, but the memory of Carson's air horn wailed in my head. I was part of this kindrily. I was allowed—and expected—to ask questions. I stood tall and walked into the living room. "Can't accept what? What are you two talking about?"

They both look surprised, obviously not expecting me to overhear them.

Krista sighed. "Nothing."

"We should tell her," Louise said. "She has the right to know."

I fought my urge to apologize for eavesdropping and go to my room. Instead, I leaned on the sofa. "Tell me what?"

Louise squeezed Krista's arm before rising from the couch. She smiled almost pitifully at me. "I'll leave you girls alone to talk."

Krista patted the couch so I sat beside her. "There's something about my gift that you should probably know." She crossed and uncrossed her legs. "My last life, it ended because I…well, because I saved Sheila."

Sorting through the puzzle pieces of what I'd learned about everyone, I tried figuring out what she meant but came up with nothing. Krista read my silence correctly and continued explaining.

"Sheila was sick. Very sick. Medicine was not what it is today, and my ability wasn't nearly as strong back then as it is now. Remember, I wasn't technically an Element until this life."

I nodded.

"Well, Helen told me about a mixture of herbs she thought might help. You and I traveled to a different town to get them. We were only gone half the day, but when we returned to the house…" She crossed her ankles and shook her feet. Her fidgeting was making me nervous. "Sheila had passed away."

"What?" That couldn't be right. "But Sheila is ninety-nine. She hasn't died since—"

"She did die. In 1938."

"But—"

"I didn't know what I was doing," Krista rambled emotionally as if reliving the past. "I was hysterical. I desperately wanted to heal her. I couldn't accept her death, so I gave her all the healing energy I had. And I mean *all* of it. She started breathing again. The color slowly appeared in her cheeks." Krista wrung her hands in her lap. "Only you, Nathaniel, Sheila, and I knew the truth about what happened. As happy as I was that Sheila was alive, I felt sick and drained so I fell asleep beside Sheila, still giving her whatever healing energy I could. You never left our side." She closed her eyes and swallowed hard. "After a while I didn't feel weak or sick anymore, and my mind felt stronger than ever so I kept pouring every ounce of energy I had into Sheila."

"That's amazing, Kris. You brought her back to life. You saved her."

Krista's big puppy dog eyes met mine. "There's more. You pressed your hand to my forehead and called out my name. I was confused when I saw the shock on your face. I couldn't figure out why you kept yelling my name and shaking me, until I realized I wasn't connected to my body anymore."

I froze, replaying her explanation. "I'm confused."

"So was I. It all happened like a hazy dream within a dream that made my soul feel better than ever. I had no idea what I was doing at the time but...giving Sheila enough of my energy to bring her back to life meant I gave up my own."

My chin jutted forward. "You died in her place?"

Krista nodded.

"Oh, Kris." My eyes stung. I couldn't imagine losing Krista. Ever. A past me did lose her, but I didn't remember experiencing that loss, nor did I want to. We both sat there in silence. "You aren't thinking of doing it again are you?"

"I can't find anything wrong with her. I've been trying relentlessly. I've even focused randomly on common health problems, but nothing works."

"Wait, why are you trying to find something wrong with her? She seems perfectly healthy."

"Because her death is inevitable, and it will be here soon."

I couldn't imagine living to be almost one hundred like Sheila. That length of time was almost impossible for me to comprehend. I'd have to come to terms with it sooner or later because I would never erase again, but in my current limited state of time perception, living to be one hundred seemed so long. "She can't live forever. But when she dies she'll reincarnate and start a new life with us."

Krista shook her head, not meeting my eyes. "No, not with us."

"Why not?"

"She's going to erase."

I felt like I'd been smacked across the face. Sheila knew what my erasure had done to this kindrily. How could she possibly think of putting them through that again? "But she can't."

"It's her decision and she already made it." Krista brought her hands to her lips in her signature prayer position. "When she dies, if I give up my life for her again—"

"No. Krista, no!"

"Calm down. You're thinking with your limited mind and emotions, but look at the bigger picture. I'm an Element. It doesn't matter if I die. I'll be able to come right back. It will buy us time."

"Time for what?"

"For you to strengthen your ability. If you prove to Sheila that you can astral travel then she'll retain, but not until she knows for certain you can find her when she's reborn again."

My stomach clenched. "She's erasing because of me?"

"Don't look at it like that."

"What other way is there to look at it? It's bad enough that I can't locate Gregory for Harmony, but now this?" I stood up. "You and Sheila have been together for almost a hundred years. You gave up your own life for her. And now, because of my awful, horrible, forbidden decision to erase, she's going to be separated from us forever."

"Please don't say forever. I can't even think about it."

"How long do I have to master astral traveling?"

Krista bit her lip but didn't answer.

"You said you can't find anything wrong with her, so maybe we have years," I said optimistically. "I'm sure I'll figure out my ability by then. Heck, with Carson's help maybe I'll be able to do it in months."

Krista's voice hitched. "She said she's going to die this week."

I gaped at her. My heart pounded in my throat so hard it took me a minute to swallow it down and speak. "This week? How could she possibly know that?"

"She saw it in her tea leaves."

"Tea leaves?"

"I know what you're thinking, but her readings have always been accurate."

My hands flew up at my sides "We're getting all worried and worked up because of tea leaves?" I turned to walk away, but turned back again. Krista wouldn't be so upset if she didn't think there was some truth to this crazy prediction. I didn't want her stressing out over this. Sheila was healthy, but maybe she wasn't as mentally sound at her old age as we thought. I needed to speak to her and debunk this death forecast. "Where is Sheila?"

"At Edgar and Helen's resting."

I stormed out onto the deck and down the pathway to Edgar and Helen's cottage. No way was I going to let Krista and Sheila stress out and plan their goodbyes because of some silly tea leaves. Helen's recipes were extremely powerful, and Sheila must have consumed so much Chamomile or whatever that it made her delusional.

∞

I knocked on Edgar and Helen's door.

Helen answered within seconds. "Maryah," she said warmly. "What a pleasant surprise. Please come in."

Edgar and Helen's home always smelled of spices. Their cottage was styled similar to the main house, but in a condensed version. It was still open and mystical looking, but it didn't quite have the same wow factor. Cozy was a good word for it.

An old record player spun as violin music filled the air. Their fireplace crackled in the living room. On the other side of their large windows, Edgar sat in a rocking chair reading on the back porch.

"Would you like some tea?" Helen asked.

If I hadn't known better, I might have thought she was mocking me. "No. No tea for me, but thank you. Krista said Sheila is here."

"She is. I believe she's finishing her bath."

Even though I didn't believe the tea leaves prediction, thinking about Sheila alone in the bathroom with a wet tile floor made me uneasy. "What if she slips and falls?"

Helen rested her hand on one cocked hip. "What if any of us slip and fall?"

"We're not as old as she is."

"We're all *much* older than she is."

"You know what I mean. Physically."

"Sit down and try to relax." She pulled out a chair from the kitchen table and I sank into it. She ran her fingers over the end of my ponytail. "How about some hot cocoa?"

"I would love some." Helen's hot chocolate had become my new favorite indulgence—aside from Nathan.

Helen tied on an apron and went to work. "I gather you heard about Sheila's upcoming departure?"

"I heard she has convinced herself and everyone else that she's dying this week based on tea leaves. Which is crazy."

"What's so crazy about it?" She pulled a container of cream from the fridge. My mouth was already watering.

"Tea leaves? Come on. She's not even sick."

"Tasseography has been around for ages. The power isn't in the leaves; it's in the clairvoyant ability of the person reading the leaves." She turned to face me, hugging her large mixing bowl under one arm and whisking her ingredients together with the other. "Let me get this straight. You believe Sheila can read a soul and see its history, like she did with Michael, but you don't believe she can see omens in tea leaves?"

I opened my mouth to explain the difference, or give a reason, but I couldn't come up with anything.

Helen's thinly waxed black eyebrows arched higher. Then she looked past me. "Ahh, there's our girl. How was your bath, Sheila?"

"Delightful." Sheila shuffled into the living room tying her fluffy robe. She wasn't even using her cane. She looked healthier than she did yesterday. Her blended British and Irish accents seemed heavier than usual. "Your salts do wonders for old bones."

She fanned her delicate fingers. "Hello, Maryah."

I stood and walked into the living room. "Sheila, do you need any help?"

"I'm all right for now. " She lowered herself into Helen's padded rocking chair and sighed. She motioned to the sofa beside her chair. "Sit a spell. We have some catching up to do and time is ticking away fast."

"Don't say that." I sat on the edge of the cushion closest to her.

She reached forward and held my hand in hers, flipping my palm up and studying it. "Yer lines have changed."

"You said that before, but you haven't told me what it means."

"It means you changed the fates. See this line?" She ran her crooked pinky along a deep curved line below my fingers. "It's yer heart line. Same as it was when you were Mary. But these," she traced two shallower lines that formed an X. "Yer head and fate lines have changed. You created a crossroads."

I searched her brown eyes. Even with wrinkled skin and her white and gold hair wet from her bath, she was still luminous. "Because I erased?"

"Partly. But see how another line forms here, running parallel to yer fate line? That's new."

"What's it mean?"

She closed my fingers into a fist then pressed my hand into my lap. "I can't say, but when the universe feels the timing is right, the answer will reveal itself to you. Until then, it's a secret between you and yer soul."

I opened my hand and studied my lines again. "A secret with myself."

"You and I used to share many secrets."

"We did?"

Sheila's head rested against the back of her chair as she rocked. "We did indeed. Drove Krista mad when you confided in me and not her."

Helen joined us long enough to hand me a mug of cocoa. I thanked her and tried making sense of what Sheila just said.

"I know what yer thinking," Sheila continued. "Now you tell Krista everything. You can't imagine ever keeping a secret from her. And that's grand. You should share secrets with her. She's the most trustworthy soul I know." Sheila stopped rocking. "A secret shared between two people is a powerful bond. Some are good, some are bad, but the secrets of life and this world are what make it so fascinating."

"Sheila." I sat forward, hopeful that Mary had told Sheila the answer to everyone's big question. "Do you know why I erased?"

"Of course I do." She sat forward too. She looked me in the eyes and her wrinkles deepened. "To save yer kindrily. To make the world a better place."

"Can you be more specific?"

"No. That's all I know."

I let out the breath I'd been holding. Her answer was as clear as mud. Probably as clear as her tea. "And what about you? Your tea leaves showed you a secret much more telling than the lines on my palms."

"Yes, my sojourn in this body will end any day now."

"How can you say that?"

"Because that blasted raven appeared in my tea again."

"Raven?" I thought of Mikey's hat that I wore every day when I first moved to Sedona. The Ravens were our hometown football team. They reminded me of Mikey, not death.

"He floated at the top of my tea cup, flapping his wings. Same wretched way he did when he came for me the first time."

Krista's story about Sheila dying made my chest tighten. "You saw a raven in your tea before you died last time?"

"The very same one." She leaned back in her chair, looking almost happy. "But this time, beneath the raven was a scarab, and the sight of her brought me peace."

"Scarab? A beetle?"

"A sign of eternal life."

My focus drifted to the floor. As odd as the beetle theory sounded, something about it whispered at a memory I couldn't quite latch onto. I sipped my hot chocolate and couldn't help looking inside my mug to check for birds or bugs.

"You know," Sheila said. "Deep down you know it too."

"Know what?"

"That my time has come. Erasure or no erasure, our souls are tightly bound. Yer being senses our upcoming separation." Her words caused tears to pool in my eyes. "See," Sheila said. "You might be in denial on the outside, but inside you know the truth."

"Please stop talking like that."

She moved to sit on the sofa beside me then touched my cheek. "Don't avoid the truth, love, even if it's painful. Fate and truth are two powers you should never fear. You were the one who taught me to listen to every internal whisper—every gut instinct. No matter how farfetched or impossible it seems, listen close. Then act with faith and love. Now it's my turn to tell you to do the same." She patted my knee. "Circle of life."

We stared at each other. It wasn't uncomfortable or awkward; it was like my soul knew to drink in this moment with her. Words escaped my mouth without me thinking. "You have to retain. I promise I'll find a way to find you."

She closed her eyes for a long moment.

"Sheila, please. Promise me you'll retain."

"I can't promise you that."

A tear streamed down my cheek. "You have to. Don't make the same mistake I did."

"I've had a splendid run. You were a wonderful mother to me. I know you have no memory of it, but my childhood with you and Nathaniel are some of the most cherished moments of my long life."

"Then don't erase them," I pleaded.

"And what if I'm born to parents who abuse me or do other horrible things? How could I live through that agony with memories of what a glorious life I once had? I would be a prisoner to whatever fate handed me. Yes, there's a possibility it would be good, but the possibility of it being bad is too frightening to consider."

"But we'll find you."

"How?" she asked, already knowing I had no answer.

"I don't know yet, but we'll find a way."

She placed her soft hand on top of mine. "Some ideas, while brave-hearted, are impossible to turn into reality. My path is meant to lead me where it will, but my soul will be forever graced because for many years I knew what love and family truly meant."

I stared into her eyes again, examining every line, speck, vein, and vessel, trying to memorize every detail so I could find her soul again. "I can memorize your eyes. You wouldn't be sent back immediately. I'd have a minimum of nine months, probably longer. I will have mastered my gift by then, I swear."

"You can't swear such a thing. You have no idea what the future holds."

An invisible hour glass sat beside us with sand quickly disappearing into an unknown eternity. I had to figure out how to astral travel at will. For Sheila's sake. And Krista's. For all of our kindrily.

Sheila smiled her angelic grin. "My life has been long and I am grateful for every second of it. Death is not the end, it's a new beginning—a beginning I will embrace and welcome when the time comes." She rubbed my chin with her thumb. "Not every star is destined to shine forever. Some of us are meant to quietly fade away."

"Maybe," I agreed, "but not you. You are meant to shine eternally."

COMING ALONG

Maryah

"You look beautiful." Krista tucked a bouncy spiral curl behind my ear.

"You'll be with Sheila all evening, right?"

"Yes. Go out, don't worry, and have fun."

How could I have fun or not worry? All I could think about was Sheila and how confident she was that she'd be dying soon. "What if she—"

"Stop it. Enjoy this momentous event with Nathaniel."

"It's just a date."

"It's your first real date with your soul mate." She added, "That you can remember."

I kissed her cheek and headed down the hall to Carson's room. I had to check on one important thing before I left. His door was open and he was on his bed reading.

"Carson?"

He lowered his magazine. "All ready for your big night out?"

I blushed. "It's our first date."

"Try your millionth date."

"Not for me." I smoothed down my dress. I couldn't figure out if the dragonflies flitting around my stomach were because I was going on a real, high-pressure date with Nathan, or because I was so worried about Sheila. "When do you think your plan, or whatever, will be ready? You know, to help me sensperience and get my ability under control?"

"In a rush because Sheila's about to kick the bucket?"

"Carson!"

"What? It sounds better than 'she's about to die.' Or croak. Or—"

"Okay, enough! Just hurry along your plan if you can, please. I'm eager to get started."

"As if I'm not moving as fast as I can?"

"I've seen you move much faster than this." I nodded at him lounged on the bed doing nothing.

"You go flit about town with lover boy and leave the real work to the multi-gifted."

I fought back a smile. "Thanks, Car."

He waved his hand like he was annoyed. He could pretend all he wanted, but we had grown fond of each other.

The doorbell rang and my pace quickened down the hall. I hadn't seen Nathan all day. When I called him for the tenth time, he politely said he was too busy to talk but he'd see me this evening. We had to talk about the Shelia crisis, and we had to figure out a way to kick my astral traveling ability into high gear ASAP.

As I passed my room, my foot slipped and my ankle rolled. My heels weren't high, but they weren't the sandals or sneakers I usually wore and I cursed Krista for making me wear them. I doubled back to my room, kicking off my heels, and grabbed my ballet flats.

The front door opened and I heard Louise say hello to Nathan. I jogged down the hallway but slowed when I reached the kitchen.

Being so eager to see him probably wasn't proper first-date etiquette.

Anthony and Krista stood at the island watching me.

"You look lovely," Anthony told me.

"Thanks."

"Good Evening, Krista." Nathan stepped into the room and my heart stopped. He was wearing a dark gray suit over a crisp white shirt that fit him perfectly. His blue and green tie made his green eyes even bolder. The epitome of handsome and debonair, he put James Bond to shame.

He bowed slightly. "Mr. and Mrs. Luna."

"Nathaniel, nice to see you," Anthony said.

The formal good manners were sweet and endearing, but I couldn't focus on anything but how amazing Nathan looked.

He stepped closer to me. "Maryah, it's a pleasure to see you." He gently took my hand and kissed the top of it. Whatever cologne he was wearing smelled delectable. "You look enchanting as always."

"Thank you. You look..." *Hot as hell. Unbelievably gorgeous. Good enough to eat.* "Very dashing."

"How kind of you to say so." He straightened and turned his attention to Anthony. "We should be on our way if we want to be on time for our engagement."

I gasped. "Engagement?"

Louise grinned at me. "Your date."

"Oh." My cheeks warmed. As if Nathan would propose to me so soon. "Right."

Nathan raised his elbow and offered me his arm. My heart ached because I wished my mom could have seen me off on my first date. She would be so impressed by everyone being so proper and genteel.

Nathan and I walked to the front door.

"Good night," I called over my shoulder to Anthony, Louise, and Krista. Louise and Krista waved and wished us a fun evening, but I was surprised when Anthony followed us out. I looked ahead as we made our way to the driveway, but Anthony's footsteps followed behind us.

When Nathan opened the passenger side door to his Mustang and Anthony climbed into the backseat, the disappointing realization of what was happening hit me.

I turned to Nathan. "Is he—?"

"Our chaperone for the evening? Yes."

My mouth fell open. "Chaperone?" I whispered. "Seriously?"

Nathan leaned close and spoke under his breath. "A lady and gentleman should be escorted by a chaperone the first time they appear in public together."

"This isn't the early 1900s, or our first time together."

"Oh, but it is our first time. Officially."

I glanced at Anthony sitting patiently in the back seat. Just when I was starting to appreciate how cool it was to be part of a centuries-old family, they had to go and ruin it with Anthony crashing our date.

I tilted my head so Anthony wouldn't overhear me. "Guess there won't be any kissing tonight."

Nathan faked shock. "And tarnish your reputation? I would never."

Oh boy. We were in for a very long night.

∞

The first thing I noticed on our drive into town was the absence of hot chocolate. As thoughtful as Nathan was, I assumed he'd remember to bring me hot chocolate, but nope. And the radio softly played whatever song the DJ selected to blast over the airwaves, definitely no Ella Fitzgerald. We were off to a disappointing start.

We pulled into the parking lot of a restaurant whose sign advertised a supper club tonight. A supper club, if memory served me correctly, was dinner and music or a show of some sort. At least we wouldn't have to talk much. Having any conversation with Anthony tagging along would be awkward.

Nathan shut off the engine and climbed out of the car. I opened my door and Anthony grunted. "You should let Nathan get that for you."

"I can still be a lady and open my own door." The novelty of this old-fashioned stuff had worn off. I just wanted to get through our date and get back home where Nathan and I could be alone.

Nathan offered me his arm again as the three of us walked into the restaurant. Anthony hung a few steps back.

A cute blonde hostess welcomed us by practically swooning. "Nathan Luna!"

I glanced at Nathan, but he was calm and cool as usual. "Good evening."

"We had a class together last year. I'm Kelsey."

"Of course. How are you, Kelsey?"

"Great. I heard you moved to Colorado. Are you back?"

"I am back. For good." His hand rubbed the small of my back. "This is Maryah, my reason for returning."

"Oh, hi." She glanced at me and looked sort of disappointed. River had mentioned that all the girls at school had a thing for Nathan at some point. Apparently Kelsey was one of them.

"Nice to meet you," I offered, trying not to blush from Nathan's sweet introduction.

Kelsey smiled and grabbed two menus. "My boss told me to give you the best seat in the house. Follow me right this way."

Nathan held my hand as we followed Kelsey to a table for two in front of huge windows that framed a breathtaking view of Oak Creek Canyon and the red rocks. Nathan pulled out my chair for me and I sat while scanning the restaurant for Anthony. He was sitting at the bar with his back to us.

"They play live music here," Nathan told me. "I think you'll enjoy it."

"Are we done with all the formal stuff?"

He grinned. "Would you like to be done with all the formal stuff?"

"Yes, I barely know how to act on a date in modern times."

"Just be you. That's all I ask."

I spread my napkin over my lap then read the menu.

A waiter appeared and set two waters on our table. "I'm Brad and I'll be your waiter this evening. The jazz band will start shortly. Can I get your drinks started while you peruse our menu?"

"I'll have an iced tea," Nathan replied. "And the lady will have your signature chocolate cocktail, but make it virgin, please." Nathan looked at me. "Would you prefer it hot?"

My heart warmed as if I were actually drinking hot chocolate. He hadn't forgotten. No wonder this guy was the love of my life. Correction, lives. "However they usually make it is fine."

Nathan nodded at Brad. "Chilled will do. I'm sure she'll enjoy it."

Brad dashed off while Nathan and I smiled at each other. The setting sun outside reflected off his silky tie, creating a sultry glow in his eyes. If we weren't in a crowded restaurant, I would have climbed over the table and kissed him.

"We have a four course meal ahead of us," he said, completely unaware of how badly I wanted to skip right to dessert—him being dessert. "I hope you're hungry."

"Oh, I'm hungry," I mumbled.

"Beg your pardon?"

"Nothing," I said louder.

He licked his lips while smiling then read the menu. "So jazz music, huh?" I hadn't given him enough credit in the car. He had tailored this date especially for me.

"I'm sorry it's not Ella Fitzgerald, but she's impossible to get tickets for these days."

I laughed. "I wonder who she is now. I hope she was reincarnated as a singer again."

"Perhaps she's doing something different. An Olympic gymnast or a movie star."

"Maybe she's a music teacher, teaching kids to sing—with soul."

"That sounds more likely." He set his menu down. "I missed you today."

My toes curled and I swung my feet happily under the table. "I missed you too. Where were you all day?"

"Running errands."

Brad returned with our drinks. The chocolate drizzled glass he set in front of me made my mouth water. Nathan ordered for us, somehow selecting every item I would have ordered for myself. The jazz band started playing in another room, but at a comfortable volume so we didn't have to shout to hear each other.

I almost brought up the Sheila situation, but I didn't want to dampen the mood. This was our first date, and even with Anthony sitting nearby at the bar, it was perfect. I didn't want to do or say anything to ruin it.

The sun continued setting over the red rocks, painting the Sedona sky with awe-inspiring streaks of pink and orange. I loved this town. I loved my life. I missed my parents, but in a way they would always be with me. Mikey was back for good. All was right with the world.

I studied Nathan. He was gazing out the window too. His perfectly tailored suit and the profile of his chiseled jaw was enough to make me reach across the table for him. He extended his hand and wrapped his fingers around mine without looking away from the sunset. "Pretty, isn't it?"

"Very."

His ardent eyes fixed on me. His voice put the velvety jazz band to shame. "The view doesn't hold a candle to you."

At the moment, I couldn't imagine my view, or my life being any more beautiful.

∞

I finished my second chocolate drink and pushed away my plate. "I can't eat another bite. This was a delicious dinner and an amazing date. Thank you."

Nathan leaned back, twisting in his seat to glance around the restaurant. He casually draped his arm over the back of his chair then turned to look at me. His eyes penetrated me in that same unique way they always did right before he blew me away by saying or doing something amazing. Something was coming. I just couldn't have guessed what.

The music abruptly stopped. So did every other sound in the restaurant. Fuzzy white noise rang through my ears due to the instant quiet. I glanced around and everyone was frozen in place. Patrons at other tables were paused mid-sentence, or mid-chew;

one older woman's wine glass hovered at her lips. At the next table, Brad held a tray of food at his shoulder, his friendly smile cemented in place. My eyes shot to the bar but Anthony was gone. My heart leapt into my throat, assuming the worst. *Nefariouns* was all I could think. "Why did Anthony freeze time? What's going on?"

Nathan stood and offered me his hand. "Come with me?" He was far from panicked. Clearly this was planned. My heart calmed a bit and I took his hand.

He guided me into another room where the lighting was dimmer and spotlights shone on a stage where band members stood frozen with a saxophone, trumpet, and trombone pressed to their lips. Behind them, projected onto a brick wall was a screen of white light. Nathan guided us onto the dance floor, carefully weaving between the living statues who had just been dancing moments ago.

A recorded audience applauded and a video of an orchestra on a stage appeared on the wall-screen. My hands flew over my mouth as I squealed.

Ella Fitzgerald strolled onto the stage. She was all smiles in her dress and pearls and she sweetly thanked all the ladies and gentlemen in the audience then introduced the Johnnie Spence orchestra.

"It was the best I could do," Nathan said beside me.

"Oh, Nathan, it's wonderful!" My skin tingled as her audience from decades ago roared with applause and she started singing. "She's so amazing." I turned to face him. "You're so amazing."

My head bopped along with hers and my hands swung at my sides snapping as she sang "Too Marvelous for Words." I mouthed every word. I felt sorry for the people frozen around us.

They had no idea what they were missing. Anthony was nowhere in sight. "This is why Anthony came along, isn't it?"

Nathan took my hands in his and bounced to the music. "Yes, but way back when, a chaperone *was* required on our dates."

He leaned and swayed in time with the beat then spun in place, opening his arms and taking my hands again without missing a beat.

"You can dance?"

He laughed. "I've learned some moves through my lifetimes."

Of course that made sense. But seeing him dance so gracefully made me very aware of my own lack of dancing skills. He took off his suit jacket and hung it on the extended arm of a man frozen beside us. He rolled up his shirt sleeves without breaking stride. "Dance with me."

I stepped back. "I'm not a good dancer."

"You also said you weren't a good kisser, but that was a lie."

I bit my pinky nail, watching Nathan's feet cross over each other and step perfectly in time with Ella's song. My mom and dad used to dance in a similar way and it always left me in awe. Mikey picked up on it quickly, but I usually ended up stepping on my dad's toes. Nathan was an even better dancer than my parents. No way could I move like him.

I glanced at Ella on the screen again. She drew out one low note and a burning throbbed behind my eyes. I keeled over, pressing my palms against my closed eyelids.

Nathan pulled me up, prying my hands away, and then cradled my face in his hands. "Hey, you're pale as a ghost. Breathe."

I inhaled a shaky breath and struggled to take another one. My head pulsed with pain.

"Whoa, whoa, whoa." Nathan pulled me against him, tucking my head against his chest. "Easy, baby girl. You don't have to dance. Relax."

"No," I uttered, trying to explain my sudden headache. Ella's band transitioned into a slower song.

"You're shivering," Nathan said.

My jaw was clenched shut from the throbbing in my head.

He grabbed his jacket and wrapped it around my shoulders then lifted my chin. "It's just Ella, you, and me. I would never judge your dancing abilities, and I'm sure Ella wouldn't either, but we don't have to do anything that makes you uncomfortable. This is your night."

I took a few deep breaths and pulled his jacket tighter around me. "That's not it. It's my head."

"Your head hurts?"

I nodded. He started massaging my scalp, and like magic, the pain eased. He continued for the rest of the song and when the ache had dulled enough to tolerate, I looked up at him.

His worried eyes darted around my face. "Any better?"

"Much."

"Do you want to go home?"

"No. I want to be here with you and Ella." I didn't want to ruin the special night he planned by discussing my frequent headaches. Krista was the only one I had confided in about my suspicion that my headaches were linked to my soul trying to remember my past. Soon I'd tell Nathan too, but not on our first date.

Nathan reached into the pocket of his suit jacket and pulled out a tiny remote. The video advanced a few frames and then Ella started singing "Body and Soul."

"How about we slow dance?" he suggested.

"I don't know how."

"All you have to do is wrap your arms around me. I'll do the rest. It's what all the kids are doing these days."

"I think I can handle that." I slid my arms into his jacket, loving the feel of wearing something of his.

He kissed my forehead and pulled me close. At first we simply rocked side to side, listening to Ella sing. I rested my head on his shoulder and breathed in his invigorating nectar of the gods scent. Running my hands down the back of his crisp shirt, my fingertips pressed against his muscular back. I gazed up at him. He watched me with a sexy seriousness that weakened my knees. Soon, I wouldn't be able to slow dance either.

Without thinking, I pinched my wrist.

Nathan squinted and cleared his throat. "You're still doing that?"

"Doing what?"

"Pinching yourself to see if you're dreaming."

"Can you blame me?"

"No." His smile was luminous. "I mentally pinch myself every time you look at me in that way of yours."

"What way of mine?"

"That magnetic way. Like you're analyzing my body and soul and you love every part of what you see. That way that makes everyone else disappear because all I see is you, and I know all you see is me. That way your eyes flicker with light and it makes the whole world shine and shake. *That* way." He looked pointedly at me. "The way you're looking at me right now."

I kissed him and the world did shake. It felt like a fire ignited between us, lifting us off the ground and blasting us up out of the restaurant, into the sky, past the stars, into space, and out of this galaxy.

Nathan's tender voice brought me back to Earth. Ella stretched out her last three words, *bodyyyy annnd soullll.*

"Nothing?" His fingers running through my hair felt like stardust falling from the sky. "No memories at all? Only the headache?"

"What?" I pulled back, surprised by his question and suspecting he knew about mine and Krista's headache/memory connection.

"I hoped the concert would be so familiar that it might trigger a memory from our past."

I glanced at Ella singing in front of the orchestra, then at the dark room around us. "Have we been here before?"

Nathan shook his head. "Not here." He pointed at the video playing on the wall. "There."

"At the concert?"

"Yes, 1965 she sang in London. She was your favorite singer. I had to take you."

I gasped and stared at Ella. "Wow. That must've been the best date of my lives up until that point."

The corner of his mouth lifted into a smirk.

"But now," I wrapped my arms around his neck. "You've outdone yourself."

∞

Anthony snuck away at some point after the Ella concert. Nathan and I stayed to listen to some of the current jazz band then finished the evening by sharing a scrumptious piece of chocolate cake. The drive home was much more relaxing without a chaperone in the backseat.

When we arrived back at the house, Nathan walked me to the front door. "I had a lovely evening. I hope you'll allow me to take you out again soon."

I played along. "I'd be delighted, sir."

He stepped close to me, took my hands in his, and held them against his chest. "May I kiss you goodnight?"

I wanted to kiss him until the sun came up, but I managed to demurely turn my cheek. "A lady never kisses on the first date."

His head tilted back and he smiled at the sky. "Of course. Where are my manners?"

"But perhaps next time I'll allow it, *if* I'm still as enamored with you as I was this evening."

He leaned down. His mouth was so close to mine that his fingers barely fit between us as he traced one finger over my lips. "I dream of an existence where you yearn for my kisses and are enamored with me for all of eternity."

My lips parted, aching to kiss him. I leaned forward but he stood up straight and kissed my hand. "Good night, Maryah. I'll call on you again soon."

He turned away and stepped off the porch.

"Wait," I said. "You are coming inside, right?"

The pretend formalities were fun, but Nathan lived here. We had slept beside each other every night since the Montezuma Well nightmare.

He gracefully stepped backward off the porch, slightly bowing to me. "A gentleman would never enter a lady's home at such a late hour."

"Nathan, enough. Come inside with me."

He blew me a kiss and turned away. As he walked to the driveway, he called over his shoulder, "I shall ring you tomorrow."

Tomorrow? He had to be kidding. His Mustang roared to life and I watched—worried he might have been serious—as he backed down the driveway. I went inside and found Louise, Krista, and Sheila in the living room watching an old black and white movie.

Krista used the remote to pause it. "How was your date?"

"Heavenly. But he left. And I think he was serious when he said I wouldn't hear from him until tomorrow."

"What else would you expect?" Louise asked. "I'd never allow a suitor into our home at this hour."

"He's your son," I argued.

Louise shrugged. "Society makes the rules not me."

I opened my mouth but shut it again, predicting I'd never win this silly debate. Krista and Sheila giggled. "Very funny," I said. "I'm going to bed."

"I expect details in the morning!" Krista called after me.

I walked into our bedroom, expecting—hoping—to see Nathan waiting for me. But I was alone.

As I changed and got ready to go to sleep I was on high alert for Nathan appearing, but much to my disappointment, he never came. I crawled under the sheets and hugged his pillow to my chest. It smelled like him and that made me miss him even more.

Eightball was already snoring in his dog bed. I sighed. "This sucks."

Dating in the old days must have been excruciatingly lonely.

BETTING ON HUNCHES

Harmony

I'd been helping Dylan and Amber move into their new house since the early afternoon. Anything to try to distract my mind from what Gregory might be doing with the Nefariouns. Knowing he was with Dedrick was enough to make my blood boil.

I set down the last box labeled *Nursery* next to Mikey's crib. Molokai watched me from the doorway, panting and wagging her tail. Her gray ears perked up just before the loud crash. She took off running down the hall and I rushed after her. We found Amber and Dylan in the kitchen. Dylan was laughing at Amber who had apparently fallen into a moving box butt first.

Her arms and legs flailed above her awkwardly. "Don't laugh! Help me out."

Grinning, I grabbed her hand and yanked her up out of the box as Molokai licked her excitedly.

"I know, I know. I'm fine, Molokai." She glared back at the crushed cardboard like it was the box's fault she fell into it.

"One step," Dylan said. "Throughout this entire house there is only one step into the kitchen and you still managed to fall down it."

Amber waved him off and picked up the pots and pans strewn all over the kitchen. "My socks are slippery on the tile floor."

Dylan shook his head and helped pick up pans. "Did you hurt yourself?"

"Do I ever hurt myself?"

I peeked in the box. "Lucky for you this box contained placemats and potholders. That could have been a lot worse if it was full of knives and kitchen utensils." Amber's clumsiness was a trait she hadn't been able to shake in any of her bodies, but amazingly she rarely injured herself during her trips and spills. I handed Dylan a pot that had rolled across the room. "I'm surprised all the noise didn't wake up Mikey."

"That boy could sleep through a hurricane." Amber took off her glasses and examined them, but they survived the fall too.

Nate strolled through the front door and Molokai trotted away to greet him. Dylan wriggled his eyebrows at Amber and they both dashed into the living room for questioning.

"How'd the date go?" Dylan asked.

"Brilliantly." Nate tossed his suit jacket onto the arm of the couch. He might as well have been walking on air.

I leaned against the archway connecting the two rooms. "So why are you here?"

"Because I'm a gentleman and Maryah should experience how respectful dating should be."

Dylan laughed. "You've been sleeping together in the same bed for a week."

"For the record," Nate said, "I've been a gentleman about that too. It's not what you think."

"Oh, for prudence sake," I groaned. "Seal the deal already."

"I think it's sweet," Amber said. "Maryah is lucky to have someone who isn't just trying to get in her pants."

I smirked. "I bet good money Nate is dying to get in her pants."

"Even *if* that were true," Nate said, clearing piles of bubble wrap off the couch and sitting down. "It won't be anytime soon. I'm developing this relationship slowly and genuinely. Maryah deserves nothing less."

"Shall we place bets?" Dylan said.

"We should," I agreed, digging in my pockets.

Dylan threw a wad of cash on the table. "A hundred says less than a month."

I tossed two fifties onto the pile. "A hundred says less than two weeks."

Amber scribbled on a notepad and tossed in an IOU. "Two hundred that he waits until they're officially bound."

Nate took off his shoes then reclined back on the couch with his hands behind his head. "Amber, your two-hundred dollar winnings will be a nice start to Mikey's college fund."

Amber looked pleased, but Dylan and I shook our heads at each other. Amber would surely lose the bet.

Dylan leaned over the couch arm and nudged Nate. "Shall I persuade Maryah to marry you this week or next?"

"No persuading will be necessary," Nate said. "Any and all supernatural meddling will result in a forfeit of the bet in which all monies revert to me."

Amber and I grinned, while Dylan faked disappointment at not being able to use his ability to win the bet. Dylan would never use his gift to control such an important decision.

I dug into another box and unwrapped knickknacks.

"When's the housewarming party?" Nate asked, rubbing Molokai's head.

"Ugh," Amber moaned. "I can't even think about that. The baby, then moving, all this stuff with Maryah, it's overwhelming." Big Kahuna head-butted her leg so she picked him up and sank into a chair. The other two meerkats were probably rifling through boxes somewhere. "Big Kahuna's right. It's late." Amber rubbed her neck. "Let's call it quits for the night."

"Hallelujah," I grunted. "Tell Big Kahuna thanks for stating the obvious." My fingers were raw from tearing through boxes and cleaning. Hilo was asleep on the floor so I curled up beside him. If I couldn't be cuddled up with Gregory, at least a miniature horse would keep me warm. It was nice to have all of Amber's animals around again.

"We appreciate all your help and hard work," Dylan told me.

"No problem." I watched all of them, guessing what kind of reactions I'd get when I told them my news. Time to get it over with. "I want you guys to be the first to know that I'm leaving tomorrow."

"Leaving?" Nate asked. "For where?"

"Carson and Dakota sent me searching the Internet for any leads on where Dedrick might be."

Nate rolled over and propped himself up on one elbow. "Louise has been monitoring the Internet for years and hasn't found anything."

"I know, but I had a hunch. Some reports I found led me to believe I might be correct."

"What was your hunch?" Amber asked. Dylan stood behind her looking concerned but intrigued.

"I think Dedrick is in Damanhur. We know he was obsessed with the temples in the 1990s and I have a feeling he might want to overtake them for his own."

Amber's eyes were wide. "He could never pull that off. Too many people are part of that community."

"Yes, but what if he plans to mind-control all of them the way he did Gregory?"

Dylan shook his head. "Thousands of people visit the temples every day. He'd never be able to control so many members of the public population without drawing a lot of attention."

"I'll go," Nate said. "Tomorrow, I'll walk the temples in disguise and look for anything or anyone who seems suspicious."

"Good," I said. "You can meet me there."

"There's no need for you to travel across the world on a hunch," Nate argued. "I promise I'll thoroughly investigate every nook and cranny. If I find anything at all I'll ring you and you can fly out immediately."

"What if you miss something? Four eyes are better than two."

"Harmony." Amber set Big Kahuna on the floor and he scampered off. "Explain why you think he might be there. The whole truth."

I sighed. "In London, Dedrick told Nate the Nefariouns intended to be the gatekeepers of this world. Louise discussed that with Audrey, Marcus, and members of some of the other kindrilies and they seem to think Dedrick is trying to control a soul's energy. He wants to decide which souls come and go in this world."

"That will never happen," Dylan said. "No one is that powerful. Only the infinite source controls the reincarnation process."

"Sure, *we* know that, because we aren't psychotic and delusional, but this is Dedrick we're talking about. He craves more power. Always has. He's mastered mind control. What if he manages to master something worse?"

Nate sat up. "And you think because Damanhur sits on energy lines to the cosmos that he'd set up operations there?"

"Exactly." I was making sense to Nate. I could see it his eyes. "The same reason Mary wanted to build a home in Sedona. The Earth's spiritual energy centers empower the souls who spend time there. My hunch is that Dedrick is living somewhere near the temples, hoping to infuse himself with more power."

"Why haven't you discussed this with Louise?" Nate asked.

I shrugged. "She's been researching and investigating long and hard for so long. I was worried she'd brush off my theory because it doesn't match up with any of her previous leads."

The three of them glanced at each other, silently debating whether my plan was a worthy one.

"I know it's a long shot," I said, "but please give me your blessing and support. Let me do *something*. He's my soul mate. How can any of you expect me to sit around here and wait while time ticks away? With every tick of the clock Dedrick could be making Gregory worse."

Dylan sat on the arm of the chair beside Amber and wrapped his arm around her shoulder. "How long will you be gone?"

Finally. Success. "Hopefully only a day or two," I said. "Dylan, can you handle the situation with my parents? Tell them I'm going on a senior trip or something."

He nodded.

Amber looked up at him then back at me. "Harmony, are you sure about this? What if something happens to you?"

"Please don't try to talk me out of it. If you do, I will resent you for it, and I don't want that burden."

"I'll be with her," Nate assured her. "Well disguised, of course."

"Okay." Amber didn't seem happy about my plan, and her fingers tapping endlessly on her knee meant she was nervous about it.

We sat around ironing out the details of my trip and what Dylan would tell my parents. Amber agreed to take me to the airport at noon to catch my flight.

My eyes were so tired they ached. I tried staying awake as Dylan, Amber, and Nate chatted about the drama Dedrick had caused for the temples in the early nineties, but Hilo's warmth and steady breathing lured me to sleep. I was vaguely aware of Amber covering me with a quilt, and then, as always, the memory of Gregory singing me Spanish lullabies was too solacing to resist.

EXPLORING THE HEAVENS

Maryah

I dreamed of Nathan dancing. I knew it was a dream because I danced with him, and I was good—even better than my parents. Gregory stepped onto the dance floor with us. I reached out to him, but he pulled out a metal pipe and swung at my head.

I opened my eyes and my mother was there bandaging my forehead, telling me I was okay, that all my marbles were still inside my jar. I didn't understand what she meant so I looked in a mirror. My head was a glass globe and my eyes were sideways peacock feathers. Gregory appeared again, but this time he tried helping me, shouting at me to be careful. He shook me and I watched in the mirror as glowing stars floated around inside my glass head.

"I missed you," Gregory whispered, but he sounded like Nathan.

"I missed you too," I told him.

A gun shot fired and I turned around to see Harmony barreling toward me with a cartoon pistol in her hand. She pulled the trigger and I ducked. In slow motion, the bullet—which was a silver star—sailed over my shoulder and hit Gregory between the eyes. He exploded into a cloud of glitter, but it sounded like glass shattering.

I looked at Harmony, but she stopped, lowered her gun, and kissed me on my cheek. Her lips moved, but it was Nathan's voice coming out of her mouth. "I tried to stay away, but I couldn't."

I opened my eyes and Nathan stared back at me in the dark. I blinked a few times, shaking off the eccentric dream and focusing on reality. Nathan was lying beside me in our bed. Under the covers and everything. His intoxicating smell caused my hands to clutch the front of his t-shirt and pull him closer.

"Did you say something?" I asked him.

"I said I tried to stay away but couldn't. I missed you too much."

I nuzzled into his neck and breathed him in. "Good. I promise to be a proper lady during the day, but at night I need you here with me."

He chuckled and lifted my face so our eyes met again. "That's a brilliant plan." His lips brushed against mine lighter than a whisper. "May I have our goodnight kiss now?"

I brushed my lips against his just as softly. "I've been yearning for it."

His lips closed over mine so sweetly I thought I might still be dreaming. He kissed my chin, each of my cheeks, then my lips again. If my head was a glass globe he would have seen all the stars inside swirling out of control.

∞

In the morning, Nathan and I were awakened by the blaring of a trumpet, followed by Faith's wretched attempt at impersonating Robin Williams in *Good Morning Vietnam.*

"Gooood mooorning, Ma-Ma-mam! It's training day!"

I squinted through the sunlight to see Shiloh carrying a boom box which started playing an old rap song called, "Ghetto Superstar." He and Faith danced around our bed singing and dancing. I buried my face into Nathan's t-shirt and pulled the covers over our heads.

"Are they serious?" I moaned.

Nathan ran his fingers through my hair. "Serious as a myocardial infarction."

I glanced up, giving him an unimpressed look.

"Sorry, heart attack." He cleared his gruff throat. "No use fighting it. Faith is on a mission."

The bed bounced in time with the music as Faith danced and Shiloh sang along with the song.

"Okay, okay, we're up!" I grumbled.

"Report to the living room in ten minutes," Faith ordered.

After reluctantly crawling out of bed, I dragged myself into the kitchen and made two bowls of mixed cereal for Nathan and me.

"Didn't all that racket wake up the baby?" I asked Shiloh.

"He's in his new home with Dylan and Amber. We finished setting up all the furniture yesterday."

"Oh." So many people came and went in the Luna house that it was hard to keep track of everyone, but knowing Mikey wouldn't be living here full time anymore made my mood even worse.

Harmony was sitting at the island rolling a plum across the counter. "I'm leaving the country today. Just thought you should know."

"To search for Gregory?" I guessed out loud.

She nodded.

"But Nathan said he didn't know who he was. He thinks his own name is Argos. What if he doesn't remember you? What if he..." I hesitated. "What if he hurts you, or worse?"

"He won't."

"How can you be sure?"

"The heart is a muscle," Harmony explained. "Muscles have memory. Scientists have proven that the heart retains memory function even when removed."

"I don't understand what that has to do with Gregory." I took a bite of my cereal.

She swiveled her stool so she was facing me. We were sitting so close our knees almost touched. "Imagine someone ripped your heart out of your chest and threw it in a cage. Outside the cage, vultures, rats, and coyotes circle, waiting to rip your heart apart and devour it. Worse yet, as they circle, their wicked energy surrounds the cage, tainting the pure and good soul inside. Over time your heart starts to change; it becomes evil too. Smothered by negativity, it slowly stops beating until it ceases to exist."

I had stopped chewing my food. I swallowed it down in one big gulp. "So you're saying you feel like you're trapped in a cage?"

"No." She sighed. "Gregory is trapped in that cage. I have no idea where the cage is or who holds the key to unlock it, but I will find him. And I will fight to the death against any vulture, rat, or coyote that comes between us."

Nathan stood behind Harmony and gripped her shoulder. "Just give us a bit more time. Maryah will be able to help you find him. I'm certain of it."

I nodded, even though I wasn't as confident as Nathan. Plus, I was terrified of what we might find if and when I did locate Gregory.

Harmony stood and walked toward the door. "Each day that passes I know I'm one day closer to losing him forever. I can't wait any longer. I have to find him. And when I do, even if he is corrupted, even if he is no longer pure and good, I will love him and bring him back. Because as science has proven, *the heart remembers*." She slid her sunglasses on and smiled at me. "And *you* proved that the soul never forgets."

But apparently a soul could forget, because there was so much I couldn't remember.

"Good luck," I told Harmony. But secretly I was hoping she wouldn't find them. I was hoping she didn't go anywhere near the Nefariouns. I had seen firsthand what cold and ruthless killers they were.

"I don't need luck. I have love." She opened the door and called over her shoulder, "See ya in a couple days."

Nathan stared at the empty space she left. "I was hoping she might have changed her mind after sleeping on it."

"I tried talking her out of it." Faith shrugged. "But you know Harmony."

"I'm surprised we kept her restrained for this long," Nathan said. "It will be fine. I'll look after her."

"You're going with her?" I asked.

"Yes, but I'll check in a few times a day."

As much as I wanted Nathan here with me, I wanted him to help Harmony even more. The thought of her running into the Nefariouns made the hairs on my arms rise. "Promise me you'll be careful."

"Always."

I glanced around, feeling the urge to do a safety tally on all kindrily members. "Where's Krista?"

"She's in the laboratory with the mad scientist," Shiloh said. "Carson is doing a test run on her."

"Test run?" I asked protectively.

Just then Krista and Carson appeared from the hallway to the other wing of the house.

Krista looked up at me. "Oh, Pudding, wait 'til you go in there! It's amazing!"

"Go in where?" I asked with confusion.

"Carson's sensperience room."

"Did it work?" Faith asked eagerly.

Krista nodded. "Yes. I could only do it for a few minutes, but now that I understand, my practicing will be much more productive."

Faith twirled around holding a spoon above her head. "Carson, you're a stellar genius."

"Maryah, prepare to have your mind blown." Shiloh waved his spread fingers around his long braids.

Carson nudged my elbow. "You ready to see life in a whole new way?"

I set down my cereal bowl. Mind blowing took precedence over my growling stomach. "My feeble mind has never been more willing."

Nathan held my hand as we followed Carson to the game room, but when we got to the double doors, Carson paused. "Bro, you can't go in with her."

Nathan didn't verbally respond, but his eyes said something because Carson stammered. "Try to understand—it'll be—she can't have—"

"Spit it out, Carson," I said.

"You'll be distracted." Carson explained to me. "Think about it, you're newly lovestruck right now. Nathan stands within a foot of you and you get all googly-eyed and can't think straight. I need your mind to be focused."

Nathan watched me throughout Carson's embarrassing speech. He smiled when my cheeks flushed. "He's right. You'll have to explore the heavens alone for now."

Any activity that involved the words *exploring* or *heavens* should involve Nathan, but this experiment was in the supposedly genius hands of Carson.

"I'll let you blindfold her," Carson said.

"What!" I swatted at the scarf Carson handed Nathan. "Why do I need to be blindfolded?"

"Just trust me," Carson whined.

Nathan had an overly pleased look on his face as he waved the silk scarf in front of me. I shook my head, but turned my back to him so he could tie it around my head. The door in front of us clicked open and Carson guided me blindly into who-knows-what.

Carson sat me down in what felt like a floating chair. My feet weren't touching the floor, and I bobbed up and down whenever I moved. "What am I sitting on?"

"Don't ask questions, and don't analyze everything after I take the blindfold off. Let your mind remain open. Okay?"

"Okayyy," I said hesitantly.

The blindfold fell away and I opened my eyes. It looked like the inside of Space Mountain at Disney World. The game room had been transformed into an expansive night sky. Stars floated around me: in front of me, above me, below me, literally all around me. Carson had created a 3-D planetarium.

"You did all of this overnight?"

"Pshh, it was nothing. You ready to start?" Carson's voice came from speakers somewhere above me, but physically he had disappeared.

I chuckled gazing around at the starry sky surrounding me. "Are you playing the role of God?"

"No, I'm coaching you through this. If anything freaks you out say racecar, and I'll stop."

"Racecar?"

"It's a safety word if things get too weird for you."

"Gotcha."

"From here on out don't talk unless it's to say your safety word. Now, relax your eyes and try to clear your head."

My chair started moving. I gripped the sides of its rounded edges. I was sure the floor was only inches away, but through the illusion of the darkness it felt like I'd fall for miles into the star-filled space.

"Relax, Maryah. Forget about your body and focus on the stars."

An illuminated blue and green sphere whizzed by me, getting smaller as it moved farther away. When it came to rest I saw it was Earth.

"Imagine you're no longer human." Carson's voice was in surround sound. "You're part of the heavens. You're able to see more, understand more, and experience more."

A subtle electrical current buzzed against me. I flinched but Carson continued.

"You're pure aether, light, and energy. Because you're a supernal being, you see the stars differently." I grinned, amused by Carson acting so serious and wise. He was even speaking in a deeper voice than usual.

The stars closest to me grew brighter. Hundreds of smaller stars emerged near and far. The chair continued vibrating and I wondered what Carson used to create the buzzing bees feeling.

Don't try to figure out how it works, I reminded myself. I refocused on the stars pulsating in different levels of brightness.

"Look deeper and wider. Expand your expectations of how infinite the sky is. See that a star has many dimensions. It's a living, intricately woven energy field. Now, truly look. Go further. Expect to see more."

For a few seconds several of the stars opened up like petals of a flower, exposing oscillating beams and three-dimensional—no, four-dimensional—shapes of light. Every side of the star was visible even though I was looking at it from only one angle. It was incredible, like the shapes and colors I saw in Nathan's eyes the night at Montezuma Well.

Carson's voice faded away. The stars turned into bright blue four dimensional shapes. The darkness lifted, and white light surrounded me. I watched the floating shapes morph like shimmery orbs of water. A turquoise bubble floated below me. My body had disappeared. The sound of waves crashing on a shore rumbled in my ears as more bubbles swirled around me, each of them mutating into peacock feathers.

Thousands of peacock feathers fell like rain all around me. One silver streak of lightening cut through the pearly sky, its sharp and crooked line pointed to a single feather suspended in air as the rest fell around it. The feather spun in a straight path until it stopped in front of me. When I reached out to touch it the roaring waves grew louder. Each of the feather's barbs slowly turned to black as if being painted by an invisible brush.

The black feather grew bigger and wider until it filled the entire sky with darkness. The roaring stopped. A breath blew strong in my ear, like someone had blown out a candle.

Black silent stillness surrounded me. A raven cawed.

"Maryah, you're not supposed to fall asleep." Carson shook my shoulders.

My eyes flung open. I leapt from my chair and ran out of the room, tripping over a wire or cord but staying on my feet as I stumbled to the door. I flung the door open and squinted at the blinding light pouring through the windows.

Nathan, Krista, Shiloh, and Faith were gathered outside the door. I shouldered past them and ran through the living room, out the back door, and down the garden pathway, the entire time chanting, *no, no, no* in my mind.

I threw open the front door to Helen and Edgar's cottage. "Where's Sheila?"

SAYING GOODBYE

Maryah

It all happened in ultra-slow motion.

Edgar rose from the sofa, but my feet were rooted in place. Every step he took toward me sounded hollow and amplified. Every breath I struggled to breathe sounded like a steam engine inside my head. He took off his glasses but I focused on his mouth. The two words he spoke stretched from his lips to eternity. "She's gone."

"No." My voice rumbled through me so deeply it didn't even sound like me. I would have fallen to my knees, but Nathan was behind me, holding me up. "No!"

Krista pushed past me. When she reached the living room and looked down at the sofa she did fall to her knees. She made that involuntary sound people make when they find out a loved one is dead: the pure sound of human agony reverberating off the walls, seeping through skin, rattling bones, and etching permanent cracks in souls.

It's the sound I made when I woke up in the hospital and learned my parents and Mikey were dead. The sound I was making again, inside of myself.

The room spun. My head fell back and Nathan turned me around, hugging me tight to him. He lifted me up, carrying me into the living room and stopping beside the sofa. At first I refused to look. If I didn't see her dead then I could live in denial. But that hadn't worked for me with my parents. I knew I had to face the truth, so I forced myself to turn in the direction of Krista's sobs.

Sheila lay there, stretched out on the sofa, her hands folded across her stomach. Krista pressed her forehead to Sheila's, whispering things I couldn't hear. I buried my face in Nathan's shoulder, clutching his t-shirt as if holding onto him meant holding onto Sheila too.

He pressed his lips to my ear and said, "I'm so sorry, my love."

"Stop, Krista," Edgar said. "We forbid it."

I turned my head to see why he sounded so stern.

"She's my sister!" Krista shouted.

"It was her time," Helen said calmly, struggling to keep Krista's face cradled in her hands. "You can't bring her back this time."

"I can and I will," Krista argued, trying to pull away from Helen.

I wriggled down out of Nathan's arms and knelt beside Krista. "Kris, no."

"You don't understand."

"I do." I held her hand. "I do understand, but you can't give up your life for her again."

She wiped her eyes. "I'll give up my life as many times as it takes."

"No, Kris. We already agreed on this."

"She's ninety-nine." Louise stroked Krista's back. "She wouldn't last more than a few years at most, even if you did bring her back. It serves no long-term purpose, Krista. I know this is hard, but you have to let her go. She was ready. She was at peace with it."

Krista's bottom lip quivered. She laid her head on Sheila's chest. "Don't go yet. We didn't say goodbye."

So many bodies had crowded into Helen and Edgar's cottage and surrounded Sheila. Louise, Anthony, Faith, Shiloh, me, Nathan, Krista, and in the doorway stood Carson, watching from afar.

"It's Sheila's time to pass through the unseen curtain," Louise said.

Faith sniffled. "I'll call Harmony and tell her to come back so we can all say our goodbyes."

My heart leapt in my chest. I had forgotten about Harmony's ability. She could still communicate with Sheila's spirit.

I had one last chance to convince Sheila not to erase. One chance to tell her Carson's sensperience room worked and I could astral travel. One last chance to lie and make her believe me.

∞

Everyone else waited outside as each kindrily member took their turn saying goodbye. I was second to last. I'd had a long time to plan something convincing to say. It wasn't long enough.

Harmony's dark eyes stared at me, unblinking, until finally I said, "Tell her I can astral travel."

"But you can't."

"Carson created a sensperience training room and I saw stars in four dimensions and it's going to help me astral travel."

Harmony's gaze didn't so much as flicker from me.

I glanced at Sheila's body, which still looked so alive. It was hard to believe her spirit was hovering somewhere else in the room.

"I will do it," I vowed. "I'll learn to control my ability and I will find her."

"Why are you telling me? She can hear you. Talk to her."

I rubbed my lips together. They were drier than the desert outside the cottage. I stared at the empty space beside Harmony. "Sheila, please have faith in me. I will find you. I will train harder. I memorized your eyes, I know I'll be able to find you. Just please, don't erase. If you won't do it for me, do it for Krista."

The room was so quiet I could hear Harmony breathing. She inhaled and exhaled three times before speaking. "Do you know what letterboxing is?"

"What?"

"Letterboxing," Harmony repeated.

I shook my head.

"Ask Nate to explain what it is in detail, but it's an old-fashioned treasure hunt of sorts. You got Sheila into it when she was a child. It was one of her favorite hobbies. You two kept a journal of all the boxes you found. She wants to be sure you keep the journal. Visit any of the places that seem familiar. Maybe it will help spark some old memories."

"What has this got to do with her erasing or retaining?"

Harmony smirked. "Nothing. She doesn't want to discuss that anymore."

I took a deep breath, feeling anxious and frustrated. "I don't know how this works," I admitted. "I don't know what to say."

"Say what's in your heart."

"What's in my heart is that Sheila shouldn't and can't erase, but she won't discuss it."

"Then say what else is in your heart."

I twirled my ring. Final words should be poetic and meaningful, but I couldn't think of anything to say that felt appropriate or important enough, so I just stammered whatever came to mind. "I love you, Sheila. Technically, I don't remember our past, which means we just met a week ago, and to some it might seem impossible for me to love someone I've only known for a week, but my soul loves you. I feel that and I know we're connected." I kept my focus on my ring. It was easier to talk without looking at Harmony. "And I really hope you don't erase because if you do, I'll be devastated, so will Krista, and probably the rest of the kindrily too, and then, even if they won't admit it, deep down everyone will blame me and resent me for erasing and not being able to keep you connected to us. And trust me, I feel horrible that I've screwed everything up so badly. I know asking you to take a chance on me and my abilities is asking a lot, but..." I rubbed the back of my neck. A headache pinched the base of my skull. "But I want to make things right and on some deeper level I know keeping you with us is a major key in making things right again. If you leave us forever then it's not going to work. I don't even know what *it* is, whether I mean my memories coming back, or my power, or what, but I know it's something big, and you need to be with me—with us—for it to be right."

I inhaled shakily. Where the heck did all of that come from? I raised my eyes and swallowed.

Harmony was still staring at me, but her lips were parted and her forehead was wrinkled. She didn't say anything, which made me squirm in my seat. The tense silence and Sheila's lifeless body an arm's reach away from me was too much for me to take. "I love you, Sheila." I stood up. "I'll love you forever no matter what. That's what it all comes down to."

Harmony nodded, still looking at a loss for words, which was weird for Harmony. "She said she loves you too."

"Goodbye," I whispered to Sheila's body, and then I walked to the door.

I should have said more. I *wanted* to say more, but only blank words swirled around my empty canvas mind. "Krista wanted to go last. I'll send her in."

ONE LAST TRY

Harmony

Final goodbyes always took a long time. At least our kindrily were fortunate enough to have the opportunity to say goodbye after someone departed our world.

Most people assumed they'd have more time to do things, say things—especially when it came to relationships with loved ones. Everyone thinks they're invincible, everyone assumes they have more time, until death shows up, and then all the unsaid stuff comes gushing out.

What amazed me was Sheila told us she was dying this week, yet still, conversations were put off. Things were left unsaid. We might be Elements, but some of us were most certainly still wasteful humans. Time waits for no one.

I thought I'd tap a hole through my boot waiting for Krista and Sheila to finish their farewells to each other. Normally, I wouldn't be so impatient while playing medium, but I had serious business to discuss with Sheila on my own behalf.

Normally, it was spirits asking *me* for help. Now, the shoe was on the opposite foot. I wasn't a big fan of asking anyone for help, but given my current predicament, I had no choice. Maryah's rant about how *it* wouldn't work unless Sheila was with us may not have been clear to her, but I knew exactly what it meant.

Sheila was my key to finding Gregory.

I wouldn't admit it to anyone else, but my hunch about Damanhur wasn't as strong as I would have liked. It was more like a wild goose chase. New circumstances meant a new opportunity, and I planned to embrace it.

I relayed messages between Krista and Sheila absentmindedly. If someone asked me what their final words were to each other, I couldn't say because my mind was somewhere else. Which was probably for the best anyway—almost all final goodbyes are very emotional and personal. It's why I was a big advocate for expressing feelings while both parties were still alive. Once a third party like me was brought in some feelings and sentiments were lost in translation.

"Any *final* words you'd like to say?" I asked Krista when their conversation became redundant.

Krista brought her hands up to her mouth in a prayer position. "This doesn't have to be the end, Sheila. Trust in Maryah. She has never let us down in the past."

"She said she loves you, Krista. And now she must go because the stars are waiting for her."

Krista sobbed. Tears spilled down her cheeks. While Krista was hunched over Sheila's body, hugging her, I held up my hand, asking Sheila's spirit to wait a minute.

Krista didn't walk out of the room like the other members. She said she couldn't. Even though Sheila's soul was no longer in her body, Krista sat beside her on the sofa, holding Sheila's hand as if the physical connection might keep Sheila with us. It wouldn't.

"I'll be outside," I quietly said to Krista, but as far as Krista was concerned, I had left the room a long time ago. All that existed for her at that moment was grief. She was being swallowed by the huge hole left in the world by Sheila's departure. I had been there. I knew how lonely that hole could be—no matter how many people were in it with you.

I tilted my head and motioned at the door. After embracing Krista with her energy one final time, Sheila's spirit followed me out.

"Is she okay?" Maryah asked.

"You should probably go in and be with her," I said. "Grief is lonely enough without having to suffer it alone."

Maryah dashed inside. I said goodbye to everyone else as they sat on the deck and did what they always did when a loved one passed. They told stories about their best memories of that person. And because it was Sheila they were discussing, they'd be there all day and night. Maybe all week.

I walked up the garden path and into the garage. Sheila's spirit followed and I shut the door behind us so no one would overhear me.

"I've never asked this of anyone before," I began, "but I'm begging you, please, don't cross over yet. I desperately need your help." She asked what I needed from her and I answered honestly. "To search for the Nefariouns and tell me where I can find Gregory."

She was quiet for a long time.

"I know it's a lot to ask," I said. "I'm sure you're ready to see what the Higher Realm is like, but you're the only hope I have right now."

∞

Louise called me later that afternoon.

I couldn't answer fast enough. "A new lead?"

"Nooo," she drew out the word in that authoritative tone of hers. "Do *you* have a new lead?"

"Me? What lead would I have? I didn't go to Damanhur because of Sheila's passing." I pulled the phone away from my face so she couldn't hear me swallow hard. It wasn't a complete lie, just a manipulation of the truth.

"Maybe lead isn't the right word. How about a new *source*? Or *spy*?"

I stayed quiet because I knew I was busted.

"Sheila lived a long and sometimes very difficult life, Harmony. She deserves to transition to the Higher Realm quickly."

"I know that," I offered meekly.

"So then please tell me you weren't sneaking off with her spirit today to ask her to stay in limbo and help with our search for Gregory."

Silence.

"Harmony," Louise hissed.

"I was desperate."

"You were selfish."

"It's to help Gregory. How is that selfish?"

"I won't waste my breath answering a question you already know the answer to."

I sighed. "How did you even know she followed me? You can't see spirits."

Louise's bracelets clanged together. I could picture her on the other end of the line, rubbing her forehead. She was deep in thought. "You're right. I've never been able to see spirits. But I could see Sheila's aura today just as clear as I see the auras of living souls."

"What?" I gasped. "How is that possible?"

"I haven't quite figured that out yet."

More bracelets clinking together. "Stop it, Louise, or you'll rub a hole through your forehead."

"I can't help it. This one has me stumped." She paused. "But don't change the subject. Sending Sheila's spirit to search for Dedrick is unfair to her. She was at peace with her death. She's not tethered to anyone or anyplace. What if she gets lost or disoriented and ends up stuck in limbo?"

"I won't let that happen. I'll guide her through crossing over if it comes to that."

"What if she loses track of us and we never hear from her again? We might not even know that she's still spiritually shackled to this world. She's not an Element. We'll never know where or when she returns for her next life. You have put her soul in jeopardy, Harmony."

"What about Gregory's soul? Maryah can't find him. You can't find him. All your connections haven't found even a weak lead since the London encounter. What else was I supposed to do? Just sit around twiddling my thumbs and aimlessly searching the world while Gregory is being controlled like a demonic puppet by Dedrick?"

Louise sighed. It was her turn to be silent.

"I wouldn't have asked Sheila for help if I didn't know she could handle it. She'll check in with me every night."

"So she agreed to do it?"

"Of course she agreed. She's Sheila."

Louise's worry practically buzzed through the phone. "I have a bad feeling about this."

"It will be okay."

"I hope so—for your sake. Against my better judgment, I'm waiting to tell Krista about this. Only because I don't think she's strong enough emotionally to handle it right now."

I didn't want to imagine what might happen if Krista found out I had put Sheila's soul at risk. "And please don't tell Maryah either. She'll tell Krista."

As much as I tried convincing myself it was only Krista's wrath I didn't want to deal with, the truth was I had sensed Mary's fierce loyalty bubbling beneath Maryah's weak surface today. Maryah I could easily handle, but Mary had been the only soul who ever intimidated me. And by some miracle, if Maryah remembered her past and Mary's strong will and determination returned, I did *not* want to be on her bad side.

FINISH LINES

Maryah

I curled into a ball on my bed, quietly sobbing into my pillow. I was sure Krista was down the hall in her room doing the same.

In a previous life, Sheila had been my adopted daughter. Some part of my soul must have retained memory of that love because I felt as if a part of me had been ripped away. Though all I remembered was an elderly and saintly woman who could have easily been a great grandmother to me.

So frail, so delicate, yet she depended on me to reunite her with the supernatural family who loved her. She pretended she had no fear of death when in reality, we all knew she was scared of the choice that awaited her in the Higher Realm—torn between erasing or retaining.

"Please make the right decision," I whispered into my pillow. "Please, Sheila."

I closed my eyes and imagined what the Higher Realm might be like. I envisioned a lot of puffy clouds and bright light, even pearly gates—as if my imagination could have been any more cliché. The rest of the kindrily knew what the Higher Realm was like. They had been there. They *remembered* being there. I envied them because of that. I envied them for so many reasons I had lost count.

Not even a whole year had passed since I lost my parents and Mikey. Well, before Mikey had come back. And now Sheila was gone. It was too much. Death was an unfair, merciless bastard.

Eightball whimpered from his dog bed on the floor. He waved one paw at me and whimpered again so I leaned down and scooped him up. His nubby tail wagged as he licked my face and nuzzled against the pillow with me.

"I'm sad," I told him.

He stared at me, his little bottom teeth showing because of his bulldog underbite.

"You're probably sad too, huh?" I sniffed. "Sheila liked you a lot."

His ears perked up and he licked my chin.

"We'll snuggle and be sad together." I scooted closer to his wrinkled face and petted him. He sighed and together, with our frowning faces less than an inch from each other, we fell asleep.

Sometime later, someone knocked on the door, but I didn't answer or turn around. The door creaked open and footsteps approached the bed. Nathan's strong hand rubbed my shoulder.

"Come with me," he said.

Eightball grunted and covered his eye with his paw.

I felt like doing the same thing. "We want to stay in bed."

"I know that's what you *want* to do, but I highly recommend you resist that desire and come with me."

I rolled over. "Where?"

"It's a surprise."

"Hardly seems like an occasion for surprises."

"We have our own traditional ways of mourning."

"I don't want to sit around hearing about all the great times everyone had with Sheila. It just makes me feel worse about erasing."

He reached over me and rubbed Eightball's ears. "I realized that, which is why I didn't encourage you to stay and reminisce with us. This is something different."

I swallowed. I didn't know if I could handle a viewing or a funeral. Saying goodbye through Harmony was hard enough. I believed Harmony was communicating with Sheila's spirit, but I couldn't hear her or see her for myself. And I couldn't shake the image of her lifeless body on Edgar and Helen's sofa.

"Maybe later," I said, turning away from him.

He lifted Eightball off the bed and held him in his arms. "You are part of our kindrily, and you should participate in traditional activities because it may help reignite some memories—especially this one because you used to love it."

I sighed and threw back the covers. "Fine."

He stood and walked to the door, taking my snuggle buddy with him. "Wear something comfortable. Any color except black."

I suspected that whatever we were about to do wouldn't be like any kind of funeral I'd ever experienced.

∞

I climbed into Nathan's passenger seat. The heavy thump of my door shutting ricocheted off the garage walls. Faith and Shiloh were in the backseat.

"Ready?" Anthony asked from the driver's seat of his old Mustang. Louise waved at me from the passenger side.

Nathan nodded at him.

Anthony's engine roared to life. Then Dylan's. Amber was twisting in her seat, keeping an eye on Mikey in the back. Nathan flashed me a smile as he turned his key, and our car shook and rumbled. Carson's car roared to life a second later. I looked over at Krista who was riding shotgun with Carson. Harmony and Dakota were in the back of his car.

And then just as methodically as their engines started, each Mustang pulled out of the garage and fell in line as if choreographed.

"Where are we going?" I asked, eyeing the parade of Mustangs in front of us, and Carson's behind us in my side-view mirror.

"You'll see," Nathan replied.

Faith shook my seat excitedly. "You're gonna love it."

How could she be happy or excited at a time like this? Sheila had just passed away. Sheila wasn't an Element. It's not like she'd be back in nine months. Couldn't they at least pretend to be sad for a day or two?

We drove for fifteen minutes until we reached a clearing of dirt outside of town. In the middle of absolutely nothing sat weathered wood bleachers. Louise and Amber climbed out of the cars and walked toward them. Mikey's carrier had a visor shielding him from the sun.

"Should I go with them?" I asked Nathan.

"And miss all the fun? Absolutely not."

"But you do need to let us out," Faith told me. Nathan and I climbed out and pulled our seats forward to let Faith and Shiloh exit the car. Before we were back in our seats, Shiloh had jogged around to Dylan's passenger side and hopped in.

Harmony tapped on my window so I rolled it down. "You're lucky I'm giving you my spot." She slid her black sunglasses on before sauntering over to Anthony's car and claiming his shotgun position.

I looked at Nathan questioningly.

"Harmony's been my co-pilot for the past few years."

Dylan shouted to Carson through our open windows. "I see you're sand-bagging it, little brother!"

Carson glanced at Dakota in his backseat then lifted his chin confidently. "Even with the extra weight, I'll still leave both of you in the dust."

Shiloh laughed from Dylan's passenger seat. "Gentlemen, such trash talking! It's so uncivilized."

Faith danced her way to the space between Dylan and Nathan's car. She paced out about ten feet, holding a bright flag that coordinated with her pink and white hair.

Excitement crackled in the air as the four Mustangs revved their engines. Every driver and passenger grinned—except me. Why were we racing on such a tragic day?

Faith lifted her flag into the air, its shimmering fabric rustling high above her head.

Then, suddenly, Nathan shifted into park and vanished from beside me without saying a word. For a second I panicked, but he appeared beside Faith. He grabbed the flag from her hand, said something to her, then together they jogged back to the line of cars.

"What are you doing?" Dylan yelled over the engines.

Nathan gestured to shut off the cars. The deafening rumbling quieted as Nathan reached through his window and shut off his own engine. I jumped out, worried something was wrong with him. He rested his arms on the roof of his car and pushed his sunglasses to the top of his head. "Do you hear it?"

We all glanced around, clueless.

"Hear what?" Harmony yelled from Anthony's passenger seat two cars down, but then her chin lifted and a grin flickered across her lips. "Ohh. I'll be damned."

I was confused as I listened to the silence of the desert, but every other kindrily member eventually gazed off into the distance at some imaginary object. Then, finally, I did hear it; the faint rumbling of another engine.

Nathan beamed as Edgar's vintage red Mustang crested a hill. I glanced to my right and Carson was smiling almost as intensely as Nathan.

"How in the world did you hear him coming?" I asked Nathan. He just shrugged and kept his focus on the horizon.

Edgar's old but pristine Mustang crept toward the line of cars, as if he purposefully took his time getting to us. But when he was only a few yards away, he fishtailed, coming to a perfectly aligned stop at the beginning of the line beside Anthony's car.

"Well, well, well," Dylan said. "The old man decided to come out and play."

From the passenger seat, Helen fluffed her curly black hair.

"A little fun now and then keeps us young."

"Woo hoo!" Nathan howled, clapping his hands together. "Now it's a race!"

He leapt into his driver's seat, so I followed his lead. He kissed me on the cheek as he buckled his seatbelt, which amused me. If he needed to he could vanish out of a crashing car in under a second. Knowing I didn't have such a reassuring liberty, I tugged securely on my own seatbelt. All the engines roared to life again. Louise and Amber stood on the bleachers, cheering and pumping their fists in the air.

All eyes were locked on Faith as she bounced up and down, the colorful flag waving in the wind again, as one engine after another revved thunderously. Once she whisked the flag down, it was all a blur.

My head flung back against the headrest, my hands instinctively gripped the "oh crap" handle, the wind rushed through the window so hard it felt like we were flying. There was no squealing of tires like I expected; it was one long smooth ultra-fast progression forward. I couldn't turn my head—gravity wasn't allowing it—but in my peripheral vision I could see a blur of white to my right and tropical blue to my left.

Nathan's hand reached between us, shifting as we catapulted into what felt like supersonic speed. I was shocked to hear myself screaming, but eventually I was calmed by the thrilled shouts coming from Nathan, who was demonstrating complete control of his impossibly fast car.

Finally, but almost too soon, we came to a smooth stop. A cloud of thick reddish-brown dust billowed up around us, blinding my view of the other cars sliding to stops beside us.

Nathan reached over and squeezed my thigh.

"Did we win?" I asked breathlessly, trying to loosen my white knuckled grip on the handle above my head.

He laughed adorably. "Did you enjoy yourself?"

I nodded, embracing the rush of adrenaline, instead of fearing it. "That was incredible."

He leaned across the center console, gently brushed my cheek with his thumb, and kissed me. My adrenaline soared even more.

"Bro, what did you do to your car?" Carson asked through my open window.

Nathan pulled back from our kiss. He looked past me and said to Carson, "You're not the only one who can move fast."

The dust cloud was still pretty thick, but I could make out the shapes of everyone in their cars. Anthony was leaning out his window, talking to Helen and Edgar. Dylan and Shiloh were walking around, assessing Nathan's car. The bleachers couldn't be seen through the dust cloud, but I was certain Louise, Amber, Faith, and Mikey had enjoyed the show too. I covered my nose because it felt dry and I could smell all the dirt, but the rush was worth it.

"Pop the hood," Dylan told Nathan.

We all climbed out as the guys crowded around the front of Nathan's Mustang.

Dakota hung on Carson's every word as Carson explained car dynamics to Krista. She nodded and said "uh huh" a lot while his hands whirled around pointing out parts under the hood.

Edgar revved his engine. "Shall we race back?"

There wasn't a moment of hesitation from anyone. Nathan's hood slammed shut and the guys rushed back to their cars, but Harmony was already in Dylan's driver seat.

She lowered her sunglasses and said to Dylan, "Did you really think I was going to let you boys have all the fun?"

She revved the engine and Dylan laughed while hustling around to the passenger side.

We raced back to the starting line even faster than we had the first race. It was better than any roller coaster I'd ever been on.

We had a huge lead until Nathan downshifted. Carson blew by us followed closely by Harmony.

I glanced at Nathan and he shrugged. "What's the old saying, 'can't win 'em all'?"

"But you slowed down on purpose."

"Maybe they should change the saying to 'you shouldn't win 'em all when you have a young-souled little brother who needs a confidence boost every now and then.'"

Nathan pushed a button on his dashboard and Roy Rogers sang, "Happy Trails to You." Nathan held my hand. "In honor of Sheila."

I sang the perfect lyrics. "Until we meet again."

He kissed my hand then spun the car in multiple 360s.

I felt so alive.

And maybe that was the whole point.

A LONG WAY TO GO

Maryah

That evening, Nathan and I walked along our favorite cliffs again. It was within walking distance from the house, but it felt like our own private planet looking out over the rest of the galaxy.

"Can we sit and talk?" I asked.

"Of course. Give me one second." He vanished and I cradled my arms while I waited for him to traverse back to me. He reappeared several seconds later with a blanket which he spread over the ground and motioned for me to sit down.

He sat beside me and for a long time we just stared out at the valley below us in silence. He turned and watched me in such a tender way it made me not want to speak. I didn't want our moment of serenity shattered with the wrecking ball of thoughts I'd been having.

He pushed a stray strand of my hair behind my ear. "Shall I guess what's upsetting you, or would you like to tell me?"

I sighed, already wishing we could return to the quiet stillness. "I feel like I'm letting everyone down."

"You're not."

"I am. I can't find Gregory for Harmony. I couldn't astral travel so Sheila probably erased all memory of us and will be reborn god-only-knows-where. And you. I can't even remember our past lives together. I can only imagine how much that hurts you."

"We will find Gregory. Sheila's soul will continue however it's meant to. And I'll survive."

"That's just it, you shouldn't have to survive. I should never have erased, or put you through so much worry and heartache. I shouldn't be putting anyone through any of this."

"As we have told you before, you wouldn't have erased without good reason. You did remember some bits of your past, and you'll remember more, including remembering why you erased. I truly believe that."

"But *how*? How do I do that? I've studied every photo the kindrily has. I've searched everyone's eyes over and over. I've stared at my ring, willing it to magically show me something— anything—again. But nothing has happened since Mikey was born. It's like I'm getting weaker instead of stronger."

"What about the storm of feathers you saw during Carson's experiment?"

"That was just my imagination trying to recreate something similar to the times something actually happened. I didn't learn anything. I didn't watch over anyone."

"You knew Sheila had passed."

"Because I saw black feathers and heard a raven caw."

"That's something. You saw an omen."

I shook my head. "Omens won't help me find Gregory or remember our past lives."

"Be patient. Give it time."

"I'm worried I'm never going to remember anything else, and that I'm never going to astral travel again."

"You will on both counts." He rubbed his hand up and down my back. "Carson is planning more training sessions in the sensperience room."

Sensperiencing. Another thing to add to my list of failures. I pulled at a loose string on the blanket. "What's it like?"

"Sensperiencing?"

I nodded.

"It's incredible. You connect with something so much bigger and more powerful than yourself. The energy and magic of this world go unseen and unfelt by so many. It's such a shame."

"Many just like me. I can't see or feel it."

"That will come with time too."

"When? Two or three lifetimes from now? I don't want to wait that long."

"It's really not that long all things considered."

"It's too long for me." I pivoted to face him. "Will you try to teach me?"

The corner of his mouth lifted into an almost-smile. "I thought you'd never ask."

"What? If you wanted to help me, why didn't you offer?"

"I was waiting for you to *ask* for my help."

"Waiting? Nathan, we don't have time for waiting. What if you could have helped me before Sheila passed. I could've—"

"Easy," he interrupted, taking my hand in his. "Everything is and will be exactly as it should be. The universe makes sure of that."

"Oh, sure. Easy for you to say because you and I are here, together, and safe. What about poor Harmony and Gregory? And Krista might never see Sheila again."

Nathan's lips pursed and he looked out over the valley. "You know, I love Sheila too. I helped raise her. She might as well be a member of our kindrily because she's that cherished and important to me."

I felt like I'd been punched in the gut by my own ignorant selfishness. Why hadn't I considered how hurt he would be over Sheila's death? "I'm so sorry, Nathan. I should have realized how hard her death would be on you."

His jaw flexed as he stared out at the valley. "I debated whether or not to tell you this, but I don't want to keep secrets from you." I held my breath until he continued. "I don't think Sheila will erase. Truly, I don't."

I let out my breath and let his words sink in.

He bent his knees and rested his arms on them. "My belief in the universe was thoroughly tested and broken for many years," he explained. "I was crippled in so many ways because I thought I lost you. But one of the greatest benefits of being part of our kindrily is that when one link in the chain is weak, the others stay strong so that we never separate. For years I was our weak link, but our kindrily wouldn't let me break. They stayed strong for me, and for you—for us. Including Sheila."

I focused on the tiny feather inside my ring, a dozen guilty thoughts running through my mind. I wanted to claw my way into my own soul and rip out my biggest secret. Because I didn't want it to be a secret. I wanted to know what was so important. I needed to know.

"Sheila never stopped believing in you," Nathan said. "None of them did. You made powerful promises and predictions throughout your previous lives. You kept every promise and every prediction came true. Sheila knows that. *She* was the one who recently reminded me that you, when you were Mary, believed with all your being that she and Krista were meant to be part of this kindrily. That you promised her it would happen."

"I had no right or authority to make that promise."

Nathan turned. "You're so much stronger than you believe. Sheila witnessed your power with her own eyes many times. She never lost faith that you'd keep your promise. And I believe that undying faith in you will give her the strength to retain."

His words filled me with hope. "Please help me tap into the strength you all swear I have. Carson's hi-tech room is great, but the night my family was killed, when I almost died, it was you my soul grasped hold of, it was you I astral traveled to over and over, it was you and your eyes that showed me the only glimpses of my past I've ever remembered."

"It's me that gives you the headaches."

I sat up straight. "What?"

"Your headaches."

Had Krista told him about our discussions? Did he know I suspected my headaches had to do with my soul wanting to remember my past? "Krista told you?"

"Krista? No. I'm not blind, Maryah. Our Ella Fitzgerald date induced a headache. After the hot air balloon incident you had one of your worst migraines to date. Every year on your birthday and Christmas, I'd see you or come around you, even if only for a minute. I might have been a stranger in the crowd, but your soul knew I was nearby. And you would get headaches every time, correct?"

I nodded. Every year at Christmas and my birthday without fail, like clockwork.

"You've probably had more than that. Maybe you fight off the minor ones and don't mention them to anyone, and trust me, I don't like the idea of you being in pain, but there's a connection between your headaches and me."

"I told Krista I thought it was my soul trying to remember my past."

"I agree with that theory. And I'm your strongest link to your past, so I'm a major trigger. I just wish you didn't have to suffer every time a memory tries to surface."

"If that's really what's happening, I'll endure any amount of pain to remember my past."

"I'd like to try a different tactic—the opposite of pain, but just as powerful."

I bit my lip, tingling at the thought that pleasure was the opposite of pain. *Please let me be right. Please let me be right.*

"Pleasure," Nathan confirmed. *Yesssss.* "It triggers similar reactions in the mind and soul. During our Ella date your headache subsided when I rubbed your scalp, correct?"

"Yes. Almost instantly."

"I'm assuming it's because my touch brought you pleasure, so I'd like to experiment with that theory."

"I support that idea one hundred and infinity percent."

His green eyes sparkled mischievously. "Good. Get comfortable."

"Here?"

"Yes, this is the perfect place. Out in nature."

I adjusted to sit cross-legged and rested my hands on my knees like I did when Krista, Faith, and I did yoga.

"Comfortable?"

I rolled my shoulders and scooted to the left after noticing a rock digging into my butt under the blanket. "Now I am."

"Good. Close your eyes and rub your hands together."

I did.

"Harder and faster, until you feel intense heat."

I rubbed harder.

"Good. Shake them hard then clap once and hold them apart in front of you."

I followed his instructions precisely, but so far, on a scale of one to ten on the pleasure scale, this rated a one.

"Bring them close together but not touching."

My palms and fingertips hovered less than an inch apart.

"Do you feel the energy from each hand pushing against the other?"

I concentrated. "I feel warmth. And maybe a little buzzing in my fingers."

"Good. That's a great start."

His fingers landed on my wrists as he gently pushed my hands into my lap. "Expand your awareness. Don't feel with only your hands, feel energy traveling up your arms." His fingertips brushed over every part of my body as he mentioned them. "Into your chest, pumping through your heart, filling your stomach and solar plexus, traveling down your spine and through the root of your core into the earth. Can you feel it?"

"Oh, I feel something." We had shot up to an eight on the pleasure scale. I wanted to jump his bones.

He lifted my chin. The sun warmed my face, and even though my eyes were still closed, I had to squeeze them tighter due to the blinding bright sunshine.

"How about now?"

My neck was exposed and begging to be kissed by him, but I knew that's not what he meant. "I feel the warmth of the sun."

"Only warmth?"

"Umm." I focused on my skin, trying to feel the hum of energy like I had in my hands. All I felt was warmth and a subtle breeze blowing my hair and making my scalp tingle.

"Do you smell anything?"

I inhaled. "I smell you."

I could hear the smile in his voice. "Besides me."

"Not really."

"What does the air taste like?"

I opened one eye and looked at him. "Taste like?"

"Eyes closed."

Faith had once told me that sunshine smelled a certain way and how certain snow tasted like licorice. Apparently it wasn't just Faith being eccentric. Nature had a taste. I felt silly, but I stuck my tongue out. That lasted all of two seconds because I knew how unattractive I must have looked. "Nope, I don't taste anything."

Without warning, Nathan pushed me backward. My eyes opened as his hand caught the back of my head and he laid me down on the blanket. He hovered above me, so close a breeze wouldn't have been able to pass between us. "What about now?"

My lips parted but I couldn't speak. I could hardly breathe. Every cell in my body tingled and screamed out to physically connect with him.

"You feel me, correct?" He closed the last trace of space between us. His lips caressed my jaw as he whispered. "Can you feel my aura melding with yours?"

I nodded, but my head felt like it was floating away. I turned slightly, needing to kiss him, but he lifted his chin. "Focus on what you're feeling. Every inch of you."

"Every inch of me wants to be kissed by you," I said breathlessly.

He pushed himself back a smidge, but it felt like he had moved a mile. "Focus on that. Feel the craving in your skin, your muscles, and your soul. Your being is craving a connection."

"My being is craving you."

"Yes, but I'm energy. Everything in this universe is energy. We're connected to everything. You just have to become aware of it." His hand landed on the bare skin of my waist where my t-shirt had lifted. I moaned.

"No moaning," he commanded. "I'm trying to stay clearheaded while I help you."

I had no faith I wouldn't moan, or groan, or yank him down against me any second.

"Feel my energy radiating from my fingers and connecting with your skin." His hand slid slowly across my stomach then up my ribs. My mind was spinning. He pulled his hand away. "You're still craving a connection, yes?"

I nodded.

"Now, reach beyond me. Connect with the sun's energy. Feel it warming your body the same way it warms the earth."

I opened my eyes. "I don't want the sun. I want you."

He licked his lips then placed his hand flat against my exposed stomach. His thumb brushed under the waistband of my shorts. I bit my lip to keep from making noise. His fingers felt like liquid sunshine warming every place he touched.

"Your skin is so soft," he whispered. "Just like your soul."

I reached up, pulling his face to mine.

His breath caressed my lips. "We have a long way to go."

I lifted my head to kiss him, but he pulled back slightly and said, "Don't be angry with me. I love you, and it's for your own good."

"What is?"

He dissolved into thin air.

My hands, which had just been cradling Nathan's face, fell to my chest. I lay there, looking up at the blue sky and squinting at the sun. After a minute or two I realized he wasn't coming back. My craving for him was gone. Now I just wanted to smack him.

Meh, who was I kidding? The only reason I wanted to smack him was so I could touch him again.

I stood up, gathered the blanket, and walked home alone.

∞

Nathan was in the garage, bent over the engine of his Mustang. I wanted to shut the hood on his head. "That was just cruel."

He peeked out from under the hood and grinned. "You were supposed to stay there and work on connecting with the sun's energy."

"Sunshine will never be a substitute for you."

He smirked. "I'm flattered, but if you only knew what a powerful connection you could have to the sun, moon, stars, earth, to any other natural element in this world, you would become addicted." He grabbed a rag and wiped his hands. "And then we'd have to go through *that* again."

I leaned against a workbench. "What do you mean we'd have to go through that again?"

"You were an energy addict in the first lifetime you learned to sensperience. Like a sugar-deprived child in a candy store."

"Why? What did I do?"

"More like what didn't you do? You filled our home with rocks, plants, water, animals, and anything else that gave off energy. I'd wake up in the middle of the night and find you outside, frenzied and intoxicated with the connection you made to the moon. You claimed the light of a full moon was the best thing you ever tasted." He snapped his rag at my hip. "In the early

1800s, chocolate became your favorite addiction because you said it tasted just like moonlight."

I couldn't imagine any scenario bad enough to make me give up the ability to taste chocolate moonlight. "You said in the first life that I learned to sensperience. How many lives did it take for me to learn?"

His eyes darted to the ceiling and he tilted his head. I envied his ability to think back on multiple lifetimes. "It was our fifth go-round. It took all of us a lot of practice." He shrugged. "That's the theme of life: make mistakes, keep practicing, hope to master a thing or two."

"Except our kindrily members die then come back to repeat it all."

"Not repeat. Evolve."

I had evolved. And then I flushed it all down the drain by erasing. "Your ability to traverse, did you have that right away? Or did that evolve too?"

"That took practice as well. In my early days I'd traverse and end up naked on the other side. Very inconvenient when people were around."

My cheeks warmed at the thought of Nathan naked. I was envious of anyone who got a glimpse of that. "So you figured out how to take things with you. Like clothes."

He nodded as he wiped down a wrench and hung it on Anthony's wallboard of tools.

"Krista told me you can't take people with you."

"Correct."

"How do you know?"

"I've tried many times in the past."

"When was the last time you tried?"

He sighed and wiped a smudge of grease off his arm. "A few years ago with Harmony."

"What happens when you try?"

"Nothing on my end, besides feeling frustrated and having to come right back to check on the person I tried taking with me. Harmony explained a strong tingling sensation, but she never actually went anywhere. She developed a severe headache afterward."

"Let's try it."

"The last thing you need is to participate in activities that induce more headaches."

"I'll take some aspirin later. Just please try for me." I batted my eyelashes, feeling foolish for trying to seduce him into saying yes. But his face softened, so it must have worked.

"Would it make you happy if I tried?"

"Yes."

"Would it make you sad if I failed?"

"Well, yes and no."

"And there's the rub. I would never want to do anything to make you sad."

"That's not fair. It's not a bad kind of sad. I'd be a little disappointed that I couldn't travel with you, but I'd be sadder if you didn't try at all."

He sighed again and rolled his neck. "As you wish. I'll give it a go, but afterward when you get a headache, and after I pamper you back to good health, I will say I told you so."

"Okay," I agreed, bouncing on the balls of my feet. "Where should we go?"

"How about we start small and try the driveway?" He motioned toward the open garage doors. The driveway right outside didn't seem very exciting. "That way if I lose you along the way I won't have to look far to find you."

My stomach clenched. "You could lose me when you traverse?"

"Seeing as I've never taken anyone with me, I'm not sure what might happen." He glanced at the floor in contemplation. "Dropping you into the ocean or over a mountain range could be disastrous." He rubbed his chin. "And then if I couldn't find the exact spot I lost you, well, that would be quite dire."

My eyes were wide with fear. He stared at me for a few seconds and then laughed. "I'm not Superman, Maryah. I don't actually travel across land and water. I aether travel using light and energy. I couldn't physically lose you."

I still didn't understand, but I fake chuckled, trying to erase my mental image of floating in a dark ocean with great white sharks swarming me for dinner. "Okay then, let's try it."

Standing in front of me, he looked like the gorgeous super-powered hero he just claimed not to be. He wrapped his grease-smeared arms around me. "On second thought, how about we traverse to our bedroom? That destination would be much more enjoyable."

I kissed his chin. "Take me anywhere you want."

He gripped me tight and mumbled with pessimism. "One failure to traverse with me coming up."

And then he was gone. His solid form vanished out of my arms and I was alone.

His head popped around the garage wall. "Told you," he said smugly.

I turned slowly, my mind calculating. I shook my head. "How naïve do you think I am? You didn't even try."

His face didn't change, which meant I was right.

"You said Harmony felt a strong tingling. I didn't feel anything. Just like on the cliffs when you traversed out of my hands. If you were really trying, I would have felt something."

I didn't know what was sexier, his scowl or the way he sauntered over to me. "Why must you put such lofty expectations on me? Don't I make you happy the way I am?"

"Don't use that reverse psychology stuff on me." I tried pulling away as he wrapped his sinewy arms around me again. "You know how much I adore you, but I want to see the world with you."

"We can see the world whenever we want. Where would you like to go? I can have the plane ready in a few hours."

I shot him a sidelong glare. "You know what I mean."

He kissed my temple.

"Please," I whispered. "Just try. Really try. Just once, for me." I traced a heart over his chest and attempted once last innocent pleading look from under my lashes.

"You've learned to effectively manipulate my weak side."

I smiled with satisfaction. "You can call me Kryptonite."

He laughed then kissed me. "I assume Kryptonite never tasted so sweet."

"Please try for me?"

"Okay, love." He inhaled deeply. He wrapped his arms around me again but there was something different about it, something determined, focused, and unwavering in his intensity. I took a deep breath, knowing this time he was actually going to try to take me with him. And I had faith he'd succeed.

A strong vibration hummed through my bones, like someone was jackhammering the garage floor. My vision blurred. A wave of pain pulsed from my eyes to the bottom of my spine. I jolted forward but my limbs were numb, so I collapsed onto my hands and knees. I looked up at the red door of Nathan's Mustang then turned just in time to see him rushing toward me. I tried to offer a reassuring smile, but before I could force my lips to move he slid down onto the floor beside me.

"I'm sorry," he said, running his hands over my head and examining me. "Are you all right?"

"I'm fine."

He held me at arm's length searching my eyes. "Does anything hurt?"

A headache bubbled at the top of my skull, but no way would I admit that to him. "No. I'm all good."

His face was cold as stone.

"Nathan, it's okay. I didn't really expect you to get it on the first time."

Still he said nothing.

"Nathan." I touched his cheek, but he leaned back against his car and gazed at the ceiling.

"Please don't ever ask me to do that again," he said.

"Why? I'm not hurt, it didn't—"

He rubbed his hand over his hair. "Do you have any idea how hard that was for me?"

Did it hurt him too? He never mentioned that traversing hurt him. "What do you mean?"

He turned his head, but I reached out for his hand, trying to ignore my intensifying headache. "Why are you upset?"

He let go of my hand and stood up. "In our last life, at Dylan and Amber's wedding, I attempted to traverse us to safety. I prayed and pleaded for the ability to protect you. Just once, one time, to be able to take you with me so your life would be spared." He walked hard, pivoting after only a couple steps like he wasn't sure which way he wanted to go. "I failed. Over and over I tried, while our loved ones were killed one after another."

I pushed myself up to standing but leaned on his car for support, stunned and speechless.

"I made you weaker." His hands were limp at his sides. "With every attempt I drained more energy out of you. You begged me to stop and I didn't. I kept hoping I would finally be able to take you with me." He stiffened and hung his head. "*I* was the reason you couldn't fight Dedrick. You had no strength left because of *me.*"

I shook my head, wanting to defend his actions even though I couldn't remember any part of what he was telling me.

He continued. "If I had been able to traverse us out of there, you would have been safe. Our kindrily and I would have never had to go through you erasing. I wouldn't have had to endure eighteen excruciating years without you by my side, and you would still possess all of your memories, knowledge, and abilities. You would still remember me. You'd still remember us."

He stepped toward me, a look of humility and seriousness on his face. "I failed you. I failed us and our entire kindrily. And you're asking me to relive that failure by reminding me of my human limitations."

His eyes were filled with so much sadness I felt it like it was my own. I held his face in my hands, some deep and instinctive part of me taking over my thoughts. "You did exactly what you were supposed to do. All of this was meant to happen the exact way it happened—torment, loss, and all. You're not a failure. You're my hero as you have always been and you will be for eternity."

I blinked quickly and with confusion. Nathan had a similar reaction, both of us surprised by my words and confidence.

His brow furrowed. "I haven't heard you speak so confidently since our last lifetime."

"I know. I'm shocked too. Where the heck did that come from?"

His expression was questioning but admiring, as if I had just performed an impressive magic trick. "That was the way you used to be."

The familiar cloud of sadness swept over his eyes—a look of yearning and loss, but in a purely emotional sense. I knew it was because he didn't see nearly enough when he looked into the windows of my soul. He always pushed through and assured me that the current version of me was enough, but it wasn't. I wasn't enough.

He longed to see so much more when he looked into my eyes: our history, our love, and our memories. As badly as I wanted to grant him that wish, I couldn't. Not yet. Maybe not ever.

Like the sun parting through gloomy clouds, he smiled. "You and me...then, now, and eternally."

I nodded, but silently wondered if *then* would always be missing from my memory.

EIGHT TRACKING

Maryah

The trend started eight nights after Mikey was born.

Nathan got the call from Faith around midnight. She and Shiloh were checking out of the hospital. Shiloh wrecked his truck into the cement McDonald's sign on the main street of town. They weren't hurt badly—the truck got the worst of it—and Krista could heal their minor injuries with no problem, but Faith said we needed to have a round table ASAP.

Amber set Mikey's baby carrier on top of the table. I figured Mikey would be asleep, but he was wide awake and giggling. Amber set him next to Carson, in his rightful place in the order of our kindrily. They were the last to arrive so as soon as Dylan and Amber sat down the meeting started.

"Something is happening to Shiloh's vision," Faith announced.

"What do you mean?" Louise asked with concern.

Shiloh scratched around the bandage on his forehead. "It's freaky. I was driving along, and everything was fine. Then all of a sudden my view of the road changed. Actually, I wasn't even looking at the road. I was looking at my truck from head on."

Everyone appeared confused. I'm sure I was no exception.

"Is this an April Fool's joke?" Dylan asked.

"What? No," Faith said. "April Fool's isn't until tomorrow."

"Shiloh," Helen said delicately. "Keep in mind you bumped your head in the accident."

Shiloh groaned. "I'm telling you, my vision was wacky before I swerved off the road."

Mikey giggled, causing a few of us to glance his way, but then we refocused on Shiloh's issue.

"Had you been drinking?" Dylan asked.

"No, not a drop." Faith assured him.

"So you viewed your truck as if you were standing in front of it, watching it approach you?" Nathan clarified.

"Yes," Shiloh said. "Except I wasn't standing. I was moving with it, but it kept driving toward me." He turned to Carson. "You know how when we play video games we can change the character's view to see from above, below, or behind? It was like that."

"Could you see yourself in the driver's seat?" Amber asked.

Shiloh squinted, staring up into the air. "Umm, I don't remember. It all happened so quickly."

"It was like he went blind." Faith interjected. "He veered to the side of the road and next thing I knew we were crashing into a wall of concrete."

"How is your vision now?" Helen asked.

"Fine…so far," Shiloh said. "But what if it happens again? I could have killed somebody."

Harmony snickered. "We certainly can't let you drive or operate any heavy machinery."

"Did you tell the doctor about your visual impairment?" Nathan asked.

"Why? So they can start testing me to see how many of my screws are loose? No thank you."

Mikey started fussing and let out a shrill cry.

"Sorry." Amber sprang up and rounded the table to pick up Mikey. "He might be hungry." She disappeared down the bedroom hallway. Mikey's cries faded.

Edgar continued the discussion. "It is a bit concerning, Shiloh, but I don't think there's much we can do right now to assess the situation. Pay close attention over the next week or so and let us know if there are any other changes or incidents."

Shiloh nodded. Mikey cried out again from down the hallway.

"Ahh! There it goes again!" Shiloh yelled, pushing backward and stumbling out of his seat with his eyes shut.

Everyone was on their feet at the same time, including me.

Faith had her arms wrapped around him instantly. "Don't be scared. I've got you."

Amber came back into the room, looking startled. "What's going on?"

Shiloh was breathing laboriously. "I saw them coming down the hallway." He looked directly at Faith. "It was like I stood up, walked through the kitchen, and turned down the hallway to see them."

"But you didn't," Faith whispered.

"I know!"

"Shiloh, take a deep breath," Nathan said.

The looks on everyone's faces ranged from confused to worried to astonished. Mine was probably a mixture of all three. I wanted to offer some comforting words, but I didn't understand what was going on whatsoever.

"Seriously," Shiloh moaned. "What's going on with my eyes?"

"Perhaps your gift is mutating." Edgar leaned on the table.

"Why would that happen? I like my sight the way it is."

"Look around at our kindrily," Edgar continued. "What is unique about us?"

We all scanned the circle, assessing each other.

"Me?" I offered meekly. "I erased."

Edgar shook his head.

"We're in proper alignment," Krista said.

Edgar nodded. "Yes."

"This was the plan," Nathan said. "When Maryah was still Mary she pondered what might happen if we were ever all properly aligned. Even during the horror and panic at the massacre, she was telling everyone to return in order."

"I did?"

Nathan placed his hand on mine. "You must have intuitively known it would change something."

Members started sitting down again. I glanced around, involuntarily imagining the dreadful scene at Amber and Dylan's wedding. For more than a week, I'd heard stories and seen photos of what everyone was like at the time of the wedding. Dylan and Amber were Hawaiian natives, both with dark skin and dark hair, living on the island of Oahu. Harmony and Gregory were twenty-something and visiting from Peru, where they lived with their four-year-old son Carlos, who was now Carson. Faith and Shiloh were elderly Asians, well into their seventies at the time of the wedding. Krista was forty-nine and single.

Nathan and I were only nineteen at the time. It hurt my heart to think of all of us murdered on that beach, our bodies maliciously stripped of life.

A shocking thought occurred to me. Why had I never questioned it before? Even when Nathan told me he tried to traverse both of us to safety, I never thought of such an obvious question.

"Nathan," I whispered under my breath.

"Yes?"

"You could have escaped. You could've traversed to safety. You shouldn't have been killed."

"I would never leave you."

"But if it meant saving your life," I argued.

He spoke to me intimately, as if we weren't surrounded by a dozen other people. "It was easier to let them kill me. Death by a broken heart is torturous to endure."

"People don't die from broken hearts." Even as it came out of my mouth, I wasn't sure I believed it. I could feel many gazes on me, but I didn't look away from Nathan.

"I assure you that many souls die of broken hearts, and you and I have done so many times. We never lasted a year once one of us had departed."

"Really?"

"It's the same for all of us," Louise explained. "When your soul mate dies, part of you dies as well. It doesn't take the body long to cease to exist, once your soul decides to be reunited with them. For us, it's always temporary. We know once we've both reached the Higher Realm, we choose to go back together. Twin flames are usually born within days of each other."

"This educational lesson is sweet and all," Shiloh said, "and usually I'm not a selfish person, but can we please get back to me and my house-of-mirrors vision problem?"

"Sorry," I said to Shiloh, feeling shallow and self-centered. "Yes, let's get back to you."

"It is too soon to speculate." Edgar spun his glasses between his thumbs. "But perhaps the alignment will bring about a change in all our gifts."

"But why now?" Faith asked. "Why didn't it happen sooner?"

"I hate to blow your theory out of the water," Carson said. "I was waiting for someone else to realize it so I didn't have to make everyone feel foolish, but this—" He waved one finger in a circle at the table. "This is not proper alignment."

"He's right," Harmony said. "Gregory didn't die. We're only in proper alignment until Maryah. Then Gregory throws a wrench in things."

Mikey giggled again, causing all of us to glance in his direction.

"Mikey," I whispered, walking over to him. His sky blue eyes twinkled as he looked at me. I touched his tiny hand and he held onto my index finger. "He's eight days old," I said. "You guys told me eight is a powerful number. Maybe that has something to do with it?"

"Eight days old," Amber murmured. "You're right. And eight has always had significance for you. Have you noticed any changes in yourself?"

I frowned. "Sadly, no."

"Has anyone else noticed any changes in their gifts since Michael was born?" Helen asked.

We all glanced around looking at each other. Most shook their heads no.

"Your hearing," I reminded Nathan.

He squinted then lifted his chin. "It *was* odd that I heard Edgar's engine from so far away, especially with the other cars roaring so loudly."

"That was a couple days ago, so it rules out the connection with Mikey's eight-day birthday." Edgar studied Nathan and Shiloh over his glasses. "Perhaps Shiloh's vision is naturally evolving along with Nathan's hearing."

"I hope not." Nathan slumped back in his seat. "I hear too much as it is."

"They're both air signs," Helen pointed out. "Maybe that's the connection."

"Hmmm." Edgar tapped his glasses. "Faith, you're an air sign. Have you noticed anything new or unusual with your gift?"

"No, but I hope my ability strengthens." She rubbed her hands together excitedly. "Maybe I'll be able to *make* people feel a certain way instead of just being able to sense their emotions."

"Easy, tigress," Carson laughed.

Louise tapped the table in an almost fidgety sort of way. If I didn't know better I might have thought she was hiding something.

"As always," Louise said, "time will tell."

NAILED WITH THE TRUTH

Harmony

Three days passed with no more short-circuiting of Shiloh's vision. But those few days felt like a year because there was no news or progress with the search for Gregory either.

Friday after school I went to the Luna house. Louise was planting flowers around the fountain in the front garden.

"Any news or leads?" I asked her.

She was wearing sunglasses, but she still shielded her eyes with her hand when she looked up at me. "No. You?"

"Sheila checks in every night, but so far she hasn't found any trace of the Nefariouns."

"How much longer will you make her search?"

"I'm not *making* her search. She agreed to help."

Louise turned her back to me and placed a flower in a pot.

"Any progress with Maryah?" I asked.

"Not yet."

I didn't want to gloat that asking for Sheila's help was the right decision. Maryah wasn't improving at all, so she was no closer to helping us locate Gregory and I doubted she ever would be. I knew I had done the right thing.

"Go on in." Louise patted fresh soil around the fuchsia flowers. "Amber and Mikey are here too. Anthony and Dylan ran out to get pizza."

Louise and I had been keeping our distance from each other. I expected that wouldn't change until Sheila crossed over. I almost defended my reasoning again so she'd stop giving me the cold shoulder, but Louise had an impenetrable air about her when she didn't agree with someone. We had silently agreed to disagree on this issue.

I entered the house and found Maryah in the living room with Mikey. A blue and yellow quilt was spread out on the floor under them. Mikey wriggled around on his back, kicking and cooing while Maryah lay on her stomach watching him. Eightball snored at her side. None of them seemed to notice me come in.

"You're staring at him like he's an alien."

Her head snapped up. "What? Oh, I don't think he's an alien. He's just fascinating to watch."

I smirked, wondering if she had opinions on aliens, but I didn't have the time or patience to get into a conversation that extensive. "Babies don't do much at that age. He'll be much more fun in a couple months. Even more fun in a couple years."

She nodded and placed her finger in his bouncing hand. "I'm trying to predict what his gift will be."

"We've got at least three years until we find out. Spend your time more wisely. Where's Nate?"

"Right here." He strode into the living room carrying a plate of sliced apples. "Apple?"

"No thanks. Is this what you two do all day? Sit around snacking and playing with Mikey?"

Nathan bit into an apple slice while grinning. "No, a good majority of the day we make out."

I groaned and rolled my eyes. He winked at Maryah and she smiled. I almost choked on all the love and happiness clouding up the room. I shrugged my bag off my shoulder and collapsed onto the couch. I hadn't been sleeping much at night and it was catching up to me.

Maryah was looking up at me when Mikey grabbed a chunk of her hair and yanked her toward him. She squirmed out of his grip right into the path of his kicking feet.

"Ow! He just nailed me in the mouth with his foot!"

"Maryah," I chafed. "Do you even know what getting nailed means?"

She sat up, keeping a safe distance from Mikey's bouncing limbs. "Punched."

"My, how time has a way of changing a word's meaning." I glanced at Nate and we both smirked.

"So what's it mean?" she asked.

I waved my open palm at Nate. "Clearly this is one story from your past you haven't told her yet."

Maryah turned to Nate questioningly.

"Really?" He glared at me. "Of all the feel-good stories to choose from, you want me to tell her about a gruesome one?"

"I can't help it." I clasped my hands together and scrunched my shoulders. "It's one of my favorites."

Nate shook an apple slice at me. "You, my dear, are demented."

I kicked my boots up onto the coffee table, crossing my ankles and getting comfortable. Eightball stirred awake. I locked my focus on Maryah. I didn't want to miss any of her reactions.

Nate sighed. "I was nailed once long ago. Once was enough to know I did not want to experience it again."

"Nailed?" Maryah repeated. "I'm guessing you don't mean punched or kicked."

I resisted rolling my eyes.

"Far from it," Nate continued. "Several lifetimes ago, crimes were accused based on opinion and interpretation, and punishment was very uncouth."

"Uncouth." I snickered. "Try savage."

"Times were much different back then," Nate said, putting it mildly.

Maryah's back slowly straightened. "Oh no. Please don't tell me you were nailed to a cross like Jesus."

"Not quite."

"Wasn't the pillory shaped like a cross?" I asked, half instigating and half genuinely curious.

Nate pointed at me. "Be quiet and bask in the sick amusement you're gaining by making me tell this story."

"Fair enough." I held up my hands. "Toss me an apple slice."

"What's a pillory?" Maryah asked.

"It was a deplorable device where people were publicly punished," Nate explained. "And yes, the wood beams were in the shape of a cross, but don't picture all the images you've seen of Jesus being crucified because it was nothing like that."

"Yes," I agreed. "Jesus didn't have his head and arms clamped into holes so he couldn't move."

"Oh!" Maryah said, a little too perkily. "I've seen one of those at Disney World. Mikey and I stuck our heads and hands in it and had our picture taken."

I laughed. I couldn't help it.

"What?" Maryah asked snidely.

"Did you experience déjà vu while you were in the pillory at *Disney World*?"

"No." Maryah squinted. "Why?"

"Harmony, may I continue?" Irritation bubbled in Nate's voice.

I waved my half eaten slice of apple. "Please do."

All I could think about was how much I'd enjoy telling Carson about this conversation. Mikey had fallen asleep and Eightball stretched out beside him and did the same.

Nate sat on the sofa near Maryah. "Do you want the long delicate version, or do you want me to give it to you in one quick punch?"

Maryah hugged her knees to her chest. "Quick."

Nate leaned forward, resting his elbows on his thighs. "In the late 1600s, you had a dear friend whom you believed you could trust with our secret. She told the wrong people about it. You were accused of witchcraft and found guilty. I was punished for being an accomplice and listening to your gossip."

Maryah's eyes were wide as wide could be. "We were burned at the stake?"

"No."

I snorted. "That would have been a lot easier."

Nate ignored me and continued. "You were brank's bridled."

"As if I know what that means," Maryah said.

Nate stayed quiet. I could tell he didn't want to tell her any more.

"Come on," I encouraged Nate. "Tell her the rest and stun her into silence."

Nate glared at me. "You are cruel. You do know that, right?"

I shrugged.

He took a deep breath and crawled onto the floor, almost sitting against Maryah's legs. "Back then, they had a heinous contraption which resembled an iron cage that went over your head. A heavy spiked iron bit went into your mouth as a gag so you couldn't speak or swallow."

She stuck her tongue out and quickly retracted it, covering her mouth with her hand. "Oh, good god!"

I had been wrong. *Now* Maryah's eyes were as wide as wide could be. They darted between Nate and me. "Is this a joke?"

"It gets better," I said. "Nate was sentenced to parade you around town on a chain while the bridle was on your head so your neighbors and so-called friends could beat you, throw rotten food at you, and verbally abuse you as part of your punishment."

She gasped. "What?"

"I refused," Nate said grimly. "I would never do such a thing."

"Even though they warned him of the consequences of his refusal," I added.

Maryah's voice shook. "What consequences?"

"Our punishment was the pillory together, in the town square on public display," Nate explained. "To make an example of *me*, and to warn others not to listen to your *malicious gossip*." He winked at her. "Nails were driven through my ear and I was pinned to the wood beam."

I shouldn't have been entertained by Maryah's mouth hanging wide open and her face scrunched up with wrinkles of repulsion, but I couldn't help it. This was good stuff. People nowadays didn't appreciate how civilized our society was. Humans were lucky to be able to erase memories of their past. Some of it was too terrible to think about.

"That's so...barbaric." Maryah squeaked.

"They were kind enough to offer him options," I added. "He would have been pinned there for two days with no food or water, but he chose option two."

"Option two?" Maryah said almost inaudibly.

Nate touched her pale cheek. "That's all you need to know. It was long ago and isn't important."

Maryah was subtly swaying and paler than usual. "Tell me."

Nate shook his head. "Just be glad crimes are handled differently now."

I honestly didn't mean to speak. The words came out of me with no conscious effort. "He ripped himself free."

Maryah shuddered and gagged.

"Harmony!" Nate hissed.

"Sorry. I don't know what happened. I was only thinking it but the words slipped out."

Maryah stammered through her disgusted shock. "You...*ripped* yourself free from...nails...in your ear?"

"Pain is temporary."

"Why didn't you traverse?"

"That might not have boded well for our defense against not practicing witchcraft."

"Right," Maryah muttered.

Nate pursed his lips and sighed. "We had many more good times than bad. Keep that in mind."

She silently stared at her hands in her lap as she took some strained breaths. "That happened because of me. My big mouth got us punished." She looked up at Nate. "You didn't even do anything wrong."

He held her hands against his chest. "None of that is important anymore. It's in the distant past."

"There is one importance to it all," I reminded him.

Through gritted teeth he said, "Not now, Harmony."

Maryah looked at me. "What? Tell me."

Nathan closed his eyes and dropped his head.

She needed to know. How would she ever make progress if we kept her in the dark about some of the most influential parts of her past? Nate would be angry at first, but he would forgive me when he realized it served a greater purpose. I wasn't telling her to be unkind. I was telling her because it mattered.

"The woman you told about your power," I began. "She married a prominent and successful inventor several years later. And because she was obsessed with your dirty little secret, she of course shared that information with her husband. Her husband believed in witchcraft. He believed it could make him more successful and powerful. And he has been obsessed with you and our kindrily ever since."

Maryah's eyes were glassy. She sat there quietly staring at me. Layer upon layer of realization, guilt, and regret, piled on top of one another. I could see it all building inside of her until it spilled out and rolled down her face in the form of tears. "Dedrick."

Nate wiped a tear from her cheek. "We all make mistakes."

"The Nefariouns," Maryah whispered. "The massacre, all the people they've hurt and killed. All of it. It all started because of me."

I stood up and left them to finish the discussion in private.

My work was done—for the time being.

∞

My intention for sucker-punching Maryah with the biggest mistake of her past was to spark some genuine and intense emotion so her guilt would spring her into action. Logical progression of thought would be that she'd realize her mistake caused the initial connection to Dedrick and everything that followed was partly—mostly—her fault. She'd follow the line of progression to this lifetime where Gregory was missing and she'd be more motivated to find him. To make things right. Sure, it would be out of guilty obligation, but that was good enough for me.

My plan never had time to work. Sheila succeeded with her mission.

I darted down the hall as quietly as possible then shook Faith awake. "Round-table meeting. Now."

"Right." Faith rubbed her eyes and slid out of bed. She headed toward the bathroom but stopped when she was awake enough to wonder what the meeting might be about. She turned around. "Gregory?"

I nodded.

That woke her up. "Get the car started. I'll be out in two minutes."

I ran my fingers over Dakota's closed door. I wished he was an Element. I wished I could include him in our meetings and our adventures. But this one was dangerous, and I was relieved to know he'd be safe at home.

I had already called Edgar and Anthony while waiting for Faith to come outside. I was just hanging up with Dylan when she climbed into the car, already dialing Shiloh. "Sorry to wake you, babe, but round-table meeting pronto. It's about Gregory."

As I backed out of the driveway, the car was so quiet I heard Shiloh say, "Okay. See you soon. Love you."

"Love you more." Faith hung up and looked at me. "Spill it."

I focused ahead on the empty road. "Sheila located the Nefariouns in—"

"Sheila?" Faith's mouth fell open. "You didn't."

"I did."

"Ooooh," Faith said in her best Ricky Ricardo imitation, "Lucyyy, ju got a lot of splainin' to do."

I took a deep breath. "I am well aware of that."

∞

What felt like an eternity later—even though it was only several minutes—all members were seated at the table. All but Gregory.

My hand rested on his empty seat beside me out of habit. "Dedrick is in Calgary and Gregory is with him. How long will it take to have the plane ready?"

Louise sat up straight. Anthony didn't budge as he said, "Just under an hour if we rush it."

"Let's go." I pushed my chair back and stood.

"Wait." Edgar glanced at Louise, seeing that she wasn't aware of the news and she had been the one working on tracking him down. "How did you find out about this?"

Louise didn't look up at me. I was on my own to explain.

"You can scold me and give me an ear full when I get back, but I don't have time for it right now, so I don't want to hear one word from anyone. I asked Sheila to find him and she did."

Edgar's and Anthony's brows both shot up. Helen folded her hands in front of her. Dylan and Amber exchanged disappointed glances. I didn't have time to see Maryah and Nate's expression because Krista jumped to her feet and slammed her palms against the table.

"You what?"

Carson grabbed Krista's hips. "Not now, Krista."

"Not now?" Krista hissed, pushing his hands away but keeping her angry stare on me. "You put my sister's soul in

jeopardy and you expect me to sit here and not say anything?"
Krista tried to lunge at me, but Carson held her back. "You don't
need the plane," Krista shouted. "I'm gonna kick your ass from
here to Calgary!"

I braced my arms on the table and leaned toward her. "If it
will get me there faster then I'm all for it."

"Girls," Helen said. "Calm down."

"You went way beyond selfish!" Krista yelled at me.

"I know that but I had no choice."

"Sheila didn't need to be involved. Maryah would
eventually—"

"I might be waiting forever if I left it up to Maryah!" I kicked
my chair to the floor behind me. "I said I didn't want to hear a
word of judgment until this rescue mission is over!"

"I'm judging you six ways to Sunday!"

"Shut your mouth, swallow your anger, and decide if you
want to come with us and help, or stay here and seethe."

"Of course I'm coming!" Krista snapped.

"Good! Thank you."

"I'm warning you. Wear your bulletproof vest because I make
no promises that my gun won't be aimed at you at some point."

"Krista!" Maryah gasped.

"Oh," Krista waved her hand like she was swatting a fly. "I'd
heal her afterward."

I didn't blame her. I'd want to hurt me too. "We're wasting
time. Everyone get ready."

Maryah stood up.

"Except you," I said.

"What? Why can't I go?"

Nate pulled her back into her chair. "You need to stay here
with Louise."

"That's not fair," Maryah huffed.

She had no idea how unfair the situation truly was.

STILL MAGIC RUNS DEEP

Maryah

Krista threatened to shoot Harmony. Never saw that one coming. Whether she really meant it didn't matter. I never thought I'd hear any kindrily members talk about shooting anyone. And bulletproof vests? The only protective gear that I was aware of this family owning was sunglasses.

If authorities ever questioned me and demanded to know where our weapon room was, I would have sworn up and down that we didn't have one, that my kindrily would never even *think* of owning weapons. And I would have believed I was telling the truth—until Edgar ordered everyone to the weapon room to "gear up."

Nathan squeezed my hand. "I'll be back."

"Oh no you don't. I'm coming with you. No one told me about any weapon room and I want to see it."

He grinned. "Which is amusing considering you designed it and insisted it be built."

I squared my shoulders. "Really?"

He nodded.

Astonished, I pulled up the rear as a line of us paraded down the hallway into my and Nathan's room. Anthony, Dylan, and Carson lifted the bed and moved it to the side of the room. Helen grabbed the bowl of Himalayan salt rocks off my nightstand. Louise took the peacock mirror off the wall. Faith moved books and DVDs off my ladder bookshelf.

"What's going on?" I asked Nate.

He pulled me close to his side. "Just watch."

Louise laid the mirror on the floor with the glass facing up.

Helen placed a rock around the mirror every few inches forming a circle. She stood straight and held her hands open at her sides. "Earth."

"Let Maryah help with this part." Nathan nudged me forward. "She'll represent water."

Helen waved her fingers at me, taking my hand in hers. "Nathaniel, you be air."

He stepped up beside me and squeezed my hand. "You will love this."

"Fire," Louise said, holding onto Helen's free hand.

"I'll be Aether," Carson blurred to Louise's side and linked hands with her and Nathan, closing off our circle of people around the mirror. The rest of the kindrily stood behind us creating a second circle.

Helen lifted her chin. "Aether, Air, Earth, Fire, and Water, hallowed be this hollowed ground and sacred be our supernal souls. Let us inflict no harm and keep us protected from evil. Let every kindrily member return unharmed, let our weapons be returned unfired and free from blood, and let our souls be spared from regret or hatred."

"Amen," said everyone but me.

"Amen," I added.

I could have asked what was going on, but it was all happening so fast and everyone else clearly knew what to do.

Helen squeezed my hand tighter and closed her eyes. I glanced at Krista standing behind Carson. She pointed at the floor in the center of the circle and excitedly mouthed, *watch*.

Helen began saying something in a different language. I stared at the mirror on the floor reflecting the dream catcher hanging from the ceiling above us. In the mirror's reflection, the circle of string and feathers started swinging in slow circles, but when I looked up at the actual dream catcher it was hanging perfectly still.

The rocks circling the mirror glowed pink. Helen kept chanting foreign words.

The dream catcher in the mirror swung in circles so fast that the peacock feathers became a blur of blue and green. The rocks glowed so bright they turned white. Helen's black hair blew back behind her but there was no wind blowing through the room.

This is my family, I thought to myself, glancing around at everyone. They seemed content and fixated, but not shocked or even impressed. *My supernatural family is conjuring up magic in my bedroom. Yup, this is really happening.*

The mirror and rocks glowed so brightly they blended into one circular pool of light.

Helen let go of my hand. "Open the door."

"What door?" I asked.

Nathan leaned in close to my ear. "Using your hand with your ring on it, reach inside the mirror, turn the handle clockwise, and pull up."

"You're serious?"

He smiled. "Serious as a pillory punishment."

I cautiously stepped forward. My kindrily members all watched me but none of them looked as scared or worried as I felt.

"Will it hurt?" I wasn't asking anyone in particular, but I happened to be looking at Carson when I said it. He shook his head no.

I lowered to my knees and inched my hand toward the swirling light. It was warm but not hot, and it didn't hurt at all. I took a deep breath and reached farther into the pool of colored light, wondering if I'd really feel a handle of some kind. This was my bedroom floor. I had been sleeping over this very spot every night for months. Yes, my kindred family had supernatural powers, but a magical door opened by a group ritual? Maybe they were messing with me, seeing how much I'd believe.

My hand wrapped around an unseen handle that felt like it was made of cool steel. I turned clockwise and pulled up. A large circular hatch door hinged up and out of the light.

"Holy..." I muttered. They were so not messing with me. I let go of the handle and scurried back on my hands and knees.

Louise and Carson parted and Faith stepped into the circle carrying my ladder shelf.

"Good job," Faith assured me with her sparkly grin. "We'll take it from here."

The light wasn't as bright as it had been, but I still couldn't see beyond it into what I assumed was a hole or tunnel. Faith lowered the ladder shelf, which at the moment was no longer a shelf but only a ladder, into the pool of light. The light kept dimming until I saw the opening in the floor. The frame was still there, but the glass was gone.

Nathan hooked his hands under my arms and helped me stand up. "Brilliantly done."

Carson climbed down the ladder first, followed by Harmony. They disappeared into the hole. The secret hole. In the floor. In our bedroom.

"Is this really happening?" I asked Nathan.

"It is."

Dylan and Shiloh climbed down the ladder and I craned my neck to see where they went. A light flicked on, filling the opening with regular non-magical light. Shiloh looked up at me and held out his hand. "Come on, Maryah. This was your idea. You should at least come down and see it."

I stepped onto the top rung of the ladder and carefully descended into the hole, glancing up for one last visual sweep of my room.

Nathan squatted above me. "I'll be right behind you."

"This is crazy."

"This is the lifestyle of our kindrily."

I nodded and descended into the hole. I was imagining a whole lot of dirt—an underground bunker, claustrophobic type of place, but I was way off.

The underground room was spacious and bright. Actually, it looked like a museum. The floors were shiny hardwood, and the cream-colored walls were twice as tall as me. Sleek track lighting lined the ceiling, illuminating the room, but giving off a natural light feel. Several paintings hung on the walls, classical and old looking—nothing like Louise's abstract work. A long oval table sat in the middle of an area lined with floor-to-ceiling cabinets recessed into the walls with frosted glass doors.

Edgar placed his hand on an electronic hand reader on the wall and after a melody of beeps the frost vanished from the glass. Inside the cabinets were weapons.

Lots of weapons.

I walked in front of a large cabinet, running my fingers over the clear glass. The cabinet housed a wall of assorted guns six rows tall and eight evenly spaced weapons wide. I turned and looked at the matching cabinet directly across from the one I stood in front of. That cabinet housed just as many knives, swords, nunchucks, and some other threatening contraptions I didn't recognize.

I was hyperaware of everyone staring at me watching my reaction. They were probably expecting me to be scared, or shocked, or concerned that we had our own personal arsenal hidden under my bedroom, but I wasn't any of those things. I was having déjà vu. Something was tugging at my memory, and I wanted it to break through so badly. But the more I willed myself to remember, the quicker the familiar sensation slipped away.

Nathan stood closest to me, silently observing me like the rest of our kindrily.

"You said this was my idea?" I confirmed.

Nathan nodded.

I put my hands on my hips and spun around slowly, taking it all in one more time. "I was a true badass."

He smiled. "You were."

"But it doesn't fit," I said. "We're such a peaceful group. Well," I bobbed my head in Harmony's direction. "Except for the black sheep. Why do we have so many weapons?"

"We are peaceful." Anthony pulled two more guns out of the cabinet. "Until we're threatened."

"And then we become protective," Faith said, cocking a gun like some kind of trained killer.

Shiloh took down the nunchucks and some dangerous-looking star things from their pegs. "And part of being protective is being prepared."

"We'd never fire unless fired upon." Carson handed Krista a bulletproof vest.

"Speak for yourself," Krista said, glaring at Harmony and handing the vest to her.

Harmony smirked and took it from her.

"I'm worried," I admitted. "You look like you're preparing to go to war."

I couldn't handle losing anyone else. If one more person I loved died anytime soon I'd end up in a psych ward.

"We'll be fine," Faith assured me. "We're pretty impressive in action."

I hated to point out the obvious during their moment of proud flaunting of badass weaponry, but it needed to be said. "They slaughtered us. Last lifetime they wiped out nine of us and kidnapped another. Not very impressive on our part."

"Hey," Harmony said defensively. "We had no idea they were planning an attack. And we were at a wedding."

"We learned from our mistake," Dylan said, packing a duffel bag with another vest and binocular looking things. "For all future weddings the dress code includes vests and a gun."

"Lovely," I scoffed.

There were a few chuckles and then Nathan's hand pressed against my waist guiding me past the table and cabinets.

"The weapons are a necessary evil, but there's more you to need to see."

"More?"

Carson blurred past us to the far side of the room. "Even more than you originally designed. Correction," he said. "Than what Mary originally designed."

"I'm still her," I insisted.

"You know what I mean." He ran his finger along the frame of a painting then moved to a different painting and stood eye to eye with the portrait of a lavishly dressed woman. Two beams of blue light shot out of the painting and must have scanned Carson's retinas or something impressively hi-tech because a hidden door between the two paintings slid open.

I stepped back against Nathan. "Do I want to know what's hidden in there?"

"Yes, you do." Krista grabbed my hand. "I've been dying to show you this stuff."

I glanced over my shoulder and Nathan and Harmony were grinning. Anthony strolled through the opening and Krista followed, dragging me along beside her.

We paraded down a narrow curving hallway. Many pairs of footsteps echoed behind us, but I kept my focus ahead, anticipating what would be around the corner. I was not disappointed.

"Holy bat cave," I gasped as we stepped onto a railed balcony. A few steps below us sat a plane. The sleekest, most awesome, stealthiest private jet I'd ever seen. Hands down, it beat anything I'd seen in movies. "You said we had a family plane. You didn't say it was kept in a secret underground lair beneath our house."

"You didn't ask where it was hangared," Nathan said innocently.

Anthony was already opening one of the plane doors. Dylan, Shiloh, Faith, and Harmony filed past us down the steps.

"Neat, huh?" Krista gazed admiringly at the plane too. "I love riding in that thing."

I had almost forgotten Krista's emergency trip to be with me on my birthday. I was envious that she'd been in it and not me. At least not that I could remember.

I turned around and said to Nathan, "I want to go with you."

"It's too dangerous. Dedrick tried to make River kill you. The Nefariouns know what you look like."

"They know what you look like too."

"I can traverse out of there. You can't."

"He's right," Krista said. "You're much safer here. We'll be back before you know it." She hugged me as if she were running to the mall and she'd be back in a few hours then rushed off down the steps.

"Don't worry." Carson nudged my shoulder. "I'll take care of her." He blurred down the steps after her.

"This sucks," I told Nathan. "I want to ride in the plane."

"You can go for a ride when we return."

"This is so unfair. I don't have to go after the Nefariouns with you. Once we get to Calgary, I could wait in the plane."

"No," he said firmly. "But how about I show you the inside while Anthony preps it for flight?"

He didn't need to ask twice. I rushed down the steps to explore the inside.

Shiny wood trim accented the walls of the cabin. It smelled like the inside of a new car, but better. Fourteen seats were covered in soft tan leather. Some sat facing each other but with plenty of legroom between them. Others pivoted and shifted so they could line up together and make a long sofa. Tables and televisions rose from the floor or appeared from behind sliding panels. In the rear of the plane was a luxurious bed and small bathroom.

"I could live in here," I told Nathan, running my hand along the perfectly designed interior.

He grinned and guided me back to the front. The cockpit had so many lighted buttons and switches it lit up like a city skyline at night. Screen after screen showed images that were foreign to me.

Eventually, Anthony told Nathan and me that it was time for them to take off. We climbed down the steps and Dylan raised the door. Krista waved goodbye from one of the many round windows.

Several feet from the nose of the plane, a massive system of sliding doors slid open revealing a wide open stretch of dark flat land outside. We were below the deck on the back of the house. Our house did sit high on a cliff, but it never occurred to me that something might be under it and *inside* the cliff.

Nathan and I returned to the lookout balcony and watched as the plane fired up its engines. It rolled forward and several seconds later it took off and shot through the night sky like a bullet. I'd never seen an aircraft move so fast. But then again, with Anthony and Carson's design and engineering skills, I should have expected it.

"You could have gone with them," I told Nathan, watching the lights of the plane become tiny dots in the black sky as it flew farther away alarmingly fast. "I feel bad you're missing a flight like that."

He pressed some buttons on a keypad on the wall and the doors slid shut. "I'll meet them there later." He glided over to me and turned me around so I was facing him. His hands rose on either side of me and braced the railing behind me as he leaned closer. The metal handrail of the balcony pressed into my back while the heat from Nathan's body warmed my chest. His flexed forearms made me jealous that his hands were gripping the railing instead of my body. The tip of his nose barely brushed against my cheek. "I don't enjoy traveling that slow."

"No?" I breathed, lifting my chin and closing my eyes because the closeness of him felt so good, but it also made me ache for so much more.

"No," he repeated skimming his lips against mine. "But I do enjoy moving slow with you."

I grunted, frustrated by more talk of our relationship moving slow, but also tingling all over.

He momentarily pushed himself away then dipped close again, like he was doing a standing push-up against the railing. I opened my eyes and admired his taut neck muscles as he tilted his head and inched closer to my ear. His voice was nearly a whisper. "I love that you're down here and have seen the plane and our weapon room." His lips trailed across my jaw. "Now, you're in on our secret and you participated in some of our magic."

"Some magic," I repeated, but it was hard to carry on a conversation. All I kept thinking about was how badly I wanted Nathan to let go of the railing and touch me. I lifted my hands, slipping my fingers under his shirt and letting them skate over his smooth abs. "There's more?"

His forehead pressed against mine. "Yes. Our magic runs deep." He pressed his pelvis against mine. His voice was sultry. "Very deep."

I groaned and tugged at the waistband of his jeans. "Do you enjoy torturing me?"

"More than you can imagine."

"It's unnecessarily cruel."

He lifted me up and set me on the railing then wrapped my legs around him and held onto my waist. I ran my fingers through his hair as he gazed up at me, pulling off an impossible sexy *and* innocent look. "Believe me, it's going to be worth the wait."

"So you say."

Without uttering another sound he carried me through the doorway of the bat cave, down the hallway, and into the weapon room. He lay me down on the huge table between the cabinets and climbed on top of me.

"We have about an hour until they land in Calgary. I'll have to traverse there and meet them." I didn't understand how the plane could fly that fast, but Nathan kissed me and all my thoughts vanished. He ran his finger over my lips. "Until then, I'm spending every possible minute convincing you it will be worth the wait."

"You mean you'll spend every minute torturing me."

"Convincing, torturing." He kissed my neck while his hand skillfully stroked my thighs. "It's all subjective."

BETTER LEFT ALONE

Maryah

After lots of sensational torturing and unsuccessful convincing, Nathan traversed to Calgary.

I tossed and turned the rest of the night, worrying, imagining dreadful things that shouldn't be repeated, and watching Eightball snore beside me without a care in the world. I'd close my eyes and picture Nathan's eyes in as much detail as I could, hoping to astral travel to him and make sure that he and the rest of the gang were okay. I never went anywhere. I never even saw a glimpse of them.

The superhero secret mission stuff would take some getting used to. More importantly, I would have to develop my ability or I would be left behind on every mission. It was no fun to be part of an X-Men-ish family if I would always get left out of the action.

Around 5:00 A.M. I heard noise in the kitchen so I went to see who was awake. Louise was staring at her cell phone.

"Any word yet?" I asked.

She rubbed her fingers over the screen so I guessed she was worried too. "Nothing yet, but I'm sure they're fine."

She put up a strong front, but judging from the bags under her eyes and her unwrinkled pajamas, she hadn't slept at all either.

"Do you always get left behind?" I asked her.

She smirked. "I prefer to be left behind."

"Why?"

"Sweetie, when you've lived as many lives as I have, you've seen much too much tragedy. This mess with the Nefariouns is dangerous. I usually leave the danger to those with abilities that can be useful. If I were there all I'd be able to do is see how negative and evil some of their auras are. I know enough about them that I don't want to see how tainted their light is. Or their lack of light, rather."

I leaned against the side of the fridge. "What about fighting? Your name means warrior. I imagine you'd have acquired some serious fighting skills by now."

"Don't get me wrong. I can protect myself in most situations. But I prefer to work behind the battle lines. Like you used to do."

"Me? Nathan said I was the one who wanted a weapon room."

"That's true." She filled a tea kettle with water. "You predicted there would be a day when our kindrily would need to fight an important battle. You wanted everyone protected as thoroughly as possible."

"Battle. Like at the wedding when so many of us were killed?"

"Maybe." She tilted her head while clicking on a burner. "Only you would know if that were the event you foresaw, but I doubt that was it, because if you'd have had any inkling that anyone would be attacked that day you would have warned everyone. Your psychic and intuitive power was your most useful weapon. I have a feeling it still is. You just need to tap into it again."

"Some help I was that day," I mumbled under my breath. I thumbed the glass dome of my ring. "I wish I could tap into some kind of power. I'm beyond frustrated."

"I know you are, but it will happen soon. I'm sure of it."

Amber came out of the hallway in her pajamas, carrying Mikey. "Thanks for letting us stay here, Louise. The house would feel empty without Dylan. And you know how I worry."

"What about all the animals?" I asked.

"I'll head over to check on everyone and feed them. I'm just not comfortable sleeping there without Dylan yet. I don't know why. Still getting adapted to the house, I suppose."

"We can watch Mikey while you take care of things at home," Louise offered.

"I'll take you up on that offer," Amber said. "He seems to love spending time with Maryah."

I rubbed my chin that was still sore from Mikey kicking me.

Something Harmony said had me thinking. If the soul never forgets, did Mikey know I used to be his sister? He was super smart last life. Maybe his intelligence carried over into this lifetime too. Harmony said his ability wouldn't develop until around three years old or so. That seemed so far away. I missed my brother. I wanted to be able to talk to him again, and my mind still had a hard time grasping the fact that the tiny, cooing, sometimes-smelly baby was my Mikey.

As if Amber were reading my mind she said, "I know he spends most of his time drinking, pooping, or sleeping, but this infant stage will fly by before you know it."

I nodded but lowered my guilty eyes. "I'm sort of...weirded out that my brother's soul is now in a different body. Is that normal?"

Amber grinned. "Hear that, Louise? Maryah wants to know if it's normal that she's having trouble accepting Mikey being a baby."

Louise chuckled to herself.

"It's just that he was my twin, you know. We were the same age. A year ago he was taller than me, playing varsity football, and chasing after girls. Now he's this little baby who can't talk or walk. It's not like I don't *believe* it's him. I know it's his soul. But I just feel kind of weird about it. And I feel terrible that I feel that way."

Amber dipped her teabag into a steaming mug while keeping Mikey on the other side of her body. "That's completely normal, Maryah. I faintly remember my first few awkward lives when I had to come to terms with the fact that people who I used to see as young were now old or vice versa. For many of us it takes a few lifetimes to adjust to the concept. Think about Krista for example. Krista is living this life as your cousin. She's the same age as you. But two lifetimes ago, you were her adopted mother. She had to live through you dying. And then she had to witness you return as a baby. She was forty-nine at Amber's wedding and you were only nineteen."

"At first it takes some getting used to," Louise said. "But after a few years it's like..." She glanced around the kitchen. "Well, kind of like a remodel job. When you first see your new kitchen with updated appliances, countertops, cabinets, etc., it's all so different than what you were used to. It even feels different. But over time, you learn to love the new kitchen in its changed state, and even though you remember the way it used to be, you wouldn't ever convert it back to the old version."

"Great," I said. "I'm a remodeled empty kitchen with no useful appliances."

They both laughed.

"We're all remodeled over and over again," Louise said. "It's part of the process."

Amber shifted Mikey to her other arm. "And I bet you still have all your appliances. You just need practice learning how to operate them."

I half-heartedly nodded, wishing I could be as sure as Amber sounded. Mikey cooed while staring at me. "But it does get easier, right? Eventually I won't think it's strange that this little baby used to be my twin brother?"

"What usually happens is you stop thinking of any of us as a title," Louise explained. "There is no mother, father, sister, cousin, son, daughter. We're all equals. We're all souls who share a strong love and bond. Simple as that."

"But don't you think of Dylan, Nathan, and Carson as your sons?"

"Actually, no." She blew into her cup of tea. "I know it's difficult for you to understand because this is the first full life you remember, but keep in mind that I have memories of Dylan and Nathaniel as old men, middle-aged men, young boys. I've known a few of their other mothers, their fathers, siblings, and such. I knew them when they lived in different countries, fought wars. The list goes on and on. After such a long history it's nearly impossible for me to have motherly emotions for them. I love them, and I look out for them, but there have been many lifetimes when they were older than me for long periods of time. With Carson, I only recently knew him as Harmony and Gregory's son. Yes, I feel a great deal of responsibility for teaching him right and wrong, and helping his soul evolve, but Harmony feels that way too. So does every member of our kindrily. It's hard to under-stand until you've lived a few lifetimes and retain your memories of them, but eventually you will learn that titles don't mean much to our kind."

"It's just so hard to imagine." I said quietly.

"We know it is," Amber agreed. "We've been there. Let me ask you, in the flashes of the past you saw of Nathan, was he ever old or a child?"

"No. The only two versions of him I've seen have both looked somewhere between seventeen and twenty."

Louise made her famous discerning groan. "Interesting. Does Nathan know this?"

"Yes. He asks a lot of questions. He figured out that my visions of him were from the period of time when we had married."

Married. The word stuck on my tongue. I had been married once upon a time. Many times. Bizarre but true.

"Do *you* believe you'll ever remember more?" Amber asked me.

I shrugged. "I hope so."

∞

After feeding Eightball breakfast and eating cereal, I flopped down on the couch to watch TV and try to take my mind off what might be happening in Calgary. Louise had been babysitting Mikey since Amber left, but halfway through my second episode of *The Golden Girls* she carried Mikey into the living room and handed him to me.

"I'm running into town to take care of some errands. Will you be okay with Mikey?"

"Uhh." I looked down at him and he yawned while rubbing his tiny knuckles all over his face. I had sort of babysat him before, but other people were in the house. Being alone with him felt like a lot of responsibility. What if he cried and I couldn't make him stop?

"He's been fed and changed. He'll probably fall asleep any minute."

"Okay," I agreed. Monitoring him during naptime sounded easy enough. "But I can call you if he acts up, right?"

Louise grinned. "Of course. Or call Amber. She'll come right over."

"Okay. Have fun in town."

She left and I reclined back then cradled Mikey against my chest. His eyelids were struggling to stay open. "This time last year you were my twin brother," I told him. "Now I'm holding you while you nap. Doesn't that freak you out?"

He made a soft gurgling sound then fell asleep. Eightball jumped up onto the couch and curled up on my feet. They both had it so easy. They had no idea they should be worried about the safety of so many of our family members. I turned to face the television and clicked the volume up two notches with the remote to drown out Eightball's snoring.

Rose, Dorothy, Blanche, and Sophia were sitting around their kitchen table eating cheesecake in their robes. It was an episode where the women had flashbacks to clips of past shows. My lack of sleep caused my mind to play tricks on me because Nathan appeared in the Golden Girls' kitchen and told them everyone was fine. Sophia offered him coffee while Blanche flirted with him. That's the last thing I remembered before the Golden Girls disappeared and I found myself in a men's public restroom.

Nathan stood in front of me, staring right at me. He smoothed his hand over his hair then bent forward and splashed water onto his face. I looked behind me and found a mirror with a crack in the corner. I turned back around as Nathan straightened, dried his face with a paper towel, and turned to go.

I had astral traveled. Thank the heavens! I wasn't completely broken.

"Hey! I'm here! I did it!" I shouted, but Nathan grabbed the door handle and swung it open. I followed him out into a crowded cafe where he walked to a table for two and sat across from Harmony. Heavy winter coats were draped over the backs of their chairs. A waitress refilled their coffees and Nathan thanked her.

"All checked in?" Harmony asked.

Nathan sipped his coffee "She was asleep in the living room with Mikey and Eightball. I didn't want to wake them."

"Louise will update her when she wakes up."

The phantom me did a little celebratory dance because 1.) they were safe and uninjured, and 2.) I had astral traveled. To Calgary. No airplane required.

"I also texted her," Nathan said.

"Texted?" Harmony leaned forward. "Technology has trapped you in its evil tentacles after all."

"I still consider it impersonal."

"Of course it is," Harmony agreed. "The whole damn world is becoming impersonal."

"Not the whole world, just seventy percent or so."

Harmony cradled her coffee cup. "I miss the good old days."

Nathan leaned back in his chair and draped one arm over his coat. "You should have gone home. It's useless to stay here."

"You don't know that. I might find something. They were here for a reason. I intend to find out what it was."

Nathan sighed. "And still no word from Sheila?"

Harmony looked guilty as she set down her mug and shook her head. "Not since last night when she told me they had disappeared and she'd lost track of them." She crossed her leg and bounced her knee, subtly rattling the coffees on the table. "She'll check in again tonight. She checks in every night."

"Let's hope so," Nathan practically whispered.

"Don't," Harmony said. "That's the last thing I need right now. Especially from you."

Nathan kept his gaze on her but didn't say anything.

"I know it seems like I made a selfish and risky mistake," Harmony continued. "But what other choice did I have? If you were in my position you would have done the same. My plan worked. We almost had them. If we could have been here sooner, we would have found them. We never would have gotten this close without Sheila's help."

Again, Nathan sat silent.

Harmony tapped her spoon against the table. "We've all made mistakes. We'll all make plenty more."

"Agreed."

Harmony eyed him. "What's your biggest regret?"

Nathan glanced at the people at tables around us, but everyone was occupied with their own conversations. Plus, the cafe was crowded and background music was playing. Their private conversation would have been almost impossible for anyone else to hear. He leaned forward. "Maryah erasing."

Kill me now. Even with no body the guilt flooded through me.

"Doesn't count," Harmony said. "That wasn't your fault."

"I have a feeling it might be. I haven't figured out why yet, but I sense I was a big part of the reason."

"No," I said. "It couldn't have been because of you." But of course neither of them heard me.

Harmony pointed her spoon at him. "I refuse to count that as a mistake because none of us knew she was going to erase. So you have to choose a different regret."

~ 168 ~

"Harmony, this is silly."

"Humor me. I feel like pond scum for jeopardizing Sheila's soul and I'm pissed off that we didn't get to kill Dedrick. Not one shot was fired. Hell, I didn't even get to draw a weapon."

"That's because they had already fled the country."

"I know. Worst reconnaissance mission ever." She dropped her head into her hands. After almost a minute, she looked up at Nathan again. "Just one. One regret to make me feel better about my greedy self."

"Fine." He watched people at other tables as he searched his memory. I was looking forward to hearing this bit of info too. Nathan seemed so perfect. It was a crappy feeling to be so inferior to my boyfriend. He leaned forward and folded his hands on top of the table. "Our first life together, I cheated on Mary."

If I had a jaw, it would have fallen to the floor. "What?"

"Your first life?" Harmony whined. "That doesn't count. Choose something within the last century."

"Oh, it so counts!" I shouted. I hovered close to Nathan's face and yelled, "You cheated on me? What kind of person cheats on their soul mate?"

"It counts," Nathan said. "She forgave me, but it took me a long time to forgive myself."

"I rescind my forgiveness!" I swung at his coffee, trying to dump it in his lap, but nothing happened except that I became more frustrated and upset.

The cafe spun and my vision of Nathan and Harmony blurred. Nathan's voice faded away and was replaced by loud crying. An awful smell flooded my nose.

I woke up and discovered the source of the crying and the smell: Mikey. His cheeks were bright pink and his diaper definitely needed to be changed. Eightball was pacing in front of the glass door, pawing to get out on the deck.

"Okay, okay, hang on," I told both of them. I sat up, holding Mikey with my arms fully extended. "Louise?" I called, hoping she had come home while I was asleep. Mikey cried harder. "I've never changed a diaper," I told him like that would make him stop crying.

I was so distracted by Mikey that I didn't see Eightball run out of patience. But I smelled and heard it as it was happening. "No, Eightball!"

He ran away from his pile of poop by the glass door and hid under the coffee table, snorting at me with apologetic eyes. I groaned with disgust on three different counts: Nathan cheating, Mikey's diaper, and Eightball's accident.

Definitely one of the crappiest days of my life—literally.

BEG YOUR PARDON

Maryah

I seriously considered saving both loads of crap to throw at Nathan when he returned, but I couldn't stand the smell a minute longer. After I cleaned up both accidents, I tried to flood my nostrils with the smell of baby powder and the living room with air freshener. I texted Nathan to come home right away.

Amber showed up for Mikey moments later. She sensed something was wrong and asked if Mikey had been a lot of trouble, but I told her no and shooed her out the door.

I was so furious I wanted to crawl out of my skin. Nathan cheated on me. I paced the back deck and left the door open to air out the living room. Every second I waited for him to traverse home made me angrier.

Seven minutes passed before he materialized. "How was your nap?"

"You bastard."

His eyes widened. "Beg your pardon?"

"You cheated on me?"

"What are you talking about?"

"I was there! I heard you and Harmony talking. You cheated on me!"

"Hang on. You were in Calgary? You astral traveled?"

"Yes."

"That's wonderful! Did you travel on purpose?"

"Don't change the subject!" My hands balled into fists. "I want to strangle you!"

"Maryah, the incident you're talking about was hundreds of years ago. It was a one time, wretched mistake that I learned a severe lesson from and I would never do again."

Typical guy thing to say. Next he'd tell me she meant nothing. "I can just picture you kissing some bimbo, and it makes me sick."

His eyes were wide, but he had a fascinated smile on his face. It made me even madder because it almost seemed like he was enjoying this. "Picture me? I didn't even look like this. I was in a different body. I was a foolish new soul who barely had begun to evolve."

"I just don't understand. I mean, I didn't know you were my soul mate when River kissed me, and I *barely* let him kiss me because it felt wrong and I didn't even know why. You were *with* me. You knew I was your true love so how could you do that to me?"

"Greed, lust, lack of conscience and morals, I was still struggling with all of those things at the time. I was far from perfect in many of my lives, but honestly there has been no one but you since 1138. Can you please hold me accountable only for mistakes I've made in the past five hundred years or so?"

He stepped closer, extending his arms and tilting his head in that enticing way of his, but I was angry enough to resist him.

"I don't even want to be near you right now." I stomped into the house and kept going until I reached the kitchen.

He followed. "Maryah. Please, let's discuss this. I don't want you to be upset."

"Oh, I'm upset!"

"Shh, I'd prefer Louise didn't hear us."

"She's not even here!" I positioned myself so the island was between us. If I didn't put something between us I might smack him. "Do you still think about her?"

His forehead wrinkled with confusion. "About Louise?"

"No, about *her*! The hussy you cheated on me with!"

His eyes bulged again and his head craned forward. That ridiculously maddening smile spread across his face.

I gripped the edge of the counter. "Why are you smiling?"

"Because your jealousy regarding this ancient issue is entertain, er—surprising."

"Entertaining? You were about to say entertaining! You think it's funny that you hurt me?"

"Maryah," he laughed, and I wanted to leap over the island. "It is a bit entertaining, but only because it's interesting to know who you once were and to see you acting so...*jejune* about this issue."

I huffed. "What does jejune mean?"

He inhaled, tightening his lips in a contemplative grin before continuing. "Inexperienced or—brace yourself—immature."

I grabbed an orange from the fruit basket and threw it at him.

He caught it effortlessly, visually fighting back laughter. "I meant it in a loving way."

"You just called me immature!"

"You *are* immature." I threw a plum at him but he caught that too. "You are, mentally and emotionally, eighteen years old. It seems some of your past maturity has remained intact, but by no means are your emotions as evolved as they were in our last lifetime. Keep in mind I grew and evolved with you over many centuries. You basically reset yourself, leaving me with an extremely young and callow version of you."

I squinted. "Callow?"

"Inexperienced."

"You're making it sound like you're some hundred-year-old man robbing the cradle."

He smirked. "More like nine-hundred-year-old man."

"Gross!"

He laughed again. "Well, it's the truth."

"Great. Now all I can picture is you all decrepit and wrinkled like a *Tales from the Crypt* character."

He slowly eased his way around the island, peeking up from under his lashes with a careful and calculating look. If he thought of me as a child I might as well act like one. I crossed my arms across my chest and turned away from him.

His hand stroked my forearm and my skin prickled. I hated that he could disarm me with one touch. He leaned in, lightly brushing his nose along my jawline and breathing on my neck. My knees went weak but my resolve to stay angry remained strong. He hummed lightly in my ear before speaking. "Comparing me to The Crypt Keeper is a bit insulting. How about we go into the bedroom so I can prove how lively and virile I am?"

It took supreme strength not to throw my arms around him and devour him. Weakly, I said, "No. I'm mad at you."

"Mmm." His hands slid down my hips. "That's fine because we have all of eternity for me to show you how sorry I am." He kissed my shoulder then my neck. "Even when I thought I had lost you forever, I knew I'd never be with anyone else. Never, ever, will there be anyone but you, Maryah."

I turned around and he stared at me for one intense moment then his lips closed over mine. His kiss was deep and apologetic. The usual head rush flowed through me seconds before my knees gave out. Nathan knew all too well the effect he had on me, so he caught me effortlessly. He lifted me up, set me on the counter, and eased himself between my legs. He kissed me so passionately I was sure the kitchen smoke detector was about to go off.

He paused just long enough to say, "I missed you." Then he kissed me again.

I wrapped my arms around him, digging my nails into his back and pulling him tighter between my legs. Our breaths quickened and our kisses grew deeper. His hand slid through my hair and he guided my head to whatever position he wanted as his lips and tongue worked their magic on my neck.

Beams of green and gold light flashed around us. I yanked back, placing my hands on the side of Nathan's face, half-expecting him to say he saw the same thing, but when he looked at me, I gasped. I could see deep inside his eyes, just like the time at Montezuma Well. Multi-dimensional shapes pulsed and moved through a tunnel of pulsating light.

Nathan's breathing was fast and hard. He closed his eyes again and leaned against me.

"No!" I moaned, pushing him back.

"I'm sorry." He raised his hands above his head and stepped away. "I got carried away."

"That's not why I'm saying no. Your eyes."

His green eyes were smoldering and beautiful, but the magic tunnel of light was gone.

"Dammit," I said breathlessly, kicking the air.

"What?"

"Your kaleidoscope eyes, I saw them again, but only for a few seconds."

He glided back between my legs, wrapping his arms around me. "Really?"

I nodded, running my fingers through his hair. He slid me to the edge of the counter and pulled me tight against him. "I'm sorry. I would have kept them open if I knew."

"When your eyes look like that, it's so…" I couldn't find a word powerful enough to describe it, so I went with, "magical."

"It's not me," he insisted. "It's us. Our history. Every emotion, memory, and piece of our past together is stored in my soul."

I swallowed, preparing to ask the question I'd been wondering since the night I told him I loved him. "What do you see when you look into my eyes?"

His grin faded into a grimace. His focus dropped to his hands as he rubbed my thighs.

"You can tell me," I assured him. "I can handle it."

He raised his eyes to meet mine. I blinked several times, worried that what he saw caused him heartache. "I still see the grand hall, or tunnel of light as you refer to it, it's just…well, many of the shapes and colors have disappeared, and the light has…dimmed."

I flinched with guilt. "But it's not completely empty, right? You still see some light?"

His merciful squint and tight lips told me the truth, contradicting the words he spoke. "I see enough."

"I'm a horrible person," I confessed quietly.

"No, you're my twin flame. The light of my life."

"Here I am yelling and throwing things at you because I'm angry about something you did hundreds of years ago while I committed the biggest sin thinkable less than two decades ago. And every time you look at me you're reminded of it."

"I forgave you."

"You shouldn't have. I can't imagine how hard this is for you. How hard it was the past eighteen years. How hard it still is for you."

He sighed. "True, you can't imagine, so please promise me you will never erase again."

I wrapped my arms around his neck, grasping him tightly. I didn't deserve him, but I was grateful he was mine. He was imperfect but perfect for me. "I promise you, Nathaniel, I will never erase again. I love you now and eternally."

That look flickered in his eyes again—that *almost but not enough* look that frustrated me so badly. He whispered, "One more thing."

"Anything."

"Promise not to throw fruit at me ever again."

I kissed his cheek softly. "I would never make you a promise I can't keep."

He laughed and so did I.

COSMIC CARSON

Maryah

Everyone was home safe and sound, except Harmony, but Faith assured me she'd be home in a day or two at most. I had to admit a part of me was happy the Nefariouns were nowhere to be found in Calgary. The thought of any of the kindrily being near Dedrick made me cringe with fear. I felt bad that we were no closer to finding Gregory, but we still had hope. Two hopes: Sheila and me. A burst of friendly competition had sparked inside me. I was determined to master astral traveling and find Gregory before Sheila did again. I was much more hopeful given my recent astral travel *and* glimpse into Nathan's soul.

Nathan traversed back to Calgary to convince Harmony to give up on her investigation and come home. She was determined to find out why Dedrick had been there, but her search had led her to one dead end after another.

Krista and I were supposed to have some alone time to go out for milkshakes, but Carson asked if he could come along and Krista told him yes before I could say no. As always, he insisted on driving.

I might as well have been invisible the whole time. They talked about the trip, the plane, some phone application Carson was designing that sounded too technical for me to understand, and a bunch of other topics I eventually tuned out since I wasn't involved in the conversation. The whole night I felt like a third wheel. They didn't even attempt to include me.

By the time we were on our way home, I was glad the evening was almost over.

I was in the backseat, glancing between Carson's profile and the back of Krista's head. They talked to each other even more casually than Nathan and I did. Carson was zipping along a good twenty miles over the speed limit when he suddenly came to a wheel-screeching stop. I flew forward, ramming the back of Krista's seat. Carson turned his head, looking behind us as he reversed a few yards.

"What the heck, Carson?" I cracked my neck to make sure I didn't get whiplash. I tried seeing Krista's expression in her side view mirror but she was facing Carson.

"Turtle?" She casually asked him. He nodded.

"Turtle?" I repeated.

Carson stopped the car and climbed out, leaving his door open. I leaned between the front seats and watched Carson pick up a turtle from the middle of the road. He examined it then carried it down the bank and off into an area with bushes.

"How did you know it was a turtle?" I asked Krista.

She grinned, still watching him. "The same thing happened the other day."

Carson the Turtle Saver. Who would have guessed?

Carson climbed back in and buckled his seatbelt. "He's all good. Not a scratch on him."

"So this is a hobby of yours?" I asked. "Saving turtles?"

"Good karma," Carson replied. "The worst is when they've already been hit but aren't dead. It's no fun playing God."

My eyes darted to Krista. She always said she didn't want to be a doctor because she didn't want to play God. She didn't want to decide who lived or died. I couldn't help asking, "Kris, could you heal a turtle if it were dying?"

Krista tilted her head. "Maybe. I'm not sure. I've never tried to use my ability on animals."

"Why not?" Carson asked the same question I was thinking.

Krista shrugged. "I never had any pets of my own. I wasn't ever attached to an animal that needed healing."

Carson's head snapped back against his seat. "Why would you need to be attached? You're a vegetarian. You won't even eat meat. You wouldn't heal an injured turtle if we came across one? A life is a life."

Their voices rose as they continued bickering. No way was I jumping into this argument.

"I didn't say I wouldn't *try* to save an injured turtle," Krista snapped. "I simply said I've never been in that position before and I don't know if I could."

"Which basically means you'd consider letting them die an agonizingly painful death."

"Agonizing? You're acting like you know how the turtle feels."

"I know they suffer and feel pain. Amber told me they cry and beg for help. It's awful."

Krista stared at him with the same surprised look I'm sure was on my face too.

"Amber can hear animals crying?" I asked quietly.

Carson huffed. "She *communicates* with animals. Did you think her ability only applied to cheerful chitchat? I've been in the car with Amber when she came across an injured animal. One time, this rabbit had its lower half crushed by a car, but the poor thing lay there, smashed into the road, his front feet struggling to move him to safety as he cried and pleaded for help."

Tears formed in my eyes.

"Amber had to explain to him that he was going to die," Carson continued. "Imagine what that must be like. And then, so he wouldn't have to lay there suffering, she killed him."

A tear ran down my cheek.

Carson shook his head. "I still can't get the image of her breaking that poor bunny's neck out of my mind."

My hands flew to my mouth. "Oh my god."

"Yeah," Carson said, glancing at Krista, "so if we ever come across an injured animal and you don't at least try to help it, we're going to have a serious problem."

"I'm sorry," Krista whispered. "I didn't know."

"Didn't know what?" Carson gawked. "That animals feel pain? Do you know what Amber told me about that rabbit? When she told him he was going to die, that he was going to a place where he wouldn't be in pain anymore, do you know what his last thoughts were? He worried about his family. They'd never know what happened to him. They'd be left alone, worrying, imagining the worst, and they'd never have closure."

It was like a heartbreaking Disney movie. My voice cracked. "The bunny had a family?"

Carson pulled into the driveway. He shut off the car then turned to look at us. "You two have a lot to learn about this world. Maybe I'll get you two pet bunnies and turtles tomorrow and see how you feel when they show up missing."

He got out and slammed his car door.

"You've really never tried to heal an animal?" I asked Krista.

She shook her head. "Amber can only hear animal thoughts. Gregory could only hear human thoughts. I always assumed my healing power was limited to humans."

"Well, if Eightball ever gets sick, you better try your best." I couldn't get the awful roadkill images out of my head. "I feel awful for that bunny. Poor little guy."

"As sad as that story was, I think the bunny was a metaphor for Gregory." Krista sighed. "I'm fairly certain every time Carson tries to save a life, it's for Gregory."

∞

Later, Krista and I were lounging in her bed watching television with a huge bowl of popcorn between us.

"That was pretty smart of you about the bunny metaphor," I said. "I sort of forgot Carson was Gregory and Harmony's son last lifetime. I mean, I didn't forget, but this kindrily has a lot of people and it's hard to keep track of everyone and their connections. I wasn't considering how much this must be upsetting him too."

"Yup. He's been taking it pretty hard. He puts up a strong front, but he wants to find Gregory just as much as Harmony does. Maybe more."

"You two seem to be getting pretty close. If I didn't know better, I might have thought you two were having a lover's quarrel about the saving animals thing."

Krista blushed and looked away. My stomach dropped.

I sat up and leaned across her so I could see her expression. "Krista, do you like Carson?"

Her smile answered before she did. "I do."

"You *like* like him?"

She nodded. "We've been hanging out a lot whenever you and Nathan are together."

"Kris, he's like family!"

"He's not *my* family. I have no blood ties to him."

"You have kindrily ties to him."

"So?"

"And what if you date him and it ends badly and you two hate each other? For eternity we're going to have feuding kindrily members?"

"Nah." She tossed popcorn into her mouth. "I'm sure it would only take us a lifetime or two to make up."

"I can't believe this. Not Carson. Anyone but Carson."

"Maryah, has it occurred to you that maybe Carson is my soul mate? "

I smacked my forehead. "Oh dear god, you can't be serious."

"Why would that be so far-fetched? We're side by side in the order. Maybe he was created for me."

"I think my popcorn is coming back up."

"You two may have had your issues, but he's growing on you and you know it."

"That's not the point." Krista and *Carson*? She was too good for him. She deserved someone suave and sophisticated, someone who had a wardrobe that consisted of more than gamer t-shirts and white hoodies. "He can't be your soul mate. You'd know without a doubt if you two were meant to be."

"Oh, because you were so sure about Nathaniel?"

"I'm sure I was sure in our first life together. *My* lack of intuition and insanity was because I was stupid and erased. What's your excuse?"

"It's not insane. I know what I'm feeling. I've never felt this way about anyone before."

"You've only had like three boyfriends."

"You're forgetting I lived and still remember my other lives. I've dated more than three people. I have lots to compare with. If I took all the good qualities of every guy I ever dated and combined them into one person, Carson would still be a million times better."

I held my stomach and pretended to gag. "Some of my popcorn definitely came back up."

"This is why I didn't want to tell you."

I sank back into my pillows. "He likes you too, doesn't he? I can tell he does."

"Yes, he does." She answered with way too much confidence.

"Please tell me you two haven't been making out behind my back."

She laughed. "Behind your back? Why should our relationship have anything to do with you?"

"*Relationship*? You're already in a relationship?" I pulled a pillow over my head. "I don't want to hear any more." Krista tickled my side and I squirmed out from under the pillow. "Okay, okay, I must enjoy self-torture because I have to know. Have you kissed him?"

Even her tan Egyptian skin couldn't hide the blushing of her cheeks.

I groaned. "You did kiss him! And you didn't tell me?"

"Oh, because you're handling it so well right now? Besides, *he* kissed me."

She was beaming. I could hardly believe it, but Krista was glowing as she probably replayed the memory of Carson kissing her. I didn't want details, but judging by her twinkling eyes and smitten grin it must have been amazing. "How did I not notice you two had become an item?"

"You did notice. You commented on the lover's quarrel thing."

"I mean before now."

"You've been busy getting to know Nathan again and working on your ability." Her grin fell. "And then we lost Sheila. A lot has happened."

I turned so I was directly facing her. "He makes you happy?"

She smiled in a way that reminded me of the stars twinkling in the Sedona sky. "It's more than that. It's like, I feel so good around him. I feel whole, not just the butterflies in my stomach or giddy or the stuff I felt when I was dating someone in the past. With Carson it's..." She looked at the ceiling. I looked up too as if we'd find the perfect words hanging above our heads. She linked her pinky with mine and looked me straight in the eyes. "With Carson, it's cosmic."

My eyebrows shot up. How could I argue with cosmic? That was one heck of a commendation for Carson. "How long have you felt this way?"

"I was drawn to him right away. I didn't want to tell you how attractive I thought he was because I knew you'd tease me or freak out or whatever, but ever since Sheila passed we've become inseparable."

Oh no. Just when I had started believing Krista had genuine feelings for him, and that it might be possible they were destined to be together, the truth slapped me into sad reality. She had lost Sheila—the closest bond she had—and she was trying to replace that emptiness inside of her with Carson. I couldn't point it out yet because she looked so happy, but soon I'd have to reason with her before one of them got hurt. As much as I wanted her to have a soul mate, the timing and fact that she thought it was Carson was much too convenient and highly unlikely.

Krista hugged her pillow. "I know Carson is *the one*."

LET THERE BE LIGHT

Maryah

"Is Nathan coming home tonight?" Krista asked.

"No, he's still working on convincing Harmony to come home. She's really bummed about not finding Gregory. Plus, I told him I need some quality girl time with you."

"Yay! That's exactly what I was thinking too. Mind if I spend the night in here tonight?"

"Only if you promise not to make fun of my new bedtime ritual."

Her brow rose. "Which is?"

"I've been trying these guided meditations I found on YouTube. A couple claim to help with astral travel. So far nothing I experienced has been *transcendental* like they promise, but the ambient music and soothing voice of one guru helps me relax and stop overthinking so much."

"I think that's fabulous. And I'd love to try it too."

"Cool." I grabbed my laptop to show Krista our meditation options, but I got sidetracked by an email from April.

April had texted me a few times here and there since the day she came over and we made up over the River misunderstanding. She'd ask how Eightball was adjusting, how Nathan and I were doing, the polite basics. But I hadn't received an email since I scanned and sent her my notes for a reading assignment months ago. Her long and emotional email described her mom's worsening condition. I could practically feel her hopelessness and desperation seeping through the computer screen.

I finished reading April's email and looked at Krista. "Could you heal someone with cancer?"

"Maybe. It would take a lot of sessions because it would take a lot out of me." She lifted her head from her pillow. "Why? Who has cancer?"

I didn't want to ask Krista to drain herself, but if she could help April's mom even a little bit it would be cruel not to help. "My friend April's mom. She's all April has and," I paused. "It's not looking good."

Krista sat up and scrunched her pillow into her lap. "I see."

I thought about the logistics of it. "It wouldn't work. How would we explain you needing to see a stranger multiple times? Or why she'd miraculously felt better after you started visiting her." I scratched my nail against my keyboard, not looking up. "It was a dumb idea."

"It's not dumb to want to help someone," Krista said. "Trust me, if I had enough energy I'd want to heal everyone who has cancer, or any other disease. But I'm only one soul. I can't save everyone." Her voice dripped with sadness. "Sometimes, I can't even save one."

I knew she was referring to Sheila. "You did save her. You gave her a long wonderful life."

"Not long enough."

"Like you said, you're only one soul. You can only give so much."

Krista almost nodded, but the frown lines around her mouth proved she still wasn't okay with how things turned out. "Clearly you've been giving a lot of thought to April's mom's situation."

"I just read an email from her and I feel bad. I know what it's like to lose your parents. But I can't imagine it being drawn out and watching them suffer like April's going through."

Krista pulled her long hair over one shoulder and combed her fingers through it, contemplating. "There is one thing I could do. It won't cure her, but it will help ease some of the pain and discomfort, and she'll never suspect anything."

"What?" I asked, excited at being able to help even in a small way.

"I'll make her a candle."

I sank back against my pillows. She wanted to make her a gift. "A candle. Oh."

"Don't 'oh' me. You may not have figured it out yet, but the candles I make aren't ordinary smell-good candles. They have *power*."

"Healing power?"

Krista smiled proudly. "I channel my healing power into the candles as I make them. Every time someone burns one, my energy fills the space."

"Seriously?"

"Seriously."

"Every day this family astounds me in some way."

"Yes, we're incredible." She threw the covers off of her. "Time for a late night candle-making party."

"You have stuff to make them?"

"Yes, my mom shipped me a bunch of my supplies last week."

For the next few hours Krista and I gave new meaning to burning the midnight oil.

∞

The next day we checked in as guests at the hospital.

I didn't ask April if we could visit her and her mom. I just found out if April was there and when she texted me back that she was, we drove to the hospital.

April looked even worse than I thought she sounded in her email. As hard as it was to lose my parents, I was grateful it happened so quickly and unexpectedly. I couldn't imagine how hard it was for April to worry if each day would be the day her mom would finally lose her battle with such an awful disease.

I hugged her and she was nothing but skin and bones in my arms. "We brought your mom a gift."

"You did? How thoughtful."

I handed her the bag and she lifted the tissue paper out of it and managed a tired smile. "Mm, they smell amazing."

"We made them," Krista said, "by hand."

"Even better."

"Why don't you light one?" I was eager for Krista's healing energy to start working on April's mom. "They smell so much better when they're burning."

April set the bag on the nightstand beside her mom. "I can't light candles in here, but I'm sure my mom will appreciate them unlit too."

My eyes swept to Krista. Would the candles work if they were never lit? I had no idea. Krista glanced around the room as if she couldn't believe she hadn't thought about a no candle burning policy before we came here.

"I need to step outside for a few minutes," Krista said. "I forgot about an important call I was supposed to make."

"Sure." April weakly nodded, too exhausted to suspect a thing—not that any normal person would expect Krista to have a supernatural healing power she could channel into a candle. Krista glanced at me with an *it will be fine* look.

"I'm glad we're alone," April said. "I need to tell you something."

I glanced at her mom asleep in bed. "We're not alone."

April sighed sadly. "We might as well be. They have her pumped full of so many drugs, she hardly remembers anything we talk about." She motioned for me to sit in a chair then she opened a second metal folding chair and sat beside me. "The past few days, River has called me every day."

"From jail?" I gasped. "Don't they only get one phone call a day?"

"I'm not sure, but the thing is, he keeps asking me to talk to you for him. I keep refusing, but he's relentless."

"Me? Why does he want to talk to me?"

"He says he wants to apologize, but he can't call your phone or contact you. He wants you to visit him so he can tell you something that might help you find what you're looking for."

My head snapped backward. "What? He said that?" Had he told April our kindrily's secret? Had me and my big mouth created another catastrophe that would haunt us for many lifetimes to come?

"I never have any idea what he's talking about." April twirled her hair around her finger. "Honestly, he seems like he might have lost his mind, but he always sounds so sincere and desperate. Like, he always says he is *not them*. He wants no part of *them*. But when I ask him who *them* is, he won't explain. He just says 'make sure Maryah knows I will never be like them.'"

I tried to blink and look normal, like I had no idea what River might have meant, but my mind raced with thoughts of River genuinely not wanting to end up like his evil uncle. He didn't want to be a Nefarioun.

April continued, "He swears *they* controlled his mind and made him try to kill you." She raised a brow at me. "Clearly he was doing more drugs than we knew and it burnt out his brain."

"More drugs?" I asked confused. He drank a lot, but so did a lot of kids at our school. "I didn't know River did drugs."

"Maryah." April sort of laughed at me, but it was empty and weary. "There's no way you were that clueless. River did more than his share of partying." When I didn't reply, April shrugged and closed her eyes. For a few seconds I thought she had fallen asleep, but then she continued. "Anyway, he said to tell you he wants to get away and be free from *them* and only you can help. I'm thinking it's a reference to the demons in his head or something, but who knows?"

I refused to give away any more of our kindrily's secrets so I just uttered, "Weird."

"That's what I thought," April agreed. "I knew you wouldn't want to talk to him, so that's why I haven't mentioned it to you, but seeing you here, I don't know, I figured I should at least tell you that he's still obsessed with you. You know, just to be safe."

I nodded, realizing April wasn't reading anything into River's warnings and messages. The only thing she thought about was that he still might come after me or hurt me if he had the chance. But his messages were claiming he wanted no part of the Nefariouns, even though Dedrick was his uncle. Could he truly mean that, or was it another one of River's lies and part of Dedrick's plan to attempt to kill me again? "Thanks for the warning."

"Thanks for coming to see my mom and me."

Krista came back into the room with a smiling nurse. "Nurse Melodee said the hospital is making an exception to the candle rule. As long as April is in the room to monitor the candle burning it will be allowed."

Nurse Melodee glided over to April's mom and rubbed her leg through the blanket. "A little homemade love might do her some good."

"Great. Thanks so much," April said casually, having no idea how much that candle would help her mom, and maybe her too. Nurse Melodee patted April's shoulder then left the room. I glanced at Krista's cell phone sticking out of her back pocket. I was sure if I checked her call log Dylan would have been the last call she made.

Krista lit both candles and placed them on the wheeled table beside the bed. But then Krista stepped back and placed her hand on April's mom's chest. She closed her eyes and just before April turned to see her, I grabbed her arm. "Hey, is there a drink machine anywhere around here? I'm so thirsty."

"Sure. I'll take you to it." April tried turning toward her mom's bed again. "Those candles smell divine. Krista, would you like—"

"I know what she likes." I threw my arm around April's shoulder, keeping her from seeing Krista's hands waving over her mom's torso. That would have raised some serious questions. "Let's go before I pass out from dehydration."

At that moment I was thankful April was skin and bones because she was easy to steer out of the room.

LOSS AND GAIN OF CONTROL

Harmony

66 I 'm glad you guys are back," Dakota handed Carson a game controller. "It was so boring here without you."

Dakota may have been happy that we were back, but I was not. I was angry that Dedrick slipped through our fingers again. I was so close to finding Gregory.

"It was a pretty lame trip," Carson said. "You didn't miss a thing."

"Except the plane ride." Dakota smirked.

"Probably best you missed that." Carson bumped shoulders with him.

A couple years ago Anthony busted Dakota and Carson hanging out in the plane. They both loved the plane so much that Dakota talked Carson into having a secret sleepover inside of it. Anthony didn't care about the actual sleeping part, what he did care about was they had taken snacks and sodas onboard and, as usual, Dakota was clumsy and spilled sticky soda on one of the seats and floor. He apologized up and down and Anthony made him clean up his mess—twice because Dakota didn't do a thorough job the first time, but afterward Anthony took him and Carson on a private flight. According to Carson, Dakota loved every thrilling second of it, until they landed and Dakota threw up all over the floor. Anthony partly blamed himself because he forgot to tell him about the air sickness bags in the pocket of every seat. But he still made Dakota clean the plane three more times. Dakota had a love-hate relationship with that plane.

"Did you read my comic while you were gone?" Dakota asked me, not taking his eyes off the video game.

"No," I confessed. "I ran out of here so fast I forgot to pack it."

Dakota nodded but I could tell he was disappointed.

"I'll read it soon. I promise."

Both of them were entranced by the array of sounds and images on the screen. I glanced back and forth between them and the screen. "You know these games rot your brain, right?"

"Oh god," Dakota whined. "Could you sound any more like Mom and Dad?"

"They know what they're talking about."

Carson laughed. "Technology is your friend, Harmony. Embrace it."

"Nature is a better friend. I'd rather embrace that."

"I'll make a deal with you." Dakota paused the game. "Let me come on the next kindrily adventure and I'll give up video games for a year."

"What?" Carson gawked. "That's the worst deal I've ever heard. Start with a week and maybe negotiate up to a month max, but not a year. We still have ten levels to beat on this game alone."

Dakota ignored him and looked at me hopefully. "What do you say, sis?"

"I say enjoy your video games."

"Gah!" Dakota flailed backward. "Shot down again."

"Come on," Carson urged. "Unpause it. We're wasting precious time."

After a few futuristic sounding beeps they went back to virtually blowing up stuff.

"So *nothing* happened while you were gone?" Dakota asked. "Nobody used any powers whatsoever?"

"Carson used his powerful charm to woo Krista."

"What?" Dakota dropped his remote. "Krista? You can't be serious."

"Serious as it gets," I said.

Carson kept his eyes on the game, punching buttons on his controller with his super speed. "Some partner you are. I'm beating this guy all on my own."

"Carson?" Dakota glared at him.

On the TV, a huge beastly monster of some kind let out a final roar and melted into a pool on the ground at Carson's character's feet. "Killed him!" Carson lowered his remote and looked at Dakota. "What do you want me to say?"

Dakota scrunched his nose. "You were so against dating anyone."

"I know, but that was before I met Krista."

"Aww, man," Dakota whined. "We won't ever hang out anymore."

"We're hanging out now, aren't we? Nothing will change."

"Everything will change! You'll spend all your time with her. Does she even like video games, or dirt bikes? Are you going to bring her along everywhere?"

"I'm not. Stop bitching already."

"I knew this would happen," Dakota grumbled.

It was like watching a bad reality show. So much drama for no good reason.

"If you spent more time with her, you'd understand," Carson told Dakota.

I pictured Carson and Krista sitting side by side at our kindrily's table. I had wondered once, imagined what if Krista was his soul mate, but they didn't seem drawn to each other at first—the way it's supposed to be—so I dismissed the idea. But there was no denying it in Calgary. They naturally moved together, as if they were each other's shadow. They lit up around each other.

"She might be his twin flame," I said. Carson's head snapped around to look at me. We hadn't discussed it yet, but he wasn't blushing. He didn't look away. A grin crept across my face.

"You said you'd never fall in love!" Dakota shoved him. "That all this 'soul mate BS' wasn't worth the hassle."

Carson tucked his hair behind his ears. "I know what I said. It's not like I planned this."

"She's a phenomenal person," I told Carson. "I couldn't imagine a better match for you."

"So you approve?"

"How could I not approve?"

"Because you're so protective of me." Carson glanced at Dakota who still looked horrified, but then he turned his back to him and spoke directly to me. "I was scared to tell you. I thought you'd tell me to stay away from her and focus on school or something lame and parentish."

"I'd never tell you to stay away from your twin flame. And I'm not your parent anymore."

Dakota stood up. "Why is everyone so quick to believe they're soul mates? Just because they're together in the order? What if they aren't meant to be and they end up hating each other?"

Dakota had a point. I eyed Carson. "How sure are you?"

He shifted in his seat. I could tell he didn't want to say anything else in front of Dakota. Guy code. "Pretty sure."

"See," Dakota said. "He doesn't know. I was pretty sure Emma Cohen was my soul mate last year. Until she shot me down and told me she only dates football players."

I rolled my eyes. "Emma Cohen wasn't worthy of shining your shoes."

"Whatever. I need a drink." Dakota sulked off into the kitchen.

Carson leaned toward me and whispered, "She's the one. I feel it everywhere. I'd do anything for that girl. I'd figure out a way to lasso the moon and yank it out of the sky if that's what she wished for."

I smiled. "She's a lucky girl."

He blushed. "I'm way luckier."

∞

The three of us met up with Faith and Shiloh in Tlaquepaque for smoothies. Smoothies were so not my thing, but I needed some face time with Faith and Shiloh because they were still disappointed in me for the Sheila incident.

Dakota tripped walking into the shop and probably would have wiped out face first in front of the table of gossiping girls, but Carson caught him by the shirt and up-righted him so quickly and nonchalantly that no one else seemed to notice.

Faith ordered a mixed fruit concoction then asked them to add an energy booster.

"The last thing you need is more energy," I told her.

Faith smiled warmly at the guy taking our order. "In hers, could you please add a shot of remorse and a sprinkle of common sense?"

The guy laughed at Faith then turned to make our drinks.

"I have both of those things," I grumbled to Faith. "But regretfully they're watered down by desperation."

"I forgive you," she said. She wrapped her arm around Shiloh's waist. "We all forgive you, even Krista, but you still need to make it right."

"I know," I admitted. "And I will."

I just didn't know when and the longer Sheila's soul stayed in limbo, the more at risk she would be. I tried taking the focus off of me. "How's your vision issues, Shiloh?"

Faith beamed proudly.

"Actually—" Shiloh glanced around, but no one could have heard us over the loud blenders. "I'm getting a good handle on it. I can be in the studio with my class then switch to viewing the lobby with only a blink of my eyes. It's like I'm my own multi-view monitoring system."

"How far does it reach?" Carson asked. "Like right now, can you see into a different shop or building?"

"Let me play with it."

We all watched Shiloh blink hard then his brown eyes subtly lightened. Not enough that any normal person would have noticed, but I was sure any of our kindrily would see the change. He appeared to be staring at a trashcan but then he blinked again and turned his head to stare toward the restrooms. Faith bounced up and down, giddy at witnessing Shiloh use his newly enhanced power. The blenders shut off and after one last slow blink, Shiloh's eyes returned to normal. He leaned closer to Carson and me and quietly said, "I saw outside and through the door of the shop next door, but that's as far as I could go."

"Cool," Dakota said.

"Very," I agreed.

"I made him promise not to ever spy on me again." Faith giggled and pinched his side. "After he recited a play by play of my activities in the shower which I assumed were private."

"Hey, Wifey." Shiloh pulled her close and kissed her nose. "You said I should practice, so I did. And the view was exquisite."

"Gross," Dakota groaned, turning to grab his smoothie from the guy behind the counter.

Carson's phone rang. "What's up, Maryah?"

We all watched him listen to whatever Maryah was telling him. His forehead furrowed with concern. "Bring her straight to the house. I'll be waiting there for you." He hung up and hardly explained anything. All he said was, "Krista needs me. I have to go."

I could tell it took a lot of self-control for him not to blur out of there.

FLYING TOO HIGH

Maryah

K rista told me to call Carson so I did, but he was meeting us at the house. The drive home alone with her was scary. She had started sitting up but eventually she collapsed across the front seat of my Desoto and put her head in my lap.

"Are you sure you're okay?" I asked.

"I will be. I just need to recharge." She was getting paler by the minute and the dark circles under her eyes were starting to look like bruises.

"I thought you were going to let the candles heal her."

Krista mumbled weakly, "She needed more than candles."

Krista's breaths were heavy and strained.

"Rest," I told her. "No more talking."

She didn't nod. She didn't move. She slept the rest of the excruciatingly long way home.

I never even saw Carson as I pulled into the driveway, but as soon as I put my car in park my passenger door opened and there he was. He ducked his head inside. "What happened?"

I looked down at Krista's dark hair pooled over my lap. She was still out cold. "She used a lot of energy trying to heal April's mom."

Krista's head slid off my lap. Carson's hand never let her head so much as bounce. In one graceful movement she was out of the car and in his arms. I jumped out and followed him as he carried Krista into the house.

"She'll be okay, right?" I asked.

"Yes," Carson said, but he sounded upset or maybe angry as he blurred away to Krista's room.

I stood in the kitchen, my hands hanging helpless at my side, watching him carry her down the hall.

"Everything okay?" Nathan asked from behind me. I turned and he was standing by the laundry room door holding a basket of folded clothes. Some of them were mine. "You did our laundry?"

"Yes. Was that okay? I'm sorry. I should have asked you first."

"No, it's fine. I'm just surprised."

"You don't think I'm capable of doing laundry?"

"It's not that. It's just, you're so old-fashioned."

"Old-fashioned, not sexist. I do my share of chores."

I nodded and looked down the hall again. "Krista's sick."

"Sick? She doesn't get sick."

"I mean drained. She worked on April's mom and now she's wiped out worse than I've ever seen her."

He set the basket of clothes on the counter and hugged me. "She'll be all right. Give her time to recuperate."

I wanted to stay there, wrapped in Nathan's arms, listening to his heart thump against my ear, but I needed to make sure Krista truly was okay. I pulled away. "She might want a drink or something. I should check on her."

"She'll appreciate that."

I walked down the hall to the Krista's room but stopped in the doorway. They were both lying in bed on their sides. Carson's arms were wrapped around her and he was talking so quietly I couldn't hear most of what he said, but his tone was gentle and loving. I wasn't one hundred percent sure, but I thought he called her his turtle.

∞

We checked on Krista again after dinner. Carson tried waving us away because she was still sleeping, but I went in and visually examined her anyway. The color had returned to her face and the circles under her eyes were fading.

Satisfied that she was getting better, Nathan and I left them and went to our room.

"Told you she was tough," Nathan said. "She always bounces back quickly."

"She does look almost back to normal." I shut the door behind me.

Nathan sat in the chair beside our bed and cracked his neck. He looked tired.

"You okay?" I asked him.

"I'm fine. How are you holding up?"

"No." I walked over to him. "Everyone is always focused on me, or Harmony, and today it's been Krista too, but what about you? How are *you* feeling? How are *you* doing with all this...stuff?"

"You're sweet to worry about me, but truly, I'm fine. I have you back in my life. That's all I need."

I stood there, looking down at him, thinking about how lucky I was, and how I had so much to learn about him, and how much I hated that I used to know everything about him. I ruined such an irreplaceable gift. "I wish I could make it up to you."

"Make what up to me?" He wrapped his arms around my legs, running his fingers up the back of my knees and thighs.

"Erasing and making this life so hard for you."

"You've already made it up to me." He pulled me down onto his lap and I wrapped my arms around his neck.

"I was thinking, we've been focusing on *my* pleasure in hopes of me sensperiencing, but the other night when your eyes lit up and I glimpsed into your soul, we were both all hot and bothered."

He chuckled. "Accurate description."

I ran my fingers through his hair. "I'm thinking, for the greater cause of me remembering my past, and for the good of the kindrily, we should probably get all hot and bothered again and see what happens."

He raised his chin but kept his smoldering gaze locked on me. "That's very charitable of you, to make such a sacrifice and work so diligently for the good of the kindrily."

"My middle name is generous."

"No." He lifted me up and laid me on the bed. "Your middle name is Anne, but I accept your offer of generosity."

My insides melted. I should have known Nathan would know my middle name. We weren't exactly a normal couple. Our conversations consisted of questions like "How many countries have we lived in?" Not, "What's your middle name?" But still, hearing him say it made me feel that much closer to him.

He crawled onto the bed and hovered above me.

"Wait," I said, just before his lips met mine. "I don't know your middle name."

Nathan grinned. "That's because I don't have one."

"Oh." I tilted my head. Good. The name Nathaniel Luna was too perfect to be botched up with a third name. He moved in to kiss me again.

"Wait." I pushed against his chest.

His chin jutted up and he pursed his lips. "Do you want to get hot and bothered or not?"

"Lock the door."

He vanished. He reappeared across the room, locked the door, and was back on top of me before the grin finished spreading across my face.

"Finally ready?" He asked.

"Ready. Hot and bother me."

"I thought the plan was for both of us to become hot and bothered."

"Shut up and kiss me."

He did, and I kissed him back. I was instantly hot and not the least bit bothered. I couldn't get enough of him. His lips trailed down my jaw to my neck and I clutched the pillow beside me. He gently turned my chin and kissed below my ear and down the other side of my neck. I didn't want him to stop, but his steady breath in my ear made me realize he was too much in control.

I didn't really know how to take charge in a sexy way, but I had seen enough movies and read enough of my mother's Cosmo magazines to fake some confidence. I pushed myself onto my elbows. I used a couple forceful kisses to get him on his side then I lifted my upper body on top of him. He lay on his back, looking up at me and tucking my hair behind my ear.

"You're beautiful," he said.

I had never thought of myself as beautiful. Average, yes. Beautiful, no. But when Nathan looked at me and said those words, I believed him. I actually felt beautiful. "Thank you," I said, "but you're way too composed right now."

He licked his lips and put his hands behind his head. "I'm flying."

"What?"

"The reason I love to BASE jump off mountains is for the rush. After the initial fall, I fly. I soar through the sky, free as a shooting star. Physically flying is the second best feeling in the world."

"The second," I repeated. "What's the first?"

"Love. You. For me, they're the same thing. *You* are the best feeling in the world, and right now, lying here kissing you, my soul is flying. You have no idea how much I missed this feeling while you were gone."

I tried to breathe, but couldn't. Time stood still. Not literally, like Anthony had stopped time, but figuratively like I wanted to capture that moment in a glass dome and keep it forever and ever.

Pain burned behind my nose. That pain I'd get when I fought back tears. It was the sweetest thing anyone had ever said to me, but I didn't want to cry all over Nathan and ruin the moment. Even happy tears made me snively and puffy eyed. I took a breath and looked away, making sure my tears were safely at bay, then I met his gaze again. "You leave me speechless sometimes."

He grinned with satisfaction. "You don't have to say anything. Actions speak louder than words."

I kissed him. It was unlike any other kiss we shared so far. I didn't think. I didn't worry if I should keep my tongue in or out, or if my lips were moist enough, or wonder if he was enjoying it as much as I was. I didn't think about where to strategically touch him. I didn't think at all.

I just fell into him. Like leaping of a cliff and enjoying the fall. It was our best kiss ever because I felt what he had just described. My soul flew. And it felt incredible.

"I'm flying," I whispered.

Our lips never came apart, but Nathan smiled. "Amazing, isn't it?"

I nodded and kissed him again. My hands might have raked down his back, or caressed his face, I have no idea what happened physically. I was too caught up in the rush of soaring through an infinite sky with Nathan.

"This," I gasped, still kissing him. "I want to feel like this forever."

"Forever is yours for the taking." He momentarily pulled back. His green eyes shined with longing and love. "It always has been, Maryah."

He slid his arms around me tighter and kissed me again. I understood what he meant when he said he felt like a shooting star. And what a euphoric ride it was.

Until cold hit me like a freight train.

I gasped, feeling like I'd swallowed dry ice. Wind howled around us. Nathan pulled back and yanked me up to standing.

"No," he said, panicking. "This can't be happening."

My legs felt disconnected from my body except for my bare feet. They hurt because I was standing in snow, outside, on top of a mountain.

I threw my arms over myself to cover my naked body. I couldn't breathe. The temperature had to be below freezing. And I wasn't wearing a stitch of clothes.

"No!" Nathan yelled at the sky. A white cloud of his breath rose between us. His voice echoed off the surrounding snow-covered peaks. "No no no no, noooo!"

"What happened?" I asked, my face and feet going numb.

"Don't talk." He ripped his shirt over his head and pulled it over me. "We're in Nepal. The air is too thin up here for you to talk." He lifted me into his arms and snow fell from my bare feet.

Don't talk. His warning kept repeating through my mind. My lungs felt like they were filling with frozen water. I was struggling to breathe, but couldn't fill my lungs with anything but more cold. I was so light-headed. The whole world was spinning.

"I'm sorry," he whispered. "I don't know how this happened. I didn't mean to bring you here."

I didn't need apologies. I needed to get off the damn mountain and back to some place with warmth and oxygen. I was shivering and my teeth were chattering so hard I could only manage short, painful inhalations through my nose.

"Nathaniel." My teeth rattled against each other.

"Take." I sniffed, trying to feel my nose.

"Us." I shivered and twitched.

"Home."

He kept squeezing me tight against him, whispering, "Please work, please work, please work."

Even my eyeballs were too cold and dry to keep open. I knew the feeling of blacking out all too well. I fought it hard, but I was losing all sensation in my body. I could barely feel Nathan's hands and arms against my skin. I didn't know if it was because of the cold or because I was blacking out again.

Bright light made me squint even though my eyes were already shut. I was certain a huge sharp icicle was being driven through my temple. Then warmth pelted me like I was being shot with BBs made of fire.

My eyelids flew open to see a stream of water coming from the showerhead above me. Nathan was in the tub with me, his shoes and pants still on, apologizing over and over and telling me I was home. His eyes were bloodshot—so bloodshot that I worried something was wrong with him. I tried to open my mouth and ask him if he was okay, but my lips felt frozen shut. I could feel my skin again, but the warm water cascading down on me hurt so badly.

"I know it hurts," Nathan's voice was scratchy and weak. "But we have to regulate your body temperature." He slid one arm behind me, trying to adjust me to a different position. I could feel his arm spasm and twitch like my own muscles were doing.

Then he slipped. His head made a cracking sound as it hit something above me then he fell on top of me. His bare chest pressed against my soaking wet t-shirt. Everything went still except the endless spray of water beating down on us. The water temperature grew colder. He must have hit the control handle when he fell. Exhausted beyond words, I closed my eyes. I needed sleep. Just a few minutes of sleep.

Rain.

Cliffs of red rock.

Hot chocolate.

Nathan's green eyes.

These are a few of my favorite things.

If I kept thinking happy thoughts I wouldn't shiver to death.

Water. I was aware that my body was submerged in water. Nathan was still on top of me. I tried saying his name but my lips wouldn't part. A pathetic squeak caught in my throat. I couldn't feel my limbs, but I knew they were still attached, so I focused on my right hand. Even though it weighed a million pounds, I swung it and hit the side of the tub.

Thump.

Yes. Noise. Noise was the goal. If I kept making noise, someone with working limbs and more strength than I had would come and get us out of this freezing water.

I willed my arm to swing again.

Thump. The hollow sound of my hand hitting porcelain.

Thump. I winced. That one sent pins and needles shooting through my hand.

I swallowed, but it felt like a snowball was lodged in my throat. I managed a throaty, "Help."

Whispering wouldn't help us, but it was all I could manage no matter how hard I tried. I flung my hand again.

Thump. That one sounded louder, but it stung so bad. The water level in the tub was getting higher. And I didn't think it was possible, but my body was becoming number. We would drown if I didn't get us out soon.

Move, I mentally demanded of my legs. They didn't listen.

I had to make a louder noise. I remembered the candle sitting on the corner of the tub. I lit it last time I took a bath. I had sat it on a glass plate to catch the dripping wax. It had to still be there, just to the right of my head. I couldn't see it, but it had to be there. I lifted my right arm again, pins and needles still ripping through my skin. I kept lifting my hand, toward the showerhead far above me, reaching for the sky, the stars, for a past I couldn't grasp onto.

My hand fell behind my head.

Thump. The wall. My knuckles slid down the tiles until I was sure my hand was low enough to reach the candle.

One swing, I told myself. *You've probably got enough strength left for one good swing. Make it count.*

I flung my hand and forearm. I don't know which happened first, the thump of the candle hitting the tile, or the glass plate shattering.

I did it, I told Nathan. Even though my lips wouldn't move and my voice wouldn't work, my fuzzy mind thought he'd want to know. *They'll hear us, don't worry.*

The water reached my ears and rushed in, muffling the noise of the gushing showerhead.

Swimming.

Peacock feathers.

Nathan's kisses.

The stars in the sky.

Telling death to piss off.

The shower stream finally shut off.

"Maryah? Nathan?" Krista's voice sounded a million lifetimes away. I forced my eyes open. Even my eyelashes were cold.

"Can't leave any of you alone for a minute," Carson said, lifting Nathan's limp and dripping wet body off of me.

Krista climbed into the tub and pulled me up to a sitting position. "Pudding, what the heck happened?"

I tried shaking my head but it felt more like I was having a minor seizure. Carson lifted me out of the tub and Krista wrapped a towel around my waist and legs. "Take her to the bed."

"Duh," Carson grunted.

"Watch the broken glass," she warned.

Floating across our bedroom, being set on the bed, Krista pulling off my wet shirt and Nathan's wet jeans, Carson covering us with a warm electric blanket: it was all a hazy dream. Krista kissed my forehead and I drifted to sleep. But before I slipped away completely, one thought made me mentally smile. Nathan traversed—and he took me with him.

FOR THE TAKING

Maryah

I woke up feeling almost normal. I was wearing shorts and a t-shirt. I reached under the covers and felt Nathan's shorts.

For those first few seconds I worried I had dreamt Nathan took me with him when he traversed to the top of a freezing cold, isolated mountain, and that we'd almost drowned to death in our bathtub, and that Carson and Krista came to our rescue and put us in bed. But then I sat up and saw the electric blanket covering us.

"Yes!" I threw my arms above my head.

"What are you so happy about?" Nathan asked from beside me. He was groggy and a faint bruise still existed along his hairline—I was sure Krista healed the worst of it—but he looked sexier than ever.

"You traversed. With me. You did it!"

"I almost killed us."

"By accident. Wasn't the first time and it probably won't be the last, but who cares? You took me with you!"

He touched the top of his forehead where his bruise disappeared into his hair. "Yes, and I'll never do it again."

"Nooo," I whined. "Don't you see what this means? We can go anywhere!"

He smirked. "I've always been able to go anywhere."

"But now I can go with you."

He propped himself up on one elbow. "Maryah, it took so much energy out of me that after I finally did transport you back here, I had nothing left. Well, enough to fumble through my brilliant idea of getting you into a warm shower, but then I slipped, knocked myself out—with the water running, mind you—and almost drowned both of us."

I didn't want to point out that he also managed to switch the water to cold when he fell. No use making him feel worse. "So we need some practice—maybe even supervised practice so we don't almost die again. We won't travel across the globe. We'll start small. You believe my ability is going to get stronger. I believe yours will too."

"Are you forgetting you ended up naked in the snow?"

My cheeks warmed. "You'll definitely need to work on *that*."

"That might be the only worthwhile incentive I have for practicing."

I laughed. "That is *not* how I imagined you seeing me naked for the first time. How embarrassing."

"Only embarrassing on my part because I put you in such a dangerous predicament. I'm sure you looked beautiful, but I was too worried and panicked to think about anything but making sure you survived."

I rubbed the blanket between my fingers. "So you don't remember what I looked like naked?"

"Not exactly, no, but I have spent a lot of time imagining it."

"Some gentleman you are!" I smacked him playfully. "Seriously, you can't deprive me of traversing with you. Instantly traveling anywhere in the world with you is a dream come true."

He pulled me on top of him and wrapped his arms around me. Tucking my head under his chin he whispered, "I will always do my best to make all your dreams come true."

An electrical buzz rippled through my muscles. Blinding light flooded the room. When I opened my eyes, we were in the bathroom. I stared at the mirror's reflection of us standing there, me wrapped in Nathan's arms.

I jumped back and gaped at him with so much happiness it rumbled through me in an excited purr. I was fully clothed. I felt fine. He looked healthy as could be—with the exception of the bruise Krista would fully heal soon. "You did it again. On purpose. And we're fine."

"I figured it out on the return trip—the key to being able to take you with me. I expanded my energy field so it didn't just meld with yours, but completely enveloped you. I'd never been able to do that before. But you're right, I'll need to practice before any lengthy trips."

I was so excited I jogged in place. "This is gonna be so awesome!"

He rubbed his hand over his face, trying to hide his proud smile, but there was no denying it. Nathan was impressed with his new ability.

∞

Every kindrily member wanted to be first to traverse with Nathan.

"We should proceed according to age, eldest first," Edgar said.

Helen agreed. "But ladies first, so start with me."

"Beauty before age." Amber struck a zestful pose. "I'm a glowing new mother."

"I *am* his mother." Louise rubbed Nathan's shoulders. "How could you deny taking your own mother before everyone else?"

Nathan laughed. "You don't believe in family labels."

"In this case I do."

"Your *mother* is talking nonsense," Anthony said. "Take your poor ol' dad."

"Krista and I saved their lives," Carson pointed out. "That deserves a payback and I'm cashing in first." Krista pinched his arm. "I mean, right after Krista's turn."

"You know it will be me." Dylan leaned back in his chair with his hands behind his head. "One simple sentence and Nathan will be zipping me away to..." He considered all his options and decided on, "Maui."

Faith leaned over the table on her elbows. "Nathan, don't let any of them pressure you into doing something you don't want to do. You know I've got your back. I've always had your back. Don't forget who befriended Maryah when she first arrived here and tolerated—I mean, *loved* her through her depressed, awkward, oblivious stage so that you two could be happily reunited again."

"Tolerated," I huffed. "I'll remember that, Stinkerbell."

She sat back and held her hands up innocently. "What? You were a tough nut to crack. I should be rewarded for my hard work."

"I made you those star glasses," Shiloh said. I had no idea what he was talking about, but Nathan laughed. "Yes, glasses which didn't work."

"Hey, I can't help it if your vision sucks."

"All right," Nathan said, spreading his hands flat on the table. "You know I will take each of you at some point, but I have to choose one person to go first. Some of you have made solid cases for me selecting you, and others were sad and pathetic attempts."

We all chuckled.

"I won't be traveling far at first," Nathan continued. "Traversing Maryah and I to Nepal and back caused me to pass out, so everyone's first trip will be to somewhere simple. The backyard, the garage, a different room of the house. It's not like you're missing out on being frostbitten in the Himalayas."

He nudged my leg and I shivered. "Seriously, be grateful you aren't going to Nepal."

Nathan stood. "My first victim is..."

I glanced around the table wondering who he'd choose and how he'd make his decision. Order of age did seem like the most fair and impartial way.

Nathan pointed to my right. "Harmony."

She gave one nod and stood, like she didn't expect him to choose anyone but her. He held out his elbow and she slid her arm into his.

She winked at me. "I'll try to return him in one piece."

INDULGENT PROPOSALS

Maryah

The next evening I was alone in our room finishing the second book in my new favorite series. Nathan walked in and collapsed face first onto our bed.

"Aww." I petted his head. "They wiped you out."

"They're a demanding bunch of gits," he grumbled into the blanket. "I never should have told them."

Nathan had spent all day yesterday and today traversing with each member. Yesterday, no one had been pleased with their short trips to another room, so today he agreed to take them a little farther. He could only do two trips an hour at most or he became too weak to take anyone anywhere.

I rolled him over and rubbed his chest. "Did everyone get their second turn?"

"Yes, finally. I just finished with Mikey."

"Mikey?"

"Kidding. Yes, everyone but Mikey." He grimaced. "And Gregory."

"Gregory will get his turn one day soon."

Nathan stared at the ceiling. "Actually, Gregory is the one member who most likely wouldn't ask for a turn."

"Really? Why?"

"He has always had a thing with people touching him. He wouldn't be comfortable with me having to wrap my arms around him."

"Did he let Harmony touch him?"

"Yes, Harmony was an exception to his rule."

I sat up, placed my bookmark in my book, and tossed it on the nightstand. "Jamie and Claire were doing some serious touching of their own tonight."

"Oh?" He tilted his head. "You read without me?"

"I'm sorry, but I needed to know what happens. I'll read those chapters again with you. It was so good I raced through it just to see what would happen next, so I'm sure I missed some details."

"Have I not taught you anything about the benefits of taking your time?"

I kissed his cheek. "You have tried, but I'm not entirely convinced jumping ahead to the good parts isn't the better way to do things."

"I'm older and wiser than you. You should trust that I know what I'm talking about."

I grinned. "Since we clearly aren't talking about books anymore, will you please tell me how long we're waiting?"

He acted clueless. "Waiting for what?"

"You know. *It.*"

He rolled over onto his elbow and rested his head in his hand. "It? You can't even say the word without blushing. What makes you think you're ready to actually do *it*?"

I rubbed my ring, trying not to blush like Nathan said. I failed. "We're soul mates." I almost argued against the typical guy-sleeping-around stereotype, but I decided to flip it on him. "It's not like you're some conquest for me and once I get in your pants I'll ditch you for the next hot guy that comes along."

His eyes widened and glimmered with amusement. "Well now that you mention it, that's exactly what I'm worried will happen. I intend to protect my virginity until I'm certain you want to be with me forever."

"Shut up." I shoved his shoulder. "You're not even a virgin."

"In this body I am."

"You know what I mean. And I am going to be with you forever. You're stuck with me now." My grin was so sappy I knew not to kiss him or our lips would stick together.

"Good. Then it won't hurt to wait until the moment is right."

"But *when* will the moment be right?"

"Honestly, I planned to follow tradition and wait until we sanctify our union."

"Sanctify our union? That sounds so official."

"The union I'm referring to is marriage."

"*Marriage?*" I flopped back onto my pillow. "We're waiting until we're married?" I assumed the kindrily was old-fashioned about some things, but waiting to have sex until we were married seemed like a stretch, even for someone as inexperienced as I was.

"Yes, marriage. Two twin flames joining together as one, witnessed by all of the souls we love and who love us. It's a divine event and everyone makes a big to-do about it. I look forward to seeing your reaction since it will be your *first* marriage."

Marriage. On some level I knew that would eventually happen, and that Nathan and I had been married numerous times before, but it was still jarring to think about. Heck, we'd just had our first kiss a little over two weeks ago and here was Nathan sitting in front of me casually talking about our wedding.

I was a little bit nervous but a lot giddy. "How do you know I'd say yes?"

He flinched then cocked his head to the side. "Oh. Well. Good point. That was arrogant of me to assume, um..." He lowered his eyes. I had rattled him. There was a first time for everything for him too.

"I'm kidding," I assured him. "I said I'm yours forever and I meant it. But I'm also in no rush to get married."

"Then you should be in no rush to do *it*, either."

I scrunched up my nose at him. "So tell me what happens at these kindrily weddings."

"I can't adequately describe it with words. You'll have to wait and *hope* I propose so that you can witness it for yourself."

I smirked. "Touché"

He rolled onto his back and I curled up against him, resting my head on his chest. For a few minutes we just lay together enjoying the comfortable silence. I couldn't stop thinking about all the places we'd be able to traverse too someday. Then, being the selfish, excited, determined girlfriend that I was, I lifted my head. "How tired are you?"

He looked down his nose at me. "Why?" He must have read my mind. "Oh bollocks, you too? Even my soul mate offers me no reprieve."

I kissed his chin. "Pretty please? I'll reward you with kisses. Lots and lots of kisses."

"Well, when you offer a deal I can't refuse." He leaned to his left and grabbed the edge of the comforter then leaned right and grabbed the other side. He wrapped us up, cocooning us together in the blanket.

"Ready?" He asked.

"Ready." I slid my arms under him and held on tight.

∞

We were on top of our favorite cliff, lying on our bedspread, staring up at the Sedona sky as it prepared to transition into my favorite time of the day—sunset.

"Do you see any stars yet?" Nathan asked me.

My gaze fluttered across the periwinkle sea above us. "No. Do you?"

"I see them all the time. They're dim when the sun is shining, but they're always there."

I sighed. "I wish I could see them."

"Me too. The sky would have so much more significance for you." He took a deep breath. "I need to tell you something."

Oh god. No good ever came out of conversations that started with one person saying *I need to tell you something*. I sat up and stared down at him.

"Why do you look terrified?" he asked.

"Because I'm worried you're about to tell me something bad."

"Quite the opposite actually." He sat up too. "Shiloh, you know he has the ability to see clearly in the dark, and that he sees light and color differently than the rest of us."

I nodded.

"Well, he swears he can still see your star in the sky."

"You said my star fell. That it was gone."

"I know. And I can't see it. As much as I've tried and hoped to see a flicker of light where your star used to shine, I still see nothing. But Shiloh doesn't lie. And he swears he can see something."

I lifted my face and scanned the cloudless sky above us. "What does that mean?"

"It means you erased, but you aren't gone. We know that's true because you have remembered glimpses of our past. It gives me hope that you'll remember more. I wanted to tell you what Shiloh sees so you could share that hope. Your star didn't fall from the sky like I originally believed. Erasing caused it to burn out, but I believe you can reignite it."

I looked at the sky again. I wanted to see the stars. I wanted to see my star. I wanted to burn so brightly that other galaxies could see me. But wanting and doing were very different things. *Doing*, I thought. It was up to me to *do* something. No one could make my star shine except me.

Nathan did give me hope. According to Shiloh, I still had a place in the heavens. I was determined to turn on the light so that everyone could see I was home again.

"Do you think your ability is getting stronger like Edgar suspects, or do you think you've been able to take people with you when you traverse all along, but you just didn't know how?"

"I'm not sure. But everything happens as it should."

"Maybe I'm getting stronger too. I mean, I'm starting over with a severe handicap, but if I'm getting stronger then I might sensperience or astral travel like a pro any day now."

"That's a brilliant theory. I hope it pans out."

I gave him my best enticing eyebrow wiggle. "I want to practice again. Do you need to be anywhere?"

"Nope, I'm all yours. Which would you like to practice, sensperiencing, astral traveling, or soul gazing?"

"Sensperiencing."

"Very well. Lie back."

I stretched out on my back, preparing for another round of one of my favorite activities. I was determined to make progress this time.

"Close your eyes," Nathan said quietly. "Abandon your body. Let every muscle, bone, and cell dissolve and become pure, weightless energy."

I relaxed my muscles and imagined them turning to water like the meditation guru said in her recordings.

"Float upward," Nathan continued, "into the sky. Keep floating through the clouds and out of the atmosphere and into space. Don't picture space from the outside looking in. *Be* in space. Let your soul float there in the black sky among the countless shining stars."

I could see what he described because I had seen it before. The night I almost died. The stars were so close and they were pulsing, living energy that I wanted to reach out and touch.

"Now just *look*," Nathan whispered. "Observe all the celestial energy around you. Feel your energy shining brightly just like the stars you see surrounding you."

I was there. I was in space. I saw and felt everything Nathan described as if it were the easiest task in the world. Two stars pulsed on either side of me. One was radiant and warm gold. The other burned cool blue and white.

I was aware that Nathan continued talking, but his words were like a slow comet traveling past me. All I could focus on was the energy of the blue and white star. It called to me, not with words, but with its energy. I reached for it, wanting to meld with its light, but then a voice clearly whispered words that shook every star in space, making them blur into streaks of connecting light. *Open your eyes.*

My eyes flew open.

Nathan was propped on one elbow at my side, but his head was tilted toward the sky and his eyes were closed. "Expand your—"

"Nathan."

He looked down at me. "Back so soon?"

"Did you tell me to open my eyes?"

"No. Were my directions working?"

"Yeah, and I was doing so well. I felt all transcendental, but then a voice said 'Open your eyes.' And here I am. Back on boring old Earth."

He smirked. "Earth can be transcendental too."

"Not like that," I said. "That was incredible."

"I have other ways to make you feel incredible." He reached down for my wrist and lifted my arm over my head. Slowly, he did the same with my other hand. With his one firm grip he locked both of my wrists together.

I felt vulnerable but at the same time completely safe because it was Nathan. *My* Nathan. "Do what you please with me," I said. "I'm all yours."

He gazed down at me. "Is that a promise?"

"Given our history, I'm pretty sure it's a fact."

"This," he whispered before kissing my neck.

"This what?"

He kissed the other side. "This is one of those moments when I desperately wish you hadn't erased."

"Why this moment?"

He took his time scanning every curve of my body before answering. "Because if you hadn't erased, I'd have no moral qualms about making love to you right here and now."

I closed my eyes. God, I wanted him so bad. He made love to me twenty times a day just by looking at me. How much more amazing would it feel when the physical aspects were added to it?

He released the hold he had on my wrists and repositioned himself. I opened my eyes, but his head was down. He tugged at the button of my shorts then kissed my exposed belly. I sighed dreamily and he laid his head in my lap. His breath tickled the inside of my thigh as he spoke. "You have no idea the transcendental things I'm going to do to you after we're married."

I smiled so big it reached the sky. "For the record, I have no moral qualms about making sure we're a good fit before marriage."

His head rose and he glared authoritatively at me as he lifted himself up and positioned his body over mine. Gently parting my legs, he lowered himself between them. My hips rolled forward as he pressed against me. I moaned and arched my back.

"I assure you," he whispered into my ear. "We fit together perfectly."

"Please," I begged. "I don't want to wait."

He grinned and shook his head. "I never imagined you'd become such a modern-day hussy."

I laughed and wrapped my legs around him. "Don't call me a hussy."

He rolled over onto his back, pulling me on top of him and laughing too. I sat on his lap and rolled my hips, trying to make him want me as much as I wanted him, but my shorts and his jeans between us might as well have been the Berlin Wall.

"Look at you." Nathan reached forward, holding onto my waist.

"What?" I asked, self-consciously smoothing down my hair.

"The sun is setting behind you and I swear, you're glowing like something not of this world." He propped himself up his elbows, still gazing up at me. "You look like an angel."

I leaned down and kissed him. Then I slid off him and stretched out at his side. "I used to think you were my angel of death."

He turned and faced me. His brow rose. "Come again?"

"After I was attacked, I thought you were an angel taking me to heaven. Then I kept seeing you in what I thought were my dreams. The one time, after I first moved here and set my—correction, *our*—bed on fire, you appeared again. I assumed you were trying to take me."

"Take you to...heaven?"

I nodded.

He grinned deviously. "There's a sexual joke in there somewhere about you and I setting a bed on fire and me taking you to heaven, but I don't have enough blood in my brain to deliver it properly."

I laughed at him. "Why am I even trying to talk to you if there's no blood in your brain?"

"It's slowly coming back. I can think half-straight. Continue."

I didn't like the thought of him regaining his composure so quickly. Even though I was having a conversation with him, my body still ached for him. I don't know where my courage came from, but I reached down and grabbed between his legs. He closed his eyes and groaned.

"Where's your blood flowing now?" I asked quietly.

He lay back again and pulled me down so our lips met. I kept my hand right where it was. I pretended to have some clue of what I was doing while I kissed him more intensely and squeezed him through his jeans.

"Maryah," he breathed. My name never sounded so beautiful.

I felt powerful. He always seemed to have the upper hand when it came to our make-out sessions, but now I was the one in control. And it was making him crazy, which I enjoyed.

"The first time I drank Helen's tea," I whispered, proud of myself for how composed I sounded in such an intense moment.

"You sat on the couch with me. I thought you were my angel then too. I thought the tea, and you, would be the death of me. "

"Take me," Nathan said.

My head snapped back, jolted by his words. "What?"

"That night you said 'take me,' you have no idea how badly I wanted to."

I didn't remember saying that, but he spoke about it so passionately I didn't argue. "Was that another time?"

"Another time for what?"

Just thinking about the words I was about to repeat made me eight hundred times more excited. "That you wanted to make love to me."

"I can't count how many times I've wanted to make love to you." He pulled me on top of him so I was straddling him again. He shifted his hips at the same time I did and the bulge that had just felt so good in my hand became exquisite torture between my thighs.

I was losing my mind. The feeling of control and power was slipping away into a haze of ecstatic bliss. I let my head fall back and gazed up at a cotton candy sky of pink, blue, and purple. I wanted to float up into the sky, cling to the clouds, and fly away with him.

When I looked down again Nathan's loving eyes were watching me with so much love I was almost brought to tears. His fingertips swept up and down my thighs. "Come back down here, please."

I leaned forward and he eased my head toward him until our lips met.

His kiss set my soul on fire. We were flying again.

Our mouths parted long enough for me to breathlessly say, "Marry me."

He smiled then gently flipped me onto my back and hovered above me. His lips teasingly brushed against mine. "Where's my ring?"

I help up my thumb and nodded at my antique peacock ring. "That's all I have to offer."

"That belongs on you. Always has and always will." He held my hand and kissed my thumb. "Besides, I promised your parents a thoughtful and memorable proposal."

My hand flew over my heart. "My parents?"

Nathan nodded. "Before they crossed over, I asked your father for permission to marry his daughter, and for your mother's blessing as well. One of the conditions was my proposal to you had to be grand."

A bittersweet tear escaped the corner of my eye. "What were the other conditions?"

"There was only one more—that I love and cherish you forever." He wiped another tear from my face. "Both conditions are inevitable."

BE STILL MY BREAKING HEART

Harmony

S ome of Shiloh's dance students were chosen to perform in a production of *West Side Story*. When he and Faith first invited me, I declined, but I was so restless after school that I changed my mind. I needed to get out of the house, out of my own head, and do something, even if it was watching a group of twelve-year-olds dance around and sing.

The distraction didn't work. All I thought about was Gregory.

On the ride home I sat in the back of Shiloh's truck, trying to ignore Faith and Shiloh gushing about how well Shiloh's students performed. Dakota sat beside me. He nudged my leg at one point and rolled his eyes. I shrugged. If this was all they had to get excited about who were we to spoil their fun?

We stopped at a red light. An old familiar eerie sound stirred in my ears—the sound of metal grinding together. It started faint, like the first subtle ripple on a still pond. I turned my head slightly, listening to make sure it wasn't squeaky breaks. But the unmistakable sound rippled inward, getting louder—more annoying than fingernails on a chalkboard.

I'd only ever heard the sound once before, minutes before the Nefariouns arrived at Amber and Dylan's wedding.

I shot straight up in my seat, searching the dimly lit streets outside and trying to see inside the dark cars passing by us on the opposite side of the road. My fingers flew to my ears, pressing hard to try to stop the sound from pulsing between them, but the sound grew louder. *Shit.*

I knew what it meant. I didn't question or deny it, but it couldn't have happened at a worse time.

I wasn't prepared for this. *We* weren't prepared for this. I glanced around the SUV. Quick mental tally: three kindrily members, one innocent bystander with absolutely no power to fight with. *Double Shit.*

I leaned down, feeling the top of each boot, confirming I had at least half-dressed this morning. I wasn't wearing a bulletproof vest. None of us were. When I sat up, as if by divine force, my head turned to look at the black Mercedes with tinted windows pulling up beside us.

For a brief second the flicker of a lighter illuminated the profile of a man in the backseat. Every curve and slope of his face was familiar. My hands fumbled for the door handle as the black window of the Mercedes lowered several inches. Through the steady stream of cigarette smoke I saw his snake-slit eyes.

I threw my door open just as the light turned green. The Mercedes sped off before my boots hit the pavement. I stood there, in the middle of the street, flabbergasted.

He hadn't aged a day.

"Harmony, what are you doing?" Faith yelled through her passenger window.

I leapt into the back seat, slamming my door shut as I shouted, "Follow that Mercedes!"

"What? Why?" Shiloh asked.

"Gregory is in the back seat."

I'm not sure which was louder, the gasps throughout the car or the truck's tires squealing against the road.

Faith dialed Anthony.

Shiloh tossed his phone to Dakota. "Call Nathan. Keep calling until he answers."

I kept my eyes locked on the Mercedes several yards ahead of us as I waited for Carson to answer his phone.

"What's up?" he asked.

"Gregory's here. Get to the main road as soon as possible and head west. I'll keep you on the phone until we figure out where they're going." I heard a short, shocked squeal from Krista. Seconds later, Carson's Mustang roared to life. I could imagine the look on Krista's face when Carson grabbed her and whisked her away with his sonic speed. It was like being shot out of a canon before you even had time to figure out you were moving.

My heart throbbed in my throat as the Mercedes turned onto Airport Drive.

"The airport," Faith and I both said into our phones.

Every time Dakota pushed the end button on Shiloh's phone, I wanted to scream. *Answer your goddamn phone, Nate!*

He finally had the ability to traverse people where they needed to be and we couldn't reach him. We needed Anthony to get there in time. We needed Carson too. Hell, we needed everyone and then some. We never knew what to expect with the Nefariouns.

As we rounded the top of the hill on the road climbing up to the airport, it occurred to me. "We have to hide Dakota."

Faith's head bobbed in agreement.

"No!" Dakota argued. "I want to help."

"No," Shiloh, Faith, and I all answered simultaneously.

"You need to be our lookout from a hiding place," I said, trying to give him a sense of purpose.

"Lookout for what?" Dakota argued. "We know where they are."

"More might be coming. Call out like a bird or something if you see anyone else drive up the road."

"A bird? What—?"

Shiloh stopped the truck behind a shed near the main gates to the airstrip. The Mercedes was still in view but way ahead of us. I removed my gun from my left boot and cocked it. Every head in the truck turned to look at me.

Dakota was the only one to ask. "Harmony, where did you—"

"Dakota, take this. Anthony and Carson will be here soon. If any of those nefarious bastards come after you, shoot them. Don't hesitate, they don't deserve to live. Be careful. It's cocked and loaded."

He nodded, staring wide-eyed at the small but deadly pistol. I pulled my knife from my other boot and stuck it in my back pocket. "Get out. Hide behind that shed and *do not* come out until it's over. Don't watch us. Keep your eyes and attention focused on the road, and keep calling Nate until he answers."

Dakota slid out of his seat and stumbled away from the car. "I just aim and pull the trigger, right?"

"Yes, but don't try to be a superhero, little brother." I reached over, slamming his door shut and pointed to the shed. Dakota scurried off and hid.

"Go," I commanded as Shiloh's truck lurched forward.

"Damn, they move fast," Shiloh said as we pulled through the open gate to the runway. A private plane sat with its steps already lowered.

"River," Faith hissed.

She was right, River walked beside one of the men with his hands cuffed behind his back. The first person of the group of five was about to step through the plane's doorway. And that lead bastard was Dedrick.

All three of us jumped out of the truck at once, sunglasses shielding our eyes, running as fast as we could toward them.

Gregory was second in line. My heart and lungs felt like they were trapped in barbed wire when he stepped inside the plane.

"Wait!" I yelled to River and the last two monsters climbing the plane steps. Their heads snapped up to look at us.

"There's a bomb on that plane!" I have no idea where my threat came from, but it worked. River pushed past a bald guy and a black-haired woman who looked like a witch, almost tripping down the steps. Baldy and Witchy followed him. Then the most stunning soul in the world stepped out of the plane and descended down the steps. I had missed Gregory so much it physically hurt to see him again.

Dedrick poked his slimy head out the door but remained on the plane.

It didn't take long for them to notice we were wearing sunglasses at night. But so were they. Young and non-threatening as we may have looked, they surely knew we were hiding our eyes for the same reason they were.

River ran toward us, looking panicked, but Baldy grabbed him by his cuffed arms and held him in place. Witchy strutted over to us, clinging to Gregory's tensed arm like a leech.

He doesn't like to be touched, I mentally jeered.

"Darling," she said in a sickening sweet voice. "These are the enemies we told you about."

Calling him Darling earned her first spot on my hit list.

"Enemies?" Faith laughed. "We're all friends here. Let's work out a deal."

We stood braced and ready to fight, three against four, not counting River. Judging from the pleading look in River's eyes and the fact they had him in handcuffs, I sensed he'd rather not be with them. And if he did put up any kind of fight, I'd snap him in two. Faith and Shiloh had trained in many parts of Asia throughout their lifetimes. They had fighting skills like ninjas and they weren't afraid to use them.

Witchy snickered at Faith and they engaged in a useless exchange that I knew Faith was creating as a diversion to buy us time to give me a chance to communicate with Gregory.

He stood directly across from me. No more than five long strides across the asphalt. His hair was longer, his bulging muscles were larger, and it didn't make sense that he was the age he was, but I knew he could hear our thoughts. And I knew how to make mine loud.

Hey you, beefcake, who can hear my thoughts right now. Don't do this. Those cretins standing beside you are not your compadres. We were your family once, and they kidnapped you. I don't know how or why you're still with them, but this is your chance to return to where you belong.

His sunglasses blocked his eyes but his ears pulled back slightly. A tell-tale sign he was listening. I knew Faith and Witchy's chitchat wouldn't continue much longer. If the heathens had any brains at all, it wouldn't take them long to figure out that one of us might be silently communicating with Gregory.

You and I are soul mates, I told him. *I don't know what they've brain-washed you into believing, but I swear, you belong with us. I love you more than life itself and you'll have to kill me to stop me from taking you back because I'll be damned if these lowlifes will continue to keep you hostage.*

"Enough!" Witchy hissed. "Time for you three to depart this world."

All three of us crouched. Where the hell was Anthony?

Baldy snapped his attention to Gregory. "Argos!" He shouted in a thick Scottish accent. "Which of these gangrels would you like to squash?"

I slowly stepped sideways, hoping to lure Gregory away from the others. *Argos is not your name. You are Gregory, ninth member of a kindrily of virtuous souls who love you.*

"The little dark one is mine." Gregory sneered. He unsheathed a dagger and braced himself like a bear ready to attack.

Damn right I'm yours! And you're mine. We're twin flames, Gregory. Snap out of it!

In Japanese, Shiloh warned us that Witchy had a gun tucked in the back waistband of her pants. His new vision perspective was already being put to good use.

Baldy whispered into River's ear then shoved him aside. River ambled back, almost in a daze but headed for the plane.

Baldy and Witchy jumped first, but Shiloh and Faith were faster. Faith leapt at Witchy and tackled her to the ground before she could draw her weapon. Shiloh darted side to side while advancing, confusing Baldy and avoiding every swing of his fist. I heard Shiloh's elbow smash into Baldy's jaw as my eyes landed on Gregory lunging at me.

I jumped backward. He kept coming, so I kept drawing him back. For each of his steps forward I took two or three back. I planted my feet, focusing on the dagger he'd been swinging at me. On his next swipe I kicked. My boot made hard perfect contact with his wrist and the dagger went flying.

I lunged forward and ripped his glasses from his face. His obsidian eyes were gone, replaced by something heinous. *Mi vida, what happened to you?*

He tried to grab hold of me but I slipped away. He threw a punch. I bobbed. He threw another. I weaved. I knew all his moves because we had learned to fight together.

I could hear the grunts and blows of Faith and Shiloh fighting Witchy and Baldy. Shiloh shouted out to Faith in Japanese. Faith flipped over Witchy's head, elbowing her in the face mid-flip and grabbing the gun the instant her feet hit the ground. Faith had the gun pointed at her before Witchy could wipe blood from her nose.

I landed a kick to the side of Gregory's knee. His weak spot. He dropped and I took advantage of the moment by jabbing him with a right hook. His head flew sideways, but he stumbled back up to his feet. I pulled out my knife and crouched, waiting for him to come at me again.

Shiloh had Baldy face-down on the ground with his arms locked behind him.

Gregory shook his head like he was shaking away the pain. "Is that really you?"

Yes. I answered.

He stood up straight, glancing around. Beyond him I saw a red-head glide down the steps of the plane. *Shit.*

Flames ignited from the ground between Witchy and Faith. Faith stepped back, gun still aimed at them. Gregory stalked closer to me, away from the flames.

"Let him go," Red told Shiloh in a dementedly calm tone. She waved her hand and the flames spread wider, rushing toward Shiloh and Baldy.

Shiloh shoved off Baldy and jumped back as the fire nearly singed the front of him. Baldy crawled forward and stood. He,

Witchy, and Red stood on the other side of a growing wall of flames.

"I never thought I'd see you again," Gregory said as if unaware of the fire raging higher behind him. His words jumpstarted my mind back into action. He closed the space between us in two long strides, his arms opened at his sides. My grip on my knife loosened as Gregory wrapped his huge arms around me. I inhaled. His familiar coconut scent was gone.

Eighteen years I had longed to feel his arms around me. Two, maybe three seconds of ecstatic bliss, rushed through me as I rested my head against his muscular chest and listened to his strong heartbeat. I didn't care about the raging flames. I didn't care about anything except feeling him again. *God, I've missed you.*

Gunshots fired. Faith shot at the wall of fire but the three Nefariouns were gone.

When Gregory's arm moved, I expected to feel his fingers run through my hair, or the familiar pull of his hand to raise my chin so he could kiss me. That's how it always was with us, and that's how I thought it was going to be again. I never felt him take the knife out of my hand. So the whopping thud in my upper back was a shock.

The hot searing pain and the surge of adrenaline ripped through me at the same time. I sucked in a breath through my teeth. Stabbed in the back by my own soul mate, with my own knife, how poetic. How stupid could I have been?

I should have realized he was playing me, that he was still being mind-controlled, but logic had been pushed aside for a more important matter, *love.*

Many things happened around me simultaneously, but my mind processed it all with great clarity. The plane rolled forward with its engines roaring. To my left, over Gregory's shoulder, the event I feared would happen became a reality.

I tried shouting, but my words came out quiet and ragged. "Don't be a hero!"

It was too late to remind Dakota of that. He ran toward us, yelling, with my gun pointed at Gregory's back. Faith shouted something and I was sure she was running toward us too, but my focus was glued on my little brother. Dakota's wide eyes met mine for half a breath as Gregory stabbed me again under my left breast.

The knife thrusting into me didn't hurt nearly as bad as the panic and horror on Dakota's face.

The gunshot sounded muffled, like it was farther away than it actually was. From previous deaths I knew that meant I was losing too much blood. My senses were distorting. Witchy appeared out of thin air behind Gregory and launched herself at Dakota.

I sneered with satisfaction when a bullet hit her. But she continued barreling through the air and into my little brother. He fought her off like a true superhero.

I gasped as my lung collapsed. My wind pipe felt like the size of a cocktail straw. I wheezed out the only words my deoxygenated brain could think of. "I love you, Gregory."

Visions of our previous life in Peru flashed through my mind. Did he still know Spanish? If he did, it would be the version he heard at least a million times.

"Te amo, Gregory..." I tried to look up at him one last time but my lids were too heavy.

Witchy had Dakota's head clamped between her hands. I tried to scream out and warn him, but she was so fast.

She snapped his neck like he was a rag doll.

"No," I murmured, reaching out for him.

Faith pounced on Gregory like a tiger. Gregory let go of me to fend her off and I slid to the ground.

Radiant yellow, blue, and orange light seeped out of Dakota, hovering above his contorted body as his spirit continued calling out my name.

I crawled to him. *Hang on Dakota. I'm coming.*

Witchy staggered sideways. Dakota's shot had hit her, and judging from her swaying body and the blood dripping from her mouth, it was a kill shot. She fell to her knees right in front of me. Her sunglasses slid off her face and onto the asphalt. Her eyes matched Gregory's—just like a snake's. She coughed up more blood and toppled forward, her eyes changed to a brilliant blue. They darted around then landed on me.

She was fading away faster than I was, but we were both still coherent enough to see into the windows of each other's souls.

"No!" I gasped when I realized who she was. "Josephine."

"Where am I?" she whispered. "What happened?"

Her light faded from her eyes too fast. She was gone. Her spirit expanded like a prism of light over her useless body. Over my lifetimes I had learned to appreciate the uniqueness of every spirit, but Josephine was an ancient icon of this world. Her incandescent light was like nothing I'd ever seen. I had so many questions to ask her, but I couldn't utter a sound.

Faith and Shiloh grappled with Gregory beside me, but I couldn't turn my head.

"Harmony?" Dakota's soul desperately shouted beside me. "Harmony, are you okay?"

Another death had arrived for me. After a few times, you get used to dying, but this was one for the memory books. Gregory had never killed me before. What would his warped mind think when all this was over? Because it wasn't over. It would never be over.

Even if he stayed with Dedrick for centuries, and killed me over and over, I would always find him again. He could kill me as many times as Dedrick's evil forces made him, but he would never kill my love for him.

My spirit hovered above my body. Shiloh held Gregory's arms behind him while Faith delivered a mid-air roundhouse kick to Gregory's temple.

The plane took off down the runway.

Carson's Mustang squealed to a halt and he jumped out. He blurred toward Gregory so fast that no one could have stopped him. The anger radiated off him, leaving a vapor trail, and all that rage went into the uppercut punch Carson blasted Gregory with.

Gregory was knocked out the moment Carson's supersonic fist made contact with his face, but his body still flew up into the air. He landed flat and unconscious on the asphalt.

Carson leaned over him and spat. "Bet you didn't see that one coming, did you, *Dad*?"

Mine and Gregory's relationship had always been the epitome of tough love. And it appeared Carson inherited the trait from us.

The Higher Realm tugged at me, but so did Dakota's pleading spirit.

Just like Dakota and me, the flames were dying on the asphalt, leaving nothing but smoke drifting up into the black sky.

IMPOSSIBLE CHOICES

Maryah

Nathan and I had been lost in an ebb and flow of each other. We'd let our desire build up until one of us almost couldn't take it anymore, then we'd try to calm down by cuddling or talking about the past or future, or whatever. But the touching and kissing had always reignited somehow.

"We should go home," I told Nathan. "We've been gone a long time. It's getting cold, and the mosquitoes are eating me alive." I slapped my leg, trying to kill the bloodsucker that bit my shin, but I missed. "Can you traverse us back to our bug-free room, please?"

"Your wish is my command." He wrapped the blanket around us and seconds later we were back in bed.

"That will never get old."

He didn't let go of me. "Would you like me to find some of Helen's oils to rub on your bug bites?"

"Yes, please. And you should give me a full rubdown to make sure you don't miss any."

He kissed me. His kisses would never get old either.

After only a few seconds, Nathan moaned with irritation and rolled off the bed.

"Why'd you stop?"

"My phone keeps ringing."

"I didn't hear either of our phones."

"That's because they're buried at the bottom of your purse on vibrate." He strolled over to my desk, glancing back at me with a cocky I-hear-much-better-than-you smirk. He held up my purse. "May I?"

"Of course."

He walked back to the bed while digging. He tossed me my phone first, but I didn't look at it. I rarely ever received calls or texts. He pulled out his own phone.

"Oh no," Nathan said with borderline panic in his voice.

"What?" I asked, sitting up straight.

"I'll be right back."

And then he was gone. I grabbed my phone and saw I'd missed two calls from Louise and Amber. I had one text. From April:

All over the news...River busted out of jail. Be careful!

I jumped to my feet, not so patiently waiting for Nathan to return. How could he say something like, "Oh, no," then vanish without telling me what was wrong. Why didn't he take me with him? My stomach churned with a mixture of nerves and worry. What if River showed up here while Nathan was gone? Was anyone else even home? I stared at our locked bedroom door and considered checking the house, but decided to call Louise instead.

I scrolled to her name just as Nathan reappeared.

The sight of him made my knees weak, but not in a good way. He looked like he had seen a ghost.

"Oh god, what happened?" I shouted.

There was an excruciating expression on his face. "It's not good."

"What's not good? What happened?"

He wrapped his arms around me. "It won't hurt any less if I tell you beforehand."

I held onto him tightly. With one blur of light we were gone from our room and standing on a stretch of open blacktop in the dark. I heard the sobbing before I saw her. Once my brain registered the reality of the situation, I begged for it to be a nightmare.

Dakota and Harmony were sprawled across the ground. Dakota's neck was bent in the most awful and unnatural way I'd ever seen. Harmony was covered in blood. Krista was on her knees between them. After the initial paralyzing shock wore off, I ran to Harmony.

I felt Harmony's neck. "She still has a pulse!"

Krista's arms were stretched wide, touching Harmony with one hand and Dakota with the other. She let go of Harmony and shuddered as she moved Dakota's wrenched neck back into alignment. She looked up at me with tears streaming down her face. "What do I do?"

I didn't know what to say. My hands were trembling from shock. I just stared back at her, knowing the thoughts that were going through her mind.

"Which one do I save?" she pleaded for an answer.

Tears fell from my eyes. "You can't save Dakota, Kris. He's gone. If you bring him back, you'll give up your own life."

"He's not gone yet."

I didn't believe her. The way his head had been positioned beside his neck instead of on top of it could only mean he'd been killed by having his neck broken. She was in denial.

"Kris," I murmured, not sure how to verbalize my horrid thoughts.

Carson was suddenly beside us. I had no idea where he came from.

"No," he said, cradling Harmony's head in his hands. His eyes landed on Dakota and his nostrils flared. "No way. Why was he here? He has no part in this." His voice hitched. "He's my best friend!"

"Which one?" Krista yelped to Carson. "Please just tell me which one to save. I can't choose."

I glanced between them, speechless, then down at Harmony, realizing my hand was still pressed against her neck. Except no pulse throbbed against my fingers.

"Tell me which one!" Krista screamed again. "I can't let them both die!"

I shook uncontrollably.

Krista placed her hands behind Dakota's neck and closed her eyes.

"You can save him," Carson told her. "I know you can. You can save both of them."

Nathan squatted behind Krista and pulled her hair from her face. "Dakota is gone, Krista. To give up your life for his would be detrimental to the survival of the kindrily. We need you. Harmony needs you. You need to focus your efforts on her."

Krista strangled back a sob and pressed her lips to Dakota's forehead.

"No!" Carson yelled at Nathan. "He's not dead. He can't be dead." Carson's head drooped and he murmured, "He's my best friend."

Anthony joined us. "Everyone to the hospital, now."

Shiloh had already backed up his truck and opened the tailgate.

"I'll take them," Nathan said. "It will be faster."

"Are you sure?" Anthony asked.

Nathan nodded.

"You can't take anyone to the hospital until I'm there to freeze time." Without a word, Nathan threw his arms around Anthony and they were gone. Nathan reappeared seconds later, scooped up Dakota's body, and vanished again.

Faith petted Harmony's face. "Hang in there, sis." She stood and put her hands on her hips. "Dylan is on his way to deal with Gregory when he comes to. Carson, can you stay to help him?"

Carson nodded, but then said, "No. I need to be at the hospital with them."

Nathan reappeared and lifted Harmony from Carson's hands then traversed with her. Krista stood, wrapping her arms around herself and shaking. Carson sprung up and hugged her, whispering in her ear.

Nathan reappeared and I worried because he looked pale and weak.

"Go with Nathan," I told Krista. "I'll ride with Faith and Shiloh."

Nathan didn't need to waste his energy traversing with me. Krista needed to be at the hospital much faster than I did. I still didn't know who or what killed them, but I suspected Dedrick and maybe River. I wasn't sure I wanted to know the details.

Carson handed Krista over to Nathan and she sank against his chest. His green eyes had never looked so defeated as they did the moment before the two people I loved most dissolved into the darkness.

DO OR DIE

Harmony

The great thing about being in spirit form is watching whomever you want whenever you want. No big surprise that I kept my attention on Gregory.

"Go," Dylan told Carson, shoving him toward his car. "We can handle Gregory."

"You and Amber against Gregory?" Carson eyed Amber skeptically.

She patted Molokai's head. "Her bite is worse than her bark."

"Besides," Dylan said, "he's out cold, secured and bound, and anything I tell him to do, he'll do."

"What if he's immune to your power?"

"We can handle it," Dylan insisted. Dylan's eyes rippled with light. "Go to the hospital, Carson."

Ordered by Dylan's power, Carson turned, climbed in his car and drove away.

Gregory stirred, groaning and slowly trying to move, but his focus landed on his restraints and he stilled.

"Finally. There they are," I said, hovering close to his face and wishing he could hear my thoughts while I was in spirit form. "Those warm obsidian eyes I've missed so much."

He peered through me, squinting up at Amber and Dylan. His voice was as choppy as the waves of Playa de Santa Maria. "Did I kill her?"

A jolt of grounding energy burst through me. My soul was struggling to reconnect with my body. I turned to explain what was happening to Dakota, but he was gone. I let the second jolt of energy yank me away to the hospital.

My body lay on an operating table. I looked awful. Dakota was on another table beside me. Krista stood between our bodies, her arms extended wide, one hand touching each of us.

A scrub nurse was frozen near the corner of the room. Outside in the hallway a doctor was paused mid-stride. Anthony stood in the doorway with his hands opened at his sides.

Dakota's soul materialized next to me.

The protective sister in me wanted to grab him and turn him away before he saw the scene in front of us and realized what was going on. But he was in spirit form, and so was I. I couldn't grab him. I couldn't protect him.

"Hey," Dakota said, looking me up and down. It's hard to describe what a soul looks like. I see the person as if they were human, but not solid skin and bones. Spirits are light and energy imprinted with the physical features of the last body in which their soul took residence. Sprit forms glowed, pulsed, and changed color. Dakota was radiant, but I knew he would be.

Confusion washed over his ethereal face as he glanced at the ceiling and sterile white walls. "What's...we're in a hospital?" His focus landed on our unconscious bodies on the table. "Hey, that's us. Wait. Are we...?"

"We're straddling," I told him.

"Straddling?" He looked around again, realizing that Anthony was freezing time, and that Krista was pouring healing energy into our bodies on the hospital tables. "Oh, shit. We're dead?"

"Not yet. But we're as close as it gets. We've got Krista on our side. That helps, but she won't have enough life force to save both of us. Not on her own anyway."

"What do you mean, not on her own?"

Krista turned and focused on my body. My clothes were still on, but my shirt was soaked with blood. Krista's hands swept up and down inches from my torso.

"Should I stitch up her wounds?" Nathan asked. Krista's eyes remained closed. "No, that's the easy part, but Faith needs to cut that shirt off of her. It's probably covered with bacteria."

I turned to face Dakota. "This is it. *Do or die* in the most literal sense of the phrase. Only you can decide if you want to live or pass on."

"Decide?" He floated forward, hovering over his body. "I look pretty dead. I don't think I have a choice at this point."

"Your light is still transparent. If you were dead it would be translucent. Part of your soul is holding onto your body."

"This is incredible," Dakota said in awe. "I mean, I'm almost dead, but I've never felt better. I feel so powerful, so free, so..."

"Alive?" I chuckled.

"Yeah. Why is that?"

"Serious design flaw they can't seem to fix."

"They?"

"They. He. She. It. Whatever. Bottom line is your spirit isn't bogged down with all your human worries and pains. As good as you feel right now, it intensifies times infinity in the Higher Realm."

"And I can go there?"

"If you choose to, yes, but you can also stay and fight to live through this."

He stared at his body again. "What will happen in the Higher Realm? Will I be able to stay there?"

"No, the universe will send you back in what will simultaneously feel like an eternity and a heartbeat."

"But I won't get to choose how or where I come back?"

"Sadly, no. You aren't an Element."

"But Mikey came back and he wasn't an Element."

"He was Maryah's twin. I think that might've had something to do with it."

"What about Carson?"

"Same thing, I'm guessing. Product of Gregory and me. Maybe Maryah's help too. She adored him in his first life—swore he was gifted. Same thing with Krista. All of them were loved by Mary, by Maryah."

"I should have become better friends with Maryah."

I snickered. "Maybe."

"But I could have more time if I fight to live, right?"

"Right."

"What if I don't make it?"

"What if you do?"

He studied me. "Your light is transparent. Are you going to fight?"

"Of course. I have to kick Gregory's ass for stabbing me."

Dakota weaved slowly between his body and Krista. He brushed up against Maryah, then studied Faith as she bounced in place at the foot of his table, praying. "I don't know what to do," he admitted. "I like this feeling. I feel free, but I also feel like I finally matter."

Regret tugged at my soul. "What do you mean you *finally* matter? You've always mattered."

"You're obligated to say that. You're my sister."

"I'm not obligated to say anything." I swept past Shiloh and hovered between Faith and Dakota's spirit. "You matter, Dakota. You have always mattered and you always will."

"If you were me, which would you choose?"

"Life. I always choose life when given the chance."

"Why? You said the Higher Realm is so amazing."

"It is, but...how can I make this more understandable for you? What do you enjoy more, books or movies?"

"I love them both, but I think I love books more, comic books, anyway."

"Perfect. Then imagine that you started reading the most interesting and fascinating comic book ever created. You fell in love with some characters, you hated others. Endless plots unfolded and every one was an emotional page-turner. You couldn't read fast enough because you had to know what was going to happen next. You felt like the world would end if you didn't find out how the story ended. But then you get to the end and there was no end. The author didn't finish it. You don't know if good or evil won. You don't know if the guy got the girl. You don't know any of the answers to all of your important questions. No idea what happened to all the characters that you were so enthralled with."

"That would suck."

"Exactly. And that is the system of life. In the Higher Realm, you get the choice to either forget about the comic book you'd been reading and start a new one, with no memory of the other one you read. Or, you retain the story you loved, but still get assigned a new one, with no idea or say in whether it will be better or worse than the one you were so invested in."

"Unless you're an Element. Then the fantastic story continues forever."

"But you're not an Element. Your choice would be a much harder one."

Kindrily members moved and talked around us. Nathan was helping with scientific medical methods while Krista continued her supernatural approach, but sadly, Dakota's light was becoming more solid.

"Why would anyone choose to give up a story they loved?" he asked.

"Because most likely there were also parts they hated. Most people have loved deeply and been hurt deeply. They carry that love and pain with them. Some realize they'll retain horrific memories, guilt, or sins they don't want to carry onto another existence. Sometimes completely erasing a story ensures the reader they'll never regret their decision because they'll never know they had a choice in the matter."

Carson blurred into the room. He grabbed Dakota's hand. "How is he?"

Dakota watched Nathan shake his head.

"But for me, most of the souls I love are you guys." Dakota opened his glowing arms and motioned at the hospital room. "You're all Elements. If I retained, I could find you in a few years and tell you who I am. You'd take me in and we'd be together again."

"What if you aren't sent back for a thousand years? What if by some unforeseen circumstance all of our names have changed? What if you couldn't find us?"

"A thousand years?" Dakota gaped. "It can be that long between lives?"

"Non-Elements have no say in it. The universe decides."

"That's one messed up system."

I shrugged. "For most, yes it is."

"Do you think it would be easier to erase?"

"I can't answer that because I've never chosen to erase."

Krista opened her eyes and breath whooshed out of her. "Trying to keep both of them alive at the same time is draining me. Dakota was internally decapitated, but I transfused his skull back onto his spinal cord."

Carson's nose crinkled. Dakota's light pulsed.

"Is she serious?" Dakota asked me.

"Sounds like it."

"Would I even want to live after an injury like that? What if I can't walk or talk?"

"What if you can? Only you can decide how much strength lies within you, Dakota."

Dakota studied my body. "Are you going to live?"

"I'll do everything within my power to survive."

"Am I going to live?"

I focused on his solidifying light. "Only you can answer that."

FORGIVING THE UNFORGOTTEN

Maryah

"I've stopped Harmony's internal bleeding."

Krista's eyes were cradled by circles that were almost black. "But there was a lack of oxygen to her brain that caused severe damage. It took me almost two weeks to heal Maryah from the same injury."

I thought back to my recovery from the attack on my family and me. I was clueless to the fact that Krista was the one healing me. She sat at my side every day for hours as I lay in a coma, battling with death as it tried to carry me away.

But Krista never let go of me. She won the battle.

She healed me and gave me a second chance at life. I said a silent prayer that she would be able to do the same for Harmony and Dakota.

"Exactly who did this to them?" Anthony asked Shiloh.

"There were four plus River. I'm assuming they broke him out of jail because he looked like he didn't want to be with them. Dedrick escaped on the plane with a bald guy and a red-haired woman. The black-haired one died after Dakota shot her. Gregory stabbed Harmony."

No one said anything. Anthony and I both stared at Shiloh as if trying to believe such a horrible thing could be true.

"*Gregory* stabbed her?" I gawked.

Even lying unconscious on the hospital table, her skin stained with blood, Harmony still looked tough and fearless. Any second I expected her to spring up from the table and demand to see Gregory.

"Will she live?" I asked Krista.

Krista's voice was so weak and raspy she sounded like she had strep throat. "I can't be sure about either one of them at this point."

She wiped her brow then swayed on her feet. Carson instantly caught her and held her against him. "Take a break, Turtle."

"I can't." Krista sighed, resting her forehead against Carson's. "They need me."

Carson smoothed her hair from her face. "You'll be no use to anyone if you drain yourself completely."

"Speaking of drained," Anthony said, "we need to wrap it up here. I'm not sure how much longer I can last."

Shiloh glanced around. "Do you need any supplies, Krista?"

She shook her head.

"We'll send Dylan if we need anything." Nathan leaned against the wall beside me. "We'll have to transport them to the house in vehicles. I don't have enough energy to traverse right now."

"No problem," Shiloh said. "These tables are on wheels. Let's roll them out."

Krista's eyes were closed and her head was limp. Carson scooped her into his arms. "I'll take her with me."

∞

We arrived at the house and so much was happening it was hard to keep track: bodies being unloaded and carried in, car doors slamming left and right. Louise was waiting at the door, ordering Anthony to put Dakota in their room and Harmony in mine and Nathan's. She mumbled something about those rooms having the strongest healing energy.

"Krista?" Louise whispered as Carson carried her over the threshold.

"Just drained," Carson told her.

Louise nodded and waved them in.

I rounded the corner to the family room and stumbled backward when I saw Gregory sitting on the sofa.

"It's okay," Dylan assured me. He pointed to some kind of spiked handcuffs around Gregory's wrists and ankles. "He's not moving."

Gregory lifted his head and looked directly into my eyes. His long black hair had slipped out of its ponytail, and he no longer had snake eyes, but everything else was the same: his face, his muscles, even his black t-shirt and blood-stained boots. My jaw clenched as I fought back fear and rage from the memory of what he did to my family and me. He blinked a few times, like he was confused by seeing me again, but then he stared at the floor in silence.

A dull ache pulsed behind my ears. I didn't try to fight it. If my headaches were past life memories trying to break through then I wanted them to. I'd happily endure physical pain to regain some of my memories. And I wanted to remember Gregory as someone other than a murderer, but I didn't know if that were possible.

Carson strolled into the room with his sunglasses on. Gregory looked up and rolled his shoulders.

"Enjoy the beat down I gave your sorry ass earlier?" Carson asked Gregory. I hadn't been there to see what happened at the airport—the aftermath was bad enough—but I tried to imagine Carson beating up the huge monster of a man who was still in the same physical form as Carson's father from his last life. How difficult must it have been to beat up his own dad?

Gregory said nothing, just lowered his focus to his boots.

"Hey, I'm talking to you, douche bag." Carson rushed forward at his usual unnatural speed and grabbed Gregory by the jaw. "Answer me."

Gregory stayed stone-faced and silent but didn't try to pull out of Carson's grip.

Carson took his sunglasses off and Gregory's forehead wrinkled. His wide shoulders softened.

"Carlos?"

"I go by Carson now. I'm a Scion."

"You're an Element?"

Carson let go of Gregory and stood tall. "Surprised?"

"No. I always suspected you were gifted." He leaned forward slightly, almost like he wanted to reach out and hug Carson, but he flinched and stilled. The spiked cuffs must have been as painful as they looked. "You must be furious with me."

"Furious. Hurt. Confused."

Gregory nodded. "Even more so than I am, I bet."

"Just tell me one thing." Carson squatted so he was eye level with Gregory. "Did you go willingly?"

"Absolutely not." His jaw moved side to side. "I swear to you, I fought them with everything I had. And it kills me that it wasn't enough."

"You're a Nefarioun. We should kill you."

Gregory glanced at everyone in the room. I hadn't even noticed so many had joined us. I was too consumed by Carson and Gregory interacting. Nathan, Anthony, Louise, Faith, and Shiloh were all scattered around the room. Dylan still sat beside Gregory on the sofa, and Edgar and Helen sat on each arm.

"I am not a Nefarioun," Gregory said. "But I do deserve to be killed, punished, tortured, or whatever awful thing could be done to me." He turned toward Edgar. "And the worst part is I know my kindrily won't do any of that. Living with my guilt and betrayal will be the worst punishment of all."

"Did you know what you were doing?" Faith asked, clutching his arm. Anger raged in her eyes. "When you hurt and killed all those people."

Gregory hung his head. "No. A lot of the details are still hazy. Everything is hazy. Even this, everyone in this room, feels like a dream within a dream."

Faith looked up at all of us. "He's telling the truth. He's overwhelmed with guilt, sadness, anger, and confusion." She looked down at him again. They were both silent as they stared at each other. At first I thought maybe they were speechless from so much emotion, but then it hit me that she was having a silent conversation with Gregory. He could hear her thoughts, and whatever Faith was telling him made his lip quiver.

"I need to see her," he begged. "Please. Keep me cuffed and shackled. Just please let me see my soul mate."

∞

I have no idea what happened when Carson and Faith took Gregory to see Harmony. They were the only ones in the room.

Nathan pulled me into his old bedroom. He held me against him in a comforting hug. "Are you okay?"

"Physically I am," I assured him. I sat on the twin bed and dropped my head into my hands. "My god, Nathan, we were too busy making out to know they needed us."

He sat beside me. "I know."

We didn't know what else to say. There was no righting our wrong. We had a time stopper in our kindrily, but no time rewinder. A thought occurred to me. "Do any of the other kindrilies have someone who can rewind time?"

"No one exists with that power that we know of."

"You've searched for one before, haven't you?"

"Of course. I would give anything to go back to Amber and Dylan's wedding and prevent all of us from being killed." He paused. "And to stop you from erasing."

What if a time rewinder did exist somewhere? I would be able to fix all of this. Maybe I could travel all the way back to the lifetime when I told some woman my secret and she told Dedrick about me, starting this chain of awful events. That would have to be investigated later. Nothing I could do about it right now. Nathan wrapped his arm around me and pulled me against him.

"I'm sorry," I whispered into his chest. Given his hearing, I knew he heard me. I pulled back and looked up at him. "Are you okay? All that traversing and taking people to the hospital must have wiped you out."

"I'm fine physically," he added. "This Dakota and Harmony situation is what's worrying me."

"I don't understand how Dakota could survive." I felt sick with grief. "His neck was snapped."

"There's no guarantee he'll survive, but Krista is determined to give them everything she has."

"That's what I'm afraid of. What if she gives up her own life trying to save them?"

"She won't. As tempting as it may be, she won't."

I glanced at the open door, trying to imagine what might be happening in our room where Gregory was being taken to Harmony. "What if Gregory tries to hurt her again?"

"We're taking all the necessary precautions, but you saw his eyes. He's not under Dedrick's power any longer."

"Or maybe that's part of the plan. To make us think that. What if he's still one of them?"

"He's one of us, Maryah." Nathan held my hand. "I know that's hard for you to hear, but he is still a member of this kindrily. He always has been."

COLLECTIVELY DREAMING

Maryah

No one slept much. We were like a flock of birds with clipped wings flitting around a cage and pacing our perches because we didn't know what else to do. All night people shuffled from room to room. Helen spent most of her time in the kitchen brewing teas to help ease everyone's worrying. Full mugs sat everywhere: on tables, tucked away in bookshelves, on the railings of the back deck. Most of them felt cool to the touch and had barely a sip of tea missing.

Every now and then I'd find a member lying on the couch, reclined in a patio lounger, or slumped in a chair, their gaze far away, their body unmoving, like they were sleeping with their eyes open. They were dreaming of Harmony and Dakota waking up—living, breathing, filling the too-quiet house with their voices that we hadn't heard in much too long.

We all dreamed that same dream.

But I wondered if, behind everyone's tired and weary eyes, they saw the same nightmare I did: a foolish girl spilling a secret long ago, attracting the attention and obsession of a madman who would hunt and harm her and her kindrily for many lifetimes to come. That girl was the reason nine members were slaughtered last lifetime, the reason Gregory was ripped away from Harmony, the reason Harmony, and Dakota—an innocent bystander—lay in bedrooms several feet apart both fighting to live.

My nightmare was knowing I was to blame for all of this, and wondering if everyone else in the house blamed me too. And then hating myself for being so self-centered as to think anyone was thinking of anyone but Harmony and Dakota.

Around 2, 3, or 4 A.M., Louise made waffles and pancakes. Carson ate one then pushed his plate away, leaving the other three untouched. I put myself in his shoes. He was at risk of losing two people he loved dearly: Harmony, his friend in this life, mother in his last life; and Dakota, his best friend and the only other soul I'd ever seen him interact with besides kindrily members.

Krista, his possible soul mate, drained herself over and over trying to save their lives. If she failed, would Carson blame her? Would he ever look at her again without seeing a girl who had failed to save two souls he loved?

His eyes met mine for the first time since the airport. Maybe it was sleep deprivation, or my guilty conscience, but I imagined his lips parting and him screaming, "This is all your fault!"

I flinched and looked away, fighting back tears, even though he hadn't uttered a word.

He slid off his stool and traipsed down the hallway.

For a long time, I sat there, staring at the shadowed wall of the hallway where Carson disappeared from view. Nathan sat beside me for a while holding my hand. Helen floated around the other side of the island, making more tea that no one drank. Mikey cried. People talked in quiet voices and said very little. Someone turned on the TV, and minutes—or maybe hours—later someone turned it off.

The entire time I sat in a kitchen stool, I breathed in and out, and every inhalation filled me with the guilt of what I had done.

With every exhale, I sent out prayers for Harmony and Dakota to survive.

The sun rose slowly, yet much too fast given the circumstances. The sun didn't get the memo that there was no reason to shine today.

Beams of sunlight shone through the floor-to-ceiling windows behind me. The light passed through Louise's hanging crystals, creating a rainbow on the hallway wall at the exact spot I'd been staring at for who knows how long.

I eased out of my stool and walked down the hallway to Louise and Anthony's room.

I lightly tapped on the door and pushed it open. "How's he doing?"

Carson glanced at Faith and smirked. "How do you think he's doing?"

I nodded. What a stupid question.

Faith was sitting Indian style in Anthony and Louise's king-sized bed. She stretched and cracked her neck then rubbed Dakota's chest. "I'm going to visit Harmony for a while and see if Krista needs anything." She climbed out of the bed then walked past me and touched my forearm. "Thanks, Maryah."

"For what?"

"For being so worried about my little brother."

She left before I could figure out what to say.

Carson motioned for me to sit down in the empty chair beside him so I did. Dakota looked so frail and weak. I cautiously glanced sideways at Carson. He wasn't looking at me. I hadn't noticed at first, but he was holding Dakota's hand.

"I keep praying for both of them," I said. My throat felt dry and raw. "Nonstop."

"Prayers won't help." Carson closed his other hand around Dakota's wrist. "I know Dakota. He's waiting."

"Waiting for what?"

"To decide if it's worth it to stay."

"To live?"

Carson nodded.

"Of course it's worth it."

"I'm not the one who needs convincing."

I stared at Dakota's pale face. The pink patches on his cheeks were missing. Dakota's cheeks were always speckled with blotchy patches of pink, like he'd just been crying, except the patches spread and grew pinker the bigger he smiled. The unconscious body in front of Carson and me didn't look at all like Dakota. "You think he'd rather die?"

"You make it sound like he's suicidal. That's not what I meant. Dakota is my best friend. Do you realize what that means?" Carson paused, waiting for me to answer, but I only shook my head.

"His best friend is an Element," Carson explained, "a Scion no less, with super strength and immense mental power. Dakota's only two siblings are also Elements with supernatural abilities. He has no girlfriend, mainly because he becomes bored with normal humans after spending a few hours with them. His parents are hardly ever home because they are more interested in their church than they are in their own children. Life sucks for him. He's been cursed ever since we told him our secret because it made him hyperaware of his own human limitations. As he has told me several times, for him, life is like existing in an awesome comic book; amazing things and people are always around him, but he has no role, no part in any of the meaningful plots."

"But life isn't a comic book."

"It's a metaphor, Maryah. The Higher Realm would be tempting for someone like him. It's a chance to wipe the slate clean and start fresh. He wouldn't have to feel inferior anymore."

"He really feels that way?"

Carson nodded. "It sucks. I'd give him one of my powers if I could in a heartbeat. I swear I would." Carson squeezed Dakota's shoulder. "He needs to be convinced there's a reason for him to stay, so that's what I've been doing." He motioned toward the door. "Harmony will live. She has a score to settle, so I have no doubt she'll pull through. Dakota needs a reason to fight." Carson's shoulders slumped forward. "And so far, I haven't been able to give him one that's good enough. What kind of best friend am I?"

"You're an amazing best friend, Car. He would tell you that if he could."

Carson let go of Dakota and stuck his hands in the pocket of his hoodie. "I need to check on Krista."

He stood and left, and it was just Dakota and me. He was covered up to his chest with Louise and Anthony's midnight blue comforter. Just past him, sitting on the nightstand, was a white candle burning. It was the first time I had noticed it, so I inhaled deeply, trying to determine which scented oils Krista had used to make it. I smelled vanilla, jasmine, and something woodsy. Then I felt guilty for inhaling some of the healing energy Dakota so desperately needed.

I moved over to Carson's chair so I could be closer to Dakota. Carson's seat was so warm I almost went back to my seat. I felt like I had intruded on Carson's place beside his best friend. But I wanted to talk to Dakota. I needed to talk to him. I held his hand. Leaning close to him, I spoke from my heart.

"Hey, Dakota. I'm so sorry about all this. I'm sorry you're hurt, and that you might...well, you know. I'm just so sorry because this is all my fault. My parents died because of something I did a long long time ago. Now you might die too, and, I just, I don't know how to make any of it right."

I thought back to the first time I met him. We watched *Jumper*, and he was so fascinated with superpowers. Now, it all made sense. "I know you want to be an Element. I know you want a superpower. I remember you said you'd want the ability to fly." A tear ran down my cheek.

The candle flame flickered and danced not far from Dakota's pale face. I willed the candle's warmth to turn his cheeks pink again.

"Don't fly away, Dakota. Stay here. Stay with us. Fight and survive this. That would make you a superhero. To live through something like this, you'd be better than a superhero." I squeezed his hand tighter. "I have no idea how it would happen, but if I could grant your wish to be an Element, I would. I swear, with all my being, I would. I'd gift you with a soul mate and everything, and I'd give you the power to fly, as long as you promised not to fly away." More tears streamed down my face. "Don't fly away, Dakota, please."

I wiped my eyes. I gasped when Dakota squeezed my other hand.

"Dakota?" My voice quivered. His fingers twitched. "Dakota!"

I half-stood, still keeping his hand in mine and shouted, "Dakota moved! Someone, hurry!"

Carson blurred into the room.

"He squeezed my hand." I panted, excited but also worried. I hadn't imagined it, right? Oh god, what if my sleep-deprived brain hallucinated and this was a false alarm that would get everyone's hopes up just to be disappointed again. Krista practically stumbled into the room, followed by Faith.

"What happened?" Krista asked.

Carson kneeled on the bed beside Dakota. "Wake up man. We're right here cheering for you. Wake up."

Faith climbed in beside Carson, holding Dakota's hand. "I'm not getting anything. No emotions at all."

He wasn't moving. Not one twitch or flinch. I had imagined it. Carson would never forgive me. I sank back into my chair.

Krista stood beside me and leaned over Dakota's body. I stared at her hand, moving in slow motion over the blanket. I moved out of the way as she made her way past Dakota's chest, and finally stopped at his pink cheeks.

I did a double take. His cheeks were pink. Thank the heavens above, his cheeks were pink!

The rest of the kindrily filed into the room, watching, hoping, dreaming the same dream again.

"Dakota?" Krista called gently. "Can you move for us again?"

I didn't know what I was more afraid of, Dakota dying, or Dakota waking up and being paralyzed for the rest of his life.

"Please don't let him be paralyzed," I whispered to myself, but Carson heard me.

"How can he be paralyzed if he squeezed your hand?"

Great point. Hope soared inside of me. I reached toward Dakota's feet and squeezed his toes through the blanket. "Come on, Dakota. Come on."

Krista waved her hands around Dakota's head then down around his chest. Carson continued urging him back to the land of the living while I held my breath.

His foot twitched.

"His foot!" I yelped. I stared at the lump under the blanket, begging it to move again. "His foot just moved."

"Confusion!" Faith yelled, excited to feel any emotion at all from Dakota.

My focus shot up to Dakota's face. His eyelids were fluttering.

"Hey, man," Carson said. "Welcome back."

I held my breath and wrung my hands. I'd seen kindrily members perform supernatural feats that were hard to believe, but this ranked right up there with witnessing the impossible. Dakota's skull had been snapped from his spine, but Krista healed him. He was still breathing, his eyes were opening, and his hand and foot had moved. It was a miracle.

"Hi Dakota," Krista said soothingly.

Dakota rubbed his lips together. I knew firsthand how dry they probably were because my mouth felt like a desert when I woke up from my coma.

"I'll be right back," I said, taking off for the kitchen.

I threw some ice cubes in one glass and filled another with water, then hurried back to Dakota. I shouldered past Louise and Shiloh, then squeezed in next to Krista at Dakota's side. I grabbed an ice cube and dipped it in water then ran it over Dakota's lips. He looked relieved.

"You're making us nervous," Carson told him. "Say something."

"Something," Dakota murmured.

"Hell yeah!" Carson shook his shoulder. "I knew you'd pull through."

Faith fell forward, hugging Dakota's torso. "You crazy brave idiot, you almost got yourself killed."

"So good to have you back," Krista told him.

His tired eyes narrowed on her. "You saved my life."

Krista grinned. "It's sort of my thing."

"Well," his voice was scratchy. "Thank you."

"Can you feel everything" Carson asked him. "All fingers and toes accounted for?"

Dakota wiggled his fingers and his feet moved under the blankets. "I think so. Just stiff as hell."

"It will take time to get your strength back," Krista told him.

Dakota barely nodded. He looked at me.

"Hey," I muttered.

"Hey."

I didn't know if he heard what I had said to him right before he woke up. I sort of hoped he hadn't, but he had this expectant look in his eyes like he was waiting for me to say something. "I'm so sorry this happened to you."

"I know." His eyes searched the ceiling. "Is Harmony okay?"

Krista and Carson exchanged glances.

"She's recovering too," Krista assured him.

"Good," Dakota said. "And the Nefariouns?"

"You killed the red-head," Carson told him. "Dedrick and River got away."

"That's three," Dakota said. "What about Gregory?"

The silent crowd of members shifted and fidgeted.

"He's here," Faith said. "With Harmony."

Dakota's brows rose.

"It's okay," Krista explained. "He was being mind-controlled and didn't know who he was, but he does now. He's no threat to anyone."

"Crazy," Dakota murmured. I could tell he was struggling to make his mouth move.

"Do you want some water?" I asked him. He nodded so I pressed the cup to his lips and helped him take a few sips. He let out a sigh of relief then his head fell back into his pillow. "Mind if I rest for a minute?"

"Rest as long as you need to, man," Carson said.

"My parents," Dakota started. "What—?"

"Don't worry." Krista patted his hand. "Dylan took care of it. They think you're out of town with Carson."

"Cool," Dakota said as his eyes closed.

I stared, still finding it hard to believe that Dakota survived, but grateful beyond words that he did. Now, we just needed Harmony to wake up and the world would seem semi-right again.

WASHING AWAY SINS

Harmony

I missed having Dakota to talk to. He'd returned to his body days ago, which was good, but I missed having him with me. My body was not cooperating with my soul's desire to return to it. I'd never been a fan of my current body. It was too small and delicate. Even now, it was hindering me from my simple goal of waking up.

I sat on the bed and watched Gregory. He was stunning.

Being in a new body and form while he was still in his same form from our previous life was a first for us. Dedrick had somehow figured out a way to keep them from aging. That meant he was physically twenty-two, and it meant I still knew every inch of his body, and how amazing it felt.

I was pissed off that I couldn't feel it. Or touch him at all.

In spirit form I tried touching him over and over. I tried to caress his face, run my fingers through his hair, kiss his cheek, but he never flinched. He'd just stare. He'd sit and stare at my unconscious body.

Except in the early morning before anyone was awake, and late at night after everyone had gone to sleep, he'd sing to me in

Spanish. But he'd never say a word to me otherwise. No apologies, no explanations, nothing.

Frustrated by another failed attempt to connect my soul with my body, I swung my phantom arm, trying to palm-plant him in the forehead and knock him backward in his chair. Nothing happened.

"You stabbed me!" I shouted.

He kept staring at me. Not the me who was yelling at him, but at my body.

"Just wait until I wake up," I warned him. "You're going to be very sorry."

After singing me another Spanish lullaby, he pulled back my covers. He delicately pulled my shirt over my head then removed my underwear. I knew what he was planning to do before he did it. He had done it so many times throughout our lifetimes.

He gathered me into his arms and carried my naked body into the bathroom. Still holding me, he reached down and turned on the water. After running his finger under the spigot a few times, testing until he was satisfied with the temperature, he set me in the water and placed the towel behind my head as a pillow. He grabbed a washcloth and soap then sat on the edge of the tub.

Gently, and slowly, he cleaned me from head to toe. Quietly singing, every so often he'd pause to kiss my hand, cheek, or the top of my head. It was so intimate, but not sexual. I wanted to *be* there with him. I wanted to feel his strong hands gliding the soft, warm, cotton against my skin. But all I could do was watch helplessly.

When he was done, he lifted me out of the tub. With my weight leaning against him, he wrapped a fluffy towel around me and carried me back to bed. He opened Maryah's dresser drawer and pulled out a tank top and pair of shorts. He slid them on, handling my limbs like I was a breakable doll. Before he pulled my shirt all the way down he ran his fingers over the stab wound below my breast. His eyes were glassy, but no tears fell. He leaned over and kissed my scar then pulled my shirt down over my stomach.

I lay down as if I were actually in my body. I gazed up at him. One strand of hair had slipped free from his ponytail. It draped over his chiseled cheekbone. I reached up, trying to push it away as he pulled the covers up over my body. He tucked us in—my body and my soul—then sang my favorite Spanish lullaby of all time.

He hadn't changed a bit.

∞

I flashed over to check on Dakota. He was sleeping peacefully, and he looked good—healthy. He wouldn't remember having any conversations with me in spirit form. That's just the way it worked. But I was glad he fought to survive. I needed to do the same. I'd be much better use to him as his living, breathing big sister.

I felt the jolting tug of my body trying to connect with my soul while Gregory tucked me in. I was sure I could have returned to my body at that moment. As tempting as it was, there was something I needed to do first.

Someone else needed my help.

I found Sheila's spirit wandering her old home on the Isle of Man.

"It's time for you to go," I told her. "I will forever owe you for helping me find Gregory."

Her light pulsed between dim and bright. "Forever. Such a fickle word, isn't it? So many souls can't begin to grasp the concept of eternity, not even a fraction of it, yet they toss around the word so carelessly."

I moved closer. "If I could give you forever with us, I would. All of us would."

"I know that. And I appreciate it. I'm about to travel to the place where forever begins and ends. It's the most glorious trip I'll ever take. And the saddest. Because I have cherished every moment of being part of this family."

The room was filling up with light, but Sheila glided out onto her balcony. Through her transparent form I could see the moon shining down on the whitecaps of the ocean waves. "I know it's hard to let go. I'll stay here with you until you're ready."

As if just realizing it, Sheila pulsed with surprise. "Yes, why and how are you here? You're in spirit form too." Her glowing hands flung to her mouth. "Oh, no! Harmony, you've passed?"

"Not yet. I've still got a fighting chance."

"Then what in the world are you doing here with me? Get back to that young and vibrant body of yers. Go be with Gregory! I didn't do all that work for nothin'."

"I'm okay. I have time."

She sighed again. "Oh, sweetie. That's what I thought too. That's what we all think. But there's no time like the present."

"Pot calling the kettle black considering you're still not ready to move onto the most heavenly place you'll ever see."

"Agreed." She turned and looked out at the horizon. "Just a few more moments here by the sea I loved so much. Then I'll go."

I moved to stand beside her and gazed out at the waves. "I'll stay with you until then."

"But what about Gregory?"

"Screw him," I said. "He tried to kill me. Let him wait forever."

She laughed then leaned against me, her divine energy melding with mine. "Forever comes and goes so fast. It feels like the blink of an eye."

"I know. That's why he can wait."

TOUGH LOVE

Maryah

Every night Nathan and I tried to fall asleep in his old room, curled up in his twin bed, and every night I'd end up sneaking out and falling asleep on the living room couch. I told him we weren't allowed to kiss or touch, except innocent cuddling and hand holding. I still felt guilty that the kindrily couldn't reach either of us during such an important crisis and it felt eighty kinds of wrong to make out while Harmony clung to life.

In the morning, when I woke up, just like every other morning, Nathan was asleep on the floor beside the couch. I reached down and ran my fingers over his cheek. His eyes opened and he sat up, tossed his pillow on the loveseat then went to the kitchen to make coffee.

It had become our regular routine. Continuing the routine, I got up to check on Dakota and Harmony.

Dakota was still asleep so I quietly made my way to our room.

Krista was sitting at Harmony's side just like every other morning. Except Krista looked more exhausted than usual.

"You've got to give yourself more time between healing sessions," I told her. "Your eyes are starting to cave in. Carson will lose interest if you keep looking like that."

Krista kind of laughed, but she was too tired and weak to actually make a sound. Her lips didn't even curve upward.

"Carson won't lose interest," Carson said from behind me, entering the room and strolling over to Krista. "He loves that self-sacrificing crap."

"She's giving too much," I told him.

He swept her up into his arms and sat in the chair with her cradled in his lap. "She always gives too much. It's who she is. Why try to change something so beautiful?"

I couldn't have custom ordered a more perfect boyfriend for Krista. The way she and Carson looked at each other, the way he supported her and looked after her, it was everything I'd ever wanted for her. Sometimes watching the two of them together was better than watching one of my favorite romance movies.

"You're right," I agreed. "I wouldn't change her if I could."

Carson seemed to have grown a few inches since meeting Krista. He was taller than her now, or maybe he always was and I never noticed before. He sat there holding her like she was a priceless treasure he wouldn't let anything in the world damage. He'd sit in that same chair, holding Krista after every healing session, sometimes for hours at a time, and his arms wouldn't drop, shake, or falter in any way. He'd just hold her close to him while chatting with anyone who came into the room.

"She never gets heavy?" I asked, still amazed by some of the kindrily's gifts.

"Huh? Oh." He paused, gazing down at Krista's closed eyes. Her head rested against his chest." "Nah, it's like carrying around a teddy bear. Except warmer, prettier, and teddy bears don't talk or kiss you back."

I grinned. "She's lucky to have you, Car."

"Let's not get into a 'who's luckier' debate. She and I have done that spiel too many times."

It had been only a few minutes since Carson came in and gathered Krista into his arms, but she lifted her head and looked at him.

"Something's different," she said.

Carson's brow wrinkled with concern. "What, Turtle? What's different?"

I sat up straight, worried. But as I studied her more closely I saw the healthy color had returned to her face. That usually took hours.

"Not different in a bad way," Krista clarified. "It feels like maybe...I'm recovering faster."

"Yeah?" Carson asked then kissed her forehead. "Good. Maybe that means Harmony is getting better. She's not taking so much out of you."

Krista turned to me. The healthy golden color had spread to under her eyes.

"Kris," I said. "You almost look back to normal. That only took minutes."

"Weird isn't it?"

I nodded, but as I did, a cloud of intuitive knowledge blew past me, breezing by and planting a realization in my being. I whispered, "You're changing."

Carson looked up at me.

"I know. I feel good." Krista smiled.

"No, I mean like how Shiloh's vision changed, and Nathan can take people with him when he traverses. You're recovering faster even after performing heavy duty healing. You're power is strengthening."

Her face lit up. "I hope you're right."

∞

Later that evening, Nathan and I sat at Harmony's bedside in silence.

Gregory sat with us. I was still trying to be at peace with the fact that he wasn't the same person who killed my parents, stabbed Mikey to death, and almost killed me—mainly because he *was* the same person, at least physically.

Gregory barely left Harmony's side. He even slept beside her.

Most of the day we'd all leave Carson and him alone for hours at a time to discuss whatever it was they discussed privately. Once, while I walked down the hallway past the closed door, I overheard Carson laugh. I didn't know what he was laughing at, or how he could be laughing while Harmony laid unconscious in the very same room, but Krista told me not to judge. She reminded me that just last lifetime Gregory was Carson's father and they had a wonderful relationship.

My knee had been bouncing for a few minutes before I finally found the nerve to ask Gregory what I'd been wondering. "Do you remember everything?"

He and Nathan both adjusted in their seats, looking surprised by the interruption to the silence.

Gregory squinted at me. "I remember too much."

My knee bounced faster.

Gregory clasped and flexed his huge fingers. "I've sat here with you a few times trying to find proper words to describe how sorry I am for what I did to you and your family, but I've yet to find words that would be anywhere close to sufficient."

I went completely still. "So you're sorry? You regret...what you did?"

"Mary, I regret it more than I could ever express."

"My name is Maryah."

"Right." He lowered his eyes. "Carson told me you erased. But I believe you're still just as much Mary as Carson is Carlos. The Mary I knew is still in there somewhere."

Gregory's words hit a nerve, but a good nerve.

"Yeah," I muttered, wanting to believe the same thing. Nathan reached over and held my hand.

Harmony's eyes flew open as she arched her back and gasped so loud the bed shook. We all jumped, startled by her sudden awakening.

Gregory stood. Harmony sat up and sprang to her feet, balancing herself on the mattress as if she were dizzy. She pivoted and stared down at Gregory. He kept his focus raised, watching her, his Adam's apple bobbed up and down.

"Harmony," Gregory uttered.

Harmony roared. She actually *roared* and leapt off the bed, tackling him like some kind of rabid flying monkey. I jumped backward, almost knocking over my chair, shocked by her rage and burst of energy. I hadn't even recovered from the shock of her waking up. I didn't notice how or when it happened, but Nathan was standing too.

Gregory had caught Harmony after she flew at him. Her legs were wrapped around his waist. She was only wearing a black tank top and my shorts that were so short they barely covered her butt, but she didn't seem to care. I wasn't sure if she even knew Nathan and I were in the room.

Gregory kept his head bowed protectively as Harmony's fists swung at him over and over. She hit him in his shoulders, his back, even his head. She punched him over and over.

I glanced at Nathan, waiting for him to spring into action, but to my surprise he stood there watching them with a grin on his face.

"You senseless bastard!" Harmony shouted. "How could you?"

"I'm sorry." Gregory kept his head lowered, protectively raising his shoulder the last time Harmony punched him in the back. She squirmed off him and her bare feet landed on the floor. She stepped back and he almost lifted his head but she rushed forward and smacked his chest several times with her open hands. She stood in front of him balling her fists at her sides.

He towered over her. He could have knocked her sideways onto the ground with one swing of his arm. But he didn't.

She stepped forward, standing on her tiptoes and lifting her face toward his. Even though he was three times her size, he stepped back.

"You almost killed Maryah," she said through clenched teeth.

He blinked, and although he could have glanced up and seen me directly across the room from them, he didn't. He never looked away from Harmony. "I'm sorry."

Harmony punched him in the chest so hard he let out a gush of breath. Harmony took another step, and he stepped back again, but not as far this time.

"You killed Maryah's brother," she hissed, "and her parents. You were a merciless monster."

He inhaled and his eyes wrinkled with regret. "I can't apologize enough for what I've done."

Harmony punched him again, even harder, in the stomach. He bent forward, grunting, but he quickly recovered and stood tall.

Her next words were a mix of rage and heartache. "You almost killed *me*."

He ran his hand over his mouth and down around his neck. The look on his face matched Harmony's heartbroken tone. "Te amo, I'm so sorry."

She delivered a series of punches and kicks that Gregory never attempted to block. His stomach, his ribs, his jaw. I flinched for him. Watching Harmony beat him was painful, but I glanced at Nathan again and he looked as if he were watching a beautiful sunrise.

Harmony's foot connected with the side of Gregory's knee and he crumpled to the floor.

I rushed around the bed. I have no idea why. Instinct to protect someone who was being hurt? I stopped only a couple feet away, worried Harmony would hit me if I tried interfering.

Gregory stayed on his knees with his head hung. Blood dripped from his lip onto the floor.

"How can I ever forgive you?" Harmony shouted. "How can any of us *ever* forgive you?"

"You shouldn't," Gregory said quietly. "None of you should."

"I ought to beat you within an inch of your life," Harmony snarled. "I should beat in your head with a pipe the way you did to Maryah." She leaned down and grabbed his jaw, raising his chin so he had to look at her. "I should stab you through your abdomen with a dirty splintered stake of wood like you did to Maryah."

I stiffened. I should have assumed everyone in the kindrily knew what he did to me, but hearing Harmony say it aloud sent a phantom pain shooting through my stomach.

"Then," Harmony continued, "just when you think you've survived all that, I should stab you in the back and lungs with a knife." She grabbed the neck of his shirt and pulled him forward so their faces were close. "I should kill you so slow and torturously that you'll beg to erase."

Gregory licked away the blood on his lip and swallowed. "You have threatened to kill me at least a million times throughout our history together and you have yet to follow through. This time, I give you permission to carry it out. I deserve it."

Harmony pulled him so close their noses almost touched. "Do you still love me?"

His hands lifted as if he wanted to touch her. "I never stopped."

She tackled him again, but he opened his arms and caught her as naturally as if they had planned and practiced the move. He stood as Harmony's legs wrapped around his waist again, and her arms flew around his neck. She hugged him hard then pulled back and kissed him.

"I missed you so much," she cried out between kisses.

One of his hands raked through her short hair as they continued kissing so fiercely that I had to look away.

"Let's give them some privacy," Nathan said, taking my hand.

I followed him out of the room. He closed the door behind us.

"Is it safe to leave them alone?" I asked. "I'm worried Harmony might kill him."

Nathan chuckled. "She might attack him a few more times, but he's used to it. No one can handle Harmony the way Gregory can."

"And you're sure he's not going to lose his mind and try to kill her again?"

"He's free from whatever spell Dedrick had controlling him."

A loud thump from inside the bedroom made me jump. Another series of loud bangs followed. I reached for the doorknob, but Nathan grabbed my hand.

"Leave them," he said. "They're making up for lost time."

LOVE HURTS

Harmony

We stopped pinballing off the dresser, wall, and nightstand, and finally fell onto the bed.

"Eighteen years," I gasped as Gregory kissed and bit my neck. "Eighteen years I've worried about you, and missed you, and had no idea if you were okay."

"I'm sorry," he grumbled, never pausing between kisses.

I yanked his head back by his long hair and forced him to look at me. His obsidian eyes were the strongest form of foreplay I'd ever known. We stared at each other, gazing into each other's souls while trying to catch our breath. "What happened to you?"

He swallowed hard. "It's all blurring. Like two lives trying to cancel each other out. A couple days ago, I remembered almost everything I had done. I could tell you every Nefarioun's name and their ability, but I could barely remember what happened before I was with them. Details of my time with them are slipping away, but details of you and I and our kindrily have poured back in."

"So you didn't miss me? You didn't even think about me during all this time?"

"My soul missed you. It's all hitting me at once. Two decades of missing you, all that emptiness, has rendered me useless. I've been consumed by my grief and regret ever since the spell was broken." He pressed his forehead to mine. "Mi vida, I wanted to die. When I snapped out of it and realized I had stabbed you, that Maryah was Mary, and I had almost killed her, that Mikey was the kid I killed in Maryland, I contemplated walking right out in front of a truck and clawing my way to the Higher Realm and demanding to erase."

I grabbed his face. "Don't you ever."

"That's how much I despise myself for what I've done. I don't know how it can ever be forgiven. Every time you punched or kicked me, all I could think was that it wasn't hard enough. No amount of pain you inflicted on me would be enough."

We had so much to discuss, so much healing to do. Millions of questions and thoughts raced through my mind, but none more important than being with Gregory again. My need for him was primal.

I took his hand and pressed it against my cheek. "We're together again. That's all that matters."

"I'm not worthy of you anymore."

"The universe disagrees."

I gripped his face and forced him to stare at me. "I give you permission."

He lowered his eyes. "Don't. I don't deserve to hear your thoughts."

Long ago he promised me he'd never listen to my thoughts without my permission. He had a way of controlling who he listened to. For the wellbeing of our relationship, I forbid him to eavesdrop unless I said it was okay.

"I want you to hear my thoughts," I said. "I want you to know how much I missed you, and how desperately I need you. I need you to know that this didn't destroy us. Nothing could ever destroy us."

He kissed me. His hands ravished every inch of me, trying to learn every curve of my new body in one fast crash course. *Yes, Gregory, yes. You have no idea how much I've missed your touch.*

His hand slid inside my shorts and I groaned, urging him to rip them off, but he pulled back and held up his hand as if he'd committed a crime. "I'll understand if you don't want to be intimate with me. I shattered your trust."

He still wasn't listening to my thoughts, even with permission. One dreaded question hit me in the chest like a wrecking ball. I had to ask. I had to know. "Gregory, were you with anyone else?"

"No," he said sternly. "I swear, not once. I was evil, but I was faithful. You know my pet peeve about people touching me."

I kissed him to hide my relieved smile. "Except for me."

"Yes, mi vida, except for you." He nuzzled the sensitive place between my neck and shoulder. It had been the sweet spot of my last three bodies, and it was on this one too. I purred and pressed my pelvis against him.

He rose up on one arm. "Does this mean I'm allowed to do more than just kiss you?"

"You better do more than kiss me. Haven't I waited and suffered long enough?" A bittersweet smile spread across his face. I kissed the corner of his mouth. "Physically you haven't changed a bit. I know what this body is capable of and I'm dying to get reacquainted with every part of it."

His grin stretched wider. "Your body is so different from your last." His hand almost covered the entire length of my thigh as he rubbed his thumb along the edge of my shorts. "You're so small."

"Small but not weak," I assured him.

"You could never be weak." His knuckles brushed against the thin cotton between my thighs, making me ache for him even more. "But I am worried I might hurt you."

"I'm a virgin, so of course it will hurt, but I don't care. I need you." I reached down and grabbed the bottom of his t-shirt then pulled it over his head. His tan rippled chest looked so good it took my breath away.

He lifted my chin so our eyes met. "I didn't mean hurt you in that way. I meant because of your stab wounds."

"Considering *you* gave me those stab wounds, I suggest you make up for them in the most sensual and selfless way you can."

His eyes lit up and he licked his lips. "Right now?"

"Yes, right now. I'm healed. You bathed me every damn night. No reason to wait."

He caressed my cheek. "I knew you were watching."

"Then why didn't you say anything to me?"

"I did. I sang to you." He cocked his head to the side. "You don't remember, do you?"

"Remember what?"

"Last lifetime, when Carlos broke his leg, you blamed it on me. You were so angry with me, you told me not to speak to you for two weeks or you'd cut out my tongue."

I laughed. "I forgot about that."

"I didn't speak a word," he continued, "but I sang to you every morning and night. You allowed that because you knew it was my way of apologizing."

I blushed as it all came back to me. "You sang to me because you wanted sex."

"And it worked."

"It did. I've always been a sucker for you." I laughed again. "So every time you sang to me these last few days, it was only because you wanted to have sex with me?"

"Sex isn't just physical with us. It's our souls melding together. The physical pleasures of it are an exquisite bonus."

My entire being ached for him. "These past few days you sang with the hope that our souls would meld together soon."

"Yes," he whispered, kissing a trail down to my chest. "Hearts, souls, and bodies."

I ran my fingers through his long silky hair and arched my body against his. He pulled my shirt off over my head and pressed his bare chest against mine, watching me carefully to make sure my stab wounds didn't hurt. I nodded, letting him know I was fine.

He kissed me and his huge, heavy frame lowered between my spread legs. I couldn't wait any longer. Even if it did hurt, it would be the most glorious and highly anticipated pain I'd ever felt.

He gazed into my eyes, into my soul, and whispered, "Te amo, mi vida."

"I love you too. Now, take off your pants," I demanded.

"Yes, ma'am."

BETTER THAN CHOCOLATE

Maryah

Nathan had been out all day, but he wouldn't tell me where.

After my level of missing him became unbearable, I texted him. *Wish u were here.*

My phone chirped after only a minute. *I will be soon. And you misspelled YOU.*

I giggled, feeling brave and bold since we were only texting. *Perhaps YOU should hurry home and teach me a lesson on how to properly handle YOU.*

I waited. I second-guessed my own flirtatious joke and whether it even made sense. My phone chirped. *That's a complicated lesson and would need to be taught in many parts.*

I bit my lip, fighting back my giddiness as I typed. *I want to learn how to handle ALL your parts.*

A few seconds later I received a response. *Careful what you wish for.*

We had barely touched each other since the night Harmony and Dakota were hurt. I still felt bad about us not being there, but I also really missed being physically close to Nathan. This was the most we'd ever texted before and since it was only texting I felt like I could say anything. I nestled into the sofa and tried to think of something clever and flirty to respond with. I typed, *Maybe you should...*

But Nathan appeared, standing next to me. He pivoted and lowered himself onto the couch on top of me. It happened so fast I barely had time to breathe before his lips closed over mine. He pulled back just long enough to slide his hands around me. "Hang on tight."

In a flash of light we disappeared from the living room. We reappeared somewhere outside, standing on a deck, looking out over snowy mountains. It was cold, but not Nepal can't-breathe-or-feel-your-face kind of cold. Plus, I was wearing clothes.

"Yes!" I shrieked, letting go of him and spinning in a slow circle, taking it all in. "Now this is what I'm talking about. Where are we?"

"Sundance, Utah. We're in a private cabin that a family friend loaned to us."

The deck we were standing on was red cedar and butted up against a steaming pool lined with rocks and boulders. The cabin itself was two stories high and built into the side of the mountain. Massive windows covered the entire exterior and reflected the sun setting behind us.

I turned to look out at the view again. It was so pretty it could have been a picture. Framed between two mountain slopes that felt close enough to touch were more snow-covered mountaintops towering above varying shades of rolling green trees. I scanned and searched as far as my eyes could see, but I couldn't find one other house or building.

The pink sky, as pretty as it was, seemed to shy away and hide behind the mountains, knowing it paled in comparison to the majestic landscape below. "It's...I'm speechless. I have no words to describe how beautiful this place is."

"This is where we celebrated our one-year anniversary last lifetime."

"Really?"

He nodded with a satisfied smile. "You made me promise to bring you back here, so...welcome back. I kept my promise."

"How long are we staying?"

"As long as we want. I told Louise and Krista to call my phone if they need us for anything, and I promised that this time one of us would answer immediately."

"But I didn't bring anything."

He shrugged. "We can go back and get whatever you need whenever you need it."

I was sure I'd never want to leave this place, but now hardly seemed like the time to be taking a vacation. "What about Harmony and Gregory, and Dakota?"

He stepped closer and took my hands in his. "Gregory and Harmony will most likely go off somewhere private for at least a week, or month. Maybe a year. As I said, they have a lot of making up to do. And Dakota is fine. Carson and Krista are keeping a close eye on him until he's completely back to his old self, but you've seen him. He's doing great."

Nathan placed his hands on my hips and pulled me against him. "We've barely touched the last few days. We were both feeling guilty, and rightfully so, but everyone is fine, and we can learn from our mistake. Can we please stop punishing ourselves now? I'm so stiff from sleeping on the floor."

"Okay." I wrapped my arms around his neck. "I do believe your text said you had multiple lessons to teach me?"

"I do. I just wanted to make sure you were ready to handle them."

"Oh, I'm ready." I grinned. "Mentally *and* physically."

"Good. Come with me. Dinner is waiting for you."

I wasn't really hungry, but he looked so pleased with himself that I grabbed his hand and followed him through the sliding glass doors and into the cabin.

The inside was almost as pretty as the outside. It was a true cabin with wood everywhere, but all the furniture, artwork, and decorative details gave it a luxurious feel. Nathan guided me through a living room with a crackling fireplace. I glanced behind me as he continued pulling me along because for a second I had a feeling of déjà vu.

I began to tell him about my almost-memory, but we stopped as we crossed into a formal dining room, and the spread on the table made me forget all about my déjà vu.

"Oh my gosh," I whispered, creeping forward because I was afraid if I moved too fast it would disappear like a mirage. My mouth was watering. "For the love of chocolate."

Nathan opened his arms proudly. The table was filled end to end with chocolate. A three-tiered chocolate fountain sat in the center, framed on either side with white chocolate flowers in dark chocolate vases. There were boxes of assorted chocolates, chocolate bars, chocolate truffles, chocolate drinks, and tins with open lids revealing brightly wrapped candies.

I was going to overdose. I had cheated death up until this point because *this* was how I was meant to die: a glorious, delicious death by chocolate.

And I was ready.

"Let me explain," Nathan said, side stepping toward the table while watching me. "You have always loved chocolate. Everywhere we ever traveled, you insisted on trying chocolate from that place. Country, region, providence, state, next town over, it didn't matter. If we went someplace new, you tried the local chocolate. *And...*" His brows raised and his face lit up even more, like what he was about to say could be any better than a table big enough to seat ten about to buckle under the weight of so much chocolate. "You could taste and pinpoint the difference in tastes between every kind of chocolate you tried."

I reached over a chair for a truffle with a pink drizzle.

"Wait!" He grabbed my hand. "I thought you could sit down and I'd bring you a sample from each place and tell you where it's from."

"I don't care where it's from. I just want to eat it." I pulled away from him and swiped for anything I could reach, but he grabbed me by my waist and lifted me away, just as my fingers brushed the smooth surface of a candy. An oval piece of milk-chocolate rolled off the table and onto the floor. *Tragic.*

"Nathan," I grunted, kicking my legs so he'd put me down. "Don't make me kill you in this beautiful cabin."

"Okay." He conceded, laughing but setting me down. He grabbed a petit four with an intricate flower design on top and handed it to me. "One initial offering to tame the beast, but then please, let's try my plan. Remember, the anticipation and build-up is usually the best part."

I sank my teeth into the fondant covered square of cake. *Dear god in delicious heaven.* "No," I said with my mouth full. "This is the best part."

He watched me, his eyes twinkling, and his grin unfaltering. I eyed all the chocolate waiting for me on the table and tried convincing myself there was enough to share. That I should share. Reluctantly, I admired the half left in my hand and offered it to him.

"No thanks," he said. "Paris wasn't my favorite place."

"This is from Paris?" I scanned the table again. What he had just told me about trying chocolate from everywhere we'd ever been sank in. I wiped the corner of my mouth. "Is this where you were all day? Traversing around the world buying chocolate for me?"

"Yes."

I grabbed his face with my sticky fingers and kissed him. His thoughtful surprise proved, beyond any question, that he was perfect for me.

He pulled back, still smiling, and wiped his cheek. "I'd like you to start our tour with a British chocolate."

"Because we used to live there?"

He pulled out a chair and motioned for me to sit down. "Because it's the best."

∞

After trying a chocolate-covered wafer from Belgium, we decided to call it quits and save some for tomorrow—or later if I woke up with a midnight craving. I could taste many differences in all the chocolate I tried, but sadly, none of the treats, or the stories Nathan told me, triggered any past-life memories.

We curled up in front of the fireplace for a chocolate-induced nap, but after lying there for a few minutes I became restless.

"What else did you have planned?" I asked Nathan.

"Why would you assume I had anything else planned?"

"Because I'm onto you. I'm learning how your mind works."

He laughed but didn't make any sound. "I have something planned for tomorrow, but we can only do it at night."

"Why can't we do it tonight?"

He rubbed his lips together and squinted, like he didn't know whether or not to tell me.

"Come on," I urged. "If it's something that might spark some old memories then I want to try it now. Unless you have to gather supplies from around the world again."

"No, this one is fairly simple."

"Then let's do it."

"All right." He stood up and offered me his hand.

He led me outside onto the deck. The small pool was lit and steam drifted up into the cold air. The stars in the sky looked so close I reached up to see if I could scoop some out of the sky. I couldn't, but they were still enchanting.

I spun around to face Nathan. "Star gazing?"

"Yes, in there." He pointed to the pool. "It's a natural hot spring."

"But it's cold out here."

"It's warm in there."

"We'd have to go back and get our bathing suits."

He frowned. "Right. Of course. Well, that won't be a problem."

"Wait." I glanced at the inviting steaming pool then back at Nathan. "Were you planning for us to go in..." My cheeks warmed so much I worried they might be steaming too. "Nude?"

"No, of course not. We'll nip back to the house and get our suits." He reached for me, but I stepped back.

"Did we wear suits last time we were here?"

His eyes gleamed. I wished I could recall the memory he was seeing in his mind. "No, we didn't."

I swallowed, regretting that I didn't do more yoga this week. "Right." I could do it. I had already been naked in front of him. Sure, it wasn't planned or romantic and I almost died of hypothermia, but still, he had seen me naked. "Then we don't need suits this time either."

"Maryah, I don't want you to be uncomfortable."

"I'm not." I swallowed again, but my mouth was dry. I scanned him quickly, imagining what he'd look like without his jeans, and shirt, and boxers. I bit my lip. It would be *my* first time seeing *him* naked.

"Honestly," he said, "I don't want you to feel pressured. My reason for getting you into that pool is because it's where you had one of your greatest intuitive epiphanies. You said you suspected it had to do with the powerful energy of this place, combined with the restorative minerals of the hot spring. I was hoping you might have a breakthrough here."

"Really?" I stared at the pool, drawn to the water and the thought of it washing up some old memories. "So it wasn't just a ploy to see me naked?"

"If I wanted to see you naked I could have left your clothes at the house and claimed it was a traversing glitch because we traveled so far."

I opened my mouth and pretended to be offended. "My, my, aren't you a cunning mastermind."

He smirked. "I said I could have, but I didn't." He walked over to the pool. "I have an idea." He flipped a switch and the perimeter lights shut off. The pool was so dark the steam looked ghostly white against it. I'm going inside to get us orange juice, just like we drank on our anniversary. You get in the pool while I'm gone. That way I won't actually *see* you naked."

"But you'll have to get in naked when you come back."

He raised a brow and kissed the tip of my nose. "You're not obligated to look."

I tried not to let my shy grin reveal what a nervous mess I was.

"I'll be back in five minutes," he said, backing away.

"Nathan, wait." He stopped. I cocked my head. "We drank orange juice to celebrate our anniversary?"

He grinned. "Combined with champagne, but back then you were an experienced drinker. Now you're not."

What a crazy system of life we lived where in the past I was experienced enough to drink but in the present I wasn't. "Do you have any way of getting champagne?"

He stepped forward, rubbing his jaw and fighting back a smile. "We're only eighteen. Are you asking me to break the law?"

"Only for the sake of reenacting the same scenario as when we were here before. We should drink the same thing we drank back then if I'm expected to have another great epiphany."

"Maryah Anne Woodsen, I do believe you're trying to corrupt my innocent mind."

"Payback," I said.

"Payback for what?"

"Corrupting my innocent body."

He crossed his arms over his chest, but his eyes glinted with playfulness. "There are many things I want to do to your innocent body, but corruption is not one of them."

My insides danced with excitement. "Champagne, please."

He shook his head, grinning impishly, then vanished.

I stuck my toes in the pool. It felt amazing. I glanced around, making sure Nathan hadn't snuck back while I wasn't looking. When the coast was clear I pulled my shirt off then wiggled out of my shorts. I unhooked my bra, and almost took of my underwear but I just couldn't do it. The cold air sent me jumping quickly, and ungracefully, into the steaming water.

If heaven was a body of water on Earth, I had just plunged into it, and I never wanted to leave.

Several minutes passed before I heard glasses clinking together inside the house. My heart sped up at the thought of Nathan walking out onto the deck naked. I wanted to look at him, but I'd be so embarrassed. What kind of facial expression was I supposed to make when I saw him naked? Would I be able to keep my focus above his waist? I dipped below the water, trying to clear my mind and calm my nerves. It didn't work.

I swam closer to the edge and held onto a large smooth rock, keeping my body as close to the wall as possible so Nathan wouldn't catch a glimpse of me through the water. I rested my arms on the ledge and nestled my chin on my forearms, watching the glass doors, where any second Nathan would appear with our drinks—and possibly be naked.

Dragonflies danced in my stomach. Maybe he'd come out with clothes on and I could turn around as he stripped out of them. Yes, perfect. I'd suggest that. *If* he came out with clothes on. Oh god, why was I so nervous about this?

His lips kissed the back of my shoulder. I spun, my heart racing for more than one reason. He held a full flute glass in each hand above the water, but he was submerged up to his chest. My eyes glanced down, panicking at the thought of him actually being naked, but it was too dark for me to see much of anything. Still, we were only inches apart and that was dangerous.

"Cheers." He handed me a glass, but I didn't take it. My arms were plastered over my breasts in an attempt to keep myself covered. I sank into the water up to my chin. I could tell he was fighting back an amused smile.

"I didn't know you were traversing back here. You surprised me."

"I'm full of surprises." He narrowed his eyes. "You're disappointed because you didn't get to see me strip out of my clothes and strut in here?"

I was a little disappointed, but no way would I admit it. My cheeks felt like they were on fire. I tried changing the subject. "Did you find champagne?"

"I did." He extended the glass to me again. I managed to peel one hand from my chest and take the drink from him. "It's very irresponsible of me to allow you to drink alcohol at your age. Please don't tell your godmother. Or my mother. She'll ground us."

I rolled my eyes at him and took a sip. It was delicious. Nathan took a swig of his drink and drifted toward me. I moved sideways and he laughed.

"Maryah, why are you so nervous?"

"I'm not," I uttered, but not convincingly.

He drifted close to me again, but this time I managed to stay in place. I held my breath because his body was so close to mine. His *naked* body. I could not stop the word *naked* from playing obsessively in my mind. His lower body had always been clothed in our previous encounters. How could a layer of fabric be so vital to whether or not my composure unraveled?

"What happened to the brave soul who texted me about teaching her a lesson and mastering *all* of my parts?"

I tried channeling that brazen part of me who wasn't afraid to be intimate and flirty. I failed. "I'm not sure who that was."

He chuckled and pried my glass out of my nervous death grip. He set our drinks on the edge of the pool then reached out for me. "Come here."

"I'm not sure that's a good idea."

"Trust me."

I did trust him. Completely. So I extended my hand and he pulled me to him. He held my wrist and guided my hand underwater, closer and closer to his lower body.

Oh god, my hand had to be so close to it. It was one thing to feel it through his jeans. It was a very different thing when he was naked. My knees went limp underneath of me. "Nathan, I—" My fingertips brushed against wet, soft, fabric on his upper thigh. The breath I'd been holding whooshed out of me. "You're wearing boxers."

"I suspected you weren't as ready as you pretended to be for *all* of my parts."

A mixture of relief and disappointment spread through me. As chicken as I was, I sort of wanted to work through this awkward first time with him.

"You look disappointed," he said.

"I sort of am. It's not like I was expecting to have sex or anything, but shouldn't I be comfortable enough to be naked with you?"

His brow rose and his hand slid down to my butt. My panty-covered butt. "That would be a valid question *if* you were actually naked." I lowered my eyes, embarrassed that I didn't have the guts to be entirely naked. Underwater, he patted my butt then brought his arms up, splashing water on his face. "I forgot how good this feels."

"How good what feels?"

"Firsts with you. It's been so long, but you're just as cute and shy as you were in our first lifetime together."

"So you're not taking off your boxers?"

He pulled me against him and our bare chests pressed together, silky and smooth beneath the water.

"No," he breathed against my neck and I shivered. "You haven't known me very long, and I don't show off my valuables to strangers so soon."

I suppressed a laugh, mainly because he had known me longer than I could comprehend, but also because I didn't want his mouth to budge one inch from where it was. The air was so cold, but his breath and the water were so warm. Goosebumps spread all over me. "I love you, Nathaniel."

Much to my frustration his lips moved away from my neck. He looked into my eyes. "I love you more."

I inhaled a shaky breath.

"Are you ready?" he asked.

"For what?"

"An epiphany?"

"Yes. What do I do?"

"Float on your back and relax."

"Ha. Easier said than done. You'll see my boobs."

Deliberately yet so gently, his hands closed over my breasts. I turned my head slightly, unable to look at him because he looked so confident and sexy, and his hands felt *so* good. The combination was overwhelming.

He pressed his warm lips against my cool cheek. "First of all," he said, all playfulness gone. His voice was hushed and raspy and it made him a million times sexier. "I love your body. I love you. Every single part of you." He looked down and rubbed his thumbs in spiraling circles.

I couldn't hold my head up. He looked at me and my forehead pressed against his.

"Secondly," he breathed, "we're submerged in a powerful hot spring from the mountain of this earth." He glanced at the sky. "The stars, the moon, and the air all around us, you'll experience all the elements at once. This is your best chance at truly feeling the energy and magic of this universe." His thumbs circled slower. "And I want you to feel it *everywhere*."

I was breathing heavy and I groaned when his hands slid away from my chest. He shifted to stand behind me.

"Do you feel that?" he asked. "How alive and energized your skin feels?" He pulled me back against his chest and my legs naturally floated out in front of me. My upper body crested the surface. "Relax," he whispered. "I promise to keep my eyes closed."

I believed him, so I relaxed my body and stopped worrying about my boobs poking out of the water. I floated on my back with Nathan's hands underneath me.

"Is some of your skin exposed to the air?" he asked from behind me. Either his eyes were closed or he was a great pretender.

"Yes," I answered.

"Close your eyes and feel the difference between the sensation on your skin underwater, and your skin exposed to the air. The warmth of one, the chill of the other."

I nodded. The back of my wet head rubbed against his shoulder.

"Now," he whispered, "focus on the parts of your body underwater. The hot springs contain healing and restorative minerals. Can you feel all the tiny bubbles kissing every cell of your skin with the energy of earth and water?"

I nodded again and my hair swept across my bare shoulder, even that tickling sensation felt amplified.

"Try to hold onto that awareness of your entire body, but open your eyes and focus on the moon."

I opened my eyes. The thin crescent moon floated in the tranquil black sea above me.

"In your own words from previous lifetimes, the moonlight tastes like chocolate. Try to taste it."

I licked my lips. Either the taste of chocolate remained from our feast earlier, it was my imagination, or I really did taste the moonlight.

"The moon's energy is caressing every part of your skin that its light touches." Nathan drifted out from behind me and moved to my side. I stole a sidelong glance at him and his eyes were shut. My ears dipped into the water and the subtle sounds around us were muffled, but it helped me relax even more.

His fingers skimmed down my back then his hand pressed firmly, lifting me and exposing more of my skin to the cold air and moonlight. His other hand brushed lightly over my stomach. He sounded like he was in a tunnel. "Feel the moon's energy kissing you here." His fingertips brushed over my hips and down my thighs. "And here."

I sighed dreamily. "I feel it."

I couldn't resist looking at him. His face was tilted toward the sky. I couldn't see if his eyes were still shut but I didn't care. This experiment felt incredible. I wanted to float like this all night.

"Focus on the stars," Nathan's water-muffled voice said.

I searched the sky for his star. I thought I had found it, so I relaxed my focus and the thousands of twinkling stars blurred and created a cloudy web of connecting light. It was breathtaking.

"Breathe," Nathan said. It took me back to our first kiss when he said the same thing. My body relaxed even more. "Smell the air, the water, the moonlight. Taste it. Feel all that energy against your skin, all at once but as different sensations."

Every detail he described linked together and connected in a way that charged my entire being. I couldn't take my eyes off the sky, even as Nathan moved beside me. I didn't know what he was doing, but it didn't matter. I wanted to keep feeling *it*, whatever *it* was.

My body hummed. The feeling wasn't sexual. It wasn't pain or pleasure. It was like I was connected to pure energy. It was...magic, but even that word didn't seem adequate. It was better than chocolate.

The bright web of stars pulsed with different colors. I felt like I was floating into the sky, drifting between the glowing strands of starlight. They were so close I could touch them.

The sensation was familiar. I had experienced something similar the night I almost died. But even that thought didn't panic me. I stayed calm and peaceful. I reached out to touch a star that opened like a glowing flower right in front of me.

I dove inside of it, bathing in liquid energy that lapped against my arms and legs. I was swimming through a pulsing wormhole in the sky. Voices whispered unintelligibly all around me but it sounded like tranquil music. Then I stopped moving. I hovered in front of a radiant green light that morphed into different shapes, finally settling into a circular form. Stars swirled around inside like a snow globe; it was hypnotic.

I squinted, catching sight of a black feather caught in the swirling lights. Another black feather appeared. Then another. Soon, the globe of swirling color was darkened with endless black feathers.

The globe shattered and feathers poured out, spiraling through the sky. I held out my hand and one single feather landed in my palm. From nowhere I pulled a fan full of peacock feathers from behind my back and slid the black feather into the shimmering blue and green bundle.

Rainbow colored light exploded from the feathers like sparklers.

I turned around, sensing something behind me. Black feathers still spiraled through the air, but they landed and gathered around a glowing orb. The orb slowly morphed into a young girl's face. The feathers changed into black hair. She floated backward and walls of stone rose around her. One of her eyes peered out at me through a small round opening. I moved closer, wanting to see what color her eye was, but someone, or something pulled her away.

The hole opened wider and Dedrick's face appeared. I leapt backward.

I was yanked down, spinning in fast circles like I was caught in a drain. A black tunnel formed around me, swirling and closing in on me tighter and tighter until I couldn't breathe.

"Breathe, Maryah!" Nathan's voice demanded. His hands gripped my shoulders as he shook me. "Open your eyes and breathe."

I forced my eyes open and when I saw his panicked expression I sucked in a much needed breath of air.

"Again," he said, smoothing down my hair and holding my twitching face. "You're all right."

I felt the sandy bottom of the pool beneath my feet. I pressed off of it and grasped Nathan, wrapping my arms and legs around him. He held me back just as tight.

I was trembling. "I saw Dedrick."

"Where?" he asked calmly.

"Through a window. In a room made of stone. Like a castle of some kind."

"What else?"

My chest rose and fell fast against Nathan's. "A young girl with black hair."

"Did she look familiar?"

"No, I've never seen her before."

"Anything else?" I pulled back and looked at him, grounding myself back in reality. "Before that it was amazing. I floated in the sky with the stars and swam through webs of light."

His grin was bittersweet. "It worked. You astral traveled."

I wiped water from my face. It wasn't quite the proud and celebratory moment I had imagined. I was still trembling.

"Maryah?" Nathan lifted my chin to look at him. "Why were you looking for Dedrick? Gregory is back."

I shivered and Nathan sank lower. The warm water lapped at my chin. "He might still come after us. He might try to kidnap Gregory again. What if he slaughters all of us again like our last life? What if he still wants me dead?"

"We're stronger than we've ever been. If you're ever in danger I can traverse you away from it instantly."

"And what about the rest of our kindrily?"

"We all protect each other."

"But we don't have a definite plan."

Nathan's head tilted. "A plan?"

I nodded.

He kissed me, but it was too quick. My lips felt so cold after he pulled back. "Did you remember anything? Any memories from past lives?"

"No. Why?"

"Because you just sounded like your old self. You always had a plan."

"Maybe all this metaphysical training is starting to work."

"I think it is."

"It's because of you." I flicked my head, motioning to the scene around us. "Bringing me here was a brilliant idea."

He kissed me. "I'm so proud of you."

"Let's try it again!" I said excitedly. "I'm going to focus on someone else. Maybe Krista." I reconsidered that idea, worrying I might see her and Carson doing something that would scar me forever. "On second thought, maybe Eightball."

His head fell backward. "And the addiction starts."

I kissed his neck. It was too tempting, all wet and shiny in the moonlight. He moaned. "How about you try traveling again tomorrow?"

"Why can't we do it now?"

He pushed me away until my legs floated free from his waist, then he swept them to the side and scooped me up in his arms. He glided across the pool and climbed the steps, carrying me. "Because it's late and I was looking forward to falling asleep with you in my arms."

I shivered from the cold air and burrowed tight against him. Suddenly my goal shifted to getting warm. "Can we have some hot chocolate first?"

"Certainly." He carried me into the house then set me down and wrapped a quilt around me. "Would you prefer it be from Vienna or New York City?"

"Ooh, tough decision. How about a little of both?"

LEAVING SCARS

Harmony

I sat at the edge of the pond, watching the koi swim around and bump into each other. Krista lowered herself down beside me. "You wanted to see me?"

"Before the meeting began, I wanted to talk to you privately." My hand unconsciously rested on my ribs. "I wanted to thank you for leaving my scars visible."

She smiled while sipping her lemonade. "I thought you'd like that. I figured you'd want visual reminders so he'd never forget what he did."

"You know me so well."

Krista shrugged.

"One day," I said, "many, *many* years from now, if I ever do want to erase them, would you be able to?"

"Honestly, I'm not sure. I've never tried to heal old scars."

"That's okay. I'll probably want to keep them forever. Men need a good guilt trip every now and then."

Krista chuckled.

"Seriously, Kris. Thank you for saving my life. For allowing me to be with Gregory again. I'm not sure I can ever repay you."

"You would have had many more lives even if I didn't save this one."

"But I would have had to wait much longer to be with Gregory."

She nodded. I could tell from the sad faraway look in her eyes as she glanced out at the red rocks that she wanted to ask about the other person I needed to discuss with her.

I beat her to the punch. "Sheila crossed over."

She closed her eyes. Her skin glimmered in the sunlight shining down on her. After a long moment she nodded. "Good."

Even though they had shared a long final goodbye, I sensed her wish to have had one more. Everyone wished to have one more.

I placed my hand on her knee. "She said to tell you goodbye, that she loves you, and that the stars were waiting for her."

Krista choked back a silent sob. She wiped one tear from her eye then lifted her face to the sun again. "Thank you, Harmony."

I stood and brushed myself off. "I'll see you inside for the meeting."

∞

I had never lit the candles of the chandelier before. Ever. But as I stood on the table and lit the last one, I grinned. The burning flames swayed and danced, waving to the star-shaped colored glass above them.

"I dreamt of that skylight while I was with Dedrick," Gregory said, staring up at it. "I don't remember when or why, but the memory just came to me."

I handed him the box of long matches and he set them on the table then offered his hand to help me down. I squatted, wrapped my hands around his neck and leaned over him. With hardly any effort he slid me off the table and into his lap.

"For these meetings," I told him, "I give you open access to my thoughts. I might need to explain things to you that you've missed or won't understand, and I know asking lots of questions makes you uncomfortable."

He nodded then kissed me. We were still kissing when members started arriving.

"I don't know," Carson teased. "I'm still not sure he can be trusted."

"There's no doubt he's himself again." I flashed Gregory a sultry grin as I slid off his lap and into my seat. "I promise you that."

Amber pushed her glasses up her nose. "Can I just say how happy I am to look across the table and see you in your seat, Gregory? It was empty for much too long. And a huge part of Harmony was empty too."

Amber was right. Two empty seats used to separate Nathan and me. Recently, Maryah had returned to hers, and while I was happy for Nate, it made the empty seat left between Maryah and me feel like a black hole that would never be filled.

The black hole was gone. Stunning light now filled it. My twin flame completed our circle.

"Look at us," Louise opened her hands. "Every member present and accounted for. I'll admit I worried I'd never see that day again."

"Plus one new member." Krista shook Mikey's foot as she set his carrier on top of the table.

Edgar cleaned his glasses with a handkerchief. "I documented a lot of Gregory's information when he first arrived, but I wanted a round-table meeting so we could brainstorm and see if we have any more questions Gregory might be able to answer before the details of his time with Dedrick fade to a point where he can't recall them anymore."

"They're fading?" Maryah asked.

Gregory leaned forward and placed his elbows on the table. I held onto his strong bicep. I couldn't not touch him. I had an irrational fear that if I didn't have some sort of physical contact with him at all times he'd disappear.

"It's hard to describe," Gregory started. "It's almost like recovering from being drunk. You know you said and did stupid things, but the more the alcohol is eliminated from your system, the more the details of your intoxication become hazy."

"What about your memories from before you were abducted?" Maryah asked. "Do you remember everything before that?"

"Yes," Gregory told her. "And don't worry, you will too."

My head snapped left to look at Gregory. Other members must have picked up on his certain tone too because several of us shifted.

"Why do you sound so sure?" Maryah asked him. I was proud of her for asking important questions.

Gregory shrugged. "You promised me you would, and I've never known you to break a promise to anyone."

"When?" Maryah pried. "When did I promise you that? And what exactly did I promise?"

I glanced across the table. Edgar, Helen, Anthony, and Louise were all leaned forward as enthralled by this conversation as I was.

Gregory's ears pulled back. He was listening to someone's thoughts, or trying to block out some of us. I was certain we were all asking a million mental questions. He lifted his face and scanned the table. His attention locked on Amber. I could tell whatever Amber was thinking was the bit of information Gregory needed.

"Mary didn't die on the beach at the massacre. Everyone knows that, right?"

My breath caught in my healed-but-still-tender lung. "No one knew that," I said quietly. "When did she die?"

Gregory turned in his seat so he was facing Maryah directly. "You were with us. For the first few months you were a prisoner of Dedrick's too."

My mouth dropped open. I stared around Gregory's back at Maryah. She was frozen with shock.

"No," Nate said, looking just as miffed as the rest of us. "She slit her own throat with Dedrick's knife."

Gregory nodded. "I remember that, but Dedrick's healer didn't let her die. They took both of us."

Nate dropped his head in his hands. "Dear god." He had told us he watched Mary slit her own throat with Dedrick's hand. He'd already been stabbed and was bleeding out when it happened. He lifted his head and stared at me. His eyes were like daggers stabbing me even harder than Gregory did. Nate's words were laced with venom. "How did you miss that, Harmony?"

"I...I—" I had told the story a dozen times. To Nate. To Edgar. To whomever asked. I told them every member's soul solidified with light and crossed—except for Gregory's. We were Elements. We didn't have reasons to linger. We always crossed to the Higher Realm quickly so we could return quickly. But the Nefariouns had Gregory—alive—so I stayed. My spirit followed them, to see where they would take him, what they would do to him. Two of them hauled him away before Maryah slit her throat. I never saw her die because I was watching over Gregory—until Gregory and his captors vanished into thin air. I searched everywhere. For days I searched and searched for him. When I found no trace of him, I assumed they killed him too. So I crossed over.

"You told us you saw *every* member cross except Gregory," Nate said.

I raised my guilty eyes. "I made a mistake. I left before you and Mary died."

"You lied," Nate hissed.

I had lied. At the time it hadn't felt like a lie. Mary *had* died, and she had reincarnated as Maryah. Everyone believed she had died on the beach with the others. *I* believed that.

Gregory was listening to my thoughts. I could always tell when he was in my head. He held my hand and defended me. "She wouldn't have intentionally lied about that."

"I didn't know," I confessed. "Truly, I assumed she died and crossed over quickly like always."

Nate had never looked at me with so much disappointment. "But you didn't actually see her cross over like you told us you did. You lied to me—about the most important turning point of my existence."

My chest hurt. My hands felt so tiny and weak. "I'm sorry, Nate." I looked at Maryah. "I'm so sorry."

Maryah turned to Nathan. "But weren't we in the Higher Realm together? Didn't you see me?"

He shook his head. "I've told you, once we reach the Higher Realm linear time doesn't exist. Our soul is there to make decisions and plan our route back. We're there and gone in what would feel like the blink of an eye here. Our souls communicate with the source, not other souls. It's why we always choose to come back. As glorious as the Higher Realm is we choose human existence for the interaction with others."

Maryah turned back around. She glanced at Gregory's hand holding mine, then her eyes met mine. "You didn't see what happened to me because you were watching over Gregory, right?" I nodded. "Understandable. I would have done the same if they had taken Nathan. It's okay, Harmony."

Maryah might have forgiven me, but would Nate?

"Gregory?" Maryah's cracking voice asked. "What happened to me while I was there? With Dedrick?"

"Let me think." Gregory pressed his palm to his head like he was trying to shove the memories back in. "I traveled a lot, so I only saw you a couple times when we went back to the house. He'd send me in to read your mind, but you had mastered staying mentally quiet. You mentally told me off every time I tried to read you. And you were sick, I think. You didn't look good at all. You were always in bed. Strapped to a bed."

"Strapped?" Maryah gasped.

Gregory nodded. "At the time I must not have questioned it because of Dedrick's mind control, but yes, you were always strapped to that bed."

"I'm going to kill him," Nate snarled.

"No, Nathaniel," Gregory replied to Nate's thoughts. "It's not what you're thinking. I doubt Dedrick ever forced himself on her physically. Even if he did, he couldn't have done *that*."

We all knew what Nate was thinking. And the thought was horrifying. Gregory shifted in his seat and his hand protectively dropped to the crotch of his pants. "Dedrick isn't...fully equipped."

Faith and Amber laughed.

Faith held up her hands. "Okay, let's pause for one moment. As interesting as this long awaited information is about Mary, I have to know how evil, egotistical, power-hungry Dedrick has no physical manhood."

Gregory smirked. "Some thoughts I overhear leave too memorable of an impression to forget. Many decades ago, Dedrick was castrated by a member of another kindrily when he attempted to rape her while kidnapping her."

"Karma is a beautiful thing," Krista said, grinning.

"No wonder he's obsessed with forcing souls into his circle," Carson said. "He can't ever have little spawns of his own."

Nate put his arm around Maryah and pressed his lips to the side of her head. I could tell he was still upset, but at least the possibility of Dedrick raping Mary had been eliminated.

"As rewarding as that bit of information was," Maryah said, "let's focus on what happened to me while I was there. This could be the key to understanding why I erased."

I glanced at her when she said "me." She said it so casually. I hoped her connection with her past lives was strengthening.

Gregory pressed his palm to his head again. "One of the times I came to see you, you were crying."

"Crying. So?" Maryah said confused.

"As Mary, you rarely cried," I explained.

Nate squeezed her shoulder. "For you to cry in front of Dedrick you must have been extremely upset."

"Why was I crying?" she asked Gregory.

"I don't think you told me or let the thoughts come into your head, but that's when you promised me you'd remember. You told me no matter what you chose, you would remember again, and you'd find a way to make it right. I didn't know what you were talking about at the time. I didn't know anything I was doing for Dedrick was wrong. I relayed what you said to Dedrick and I moved on to my next assignment. A few days ago, when I figured out who you were, and Carson told me you had erased, it all made sense. You said *no matter what you chose, you would remember again*, and you chose to erase. You promised to remember, so I know you'll find a way."

"But you have no suspicions about why she would have erased?" Louise asked.

Gregory silently stared at the table for a minute then shook his head in frustration. "No. We were told you were dead the next day. And that was it. No further details or explanations."

Maryah sank back in her chair.

"It explains why you're months younger than I am," Nate said to her. "I assumed you stayed in the Higher Realm for longer than usual and I tried discerning how or why that would happen. I never guessed you were kept alive after the massacre."

Edgar laid his glasses on the table. "It frustrates me to no end that none of these events are recorded in the Akashic Records. What kind of power must Dedrick be harnessing to shield events like this from being recorded in such a universal recording device of history?"

"As I told you the first day we discussed this," Gregory said to Edgar, "Dedrick has some of the most gifted souls tethered to him as puppets. I met only some of them. He probably has his most prized possessions locked safely away."

A detail flashed into my mind from the night I almost died at the airport. "I almost forgot! Josephine was the Nefarioun Dakota shot and killed. Right before she died her eyes cleared and I saw who she was."

Louise pressed her hands over her chest. "Josephine of Ancient Greece?"

"Yes," I admitted, already knowing what everyone was thinking and hating myself for not remembering to tell them sooner.

"Harmony," Helen gasped, clutching Edgar's arm. "Josephine could read the Akashic Records."

"I know," I confessed. "I don't know how it slipped my mind. So much has happened."

Someone should have punched me. Nate, Louise, everyone. I deserved it.

Helen stood. Edgar rose to calm her.

"It will be okay," Edgar tried assuring her.

"We took his reader," Helen bellowed. "He'll need someone to replace her. Edgar is the *only* other known reader."

"Oh god," Maryah said, her voice almost trembling. "He'll come after Edgar."

"Any other crucial tidbits of wisdom you'd like to share with us, Harmony?" Nate asked with ice in his voice. "You seem to be on a roll today."

"I'm sorry." I pushed my chair back and braced my hands on the table. "I didn't keep either of those things from anyone on purpose. I made some mistakes. I'm only human."

BODY AND SOUL

Maryah

Nathan tossed another log into the fireplace. My head had been hurting since the round-table meeting, but I was actually welcoming the pain. I wanted memories from my time with Dedrick to break through more than anything.

"This is the key." I paced behind him. "I feel it. Something happened to me during my time with Dedrick that made me erase. Or maybe *he* made me erase? Is that possible?"

Nathan stood and leaned against the mantle. "I don't think so. Your soul is your own in the Higher Realm. He couldn't control your actions once you were there. At least let's hope not. That much power shouldn't be allotted to anyone."

I ran my hands over my arms trying to rub away my chills. "We're so much closer to solving the big mystery though. I can feel it."

He sat on the sofa and dropped his head into his hands. "I keep picturing you strapped to a bed and it infuriates me."

I ran my hand over his hair. "It's in the past. Nothing we can do about it now. At least we know he didn't rape me."

Nathan's eyes met mine. "But what else might he have done?"

"Again," I tried to assure him. "It's in the past. Even if he did something awful, I don't remember it, so I win."

"That. Did you just hear yourself?"

"What?"

"Even if he did something awful, you don't remember it. Endless scenarios have been running through my mind about awful things he might have done to you, and how horrific they must have been to make you choose erasure. Maryah, you were so strong and stubborn. I don't want to imagine what it would have taken to break you and make you erase."

I took a deep breath.

He stood and held my hands. "And if his actions made you erase, then he did win. He took so much from you and me, and our kindrily. He won. And we don't know if we'll ever get back what we lost."

"But I'm right here."

His eyes flashed with sadness. "A miniscule part of you is here. And while I love you, I hate him for taking away so much of you—and our history together."

Nathan looked away but I turned his chin to face me again. "I'm going to remember. I'm determined. I astral traveled last night. I'm going to again. I'll get stronger, and I'll find a way to recover my memories. I've never been more determined about anything in my life."

My very short life, I thought to myself.

Nathan nodded, but he didn't look convinced. "I'm glad to hear you being so confident." He caressed my brow. "Do you feel okay? Your eyes look strained like you're in pain."

"I have a minor headache, but I think it's because I'm trying so hard to remember what happened with Dedrick."

He frowned and ran his fingers through my hair, massaging the back of my scalp. "I hate that you're in pain."

No memories were coming through due to the headache phenomenon, so I figured trying our other theory would be much more enjoyable. "I had an idea at the meeting, but I need your help."

"Of course. Anything."

My cheeks blushed thinking about it. "You'll have to be super strong and have amazing willpower."

His brow rose. "Will I now? What exactly is this plan?"

"The flashes of my past lives have hit me only while we're in a place we've been together before at a significant time, or while we're making out and it gets hot and heavy." He grinned with such satisfaction it made me smile too. "Don't let your ego get too big when I say this, but my theory is that I'm most connected to you when our physical intimacy gets intense. But you don't want to have sex until we're married, and the more I live with that plan, the more I think that is the right thing to do. I want to stick to that, but I also don't want to rush into marriage just so we can have sex because that feels trashy, and like you've said, our relationship deserves better than that." I paused. "Why are you smiling so big?"

"Because you're rambling nervously and it's adorable. And I can see where you're going with this but you're taking an awfully long time to get there."

The tips of my ears were burning. "You do know where I'm going with this?"

"I think so." He kissed each of my fingers as he spoke. "We're here. In one of your favorite places from our last life. And we already had success with you astral traveling, so clearly this place is powerful. Your rant about flashes of your past happening while we make out means you want to push that envelope further and see if more memories flood back."

I swallowed, wishing he'd say it so I didn't have to.

"Tonight," he continued, "you want us to get exceptionally *hot and heavy* as you call it, but you're depending on me to be strong-willed enough to make sure it doesn't go too far and..." He tucked a strand of hair behind my ear and spoke in that confident and sexy way of his. "...turn into full-blown, mind-bending, star-shaking, more-pleasure-than-this-earth-can-contain, universe-altering, hours upon hours of us making love."

A huge breath whooshed out of me. It took me a few seconds to speak. "You're setting a very high bar for yourself."

"I've had centuries of experience. I'm more than confident that the bar is so high it's out of this galaxy. And I can still reach it with ease."

I swallowed hard. "Maybe this plan is a bad idea."

"Your plan is a brilliant idea."

"I'm probably going to want to take it too far."

He kissed my shoulder. "You most certainly will."

"I'll probably end up begging you for it."

"Yes, you will."

"You'll have to be strong enough to tell me no."

"I know."

"And you think you'll be able to?"

"I will."

"How can you be so sure? I've seen how worked up you get. You want to just as much as I do."

"That's not true. You don't remember what it's like when we make love. I have endless memories of us ravishing each other. Therefore, I want it infinitely more than you do."

My body screamed for him. "Then how can you promise you'll be strong enough to stop before we go too far?"

"Because I love you so much that my respect for you, your honor, and your soul, is more important than satisfying my urgent, intense, and overwhelming need to penetrate your body."

Breathe, I reminded myself. *Just breathe.* "If you talk like that during our experiment you're going to make it even harder on me."

"Everything about this experiment is going to be extremely, painfully, and ecstatically hard."

I smirked, anxious and excited about getting started, but first I wanted to shower, shave my legs, and make myself look as cute as possible.

Nathan adjusted his jeans. "What time is our rendezvous with temptation?"

It was only noon. "I want the stars to be out, so maybe around eight or so?"

"Maryah, the stars are always out. You need to look more closely. But eight it is." He kissed my forehead then walked rather awkwardly across the room.

"Where are you going?" I asked.

He called over his shoulder, "To take a long cold shower."

I smiled, very pleased with myself.

∞

I was so nervous but so excited. Those two emotions tangled and twisted my insides until I thought I might explode. I sat at a table by our private pool, gazing up at the stars in the sky.

Nathan walked through the sliding glass doors holding one perfect and gorgeous peacock feather. "For you."

"Thank you."

He squatted between my legs and held onto the arms of my chair. "You're breathtaking."

"So are you." He was wearing khakis and a white button down dress shirt. His hair was freshly cut, and somehow it made his eyes even more intense. They almost matched the color of my sundress. I made sure to wear a pretty bra and matching underwear.

Every other time we made out it happened naturally. This preplanned thing had me nervously salivating with anticipation, but I tried to play it cool. Nathan ran his hand up my calf, squeezed above the back of my knee then let his hand travel up my thigh just past the hem of my skirt. I tingled with anticipation.

But then he stood and walked over to the pool, leaving me sitting there wanting to shout at him to come back. He dipped his toes in then stared up at the sky. He closed his eyes and clasped his hands together in front of his chest.

After a minute or so I asked, "Are you praying?"

"Yes."

"For what?"

He kept his head thrown back toward the sky. "For the strength and power to not make love to you tonight when you beg me to."

I laughed. We both might need to acquire a new superpower before the night was over. I stood and walked over to him. "We're going to make serious headway tonight. I can feel it."

"Headway," he repeated. "With your ability and memories, right?"

"Among other things."

He pulled me close to him in a dancing stance. I linked my fingers through his raised hand and he led us to start slow dancing.

"There's no music," I pointed out.

"There's always music, you just need to listen."

I rested my head against his chest, listening to his steady heartbeat that always comforted me and lulled me to sleep. He began humming the song, "For You, For Me, For Evermore." I pulled back and gazed up at him, loving the sound of the deep and perfect vibration, but then he sang the words to me.

"You might sing that better than Ella."

"Now that's a compliment." He continued singing the lyrics that seemed like they could have been written especially for us.

When River sang to me it was awkward and uncomfortable, and it felt so wrong that I almost threw up, but this was different. This was romantic and amazing because it was Nathaniel. Because it was Nathaniel, it was perfect.

He kissed my forehead. "Your dancing is improving."

"I have a strong partner."

He smiled. "So do I."

We continued dancing around the deck while Nathan sang to me. As sweet as it was, I wanted to get to work. "I do believe you're procrastinating."

"It's not procrastinating. It's foreplay." That one word sent a warm rush through my body. "Enjoy the anticipation and build up, Maryah. It will make the climax that much more enjoyable."

He needed to stop saying words like foreplay and climax or I was going to stop acting like a lady and rip his clothes off.

"What exactly is the climax for us tonight? We're not going all the way, so where do we stop?"

The corner of Nathan's mouth curved upward. "Where do you want to stop?"

My heart was thumping excitedly. "You know the bases much better than I do."

"The bases." He chuckled. "Tell you what." His eyes gleamed as he licked his lips. "I'll stop right before I slide into home. Even though you'll be begging and pleading and trying to wave me in."

"You're so confident about me begging for it."

"I am."

"What if I don't beg? What if I'm the strong one tonight?"

"Then you're right, you'll have made serious headway, because I've always been your greatest weakness." He leaned down and kissed me, gently and sweetly. His lips moved to my neck and I melted. I didn't notice he had turned me around until I opened my eyes and saw I was facing away from him. He stood behind me, lifting my hair while kissing the back of my neck and shoulders.

His breath was delicious fire in my ear. "Most men never master the art of undressing a woman. It took me two lifetimes to realize that *slow* meant barely moving, and *gentle* meant skin whispering against skin."

He slid the straps of my dress down so *slowly*. His lips and tongue trailed along the curve of my neck. Painstakingly slow was an understatement, but my god it felt incredible. With one hand he pressed against my hip, pressing the back of me tightly against the front of him. His other hand masterfully, and supernaturally slowly, peeled one of my bra straps down my shoulder.

His mouth kept working miracles along my shoulders, neck, and back, and the cool air around us left a path of chills everywhere he had kissed. The mix of hot and cold had my mind blurring and my body aching.

My dress slid down my body barely an inch before he caught it with his fingertips. The fabric lowered less than a centimeter at a time, feeling like one long smooth kiss of silk against my skin.

"Dear god," I whispered.

The dress kept sliding down my body, the cool air caressing me as more and more of my bare skin was revealed. I was glad my back was to him, and my face was lifted to the sky, because my eyes continuously rolling back in my head could not have been attractive. Just when I thought I couldn't take any more of my dress teasing every cell in my body, Nathan let it drop into a pool of fabric around my feet.

I sucked in a surprised breath at feeling so exposed, but then his soft shirt pressed against my bare back, warming me. The bulge in his pants pressed against my silky underwear. I moaned as his hands skimmed my stomach and trailed down to my hips. He spun me to face him and I was dizzy from how good I felt. I was mentally aware enough to locate the seam of his shirt. I tried unbuttoning the one at his chest but my fingers were jelly. I grabbed hold of both sides and ripped it open, sending buttons flying.

"Sorry," I murmured. "I'm no master at undressing you."

"That was pretty masterful." He kissed me hard and lifted me up. I wrapped my legs around his waist, groaning when our chests pressed together.

I didn't realize he had carried me across the deck until he laid me down on the double lounge chair. He lowered himself on top of me, kissing my neck and chest. His hand slid up my thigh and traced lines along the crease of my leg. I promised myself I wouldn't beg or plead just to prove him wrong, but *yes* and *please* slipped out of my mouth over and over.

"Open your eyes," he whispered.

He had repeated those same words to me over and over while I was in a coma. Those words gave me hope, saved my life, and right now, if I opened my eyes and saw his green eyes staring back at me, I knew they'd send me over the edge.

"Maryah, please, open your eyes."

I whimpered but opened them. Holy celestial universe, he was breathtaking.

"I need to know you're all right with what I'm about to do."

"I am." I nodded, running my fingers through the back of his short hair. He could do whatever he wanted and I would be more than okay with it.

His fingers made tiny circles against my underwear. "You're certain?"

"Yes, yes times infinity, yes. Please, Nathan."

He kissed me deeply. And then his fingers weren't just teasing me anymore.

"Nathaniel," I gasped, bucking against him. I didn't know what base we were rounding but it was my new favorite. His fingers weaved magic that spread through every cell in my body. The stars shone bright above me. They were a blur of twinkles between my eyelids fluttering open and shut. Every nerve ending in my body had just found a new and beautiful beginning.

I raked my fingers down his back. His green eyes were two irresistible beacons that reigned me in deeper as we kept moving together in perfect rhythm.

"What do you want, Maryah?"

"I want you," I managed between gasping breaths.

"Just this me, or every version of me I've ever been?"

"All of you."

"Then you need to search deeper. You need to truly see me. All I've ever been." His eyes filled with light. I was pulled into the familiar magical tunnel.

It's working, I thought.

Flashes of glowing color swirled around me. A memory poured in.

Nathaniel's same green eyes shone as he smiled at me from a different body. Kindrily members were circled around us. We stood on the same Sedona cliffs where the current Nathan and I had lain and talked so many times. He wore a suit. I was in a white dress. Our hands were being tied together with fabric. Our wedding.

"I love you," I told him. "Then, now, and eternally."

He kissed me and I felt all the energies of this universe. Sunshine spun its way through every part of my being. The air tasted like honey. Millions of stars floated above us even though the sun was shining. The red rocks around us hummed a tranquil tune that warmed my soul. It was the most perfect moment I'd ever experienced. And I remembered it.

I remembered living that moment like it was yesterday.

I was pulled backward out of the tunnel of light that was Nathan's eyes. My nails were digging into his back but his face showed nothing but love and happiness. He was caressing my face with one hand and his other propped him up as he gazed down at me.

"It worked," I said breathlessly.

He grinned bigger. "I know. I saw it in your eyes."

"I remembered our wedding."

"Which one?"

"On the cliffs. Our cliffs."

"That was our last life."

"I remembered." I squealed with joy. "I'm not drugged, or in danger of dying, but I remembered." I held his face in my hands and breathed deep, still tingling from how amazing everything felt. "I was so...confident. I felt secure and strong, and so sure of everything."

He nodded.

"I'm going to remember more," I vowed. "I want to remember everything, every single past life."

He kissed my hand. "I have complete faith that you'll succeed."

"I will. I know I will. We figured it out. We'll need to do a lot more of this because apparently it helps me remember."

Nathan chuckled. "I think you could remember without all of this, but I won't argue. I am at your service whenever you need me."

I could feel the shift in me. My connection to my power and my past was rekindled and I intended to keep feeding the flame until it became an unstoppable wildfire. Dedrick would be burned to ashes if he crossed me or messed with my kindrily again.

Nathan's green eyes sparkled as he stared admiringly at me.

I wanted and needed so much more of him. "I never thought I'd be one of those girls who want to rush into marriage, but I totally am. I'd marry you tonight."

He smirked. "That's just your hormones talking."

"Seriously." I sat up. "How long will we wait? We're going to be together forever. It seems silly to wait."

He rubbed his thumb along my chin. "I'm old-fashioned. Let me do this my way. Let me give you everything you deserve without you having to plan or ask for it. Please allow me that."

"Okay. I won't say another word about it. But just so you know, my answer will be yes. Whenever you do ask, it won't be too soon. My answer will be yes no matter what."

He grinned. "Some things never change."

We kissed again and I felt as if I were still sensperiencing all the energy around us. I was wrong. Our wedding wasn't the most perfect moment I had ever experienced. This night was.

Connecting with Nathan was the key to my past, present, and future. And what a breathtaking key he was. I intended to keep turning that key until I unlocked every power I possessed, every secret in my soul, and every door to my past.

NOT THE END...

Dear Reader,

The Kindrily series is a never-ending story in my mind, so it's difficult to know where to end each book. I could have ended *Taking Back Forever* right here, but a few more short chapters were begging to be told. Harmony wanted to hint at what happens in book 3, *Fighting for Infinity*, but if I allowed it, the ending would be a cliffhanger.

I tossed and turned many nights over whether or not to end this book with a cliffhanger. The old and very true saying, *You can't please everyone*, kept echoing through my mind, but truly, I don't want to disappoint my readers. I knew many would be okay with a cliffhanger, but many might be upset. These characters are near and dear to my heart and soul; therefore, so are the readers who love them. Your enjoyment of their story is important to me, so I wanted to make the right decision.

To solve my dilemma, I'm letting YOU decide for yourself.

If you dislike ending a book on a cliffhanger, stop reading now. You can catch up in book 3.

If you want to read more, and you're okay with cliffhangers, continue reading.

The choice is yours.

For anyone planning to review *Taking Backing Forever*, please don't mention what happens in the following bonus chapters. Respect other readers by not posting spoilers and jeopardizing their enjoyment of the story. *Please* respect the decision of those who decide to stop at this point and not be left with a cliffhanger.

I appreciate each and every one of you. The support and encouragement from my readers is what makes my job as a storyteller the most rewarding profession in the world. I am honored that you choose to spend time reading about the kindrily. Thank you times infinity. And may you shine forever.

Sincerely,

Karen

MIND THE GAP

In London, when riding the Tube (aka train or rail system) a famous warning is played as a public safety announcement. *Mind the gap.*

Those three words warn you to be careful of the space between the platform and the train, that brief, yet potentially dangerous space between where you were and where you're going. The following chapters take place in the space between books 2 and 3, so as they say in London...mind the gap.

And enjoy the journey.

SKETCHY AT BEST

Harmony

Dakota was in his usual spot, hunched over the desk in the library drawing furiously. I brought him a soda and set it down in front of him, but he didn't look up from his work.

"Take a break," I told him.

He glanced up as if finally realizing I existed. "I can't. I have a lot of work to do."

I worried about him more and more. Since his near-death experience he'd been obsessed with his comic creating much more so than before. And then there was the issue of him believing he was an Element. He told Faith, Carson, and me that he was a changed person. He claimed he was one of us, and he believed—with all of his dear and hopeful heart—that his ability was creating reality through his comic books. If he drew it, it would happen.

I sighed and reached for his hand to stop him from drawing. "Dakota, you need to stop this."

He tried pulling free, but I kept a tight grip on him. His eyes locked with mine.

"It sucks that you don't believe me. But I know what I'm doing. You guys could help me by telling me what I should draw, but instead you're probably talking behind my back about how nuts I am."

"We'd never talk about you like that."

We had talked about him a lot, but more out of concern for his wellbeing.

"I wish you'd believe me," Dakota pleaded. "I feel it, Harmony. I'm different."

"You almost died, Dakota. Of course you feel different."

"Not different in the way you see people talk about on television documentaries. I didn't see the light and suddenly have a new appreciation for life. Different as in I feel my power coursing through me. I'm part of the kindrily now. I'm meant to help save our members and the world."

Save the world. He'd been saying stuff like that since he woke up. He barely slept. He hardly ate or drank. He was so skinny he looked like he was on drugs.

For years Dakota's only wish was to be an Element. His encounter with almost dying left him feeling invincible. And his damaged brain stem had probably created an alternate reality where his wish finally came true. No Element in all of time or existence had drawing the future as a supernatural ability.

"I miss spending time with you," I said. "Let's go ride dirt bikes."

He tried pulling his hand away again, but I didn't let go. He squeezed his pencil so tightly it snapped. "You should hang out with Gregory."

"Gregory wants to get to know you. Why don't you hang out with us?"

"After I finish this."

But that was the problem. He never finished. Even when his body did finally run out on him, he'd toss and turn in bed with his pages clutched in his hands. He'd mumble in his sleep about saving the world and needing more pencils. It was disturbing to witness and I didn't know what to do to help him move past it. Worse, what if he never moved past it? I kept imagining him in a psych hospital, sedated and drooling all over himself.

"Please," I pleaded. "Finish it later. Come hang out with me and get some fresh air and sunshine."

"I can't. Too much work to do and not enough time."

I let go of his hand and sank back in my chair. He immediately started sketching again. His hand swept over the pages with such desperate purpose. I took a deep breath. I hated myself for what I was about to do. "I have a feeling there's something we're supposed to see or find if we go out, something that will help with your comics."

His pencil paused, hovering over the page. Only his eyes lifted. "Really?"

Reluctantly, I nodded. "Really."

"Like an answer from the universe?"

"Yeah, the universe always gives us what we need. But you're making it difficult to reach you because you stay cooped up inside all night and day."

Dakota glanced around the library. "You're right. Okay, where are we going?"

"I'm not sure yet," I said, relieved that as awful as my fake belief was, it worked and he'd finally get out of the house and back into real life. "We should stay open to wherever the universe wants to take us."

"Sounds good." He stood but grabbed a pad of paper and tucked a pencil behind his ear.

"You're taking those with you?"

"I'm sure I'll need to jot stuff down."

I sighed. My plan wasn't as brilliant as I thought. "Okay, let's go."

"Wait. I need sunglasses." Dakota ran out of the library. I traipsed out into the living room and waited, wondering if my plan would help or only make things worse. He came back wearing Carson's shades. "Don't want to chance the Nefariouns knowing who I am."

"Right." I nodded, putting on my own sunglasses.

We had created a delusional monster.

∞

Riding was uneventful—especially since I was the one who rode while Dakota sat on the ground sketching.

We returned to the house for our usual evening round-table meeting and Dakota dragged in a stool from the kitchen and sat behind Carson. No one questioned his attendance anymore. The whole kindrily was aware of the problem, and since Dakota never said a word during any of the meetings, we allowed him to sit and sketch while we talked.

"The big question is will Dedrick come after any of us again?" I said. "Yes, it's wonderful to live here together as a tightknit group, but it makes us a much easier target."

"My worry is that he'll retaliate," Louise said. "We took Gregory from him."

"No, he took Gregory from us," I clarified. "We took him back."

Gregory squeezed my shoulder. The feel of him being next to me was still surreal at times.

"And we killed one of his valued members in the process," Carson added.

Dakota's head snapped up. He was smiling. I don't know what made him happier, that Carson mentioned what Dakota did, or that he referred to Dakota as one of us. "I doubt he'll just accept that and leave us to live in peace."

"And I still believe he's obsessed with Maryah," Nate added. "I'm worried he'll still come for her."

Maryah took a deep breath. Her confidence had grown leaps and bounds over the last couple of days. I didn't know what she and Nate were doing while they were away together, but whatever it was seemed to be working.

"He knows I erased," Maryah argued. "Therefore, he thinks my ability was erased too. And River will confirm that I was clueless about our way of life and my power. Maybe Dedrick won't care about me anymore."

"Which brings me to my next question," Faith said. "Why did he take River and what does he have planned for him?"

"River never demonstrated any kind of power while you were with him?" Louise asked Maryah. "Not even a hint of something supernatural?"

"Super strength douchiness," Faith huffed.

"No," Maryah said. "But April told me something last week when I went to visit her and her mom. River had been trying to contact me through her. He wanted her to tell me he didn't want to be one of them."

"April knows about us?" Amber asked with concern.

"No," Maryah assured everyone. "I didn't tell her anything. I spilled our secret in the past and created a never-ending chain of problems. I wouldn't make that mistake again. April had no idea what River was talking about. She thinks he's crazy. But obviously River meant he doesn't want to be a Nefarioun."

"He wants you to *think* he doesn't." Faith crossed her arms over her chest. "He tried to kill you. That's as nefarious as it gets."

"But Dedrick made him. We know that. The same way Gregory almost killed Harmony."

"You said his eyes weren't snakelike," Nate pointed out. "His mind wasn't being controlled."

"Yes, but Dedrick had other ways of controlling him." Maryah glanced around the table. "River depended on him for money and a place to live. Dedrick threatened to take all that away."

"Ahh, yes," I quipped. "Murder in exchange for food and shelter. Seems fair."

Krista leaned forward. "Maryah, I know you always want to see the good in people, but River is no good. Now that he's back with Dedrick, he'll be even worse. Let it go. We need to focus on protecting ourselves. River can do the same."

Dakota had stopped sketching. "Maryah," he said. "If you could choose, would you want River to be good or evil?"

We all glanced at each other, not knowing what to do or say.

"Good," Maryah told him. "Of course I'd want him to be good."

Dakota nodded then went back to sketching. If only it were that easy.

RISING TO THE CHALLENGE

Maryah

I woke up in the floating chair of the sensperience room. The stars twinkled all around me.

"Carson?" I called out into the darkness.

No answer.

I had astral traveled again. Only to the garage to watch Nathan work on Anthony's Mustang with him and Dylan, but it was another successful training session. I had astral travelled three more times since the initial time at the cabin, but I must have fallen asleep again because Carson had left the room.

I slid off my chair and walked to the door, squinting at the bright light as I headed for the living room. I pretended to still be blinded by sunlight when I saw Carson and Krista kissing. I cleared my throat and they pulled apart.

Krista wiped her lips and fiddled with her hair. "How'd it go?"

"Good." I stretched my arms behind my back. "Traveled to the garage and watched the guys work on Anthony's car."

Carson rolled his eyes. "How ambitious of you."

"Hey, we don't all move at rapid speed like you. I'm easing into this traveling thing." I walked to the kitchen to get a drink.

Astral traveling always made me thirsty. I called over my shoulder. "And what's up with leaving me alone in there?"

"There's no way to tell whether you're asleep or traveling. If you were traveling, I didn't want to wake you. But hanging around watching you do absolutely nothing is not how I want to spend my day."

I grabbed a juice from the fridge and rejoined them in the living room. "You mean you just wanted to make out with Krista."

Krista giggled.

"Like I said." Carson smiled. "I had other plans for my day, and every other day."

"Thanks for the support," I chided.

"Whoa, Sparky, don't forget I'm the one who built you the sensperience room that started this whole regaining your ability thing."

"Noted, and thank you," I said. "But don't forget I'm the one who forced you to come up with a way to help me sensperience."

Krista glanced at Carson who was speechless then she smiled. "Oooh, good one, Maryah. That deserves a whole box of chocolates."

"Noted," Carson nodded at me, narrowing his eyes. "But I'm still smarter than you."

I smirked. "I'll catch up soon."

I'd never be as smart as Carson, but my confidence and abilities were strengthening. My intense make-out sessions with Nathan resulted in me remembering a couple more flashes of my past lives. My plans were working.

"Have you tried finding Dedrick when you're traveling?" Krista asked.

My head snapped up. I hadn't tried to find Dedrick since the one short moment when I'd seen him and the girl in the window. I wanted to master waking up from my travels at will before I went searching for him. I didn't know why I was nervous to be stuck spying on Dedrick, but only because I felt like I was truly *there* when traveling—*there* being wherever I traveled. I wasn't quite ready to be alone with Dedrick. Being around kindrily members felt safe, but it wasn't like I could take anyone with me in my travels. I had already asked Edgar if he thought that was possible, and he assured me it wasn't.

"Not yet," I answered Krista honestly, "but I will try to track him soon. I wanted to wait until I mastered returning to my body. So far my tendency is to fall asleep."

"I'm sure it takes a lot of energy out of you," Krista offered. "Your body probably falls asleep from exhaustion."

"Yes, but the clock is ticking," Carson said. "Time to put on your brave girl panties and try to find Dedrick."

Louise rounded the corner carrying her laptop under one arm. "Hello, all."

"Any news to report?" Carson asked her.

"Nope," Louise said. "Still too quiet out there."

Krista and I exchanged worried glances. Most of the kindrily pretended not to be concerned that we hadn't heard one word about the Nefariouns. But I was worried. It had been more than a week since the battle at the airport. I had a gut feeling Dedrick was waiting to make his next big move. Not knowing what or when that move would be had my stomach in knots. Carson was right; I needed to be brave and take the plunge into trying to locate Dedrick again. I was the key to knowing what he was doing and planning.

"I traveled again," I told Louise.

Her face lit up. "You did? Where to?"

"Just the garage," I admitted. "But I'm getting better at it."

"Wonderful." She hugged her laptop to her chest and her lips parted like she was about to say something else, but she stopped. What she probably wanted to say was that it would be helpful to know if Edgar was next on Dedrick's wish list.

"Tomorrow," I told her. I couldn't wait any longer. "Tomorrow I'll attempt to find Dedrick."

The worry lines framing her mouth loosened with relief. "Good. It would be nice to have some clue as to what he's up to."

Krista reached over and squeezed my hand—her unspoken way of telling me she was proud of me for being brave. I squeezed back because the thought of actually locating Dedrick scared me, but I was determined to conquer my fear.

DIVING DEEP

Harmony

G regory set his sunglasses on the patio table between us. "I'm going to have to meet your parents someday,"

"Yes, but not today." I finished the last bite of my sandwich. "Or tomorrow."

As far as my parents knew, Dakota and I were on an educational trip for school that was earning us extra credit. Dylan persuaded them to not only believe it, but also to support my decision to go on the trip, so I was embracing the freedom to stay at the Luna house with Gregory.

"Dakota is going stir crazy being cooped up here," Gregory said. "He needs to go home."

"I know." That was one of my major concerns about us returning to our routine at home. I wouldn't get to spend as much time with Gregory, and my parents would surely notice the change in Dakota's mental state. I could ask Dylan to persuade them to believe Dakota was fine, but that didn't seem fair to anyone.

"What's going through that magnificent mind of yours?" Gregory asked.

"I'm enjoying my time with you. I'm not ready to give that up yet."

"We'll still be together. It will be fun. I can date you and try to impress your parents. Make them wonder if I'm good enough for their daughter."

I grinned. "You're not good enough for me."

"I know that, but the key is getting *them* to believe I am."

"And what about at night? We won't be able to sleep together."

He waved me over to him and I sat in his lap. "Your bedroom has a window, right? I'll sneak in."

"Ooh, that does sound fun. Real teenage shenanigans."

He pulled me closer and gently bit my lip. "The possibility of getting caught will make it that much more exciting."

"My parents would die if they found you: a towering, muscular, long-haired, Spanish twenty-two-year-old naked in my room."

He wiggled his dark brows. "I look forward to hearing all the shocked expletives running through their head when they catch us."

"That would be a true test of my dad's preaching about remaining peaceful and always acting with love and compassion."

"He sounds like a good man."

"He is." I fed him another potato chip. "Both of them are great."

"Why'd you choose them? And how did Faith become your twin sister?"

I shrugged. "They were close to Louise and Anthony. Mary told us to choose so we'd be close together. Apparently Faith chose the same parents. She requested to be sent back right after me. The time line was close enough that we could be twins."

"Fascinating."

"Some days I think Maryah is determined to build an army— or Mary was anyway. First Krista and now Mikey."

He squeezed me tighter. "We contributed to the army with Carson."

"Carson is something special," I said. "He probably raised hell in the Higher Realm until they granted him Element status."

"He must have inherited his ability to raise hell from his original mother."

"Or his father."

Gregory's eyes lowered. "I sense it's a bit weird for him. I'm in the same body as I was when I was his father. Sometimes when he looks at me it feels like he's watching a ghost."

"I'm sure it's strange for him, it's strange for me too, but in a good way. Carson will get used to it. Isn't it hard for you too? Physically you're not much older than he is."

"That's not strange. The really disorienting part is my last solid memories of the kindrily—before the day I stabbed you of course." I squeezed his side where he was ticklish and he squirmed but continued with his thoughts. "There was Amber and Dylan's wedding. Then things go blurry, and bam, here I am with you, and you're in a different body—hell, almost everyone is in a different body—and I've missed two decades of what's been going on with my own kindrily. The time I was gone is slipping away from my memory more each day. Years of my life are being slowly erased."

My chest tightened at the word *erased*. "Oh, no." I sat up straight. What if Dedrick had the actual power to erase memories? "What if Dedrick erased Maryah's past? What if he's planning to erase all of us? What if you forget our past lives together?"

"That won't happen."

"How do you know? We have no real idea of what kind of power Dedrick has at his disposal."

"I remember everything from all my lives. Just a lot of the time I spent with Dedrick is unclear. And if he has the power to erase all of those memories from my mind then I'll thank him for it."

I traced my fingers around Gregory's obsidian eyes. He knew what I was doing, that I needed to gaze into the windows of his soul and see for myself. That I needed to know every bit of our history was still intact.

He lifted his chin and relaxed back into his seat, knowing it would take a while. "Dive on in. The waters of my soul are fine." I kissed him then went deep beneath the surface. I needed to make sure our history was still there. Every part of it.

Thankfully, nothing had been lost—except almost two decades together. And while losing that time was painful and awful, I had him back—forever. And that's all that mattered.

∞

Gregory and I brought in our lunch dishes from the deck. Louise and Helen were pacing the kitchen.

"Still waiting?" I asked.

Louise nodded. "I hope she locates him. At this point any bit of information is better than nothing. Even members of the other kindrilies are worried about how quiet it's been."

"I'm going to sneak in and see how it's going," I said. "I'll report back in a minute."

I crept down the hall and turned the doorknob to Maryah and Nate's room slowly and soundlessly. Krista looked up as I tiptoed into the room. Already knowing the question on everyone's mind, Krista shook her head.

"She's been under a long time," Nate said.

Krista sat on the bed beside her. "I was just thinking the same thing. But she's been falling asleep after she travels. Maybe she's asleep."

I stepped closer. "Or maybe she found him and she's finding out a lot of useful information."

Nate looked at me as if considering my reasoning, but then he shook his head. "Something's amiss. I can feel it."

I leaned against one of the branch posts of the bed. Maryah looked peaceful. "She'll be pissed off if you wake her up right before she discovers a plan or something else important."

Nate stood. "That's fine. It wouldn't be the first time I made her angry." He rubbed her arm lovingly. "Maryah, come back. We're concerned." He gave it a few seconds then nudged her shoulder and patted her cheek. "Angel, we need you back here. Time to come home."

Krista glanced at me, then back to Nate as he continued trying to wake up Maryah.

Maryah wasn't budging.

Krista snapped her fingers in front of Maryah's face. "Pudding, wake up." She clapped her hands. "Come on. You're freaking us out."

Nate looked up at me. I shrugged. "Don't ask me."

"Krista," Nate asked, "will you check to make sure she's okay physically?"

Krista held her hands over Maryah's body and closed her eyes, scanning every inch of her. "She's perfectly healthy."

"Where's Carson?" Nate asked. "Perhaps he can figure it out."

Krista sprang up. "I'll go get him."

Nate caressed Maryah's cheek. "Maryah," he pleaded, "wake up."

Carson blurred into the room and halted at the side of the bed. "She's probably asleep."

"We tried waking her," Nate said. "It's not working."

Krista ran in and stood beside him. Carson blurred away again then came back with a glass of water. He dumped it on Maryah's head.

"Carson!" Nate yelled.

"What? It should have worked."

The worry was spreading through all of us. I could feel it filling the room.

Nate dried Maryah's face with a blanket. "Wake up, Maryah. Please, open your eyes."

LOST IN THE DARK

Maryah

It was like a dream, a terrible but extremely rewarding dream.

I found him. I found the monster. As terrifying as that was, I kept reminding myself that only my spirit was with him. He wouldn't even know I was there.

I tried to observe and make a mental note of everything. The young girl I'd seen in my other travel was with him again. They were in the same place. This room was made of stone and had no windows, and it was dimly lit by candlelight.

The raven-haired girl was sitting at a table in front of an old thick book that called to me. I hovered over it, wishing I could open it and scan through its pages, but with no physical form that was impossible.

"Well hello there." Dedrick looked at the book then sneered. I could almost smell his rotten breath just by looking at his crooked yellow teeth. "We knew you'd be joining us soon."

I scanned the area around me, but no one else had entered the room.

"Yes, Mary," Dedrick said, "or should I say *Maryah*, I'm speaking to you."

If I had a body, it would have gone rigid. He couldn't see me. That was impossible. But Dedrick's eyes penetrated me as if I were flesh and bone standing in front of him.

He walked over and ran his fingers through the girl's black hair. "She's irresistible, isn't she? Once you've seen her, you're forever drawn to her."

He yanked the girl to her feet and shoved her aside. Her expression was cold and emotionless. "She's my tempting flame and you're my predictable moth."

Her black eyes met mine as if she could see me too. Her eyes weren't snakelike. She wasn't under Dedrick's mind control, but something about her was chilling and eerily familiar.

"Maryah," Dedrick barked, snapping me out of my intense study of her. "Meet Rina. I think you two will become great friends."

I hated that he was speaking to me as if I were really in the room.

I wanted to find out more about where they were, and Rina, but I didn't feel safe with Dedrick speaking directly to me, so I tried returning to my body. Nothing happened. I grappled for the cords of energy that usually connected me with my body, but my connection was gone. I tried again, and again, getting more anxious and desperate with every attempt.

"Come, now, Maryah. You didn't think it could actually be that easy, did you? Didn't Gregory's capture seem a bit too convenient?" Dedrick sat down, kicked his dirty boots up onto the table, and laughed. "All this time, I've thought I needed you—the physical you. But I came to realize your body isn't important. Your soul is what I require. And now I have it."

Rushes of painful energy lashed through me like a lightning storm. I kept opening up my awareness, my energy, my soul, trying to reconnect with my body. I stared at the feather on my ring, willing to see its light, pleading to form a bridge back to my body. I pinched my phantom wrist as hard as I could.

"Look at you." Dedrick snickered. "Like a lightning bug trapped in a glass jar."

I darted around the room as if I could fling my spirit into a wall and a secret door would open so I could fly out. I caught a glimpse of light in a glass bookcase and I slowly moved toward it.

Reflected in the glass was a glow of gold, silver, and green light in the vague shape of me. I moved side to side and so did the light. Around the glow was a translucent bubble.

"Pretty isn't it, Rina?" Dedrick cooed. "Like our own life-sized snow globe."

She nodded while wringing her hands and keeping her eyes on her bare feet.

Was I really trapped? How was that possible? Harmony's words echoed in my head: *Imagine someone ripped your heart out of your chest and threw it in a cage. Outside the cage, vultures, rats, and coyotes circle, waiting to rip your heart apart and devour it. Worse yet, as they circle, their wicked energy surrounds the cage, tainting the pure and good soul inside. Over time your heart starts to change; it becomes evil too. Smothered by negativity, it slowly stops beating until it ceases to exist.*

I wanted to cry.

"Let me go!" I shouted.

Dedrick folded his hands behind his head and smiled. "You aren't going anywhere for a very, very long time, Maryah. Might as well make your soul comfortable."

NOT THE END

Follow the journey in book 3,
Fighting for Infinity

Want updates and behind the scenes information about the
Kindrily series?
Follow the Kindrily Facebook page at
www.facebook.com/Kindrily

ABOUT THE AUTHOR

Karen was born and bred in Baltimore, frolicked and froze in Colorado for a couple of years, and is currently sunning and splashing around Florida with her two beloved dogs. She's addicted to coffee, chocolate, and complicated happily-ever-afters. She is a co-founder of the teen focused blog, YA Confidential, and a proud member of The Indelibles.

Find more information about Karen Amanda Hooper
and her books at
www.KarenAmandaHooper.com

CPSIA information can be obtained at www.ICGtesting.com
Printed in the USA
LVOW120049140613

338562LV00001B/2/P